Anna Mantovani

The Dragon Plague

Trilogy of Europa
Book 1

© 2019 Anna Mantovani
Editing: Word for Word Editing and Proofreading Services

Prologue

"Dragon eggs found in Scottish islands? The discovery of mysterious eggs leaves the scientific community in bewilderment.

The remains of a previously unknown reptile were discovered by researchers at the University of Edinburgh in the South Sandwich Isles. The expedition also found fragments of a hatched egg, whose original length was estimated between eighty and one hundred and twenty centimetres. Along with it, an unhatched intact egg was found. An X-ray analysis of the egg showed the lifeless body of a reptile embryo with wings and a long tail. Initial laboratory analyses seem to determine that the chemical composition of the animal's organs allowed high resistance to heat and all kinds of radiation, which would explain the miraculous discovery within the quarantined territories. The characteristics of the reptile make it strikingly similar to the mythological animal popular in the recreational literature of the Old Era. The scientists involved have not yet made any official statement on the subject."

The unbreakable glass wall between them shattered with a deafening noise.

Dr Kathleen Anderson felt the panic mount in the pit of her stomach.

The whole room bore the marks of his fury.

Oxygen erupted from a cylinder with a shrill and constant whistle and piles of shredded paper were everywhere.

He was going to get out.

She had spent the last eighteen years trying to prevent it; if he went out and infected the others… there would be no controlling it. It would be the end.

He moved towards her, and instinctively Kathleen took a step back.

She wasn't scared of the disease, of course, but the bond with the dragon gave him a powerful and uncontrollable force that his body normally could not even hope for.

In that moment, at one of his crises, he seemed more alien than ever, with cold, snake-like eyes and the scales on his elbows and knees in full view.

"Mum," he said, his voice whiny.

The appellative sounded wrong, obnoxious.

It had been a mistake from the beginning; but passing him as her son spared her many questions.

At the beginning she didn't even think about it: he was born in the lab, the only survivor of a series of tests that had killed all the other subjects. The miracle child, whose blood could hold the key to the riddle of the bond with the dragons.

An experiment, the most interesting and exciting that she had ever undertaken, but still an experiment.

When she brought him home, David looked at her wide-eyed and full of hope.

"Is he my little brother?" he asked.

David was such a lonely child.

His illness had prevented him from going to school or even playing with his peers.

Even after he had healed, he was always a little shy, as if the other children were interesting but dangerous animals that he preferred to observe from a safe distance; and the new-born could not infect him, not him.

It would be easier, no authorizations to sign, nothing to hide, just another sickly child who would not leave the house very often...

"Yes, David," she replied, and saw his face light up with joy, "That's your little brother."

She should have known, should have foreseen the dangers to which she exposed her son. At first, it had worked well: as a child, that being was surprisingly normal, even cute.

She remembered his toothless smiles and how at times, just for a moment, she thought that perhaps in the end she might even feel affection for him. She had tried to treat him well.

Not the same way as David, no; that would never have worked... but at least as if he were like all the other children.

But there was something evil, corrupt in him. It was in his blood, just like the dragon. And David... in the end it was him who had paid the price.

It was all her fault, she knew... but now she couldn't let him go: he was too dangerous.

"So you want to escape? And where would you go?" She urged him, her voice trembling.

He did not answer.

"Perhaps you think you can mingle with other people? But look at you!" she taunted him. She didn't even try to hide the contempt in her voice; it no longer mattered.

"You couldn't hide even for a day".

He shook his head in a gesture of annoyance, as if he didn't want to listen.

"Listen to me," she said, "You cannot be with other people. You are contagious. Anyone who touches you will die. Is that what you want?"

He rubbed his arms where, on the pale skin, the bruises of the syringes and the IVs stood out - an annoying and childish gesture that he often did when he was nervous. Kathleen noticed that his pupils were again rounded, and the irises were losing the cold, greenish shade. She sensed that the fury was flowing away from him; without it, he was harmless.

I can still control him, she thought... not all was lost.

Trying to remain calm, she pulled out a syringe of sedative from the pocket of her white coat and hid it behind her back.

"Now stand still. Calm down," she said, slowly approaching him, "Breathe."

He continued to shake his head.

"Come here. Trust me," Kathleen continued. She was just a few feet away from him. "Tomorrow it will all look like a bad dream."

She reached out to him... it was almost done... for a moment it seemed to work.

He allowed her to touch him, grab his arm.

However, when he saw the syringe, he snapped: "No!"

He lifted his gaze, and she saw the eyes of the dragon again.

His stubby arms pushed her with an inhumane strength.

Kathleen was thrown across the room. Upon hitting the floor, she felt something sharp sticking in her back, then through her chest. When she looked down, she saw her own blood on the white, immaculate coat.

She tried to get up, but her strength was leaving her rapidly.

His face was above her, looking confused and horrified.

"I'm sorry, I..." he said, looking at her wound with his reptilian eyes, apparently not knowing what to do.

"Don't touch me," Kathleen managed to hiss. Terror made her rude, but now it no longer mattered. Her head was spinning, and her vision was becoming foggy.

The last thing she saw was her stepson forcing the laboratory door and running away as fast as his legs could carry him.

It's over, Kathleen thought, while all went dark around her.

All was lost.

Chapter 1

Twenty-five years later

Sophie Weber entered the waiting room and, like every day, stood still for a moment, hit by the strong, feral smell of too many people crammed in the same space.

Anxiety made her heart hammer in her chest.

She shook her umbrella and left it near the door, then did the same with her parka and her hat. A thin but persistent drizzle was falling, which would have been quite pleasant against her overheated face, if it wasn't for the slag danger that the news kept warning about.

She hastened to carefully wash her face and hands with a clay-based soap: it was said that it contrasted the accumulation of radiation, but she had the impression that it was only a palliative. In any case, her morning routine was somehow reassuring.

She looked in the mirror, tidying her dense, curly hair, then slipped on her coat and walked into the doctor's office.

"You're late," Dr Solarin received her, without looking up from the patient whose back she was auscultating.

"Sorry... A traffic block at the North door," she explained, then took a deep breath: "An infected."

The doctor froze but did not answer.

The patient, a man with very thick glasses, was startled: "Really?"

Sophie suppressed a shudder, thinking back about the ambulance, the police in riot gear and the yellow tape with the biohazard symbol. The idea of an infected so close to them was disturbing.

The disease that twenty years earlier had decimated the population of the city was officially named DH16N10, but most people called it the "dragon plague".

It all started with a fever, a burning fever that devoured the body from the inside and that no drug was able to reduce. The patients gradually lost their sight, and later perhaps also the other senses, but they all raved too much to give a comprehensible report. Then the skin would begin to dry up, and the swellings start to emerge, wide, thick and dark, covering large areas of the body, particularly on the bones.

When they burst, they revealed scales like those of a snake, but at that point, in most cases, the patient was dead.

However, compared to a few years ago, the disease was almost completely contained. Safe areas had been established within the city, and every citizen was periodically tested to detect the incubation of the disease. That morning all who entered in the central city, including her, had been subjected to blood screening. She was clean, she had discovered; at least for now. If the virus had returned to the city...

"What happened to him? Or her?" Amanda Solarin asked, shaking her from her thoughts.

"What?"

"The infected? Did they get him?"

Sophie shrugged: "I don't know. But if they haven't caught them yet they will do it soon: there are blocking points all over the place. It will be fine," she said, more to convince herself than to anyone else.

"Poor soul," the patient said, getting his clothes back on.

Sophie shrugged: "Better not take risks, don't you think?"

She had little compassion for those who risked spreading the disease.

Dr Solarin prescribed the man a syrup for coughs and dismissed him. With a little luck he would even be able to obtain it; medicines were increasingly scarce and difficult to find, and the waiting lists could drag for months, but his coughing seemed alarming enough to give him some priority.

Sophie had worked under Amanda Solarin for the past two years.

Before that, she attended a medicine course for three years, and for two years before that she did an internship in a large hospital in the fourth ring. She knew that once, before the plague, the future doctors studied for many more years, but times had changed: now the knowledge was gained mostly on the field.

Sophie considered herself lucky to be working under Amanda, who had been a doctor for many years, studied in a real university, and had a real higher education.

Amanda Solarin was forty-six years old; she was brown-skinned, tall and athletic-built and would have seemed much younger, if not for her short, greying hair.

Sure, she didn't have a very easy-going personality: on many occasions she was abrupt and despotic, and this was the reason why the previous three aspiring doctors left their place. The first day of work, Sophie came home in tears and by the end of the first week she was cultivating murderous fantasies.

However, she didn't want to give up her desire to become a doctor; she had worked so hard to get to that point and she certainly wouldn't give it all up because of some interpersonal difficulties.

After a couple of months, she began to realize how to behave around Amanda, what made her angry and what mollified her; she had begun to appreciate her caustic sense of humour and, surprisingly, she found, that after all, she actually liked Amanda. From then on, they began to get along; which, Sophie had to admit, was a relief.

After all, the two of them spent most of their day in the medical centre, and, at that time, a job was too precious to give it up lightly. Not to mention that, for the first time in years, she had found a friend.

Meanwhile, the news of the infection had spread in the waiting room, and so did the panic. No one could think of anything else, it seemed. The air was charged with nervous energy.

That day Sophie treated a number of patients. She stitched up a bad cut on an arm, plastered a fractured finger, prescribed medicines without knowing that they would ever be obtained.

She checked on Mr Verlinden, a man in his seventies who went to the medical centre virtually every week, for real ailments or, more frequently, for diseases that he imagined having.

That day he was sure he was on the verge of a heart attack, although his electrocardiogram argued the opposite. His problem, Sophie thought, was that he had a vivid imagination and too much free time. Like many of their elderly patients he preferred to be examined by Sophie rather than Amanda, because she was more patient and listened to him.

Amanda, despite being a brilliant doctor, did not really want to spend time listening to old people's complaints.

"Once you understand what ails them, cut them short," she always warned, "We are the only medical centre in the radius of fifty kilometres, we cannot start providing psychological support too."

Sophie knew she was right, but she always found keeping the hard line difficult. In any case, on a day like that, the presence of Verlinden was almost a welcome distraction.

During the whole day Sophie tried to keep herself busy and not think about the infected which had been found just a few blocks from there.

She washed her hands repeatedly, as if the gesture could keep away the virus.

She knew it wasn't so: the disease was transmitted by contact, even through fabric, and once it had settled on the skin there was nothing left to do.

The incubation lasted about a month, without any discernible symptoms, but it was highly contagious. When the fever began to rise, it was already too late.

Not everyone caught it, however: there had been a long debate about people immune to infection, although many doctors claimed that it was an urban legend. Some said that anyone who came into contact with the pathogen agent became ill, but that did not stop people like her hoping to save themselves.

Maybe she *was* immune... maybe she shouldn't worry, maybe...

"What are you doing?" Amanda interrupted her, approaching the basin.

"Just washing my hands..." she answered.

Amanda raised an eyebrow: "For a quarter of an hour?"

Sophie didn't answer.

It was stupid, she knew. But she had to do something to reassure herself she is keeping the disease at bay.

Amanda rolled her eyes: "You were tested this very morning. You are not infected."

"I know." She nodded.

Actually, she had come in contact with at least fifty people in the course of the morning.

"Anyway, paranoia is useless."

"I know," Sophie repeated.

"If you are so scared of diseases maybe this is not the right job for you."

"I'm not scared," Sophie interrupted her. "I am just worried because of the dragon plague, like anyone with some common sense."

Amanda sighed: "Put the plastic gloves on, they prevent the passage of the virus."

Sophie shrugged: "Yeah, I always do, but it is not certain they prevent it... some say there is no way to stop the virus, that the gloves and such don't really offer any protection..."

"They do work, don't worry," Amanda assured her, looking smug. "When you're done come to the lab, Lukas has got coffee."

Sophie opened her eyes wide: "Real coffee? Wow."

The ration cards rarely allowed one to purchase luxury products like coffee; while commonly found in the black market, it was quite expensive.

Lukas Bonnet, the lab technician, was in charge of the analyses; he was tall, blond and rather handsome, as many of the patients had noticed.

It was such a pity that his work did not include any contact with the public, Sophie thought, because his presence would be a great advertisement for any commercial enterprise.

"Lukas, have you finished the analyses that I asked you to do yesterday? They are very urgent," the doctor said, entering the lab.

He smiled proudly: "They've been ready since last night!"

"But... why didn't you tell me?"

Lukas' smile faltered: "I haven't thought about it... "

While the technician went to get the papers, Amanda whispered: "Remind me why I hired him?"

Sophie shrugged. "He's ornamental," she said.

"Yeah, there's that," Amanda sighed, "He can't be clever too, it would be unfair."

After accepting the papers from Lukas, Amanda poured out three cups of coffee.

It was strong and dark, and its aroma made Sophie's mouth water.

"Hmm, this is really good," she said after the first sip, "I haven't tasted coffee in years!"

The coffee had an intense, exotic flavour, completely different from the bland lukewarm beverages she was used to. It seemed absurd that there was a time when people drank it every day. Its powerful intensity made her head spin.

"Where did you find it?" she asked.

Lukas smiled: "A gift. The girl who works at my favourite food distribution centre, in the sixth ring, is always so nice to me."

Sophie wasn't surprised.

"So, what do you think about the infected?" Lukas asked. "Do you reckon it got caught?"

Amanda snorted: "This bloody infected again! Isn't there anything else to talk about?"

Lukas looked surprised: "Are you really not worried?"

"I just think that we're worrying more than we should, that's all."

Sophie sloshed the coffee in her cup: "There is no cure and no way to stop the disease. It seems to me that our concern is perfectly justified."

"There are ways to contain the disease…"

"The plastic gloves? And what else? Homeopathy?" Sophie teased her.

The doctor shrugged: "Yes, plastic gloves, for example. It's a virus, and as such it has limits, there are materials in which it can propagate and some in which it can't. I think that there's no point in talking about it as if it were a magical, mighty entity. Such an attitude won't help us combat the epidemic."

"It will not be over while there are still cases of the plague," Lukas said.

"It will not be over until the last dragon is killed," Sophie corrected him.

Dying of the plague was the lesser of two evils: those who survived suffered worse. There was no cure; the few survivors would never go back to what they were before, nor would cease to be contagious.

It was from those damned dragons that the plague had come, bringing with it all this pain and destruction.

If Sophie had to imagine an ideal world, it would have been a world without dragons.

Lukas drank his last sip of coffee. "Come on, Sophie. The police are doing all they can to get all the infected. They have already eliminated most of them."

This much was true: the arrest of an infected these days was groundbreaking enough to be widely broadcasted across all media. Everybody knew, though, that the infected had a network of spies and contacts that helped them in their evil plan to spread the disease across the entire population.

"In any case," Amanda snapped, "living in terror is useless. Take the necessary precautions and try to move on with your life. That's the only way."

Sophie swallowed what was left of her coffee: "I guess it is."

That evening, Sophie wished Amanda and Lukas a good week end. When she stepped on the crowded train that would take her home, she could not help but stare at her fellow passengers.

A lot of people, she included, wore hats and gloves to protect themselves from the rain, and many of the faces couldn't be seen very well.

How many of them could be infected? And how many shoulders, how many elbows, backs and hands had she inadvertently touched to get on the train, while grasping the handles to avoid falling as she scrambled to her seat? How many people had sat there before her?

It was simply terrifying.

She tried to focus on the city scenery rolling outside the window.

Europa was the last city that the world knew: it was the largest, once, before the Great War and the devastation that followed it. It covered an area of fifteen thousand square kilometres, an area that apparently centuries before was divided between France, Germany and Belgium. The buildings were tall and grey, and illuminated by the evening light they had a spectral beauty of their own. The city stretched endlessly, not only around but also upward: in that area few buildings had less than fifty floors.

It was said to be the last bastion of a civilization that was nearly lost and forgotten.

The train went through the second ring, then the third and fourth. The first ring, the richest and most ancient part of the city, was not accessible to most citizens; it was divided from the rest of the districts by a high wall topped with barbed wire and guarded by soldiers with machine guns ready to fire. The buildings were lower in there and there was more space between them.

However, few people lived in the first district: it was an area mostly dedicated to government buildings, ministries and offices. Sophie didn't think too much about it; it was as if on another planet.

The train ran along the suspended tracks between the blocks. Under the city there still existed a network of tunnels and tracks dating back hundreds of years, but it was mostly unused these days: it had become too dangerous.

The underground spaces provided shelter to the poorest, those who had no jobs and no access to the food distribution or social accommodations, so they could only live by their wits. No law existed down there, and theft and murder were everyday occurrences. There were roads and tunnels that crossed the entire city, linking each street with the buildings, stations, sewers and rivers.

One could live their entire life in the underground city, they said, without ever leaving: women gave birth there, and their children could live for years without ever seeing the sunlight.

Sophie shuddered.

She arrived at her station in the fifth ring, got off the train and walked home.

She lived in a tiny apartment in a building with hundreds of housing units. Since she had neither a partner nor children, according to the law she was entitled to a room of four by four meters: enough space for a single bed topped with shelves full of books, a folding table, sink and stove, a television hanging on the wall opposite the bed.

With her savings from the first year of work she had purchased the installation of a small bathroom divided by a sheet metal wall: it was little more than a meter and a half square, but at least she could avoid the long lines at the common bathroom.

During the years, she had made the little place as cosy as she could, painting the walls in a bright shade of yellow and buying a colourful blanket that she hoped could counter the greyness and darkness that penetrated through the window.

Once she walked in, she stroked the stunted lettuce that grew in a small vase on the sill of her one skimpy window. She carefully watered the pitiful little plants.

"How are you, babies?" she greeted them affectionately "Am I wrong or have you grown a bit?"

She had read that talking to plants would help them grow, so she often engaged in long conversations with her lettuce.

Most people tried to grow some kind of food themselves, but the lack of light was a big problem. The houses were crammed too closely to one another to allow the passage of natural light to any significant degree.

"If I manage to put aside some money this year, I'll buy some nice cultivation lamps for you," she promised.

She opened the fridge and realized that she had to go to the food distribution as soon as possible, as there was almost nothing left.

That night she was too tired, though.

She put together a sandwich of stale bread and a protein substitute (a burger with a cardboard-like consistency) that she accompanied with a strawberry-flavoured drink.
Sometimes she wondered if the strawberry flavour of soft drinks and snacks was the one of real strawberries, as she had never eaten one.

A lot of foods were strawberry-flavoured, but they were all slightly different from each other... who knew which the real one was?

In any case, the sweet drink and humble meal made her feel better.

She turned on the television. All the channels showed updates on the case of the plague reported that morning.

Then a message from President Hartmann was broadcasted. In his missive the President reassured the citizens and stressed that the disease had been contained.

The President was an elderly man, with a white beard and a deep, comforting voice; if he said that the emergency had been contained, it was probably true, Sophie thought. Perhaps there were many people who could lie in front of cameras, but Hartmann surely was not one of them.

After the presidential message, there was a broadcast that showed the brutal assault of a dragon on the edge of the quarantined areas: raw and disturbing images with vehicles exploding and trees going up in flames like matches.

Everything was taken from a distance, so the dragon looked like a dark and blurred shape, which made it even more terrifying.

Sophie sank into the comforting warmth of the blankets.

She lost her parents and brother during the first wave of the plague, when she was a child. Actually, she had very few memories of her family. She could remember their faces only thanks to the photographs preserved in an old, yellowed album. It was her paternal grandmother who had raised her until she was twelve.

She was lucky: thousands of children like her, at that time, had been infected, or locked up in state institutions more similar to prisons than to orphanages.

She had ended up in one of those places herself, though fortunately for no more than a couple of years.

It was a period of her life that she didn't like to dwell upon. On her fifteenth birthday she was deemed fit to live alone and was given a housing unit and the credits inherited from her grandmother.

In any case, seeing the world around her collapse because of an epidemic had instilled in her the desire to become a doctor. She had always known that this was the mission she wanted to dedicate her life to: what was the point of doing anything else, if a single virus could wipe out every human effort?

Amanda had been working for some time on a research project focused on finding a vaccine against the disease. At first Sophie had to take care of the patients in the study, but this left her with a certain amount of time to help Amanda.

One of the most annoying bureaucratic hurdles was acquiring the authorization to obtain samples of infected blood, a procedure that took many months and never resulted in the requested quantity.

To be honest, Sophie had no illusions that she would find the cure for the dragon plague herself. She was aware of her limits: the way she saw it, some people had a quick, brilliant mind... they had insights.

She was not one of them. She had never thought of herself as stupid, but she didn't have that spark of genius that she saw in other people... in Amanda, for example.

She might find the cure, Sophie was certain; one of the reasons why Sophie loved working with Amanda was the feeling of being able to contribute to something important. "You're a young old woman." Amanda told her sometimes, teasing her for her quiet and lonely nature. "You only lack the white hair and the knitting needles."

Sophie usually laughed it off - even though, deep down, she wondered if it might be true.

Sophie got up early the next day. She didn't have to go to work, but there were quite enough chores to attend to. This would help her keep her mind off the plague and the infected.

She made breakfast of the little food she had left (a small box of tofu and tap water), then went to the food distribution centre in her neighbourhood.

To access the distribution, it was necessary to bring a card on which each month a number of caloric units were automatically charged. The cost of these was deduced from taxes on her wage.

The food has always been subject to rationing, for as long as she could remember: arable fields were few and afar, crushed between the overcrowded urban area and the quarantined areas, where thinking of growing something was pure folly. Out there, only dry and twisted shrubs could survive, plants that seemed to live more out of will and spite than thanks to real natural resources.

The outer areas of the city, in the eighth ring, housed large greenhouses where grains, beans and potatoes were cultivated, while the food industry worked tirelessly to synthesize the vital nutrients and produce cheap food which nevertheless gave the necessary nutritional intake to the citizens.

The distributed food was practical, economical and functional, but also terribly tasteless. It was old people in particular that complained because, they said, they could remember the rich and intense flavours of their youth: her grandmother often spoke of ripe and juicy peaches that she used to eat as a girl, and about beef steaks cooked on the barbecue. Sophie found the idea a little laughable: thinking of wasting space and nourishment for all those animals was a real absurdity.

However, curious foods sometimes appeared on the black market: hot spices wrapped in packages with incomprehensible writings, vegetables and fruit with intense and exotic colours, bitter chocolate, coffee.

They were sold by shady characters who lived in underground tunnels; she had no idea where they might have got these wares from. Perhaps they found old underground warehouses from before the Great War.

Old Louis, who lived in the housing unit in front of hers and who was old enough to have outlived two wives and, a rare case, able to collect his retirement funds, often launched himself into long monologues about how people of the first ring consumed those delicacies every day and it was only them, the poor ordinary citizens, who had to settle for canned vegetables and protein substitutes.

But old Louis liked to talk of conspiracies and secrets: Sophie imagined it helped him pass the time. The truth, according to her, was out there for everyone, as boring as it was reassuring.

She couldn't understand, then, why people complained: perhaps the food was not particularly flavourful, but at least it was guaranteed. Would he have preferred to starve in the subway tunnels?

The sky was overcast and cloudy, but at least it was not raining.

The city was almost constantly topped by a dome of pollution that made the sky look dull even when the sun was shining. Sometimes, though, when the wind had been blowing for several hours and the day was clear, the light flooded everything, and the city was undeniably beautiful, with the glass of the buildings reflecting the sun like jewels and the curtains on the windows fluttering in the air.

It was worth it to withstand so many grey days for those rare sunny hours.

Today, however, was not one of those sunny ones, and Sophie walked to the nearby food centre without much enthusiasm. As she was standing in the queue, groups of people around her did nothing but chatter about a possible new wave of the epidemic.

Perfect, just what I needed, she thought.

"That's what they want," someone said, "What they have always wanted. They want to infect us all, so they'll be the ones to rule and dragons will hunt unrestricted."

Sophie tried to focus on the row in front of her to block the words out.

Still about forty people, maybe a little more. She began to count: *one, two, three...*

"I dunno..." said a woman's voice, doubtful. "When my Simon had the plague, he seemed to be recovering. The fever had begun to wane... Then came the medical police, and they put him in quarantine," she sighed. "There was nothing I could do," she added bitterly.

Twenty-five, twenty-six, twenty-seven...

"Oh dear, I'm so sorry," someone said, "but I saw a survivor before he was taken away, oh yes! A scene I will never forget as long as I live, my word."

Thirty-one, thirty-two...

"He had green scales all over his body, like a snake! And his eyes... they were not human eyes, I assure you. He had the evil stare of a beast."

Thirty-three, thirty-four...

"He ran naked through the streets, looking like an overgrown lizard, and biting all those he could get his claws on. He wanted to eat them, you know, he would have wolfed them down! He kept screaming, or perhaps roaring, who knows. An animal, I tell you, an animal!"

Sophie had stopped trying not to listen. She could not help it.

The woman who had spoken before gave a stifled groan: "Simon..." she said.

"I'm so sorry, dear," the interlocutor repeated, "But he wouldn't have been your Simon anymore."

It was common knowledge that those who survived the disease suffered an even worse fate: they turned into hybrid bloodthirsty creatures whose only goal was to escape and join their kind. Their kind, of course, were not the other humans anymore: those were the dragons.

It was said the lizard-men could hear them inside their head. They called them, whispered in their minds.

Their bodies also changed to become more dragon-like: scales appeared on various parts and they gained superhuman strength, which made them practically fire-proof.

Sophie had seen them too, in the newspapers and on television: they had almost nothing human left.

They kept a little consciousness, however, that allowed them to organize themselves: they found each other, and together they plotted to overthrow the government.

They raided the outer rings of the city where supplies were stored, riding their monstrous dragons and distributing death and destruction. They were a cross between wild animals and terrorists.

Some said that they lived outside the city, in the quarantined areas, in forests and abandoned villages; others said that they were actually there, in the midst of normal people. They hid their scales under hoods, gloves and raincoats, their vertical-pupiled eyes behind sunglasses. They roamed the city in disguise and had only one goal: to spread the disease as much as possible.

The weak would die, but the chosen would become like them, and the world would be dominated by their race, along with the dragons.

"As long as *he*'s out there, the General, no one will be safe," said the woman who had mourned Simon.

The chief of the rebel survivors had no name (perhaps none of those creatures had a real name anymore), but the newspapers called him the General.

His digitally processed identikit had adorned the walls of the city since Sophie could remember: a particularly monstrous creature, even among those abominations.

Everything about him was scary and seemed deliberately wrong: the colours, the traits, the proportions. It was said that he was the one who had spread the first wave of the epidemic, that he raided the city for months, distributing his deadly touch to all who came within range. There were different opinions about him, but everyone agreed on one thing: he was a merciless creature.

Finally it was Sophie's turn and, trying to shake off the disturbing thoughts that the conversation she was privy to had awakened, she prepared to withdraw her weekly ration: several cans of legumes, grains and canned fish, potatoes, three packs of protein substitutes, two packages of undefined green leafy vegetables (a variety of spinach, perhaps?) , seed oil, soft sweetened drinks, soluble barley, sweetener and the usual supplements.

"Only two strawberry drinks?" she observed, disconsolate. The others were lemon-flavoured. She hated lemon (or at least, its artificial flavouring).

The distribution operator shrugged: "That's all you get this week. Maybe you can try swapping with someone," he suggested.

"Thanks, anyway."

She didn't feel like talking to anyone, not even to suggest a swap of drinks, so she took the bags and walked towards home.

The identikit of the General seemed to watch her viciously from the posters on the light-poles.

Sophie welcomed the new week and the dawn of Monday morning with something like relief. She didn't feel like leaving the house during the weekend and had spent most of it watching stupid programs on television. The mindless way in which full days flowed fast while sitting in front of the television never ceased to amaze her.

She had breakfasted on a lemon-flavoured drink and a box of oatmeal, then took the first train to work.

She met a checkpoint that screened all those who entered the third ring: a nurse in the uniform of the medical police pricked her finger and a drop of blood touched the sensor.

Sophie had a moment of panic, but then a green light lit up.

"Go on," the nurse announced, smiling.

At that hour there were few people at the station, so it didn't take long for everyone to be screened. Sophie arrived at the medical centre early; she took the elevator to the basement of the building where the centre was and discovered that neither Amanda nor Lukas were in yet.

Outside the door, however, a queue of people had already formed, so she decided to open and start receiving them. Working would distract her from the dark thoughts of the week end.

The first patient was an elderly lady, with long white hair tied up in a bun and a sweet, slightly absent-minded air. She reminded Sophie of her grandmother.

"How are you today, Mrs...?"

"Lemaire," the old lady said, "Emma Lemaire. And I'm pretty good, considering what I went through!"

"What have you had?"

"At my age! By now I've had everything!"

Sophie smiled and nodded.

The elderly often had a very dramatic way to describe their symptoms. Often, she had the impression that they wanted to have a chat more than anything else.

"I came in last week and your colleague... Doctor..."

"Solarin," Sophie suggested.

"Yes, that's the one. Dr Solarin sent me to some analysis and told me to come back today for the results."

"I'll go and take them," Sophie offered.

Emma Lemaire hesitated: "I had the impression she wanted to see them herself."

Sophie smiled: "I can go through them with you, and if you still have any doubt, we will call Dr Solarin."

She went to the lab and found herself face to face with Lukas, who had arrived in the meantime.

He looked scruffy and his hair was little unkempt, as if he just fell off the bed (as he probably did), and Sophie couldn't help noticing how attractive he was.

She averted her gaze and began rummaging among the files of the analysis results. What she was looking for, though, seemed to be missing.

"Did you see Emma Lemaire's file?" she asked.

"Um... I think so, it sounds familiar..." he said, vaguely. "Ah yes, of course, the urgent analyses from last week. Amanda took them."

"Oh. I'll wait for her, then," Sophie gestured at the door.

"There was something weird about them, anyway," Lukas added.

She frowned. "What?"

Lukas shrugged. "Well, I don't remember. Something about strange plague antibodies."

Sophie's mouth dropped: "What did you say?"

"Yeah, there were some antibodies that were definitely out of the ordinary... oh, but calm down, she's not contagious!" he added quickly, noticing her bewildered expression. "If those tests had a positive result I would have done the emergency procedure. I'm not stupid."

"No, no, of course not."

Probably it wasn't anything important, but it was still worthwhile to check those tests with Amanda.

Sophie saw her entering the medical centre: she looked tired, with deep shadows under her eyes; her dark skin was marked by wrinkles of fatigue and worry.

"Amanda, hello. Listen, you know Mrs. Lemaire's blood tests...?" Sophie began.

"Is she here?" Amanda asked her urgently, grabbing her arm.

"Who? The Lemaire lady?"

"Yes, of course, her!"

"She's in there," Sophie informed her, amazed by her colleague's reaction. "She's not infected, is she?" she asked, alarmed.

Amanda shook her head: "No, no, calm down. Send her to my room and go on with the other patients. I will take it from here..."

"Because you know, Lukas said that there was something wrong with her plague antibodies..."

"Lower your voice," Amanda snapped, leaving Sophie speechless. "There is nothing strange. I told you not to worry."

"I'm sorry, I was only trying..." she began.

The doctor took a breath, as if to compose herself: "I know. I'm not angry with you. Just send her to my room and forget about it, OK? Please?"

Sophie nodded: "OK... we'll talk later, right?"

Amanda appeared annoyed: "Sophie, really, it's nothing. Come on, hurry up, the waiting room is full."

Sophie motioned to the next room where the phone began to ring. Amanda answered immediately: "Solarin Medical Centre. What?" she paused "Now? OK, yes, at once."

At that moment a noise, distant at first, distracted them. It seemed to be getting closer and closer.

A high-pitched noise, metallic, annoying. A police siren, or rather two, or even... a group of sirens? It was only when two men kicked down the medical centre door that Sophie realized they were looking for them.

"Medical police," one of them said, "Nobody move. We have an arrest order for Amanda Solarin. She's infected."

Amanda acted before the dust of the ruined door had time to settle on the floor: she grabbed Sophie's arm and pulled her inside the room where Emma Lemaire was waiting and quickly barred the door.

"Oh, Doctor!" Emma greeted her "Just the one I was waiting for! What was that noise...?"

Amanda ignored her, turning instead to Sophie: "I'm sorry. I'm really sorry I have to drag you into this, but time is short, and I have no choice. Listen..."

"What...? Are you really infected...?" Sophie stared horrified at Amanda's hand that kept its powerful grip on her arm.

"Of course not! Listen to me, I said! They mustn't take her. Under no circumstances must they take Mrs. Lemaire."

"Who?"

"The medical police! They came here for her. Her blood is the key to the vaccine!"

"Huh?" Emma exclaimed. She looked confused.

"A vaccine...? But then we have to tell them..."

Amanda rolled her eyes: "They don't want it to be created or distributed; they will do anything to stop it."

She gave her the dossier with Mrs Lemaire's analysis: "Keep her safe, they may already know her identity. In three days, Thursday at seven p.m., go to the subway station called Stuttgart. There you will meet a man called Jamie. You will easily recognize him. He will ask you for a password, which is 'Saint George'. Do you understand? In the meantime, hide in a safe place. Don't trust anybody. Get these," she put a few packs of drugs in her hands, and Sophie mechanically pocketed them.

"They will come in handy."

Someone began knocking violently at the door: "Open now, it's the police!"

Emma winced: "What's going on? What do they want from me?"

"Do you understand?" Amanda repeated, staring Sophie in the eye.

She was on the verge of tears: "I... I..."

"I'm really sorry, but this is too important. All our lives may depend on the blood of this woman. You must keep her hidden until you bring her to Jamie. Do you understand?"

Sophie nodded, sniffling: "What about you?"

"It'll be okay. Now you go," Amanda opened a cabinet where she kept the medicines: to Sophie's surprise, her colleague flicked a mechanism that made the panel and shelves shift laterally, revealing a hidden door inside. Behind it, there was a narrow, dark tunnel.

"Go on!"

Emma Lemaire seemed unsure of what to do, so Sophie pushed her inside the cabinet as fast as she could.

"Easy, easy... my legs!" the old lady complained.

Unfortunately, there was no time for apologies.

As she closed the door behind her, the one at the entrance of the room opened up.

Sophie realized she had failed to properly close the cabinet door, so there was a small crack left. She didn't know what to do, afraid of attracting the attention of the medical police if it shut with a noise.

"What's going on?" Lemaire asked, increasingly confused.

Sophie mouthed her to be quiet. Thankfully the frail old lady nodded, though she appeared terrified.

The next moment Sophie heard the voices of the police officers who burst into the room. She put one eye against the crack of the door, but all she could see was an empty corner of the room.

"Amanda Solarin, an arrest warrant was issued against you."

"On what grounds?"

Amanda's voice sounded calm and confident, but Sophie knew her well enough to realize how agitated she was.

"Contracting and spreading DH16N10," the cop answered in a flat, expressionless voice.

"That's ridiculous. I have been screened this very morning before entering the third ring. I'm clean."

The policeman did not seem to hear her: "Put your hands behind your head and come with us."

"Why?"

Some nervous noises followed: "I told you to put your hands behind you head... don't get closer!"

"Stay calm, look, I... "

"I told you not to get closer!"

Sophie heard objects falling to the ground, the wheels of the stretcher rolling across the floor, and then a dull, grim sound that she didn't recognize. It took her a moment to comprehend that it was the sound of someone being hit.

Suddenly Amanda fell on the floor, in the very corner of the room Sophie could see. She had to clamp one hand against her mouth so as not to scream: Amanda's face was covered in blood that gushed out of her nose and trickled out of the corner of her lips.

For a brief moment their eyes met, and Sophie could read a mute plea. *Go away, what are you still doing here?*

Then she saw Amanda dragged away, leaving a trail of blood on the disinfected floor.

For a few moments there were radio noises that communicated something unintelligible to Sophie, the sound of objects being moved, people walking, agitated voices from the waiting room.

Then the silence became heavy and almost unnatural.

Emma Lemaire took Sophie's hand: "We must go, my dear," she said in a gentle whisper.

Sophie nodded, pushed the door shut with a barely audible click, and followed the old lady down the dark alley that stretched before them.

Chapter 2

Officer Erik Persson shut the door of the van used to transfer the infected.

He wished he was able to smoke a cigarette.

Obviously, he wouldn't have dared to do so while he was on duty, in the street, in front of a crowd of onlookers that had assembled in front of the door of the medical centre. But damn, what wouldn't he give to be able to take just a couple of puffs.

His partner, Zoe Hernandez, was attempting to disperse the crowd, while other officers were climbing quickly into other cars.

Better not to stay too close by, in case the infected had had time to warn her friends.

Erik instinctively shuddered at the thought.

"Shall we?" Hernandez asked, climbing into the driver's seat of the van.

Their informant had spoken of an assistant and an older woman who could be located within the medical centre, but they hadn't found any trace of them.

The building had been searched from top to bottom, and now it was very unlikely that they would be found... apparently, they had been able to escape somehow.

It was too late; they would have to bear the consequences of failing to capture them.

Erik nodded and climbed into the seat next to Hernandez.

The engine roared and the vehicle headed to the police headquarters.

While the van rolled through the city streets, Erik began to feel the adrenaline drop.

Technically only authorized vehicles could circulate within Europa, but even so their pace slowed the traffic: there were police cars, of course, ambulances and the blue cars of the authorities. There were taxis for the richer, even though they were rare in that part of the city, the crossings for the trains and the tracks of the light rail. It would take a while to get the headquarters.

The operation would have been a success had it not been for the two missing women.

It had been fast, no doubt: the infected had tried to resist, but Hernandez had neutralised her with a couple of well-placed shots.

Erik knew he was supposed to scold her for her use of violence, but he was too aware of the panic that surged when one found themselves close to an approaching infected.

Zoe Hernandez had only recently joined the police, and Erik was initially dubious when she was appointed as his partner.

She was very young, and without almost any field experience. In the various assignments that they had tackled together, though, Zoe had fared rather well; Erik had to admit that, in particular, she had very good reflexes.

Once he could have said the same about himself, but that had been years ago: years that had made him slow and heavy, although he was as strong as ever.

His wife Thea liked to say to him that he could count his years on his waistline, like a tree.

Erik Persson was fifty, and he had been in the police for almost twenty-eight years: first in the normal city police, then, when the division had been created, he had been transferred to the medical police.

Once it was only the best that were assigned there, those considered smartest and most reliable, then the medical division grew further and further, to the point that they became the only true law enforcement in the city.

Erik sometimes wondered why they had chosen him at the time, as he wasn't a better or worse cop than most of his colleagues, and eventually he had come to the conclusion that it had been his hatred of the infected that had made him stand out.

When the medical police was created, his second kid, Peter, had just been born, two years after Maja, and the idea that his children should grow up and live in a world where such a monstrosity existed filled him with a terror that soon turned into anger and determination.

He had worked hard to give them a good future, a stable and peaceful life... those creatures couldn't just show up and destroy everything.

It wasn't fair.

As they turned into the junction of the ring highway the crackle of the radio pulled Erik away from his thoughts.

"Team B12, can you hear me?"

Hernandez pressed the button to enable the answer: "Affirmative."

"There seems to be a blockage in the ring highway, try to avoid using it."

"Shit," she murmured to herself, then pressed the radio button: "Too late, I'll get out at the next exit."

As soon as the line went dead, they drove up behind several cars stopped in traffic.

Some people had gone out of their cars to see what was happening.

"What's going on?" Erik asked, while his colleague slowed the van to a halt.

"What's that noise?" she asked.

As a matter of fact, Erik could also hear a sort of loud buzzing approaching.

The very second that Hernandez braked, the van shook with a sudden impact.

"What was that?"

"On the roof," Erik said, drawing his gun from its holster.

He was vaguely aware of people around them who were racing back to their cars, apparently terrified.

He opened the door that connected the driver's area to the rear, where they had put the arrestee.

She was still unconscious, but Erik saw that someone was trying to force the door.

As he and his partner came out of the van, they remained speechless for a few moments.

An old-fashioned helicopter, dating, he guessed, back to the twenty-first century, was flying above their vehicle: a man had jumped on the roof and was trying to open the rear door. The scales on his face left no doubt as to the identity of the helicopter passengers: they were infected.

Two of them had managed to land on their vehicle: he estimated that another was piloting the helicopter, and there was at least one more of them there up there, shooting towards them.

Hernandez fired first, hitting one of the infected square in the chest.

He took the blow, leaning back, but in a few moments, he was back on his feet.

Erik realized that the rebels, just like policemen, were wearing full body suits.

"Get back in the van!" Hernandez shouted.

"The road is blocked!" he protested.

"Not the other lane, though."

They hurried back into the van, and Hernandez switched the engine on.

Erik turned on the radio: "We've been attacked, asking for reinforcements. I repeat, send us reinforcements as soon as possible."

He could not interpret the crackling of the radio since he was thrown towards the back of the van as the vehicle performed a sharp U-turn.

Hernandez drove in the wrong way through the still cars, trying to find a crossing point to the opposite lane.

In the meantime, the infected on the roof of the van continued to attack the door, and Erik estimated that at this rate he would break in before long.

"I have to go back there," he declared.

"But... are you sure... the procedure...?" Hernandez objected, unsure.

"If we can't stop them, the procedure is good for nothing," he insisted.

When he noticed Zoe's anxious expression he added: "You just think about driving, get us out of this mess."

Hernandez nodded without taking her eyes off the road, while Erik unlocked the grate separating the cockpit from the rear of the van and got in the area where the inmates were usually locked. To be on the safe side, he dropped the helmet visor on his face, covering it completely.

The arrestee was lying on the floor of the van, still unconscious, but definitely alive. Erik saw her chest rise and fall while breathing.

Someone was still battering the door, and Erik realized he had better reinforce it; but before he could do anything, the door burst open.

A man stood in front of him – *no, not a man, an infected*, Erik inwardly corrected himself. He was tall and thin, with black hair and almond-shaped eyes.

The lizard man pounced, but Erik dodged him by jumping to the side, taking advantage of the creature's momentary loss of balance to deliver a blow to his legs that made him stumble down to his knees.

Like many times before, he was grateful for the police protective suit, which not only shielded him from bullets, but also covered every bit of skin that could be exposed to infection.

The infected managed to get up and attacked again, knocking Erik down. Persson felt the van jolting, and metal fragments detached from the door. The vehicle increased its speed; Apparently, Hernandez had managed to cross the dividing line and slip into the opposite lane of the highway, down which they were now travelling at full speed.

The infected staggered for a moment, struggling to keep his balance. He did not have much time: Erik struck him from the ground with both feet and managed to knock him out of the vehicle.

He heard a scream and a thud when the creature hit the asphalt, but after a blink they were too far to discern anything else.

One down, he thought.

The arrestee next to him gave a groan but didn't seem to wake up.

It wasn't over, though: another creature entered the van. This time it was a woman, at least as far as Erik could tell, given that she was completely covered by the bullet-proof suit. She was still anchored to a rope that had been lowered from the helicopter. The creature pulled out a knife: a cunning strategy, Erik had to acknowledge. If she opened a gash in his suit, he could be infected.

"Step aside, officer," she said in a resolute tone.

In response, Erik lunged at her, but she dodged, almost sending him out of the van.

Damn it, I'm getting slower and slower.

Meanwhile the creature had approached the arrestee and was checking her neck, trying to feel a pulse.

Erik tried to stop her, but she dodged him with unnatural speed and plunged the knife into his arm, tearing a long gash in the protective suit.

He clutched his arm with a groan of pain.

"So... dear officer," she said, "if you get one step closer, you'll discover how it feels to be on the other side of the barricade."

"Maybe," Erik said, ignoring the pain and placing himself between the infected and the arrestee, "but today this one remains here."

Something crackled in the lizard woman's helmet.

"No, they are almost..." she protested, obviously answering.

There was another croak from her transmitter, and then she walked over to door and yanked on the rope that was secured to her waist.

"It's not over, officer," she said maliciously, then was hauled by the rope back up towards the helicopter.

A moment later, the van entered a tunnel, rendering further assault from above impossible.

Hernandez made a sharp turn into a lay-by and stopped the van, skidding heavily aside.

Erik slid down to the ground next to the arrestee, who remained unconscious.

With a slow, mechanical gesture he pulled out a smuggled pack of cigarettes and a lighter.

He had really deserved that cigarette.

The reinforcements arrived a few minutes later, but it was too late to get the rebels: they had disappeared.

Erik was taken to hospital for the routine checks which were mandatory after a contact with an infected, and to have his arm treated. It was no big deal: the wound was superficial – he didn't even need a bandage - and his bloodwork came out fine.

At the very least, the afternoon spent at the medical centre of the police headquarters spared him from having to fill the massive amount of paperwork reporting that day's events. His partner took care of that.

When he arrived in the office, Hernandez was visibly exhausted.

"You know, I almost would have preferred to be stabbed," she commented, yawning.

Erik just grinned. In retrospect the chase should have seemed terrifying, but at the time he wasn't afraid. He had felt nothing but anger and the rush of adrenaline.

It had always been like that for him... maybe that was the reason why, despite his age, he was still considered fit for on-field missions. He didn't think he would have liked to sit behind a desk all day.

His partner was still staring at the screen on her desk and appeared lost in thought.

"What's going on? Need help to finish the report?" Erik offered.

Not that he had any particular inclination to do that, but it seemed right to offer his help, as poor Zoe had shouldered most of the paperwork.

"No, it's not that…. It's just..." Hernandez bit her lip. She seemed uncertain whether to go on.

"What?"

"Well, do you remember the two missing people?"

Erik nodded "The assistant and the patient. What about them?"

"I was expecting to get a big scolding for not finding them. You know, usually the failure to curb a potential infected is… like… the worst possible thing... "

"And what happened instead?"

"Nothing!" she exclaimed. "Nothing at all! That's so strange. I delivered the file and reported the problem, but Hoffman didn't so much as bat an eyelid."

Hoffman was the head of their division, a dapper guy more interested in politics than in the daily work of the police.

"That's not typical of him," Erik admitted.

"No, indeed. But wait, there's more. I said that I would proceed with the standard containment measures to be used in an emergency, you know, mugshots, patrols, the usual thing, but he said," Zoe mimed quotation marks with her fingers, "'Don't worry too much about it.' Hoffman! The one who is always bending over backwards to show his superiors that he's making every possible effort! This whole story makes no sense."

Erik frowned: "So what did you do?"

Hernandez seemed embarrassed: "Well, to tell the truth, I put out the 'Wanted' posters all the same. Hoffman didn't give me permission to set up additional patrols, though, so I alerted those already on the field."

Erik was confused. What could such lack of action by their boss mean?

"I have a theory," Zoe Hernandez said.

"What theory?"

She looked around, making sure no one was listening.

When she spoke, her voice was barely more than a whisper: "I think there is a rebel mole here in the police headquarters."

Erik felt dazed when he took the train home that night.

He couldn't get the words of his partner about a possible spy within the police out of his mind. It could even be someone in their division.

He probably knew the spy... but who was it?

He thought about his colleagues, but apart from Zoe Hernandez, they were all people he had known for many years.

Laurent had entered the medical police with him: he knew him very well, had spent whole evenings listening to his football obsession... he couldn't possibly be the mole.

Could it be Meyer, the beautiful officer who worked for the legal department? Erik had a kind of crush on her when she arrived in the department, almost fifteen years before. She was witty and brilliant, but a spy? *That is absurd.*

He went through a mental list of all his colleagues, but none seemed a suspect.

Unless... could Hoffman, the very head of the division, be an infiltrate? After all, he was the one who had given those inadequate orders to Zoe.

But this hypothesis was even less believable: over the years, their division was the most successful of all others in stopping the virus. Why would a rebel act so efficiently against his own cause? Sure, it might have been a clever strategy to put himself above all suspicion...

Erik realized that his thoughts regarding Hoffman were based more on gut sense than logic: as the director of the division, Hoffman held an administrative job, not an operational one. He was the only person in the division Erik had never worked side by side with, and therefore he did not trust Hoffman as much as the colleagues of his own rank.

In the meantime, Erik reached his station within the third ring. It was a beautiful, quiet residential area: the buildings were not as high and impersonal as those in the outer rings. There were even some that barely reached ten floors.

The building where he lived had twenty floors, and his apartment was on the top. He also possessed, as a privilege belonging to the officers of the medical police, a large balcony, big enough for a couple of chairs and a table.

Thea, his wife, was a psychologist who had worked with the police for some time.

That was how they met: Erik had to see her for a series of routine meetings following the clashes with the infected. Many policemen became very anxious, constantly worried about contracting the infection. Erik actually reacted quite well – he never lost sleep over fear of being infected - but the counselling was mandatory.

He had showed up at the counselling session with something less than enthusiasm, annoyed by the idea of having to waste his time. He had, however, found that Thea Kron, the psychologist whom he had been assigned, was a nice, interesting girl, with a beautiful smile and a smattering of freckles on her nose that enchanted him.

On the first day they spoke with little interest about the encounters with the infected; on the second day they mostly chatted throughout the whole time they should have devoted to the therapy; on the third, they decided to go on a date.

That had happened more than twenty years before.

Erik entered the house and discovered that Thea and Peter were already in.

Peter was seventeen, and the following year he would have to decide what to do with his life.

Erik secretly wished that at least one of his children would follow in his footsteps and join the police, and Maja had already decided to study computer science – which left only Peter.

Until that point, however, the boy had shown very little inclination to become a policeman. It was not too late, however, Erik thought: Peter was young, and a lot could change in a year.

"Erik!" Thea welcomed him "You left in such a hurry this morning. What happened?"

That morning, while they were eating breakfast, he had received a call from Hoffman, who had ordered him to proceed immediately to the other side of the third ring for an urgent arrest.

He barely had time to write down the address and rush out of the house.

"Hey dad," Peter greeted him rather indifferently, shrugging in his direction but not looking up from his handheld computer. Typical.

"We got another infected downtown," Erik announced.

Thea put her hands to her mouth: "Another? You mean... here?"

Erik shook his head and sat down on a chair next to the kitchen table. Suddenly he felt the tension of the day weigh upon his shoulders all at once.

"No, no... on the other side of the city," he reassured her.

Thea turned to her son. "Come on, put on something in the microwave for your father, can't you see he's exhausted? Stop lolling on the sofa all the time."

Peter stood up with a listless grunt and proceeded to the kitchen.

As soon as he went out of the room, Thea sat down beside Erik: "These episodes... they seem to happen more and more often. Do you think there's a wave of the plague again?" she asked with a worried expression.

"Um, it's hard to say... I don't think so, anyway. We do mostly preventive withdrawals," he explained.

In fact, they never happened to find other cases of infection in the same area where they had arrested an infected. Evidently the system worked.

"OK," Thea said, appearing relieved. "OK. What a shock!" she added with a nervous laugh, then got up and went into the kitchen.

"So everything's OK, right?" Thea called from the other room.

Erik thought of the creature's knife that slashed at his arm, and the rush of adrenaline when he pushed the other lizard-man out of the van. He thought of the expression on the arrestee's face while Hernandez hit her, and the creeping doubt that some of his colleagues, friends of a lifetime, might not be what they seemed.

"Sure," he answered, "everything's OK."

Later when they were in bed and Thea was sleeping next to him, Erik reflected on how much he would be willing to give to talk to his wife as they once did, when she really seemed to listen.

Now she always appeared too busy, as if her head was elsewhere.

Of course, she was concerned for everyone: for Maja, who lived alone near the computer company she worked for to pay for her studies, for Peter, who could hang out with bad company, and for himself and his missions.

But it seemed that once she found that each of them was unharmed, that was enough for her, and she didn't wish to go deeper. As far as Thea was concerned, if they were safe, they were fine.

Sometimes, though, Erik wondered if he had really come out unscathed from all these years on the job. Perhaps the psychotherapy sessions that he had so despised twenty years ago would have been useful now. He let the thought linger for a while.

Then he rolled over in bed, and finally fell asleep.

Chapter 3

The tunnel stretched for kilometres; it was completely dark except for the faint light coming from the street through the grates attached to the ceiling. At those points Sophie and Emma Lemaire walked hugging the walls to avoid being seen. Not that it was likely someone would look inside, but still.

Sophie walked in silence, crying softly; Emma followed her, equally silent. Every now and then the old lady threw her a concerned glance but, Sophie imagined, her companion had enough worries of her own.

It all seemed so surreal: the police, Amanda, the test results...

They do not want the vaccine to be created and spread, they will do anything to stop it, Amanda had said.

Was it really true? Sophie did not know what to believe. She had considered the option of turning herself in, but Amanda's bloody face still stood vividly before her eyes.

Was she still alive? Sophie had no idea. For all she knew, the cops had already searched the medical centre and found the secret door. Maybe they are already waiting for them on the other end of the tunnel, Sophie thought in panic.

She dried her eyes, took a deep shuddering breath and blinked rapidly to prevent the tears from coming back. There was no use in crying. She had to think.

Hide in a safe place, do not trust anyone... what was she supposed to do?

She didn't know any safe place, except for her apartment. But could she go back?

It wouldn't take long for the police to find her address... They only had to open any notebook in the medical centre, her contact information was everywhere.

Sophie and Emma had nothing with them: no documents, no handheld computer, nothing. Not even money, now that she thought of it. Where were they supposed to hide?

She sniffled: why her? What had she done to deserve all this?

Only that morning she was a normal person, with a house, a food card that would never let her starve, even her own private bathroom, and her salad seedlings...

No one would water them anymore, Sophie thought. They would die of thirst.

For some reason, that stupid thought made her cry again.

"My dear, are you alright?" Emma Lemaire asked.

"No," Sophie said.

"How long is this tunnel?"

"I don't know."

Emma sounded frantic: "Where do we go from here? What do we do? Were those people looking for me? What's in my blood?"

"I don't know, I don't know!" Sophie repeated.

The elderly woman kept looking at her expectantly as if she anticipated that at any moment she would tell her more.

But Sophie didn't know anything more, she didn't know anything about anything!

And now she also had to take care of this old lady because, let's be real, Emma Lemaire seemed very sweet, but she looked like she wouldn't last a day out there.

Not that Sophie was sure she would fare much better herself. *What a pair we make*, she thought bitterly.

"Why did you ask to have your blood tested?" she finally asked.

Maybe some talking would distract her from her gloomy thoughts and shed some light on this whole insane situation.

"Tested? Ah..." Emma seemed to consider it. "I was very ill some time ago. I thought I would die!"

Sophie kept walking: "Symptoms?"

"I had a fever... it was so high! It was like a fire burning inside me and..."

"Ok, high fever," Sophie snapped. Normally she would have been more polite, but at that moment she felt that being a little abrupt was more than justified. "What else? Cough, flu symptoms?"

Mrs. Lemaire thought about it: "I don't think so, no... but the pustules were horrible."

"Pustules?"

She nodded: "Oh yes, the pustules. Terrible, really annoying. I had them all along my spine, on the legs, and on my arms... I didn't know which way to turn when I was trying to sleep!"

There was a moment of silence, in which Sophie was acutely aware of her heart that began pounding in her chest. She breathed heavily through her nose.

She took a step back: "Get away from me," she whispered.

Emma Lemaire shook her head: "Oh no! I'm not infected! I did the tests three times!"

She made as if to place her hand on Sophie's arm.

Sophie winced: "Don't touch me!"

"Please, my dear," Mrs. Lemaire insisted, "you have my medical reports here with you. Read them, go on."

With shaking hands, Sophie opened the folder, briefly scanned the document and looked intently at the bottom line.

"Not infected," she read.

"There. There it is. I told you so."

Still, there something odd about it. "But here it says that you have antibodies compatible with the virus DH16N10..." Sophie thought aloud. "That means you came into contact with the virus…"

"...and I recovered."

Sophie frowned: "That's not possible. Nobody recovers."

The elderly woman spread her arms: "Well, I did."

Sophie stopped for a moment and leaned back against the cold wall of tunnel.

This was why this little old lady was the key to the vaccine, why it was in her blood, as Amanda said. Emma Lemaire was the only human being who had ever recovered from the dragon plague.

Amanda knew it, and the medical police had arrested her for this.

Sophie thought back about her colleague's last instructions: "Who is Jamie?" Sophie asked.

Mrs. Lemaire shook her head. "I don't know. Dr Solarin only told me not to talk to anyone about my blood tests, and that soon she would take me to a safe place."

"And did you talk to anyone?"

Emma appeared offended: "Of course not! I'm old, but I can still understand when I must keep my mouth shut."

This meant that someone had betrayed Amanda. Who could have talked about it to the police? It seemed impossible that Amanda had let the secret slip. She was very reserved.

Sophie herself knew very little about Amanda's private life, except that she was single, lived in the third ring, and had gone to the best medical school when she was young... not much else, in fact.

Did she have brothers or sisters, were her parents still alive? Was there a significant other, maybe? And who was this mysterious Jamie?

Walking in the semi-darkness, Sophie's foot bumped into something.

She discovered that they had arrived at the end of the tunnel, and the object against which she had slammed was in fact a ladder, leading up to what looked like the cover of a manhole.

"We've arrived," Sophie announced in a flat voice. *Great.*

Emma looked puzzled: "Where are we going now?"

Why did she assume that there must be a plan? Sophie had no plan. As a matter of fact, she felt utterly lost.

"I don't know... I don't think we can go to my house," she said, "or yours either. We have to avoid crowded places, because they are probably swarming with medical police, so no train stations or anything like that. We have no money or documents," her voice cracked. "I don't know what to do," she said, dropping wearily on the ground next to the ladder.

It was cold and wet, but she felt exhausted.

Emma opened an old-fashioned handbag and pulled out a wallet: "I have something here... fifty, a hundred... two hundred credits," she announced.

"Wow!" Sophie exclaimed, looking up. "Why would you carry all that money around?"

Mrs. Lemaire shrugged. "Thieves have already broken into my apartment twice in the past year. It makes no sense to keep my money at home where it can be stolen."

"I see."

Actually, Sophie didn't think a handbag was a much safer alternative, but she refrained from pointing that out.

"Well, that does help... although I don't know where we might go without documents," Sophie reflected. "We would have to show IDs at an hotel."

Emma sighed, disappointed. "Mightn't they make an exception? Maybe... I don't know, someone you know... or maybe there are places where they don't ask too many questions?" she suggested after a pause.

Sophie tried to think. According to the law, carrying identification was mandatory virtually anywhere: food distribution, controls, etcetera. However, there were probably people who *would* make an exception, in disreputable places closer to the underground city than to the central rings of Europa, places frequented by people who lived outside the law. Sophie had never been to any of those places, but she had sometimes passed them by.

"I suppose we could try in the sixth or seventh ring."

Sophie carefully lifted the manhole cover, discovering that it led to a deserted alley where the sides of the buildings were lined with trash containers.

"All clear," she said. She hoisted herself up, then helped Emma do the same.

While the old lady was brushing dust off her clothes, Sophie looked warily around the corner: there was a busy street, one she didn't recall ever seeing before.

On the sidewalk there were several stalls offering a plethora of wares, old and sagging stuff, mostly: bicycle parts, patched clothes, second or third-hand furniture.

A guy with long whiskers and a cart boasted of the delicacies he was selling; there were some skewers with unrecognizable meat on them. It obviously had nothing to do with the protein substitutes of the food distribution and smelled truly delicious.

Then it occurred to her that the only animals which could be easily found and captured in the city were rats, and suddenly the aroma of roast meat didn't seem so very appealing anymore.

"Let's go," she urged the old lady.

"Wait, dear," Emma said. "Your coat... "

Sophie lowered her eyes and realized she was still wearing the white uniform coat of the medical centre. She hastily inspected the pockets before shrugging it off and found the pill boxes that Amanda had given her. She put them in her trousers' pockets, deciding she would examine those more carefully later. Then she surreptitiously threw the coat in one of the garbage bins.

She remained wearing nothing but trousers, a shirt and a light sweater, and she shivered with cold. She regretted leaving her jacket on the coat hanger at the medical centre; she doubted she would ever recover it. It was almost new and very warm, and it had taken her several months of scrimping and saving to be able to afford it. The thought almost made the tears come back.

A man with a long beard entered the alley, pushing an old cart with squeaking wheels. Sophie froze. She turned to Emma: her companion looked just as nervous as she felt.

The man gave them a nod. Without waiting for a reaction, he headed for the garbage bin where Sophie's coat was still visible under the lid. He pulled it out and began to examine it critically.

Sophie felt her heart rate rising again: most likely their identikits had already been put into circulation. Could it be that this man had recognized them?

She mentally cursed herself for not discarding the coat earlier: she should have taken it off in the tunnel and left it there. She had been unpardonably careless, she should have...

To her surprise, however, the man emitted a grunt of approval as he held the coat and slipped it into his cart looking satisfied. Then he walked away, pushing the noisy cart before him.

"Let's go," Sophie repeated, and Emma nodded. They walked silently down the street, trying to blend in with the crowd.

"Where do you think we are?" Sophie whispered.

Mrs. Lemaire looked around, seemingly confused: "Oh, I don't know... I think... I believe we are in the third ring, not very far from the fourth."

She was probably right: they hadn't walked very far. Sophie estimated that they couldn't have gone farther than twenty blocks. They kept walking for a few minutes until Emma emitted a strangled sound, lifting a hand to her mouth.

"What's wrong?" Sophie asked with concern.

"Look!"

There was a screen on one of the buildings, broadcasting news around the clock. Sophie was so used to seeing those that she hardly noticed them anymore.

At that moment, however, the screen flashed an alarmingly blinking line: "POLICE LOOKING FOR TWO INFECTED."

Unsurprisingly, Sophie and Emma's photographs were displayed underneath.

Right there, in the middle of the street, Sophie found herself staring at her own face, as it was shown on the photo of her ID card.

Except, she realized, it didn't look like herself.

Of course, those were her dark eyes, her slightly broad face, her nose, her frizzy hair.

But all the same, surely, she didn't look so… sinister?

In the picture on the screen, she seemed to stare into space with a vacant air and looked just like she had just escaped from a madhouse. She wondered whether she might not be deluded regarding her own appearance – who knows, maybe she did look a little crazy - but then she noticed Emma Lemaire's photograph next to hers.

Mrs. Lemaire looked like a demented old woman, with feverish eyes and white hair sticking in all directions, completely different from her quiet and comfortable-looking self.

Sophie felt a stab of indignation. *How dare they!* On second thoughts, however, maybe it was for the best – such inaccurate portraits would make it more difficult for the police to find them.

"We have to take a train and get at least as far as the sixth ring," she said. In the outer rings there were far fewer medical police checkpoints and patrols.

Emma stopped at a stand and bought a hat, which partially concealed her face. Sophie found a heavy hooded sweatshirt that was slightly too large for her, but at least it would keep her warm. Then they arrived at a station and took the first train, heading south. To play it safer, they decided to board separate wagons and get off at the last stop, at the end of the sixth ring.

While boarding the train, Sophie took great care not to make eye contact with anyone while she made her way to a vacant seat. She felt that all eyes were fixed on her, but she tried to convince herself that it was only the power of her nervous imagination.

As she leaned against the window and watched the buildings and stations slip by, Sophie noticed with dismay several document control checkpoints, going inbound to the inner rings of the city, but thankfully none in the direction where they were heading. She guessed it would make little sense to put control points on roads leading out of the city: all around there was nothing but desolation and quarantined areas. No one would be crazy enough to venture there.

The truth was, there was no place to go outside Europa.

The journey took about three hours. After a while Sophie felt her adrenaline dropping. Exhaustion enveloped her, but she was too nervous to doze off as many people in her compartment did.

She kept seeing Amanda's face before her eyes, the way she looked as she was being dragged away. Again, Sophie wondered if her colleague was still alive. The events of the last hours seemed like a terrible nightmare.

She only has to hold on until Thursday, she thought. She would escort Emma to the appointment with that Jamie, whoever he was; after that she would return to her life.

She would turn herself in to the medical police and ask them to have her checked; they would discover that she was not infected, and the whole story would end there.

At the chosen stop, Sophie got off the train, but she didn't see Emma on the platform.

Panicking, she looked around feverishly, until she saw the elderly through a window, apparently deep in her thoughts.

Sophie knocked repeatedly on the glass, and Emma finally recovered, and got off the train just before the doors closed behind her.

Getting through the next three days suddenly looked a lot more difficult.

After walking on for half an hour, they finally found a street full of neon signs that promised rooms at a cheap price. Those were old buildings with rusty railings on the windows, and large patches of wall where the plaster was peeling off.

Sophie chose one at random.

"What a horrible place," Emma commented.

It didn't have a particularly welcoming look, that much was true, but they were not in a position to be choosy.

"We should take a single room," Emma went on. "I'm afraid of being alone, and we should be careful with the money."

Just three days, Sophie told herself.

Though it was a reasonable proposal, she wasn't particularly enthusiastic about the idea of sharing a room with Emma Lemaire. After all, she didn't even know this woman before this morning.

A bored-looking man with sparse hair brushed back occupied the reception desk. "Do you have any vacant rooms?" Sophie asked.

"Sure, of course... for how long?"

"Three nights, please."

The man looked surprised: "Three whole nights. Wow. Sure," he commented.

"We pay in advance, of course."

"Of course."

Emma looked around, seemingly lost.

While she was waiting, Sophie shifted her weight from foot to foot, sinking slightly into the filthy carpet. She unzipped her sweatshirt: the place was horrible, but at least it was warm. After walking so long in the cold it was a pleasant change.

"I've never seen you around here," the motel guy said as he handed her the register to sign, in which Sophie drew a scrawl that could have meant anything. Then they paid sixty credits for their three nights.

"Ah... no," she said, uneasy.

"I like your look," He said, pointing to her sweater. "Very discreet, original. Classy, I'd say."

Sophie was growing increasingly uncomfortable. "Um... Thanks."

She realized that the longer she lingered, the higher was the risk this man would remember them and might identify them in the future. It was better to cut it short.

"So, you specialize in old folks?" he continued, handing over the key to the room.

"What?" Sophie didn't understand.

"We have a number of offers for frequent customers," he explained. "I have to say that seniors are a growing industry. I imagine that you will find our hourly rates particularly interesting," he added, holding out a flier.

She blinked: "What...?" she began, but Emma took her by the arm: "Well, thank you very much, goodbye."

"What did that guy mean...?" Sophie asked, still perplexed.

"Never mind. The more we talk, the riskier it gets," Emma cut off. "Whatever he thought, at least it will not make him question why we are here."

That much was true. Better not think about it, Sophie thought, shuddering.

The room was very sparsely furnished: a greasy carpet, a double bed and a bathroom with a shower. The grey sheets didn't look as though they had been changed anytime recently.

"Well," Emma said.

"Yeah," Sophie nodded with little enthusiasm.

"What do we do now?" Emma asked.

Sophie sighed: "Now we wait."

Chapter 4

When Erik walked into the office, he found a strangely peaceful atmosphere.

Laurent and Janssen were having a hot drink near the vending machine, apparently happily chatting; Meyer was at her desk, and from what he could see on her screen she was reading the day's news with an indifferent expression.

Only Hoffman talked animatedly on the phone, but his office was separated from the open space in which the junior staff worked by transparent and sound-proof walls, so Erik had no way of telling what the call was about.

He found Zoe Hernandez at her desk, staring at the computer screen with a look of concentration.

"Good morning," he greeted her.

"Hey there," she replied, not taking her eyes off the screen.

Erik pressed the power button of his own computer and looked around while waiting for it to turn on.

It looked like a typical morning in the office: the usual hushed moments of the first half hour of work, when everyone was still sleepy and wanted to sort out their own ideas and prepare for the day that loomed ahead. Usually his colleagues would take something to drink, barley beverage or some caffeine-loaded surrogate; they would read the news or organize the meetings for the rest of the day.

Only today wasn't supposed to be like that, Erik thought. It was not a normal day: they had arrested an infected woman only yesterday, and two potential spreaders of infection were on the loose in the city. Such a circumstance, in his opinion, should have meant phone calls at five a.m., mobilized patrols, control shifts to all stations and blocking points.

And yet, nothing.

Only Hernandez looked worried.

"So," he asked, "any news?"

"Not really," she said with a grimace. "Unless the lack of any events isn't a sort of news itself."

Erik nodded: "I was thinking the same thing."

Zoe got up, took a chair and approached Erik's desk. "Can you believe that the routine investigation of looking for the two fugitives hasn't even started?" she said in a low voice.

"What?" he was astounded. "No interrogations, no special patrols?"

Hernandez shook her head: "Nothing at all."

She began drumming her fingers on the desk. In that moment she reminded him very much of Maja, who behaved similarly when she was nervous. "We just can't work like this," she said. "We can't let these two potential infected go loose around the city. They could bring on another epidemic that would spread through Europa and beyond…"

"Beyond?" Erik smiled "Are you worried for the quarantined areas?"

Zoe shrugged: "Did you know that apparently the first wave of the epidemic has been started by just one person?"

"Are you sure? I thought that the expedition that found the dragon eggs had been infected first, all together, and from there the virus had spread to various districts… "

"Yeah, I know, this is the 'official' theory," Zoe admitted, mimicking the quotes with her fingers. Then, in an even lower voice, she went on: "But I heard another rumour some time ago. They said that the disease was not born directly from the contact with dragons, but that it had been created by some kind of error in a lab. Patient Zero was just a guinea pig, but the experiment went wrong, and he found himself in the city without any control." Her voice had an anxious note. "A single person. Think what two of them could do."

Erik felt an icy chill run down his spine.

He saw Thea, Maja and Peter's faces before his eyes, and for one horrible moment he also unwillingly imagined their bodies contorted by the swellings, then the scales, and finally going cold and limp.

"I want to find out what happened, with or without an official assignment," Zoe stated. "Do you want to help me?"

Erik did not need even a moment to think about it.

"Sure," he said, "Of course I will help you."

During the morning Erik and Zoe handled all the routine work as quickly as possible, and in the afternoon they went to the former medical centre.

The area that had been used by the clinic was closed and isolated, but of course there were still a lot of people inside the building that housed several residential flats and some other commercial enterprises.

"They should have sent someone to interview the patients when they were still here yesterday," Erik said. "I thought they would do it!"

"I thought so too - in fact, I was sure. They haven't sent anyone," Hernandez said bitterly.

"Well, at this point we should comb through the records of the appointments."

They removed the tape at the door and entered the foyer of the centre, which also served as a waiting room: it was an impersonal-looking room, with walls painted in white, the chairs covered in green fabric, some posters reminding the public of the importance of this or that periodic inspection, and a faint smell of medicine that still hovered in the air.

"Where do you think they marked the appointments down?" Zoe asked.

Erik looked around and walked to the desk to the bottom of the room. He was about to open a drawer when a voice made him raise his eyes.

"Is there anyone...?"

On the threshold of the doctor's office there was an old man with a felt hat and an old brown coat; he was hesitantly looking around.

"Is the medical centre open again?" he asked, then saw their uniforms.

"I'm sorry, officers!" he exclaimed. "I thought that there was someone I could ask about the results of my blood tests... Now I'll be on my way."

"No, please, come in," Hernandez ordered. "We'd like to ask you a few questions."

Her tone was polite, but it was clear that this was not an option invitation.

The man took off his hat and sat down on one of chairs.

They discovered that his name was Hans Verlinden, and apparently he used to visit the medical centre with a certain frequency.

"I have many problems, you know..." he explained. "My heart, my lungs and... well, sure my digestion is no longer what it used to be..."

Erik privately thought that the old man seemed to have a classic case of hypochondria. "Were you here yesterday, when Amanda Solarin was arrested?"

Verlinden nodded vigorously: "To be sure... I had come to collect the results of my tests... you know, I've had heart problems lately, I always have this pain in my chest, see, right here..."

"I understand, "Hernandez interrupted him. "So, about yesterday - did you happen to see Dr Solarin's assistant, Sophie Weber?"

"Yes, of course! She was with a patient, an elderly lady. I remember the latter very well because we arrived together, but she stepped ahead of me when we took the number at the distributor at the entrance. Of course, I am an old-fashioned man - once, you know, we were taught to give way to women, it was considered common courtesy... but I must say that even so the lady could have..."

"And when did you see them last?"

Verlinden scratched his head: "Well... I think it was before all the confusion about the arrest..."

"Then you didn't see her leave the building?"

"Definitely not. I'm sure because I was in the crowd and I've been waiting in the hallway... I was very frightened, a police raid like that, you see... "

"And you walked out of the medical centre immediately?"

"Of course, I was one of the first to exit. I was near the door, although I must say, I'm not like one of those curious folks who always have to be there to watch what happens to others, as if it was a show on TV! No, no, I'm happy to mind my own business..."

"Then you can't be sure that Sophie Weber didn't exit the medical centre the same way?"

Verlinden spread his arms: "Well, at some point she must have done so, otherwise she would still be here!"

When they were down questioning Mr Verlinden, Erik glanced at the other rooms: there was only one bathroom, a lab and two rooms used for receiving the patients. One of these was the place where they had caught Amanda Solarin.

Erik noticed that the room still bore the marks of recent scuffle: objects were overturned on the floor; there was broken glass, and a sheet of paper on the stretcher was ripped out and never replaced.

A closet was open, and most of the bottles and medicines had fallen to the ground.

"It's cold in here," Hernandez said, entering.

The temperature was actually lower than in the rest of the centre, Erik agreed.

"We checked every corner in the building yesterday... She's not here," Zoe said, rubbing her hands on her arms to warm up.

"That woman must be out there somewhere, then," Erik said.

His partner shrugged, a gesture that reminded him very much of Peter: "But there is no other exit. We are in a basement, so there are not even windows facing outside."

Erik paused to reflect: could there be a door or a passage that they had not found yet?

But where could it be?

He felt a draft of air against the back of his head. It was really cold in that room. It made it difficult to concentrate.

"Maybe we could get a map of the building from the real estate agency," Hernandez suggested. "If there was another way out... "

"Yeah, let's go, I can't think with this..." he broke off, feeling very stupid. "Wait a minute."

How could there be drafts in a basement?

"What are you doing?" Zoe asked. Erik followed the draft, which brought him to the medicine cabinet that was left open. The air was definitely cooler there.

He touched the edges of the shelves, where he could feel the flow of cold air. He pressed against the closet floor, trying to figure out if it could possibly open.

"Here," his partner said, handing him a piece of plastic that had broken away from the cabinet door. Erik placed it in the crack between the wall and the closet, then pressed. The panel offered some resistance, but then he heard a snap and the back of the closet opened.

An underground tunnel, seemingly endless, stretched into the darkness.

The two partners remained speechless for a few moments.

Zoe was the one to recover her voice first: "Shit."

For a while, they were unsure whether or not to call for backup. For all they knew, at the end of that tunnel could be a room where the infected rebels gathered, some sort of meeting place. But there was no time and, given their boss's attitude in the last days, calling for reinforcements could even be counter-productive.

At the end they decided to go to the car and retrieve their suits and helmets: at least this way they wouldn't be infected by mere physical contact.

The precaution proved unnecessary, though, because after going on for some distance, the tunnel did not lead to anything other than an exit to the street through a manhole.

When Erik hoisted himself up and climbed out of the manhole with some effort, he found himself in an alley full of garbage. Zoe pulled herself up in one fluid movement, then looked around.

"Where are we?"

"Still in the third ring," he said, recognizing an area that he had patrolled many times before. He took out a cigarette from his pocket, lit it and inhaled deeply. This small thing helped him recover his focus.

He didn't ask Zoe if she wanted one: she, like most young people, considered smoking an incomprehensible habit. The times really had changed.

"We could ask around to check if anyone had seen them," she offered.

Erik slowly exhaled the hot smoke: "It's difficult to imagine that they were noticed. Rather, we could check the videos of the stations' security cameras. If I were them, I would try to go away, to the outer rings which are a lot less well-monitored."

Zoe nodded: "Ok. Back to the headquarters, then."

Erik looked sadly at the rest of his cigarette: "Guess I won't be able to smoke in the car, will I?"

She gave him a stern look: "Nope."

Once in the office, Hernandez picked up the phone, and asked to be sent the recordings of the surveillance cameras of the three nearest light rail stations. She sorted the recordings and began to watch them.

Just over an hour had passed when Lara Meyer approached Erik's desk.

"The boss wants to see you," she announced.

Erik clicked the pause button on the video running on his computer. "Did he say why?"

Meyer shook her head: "No. But I have the impression that he's in a very bad mood."

Erik winced and turned to Zoe, who was staring at him with worry.

"It must be something about yesterday's operation, nothing to be concerned about," he said to reassure her.

Then he followed Lara, who was returning to the legal department, which was on the way to Hoffman's office. Her hair, mostly black but with many silvery strands, swayed as it brushed her shoulders.

She really has beautiful hair, he thought dreamily.

Reluctantly, Erik veered toward Hoffman's office; the boss was on the phone but he gestured for him to enter and close the door behind him.

While he was waiting for his superior to end the phone call, he wondered why he had been summoned. Perhaps Hoffman was aware of the independent research that he and Zoe Hernandez had set up, and if so, was he about to be reprimanded for a deliberate breaking of orders? Technically Erik had done nothing more than follow the normal procedures for the search of an alleged infected, though…

"Well, Persson," Hoffman's voice interrupted his train of thought, "I've been wanting to talk to you for a while," he announced in an unconvincingly amiable manner.

He took off the headset he used for phone calls and set it on the desk, then carefully crossed his legs. It was clearly all aimed to pass more time and make Erik uncomfortable. This was one of the many ways in which Hoffman tried to make people feel his authority. His whole demeanour was packed with those little mannerisms; for example, the fact that he showed up at meetings always in a hurry, as if he had just come from another, much more important appointment, or treating people from which he wanted to get something like buddies, and all the rest like trash.

Erik thought it was pathetic.

In any case, he waited patiently for Hoffman to finish his little show, thinking longingly at the half cigarette that he still had in the pocket of his coat.

"The fact is..." Hoffman began, with deliberate slowness, "... that there is an issue that concerns me about this office."

"Oh," Erik merely remarked.

He had discovered long before that exhibiting a polite incredulity was the best way to make Hoffman get to the point.

"I'm discussing this with you because you're one of the few people whom I can trust... "

Probably you say the same thing to everyone, Erik thought.

"...but the fact is that I fear that there is a leak of information from this department."

Erik's back stiffened, and he immediately felt alarmed.

This was not one of Hoffman's frivolous preoccupations, but something serious. "What makes you think that?" he asked. "Does it have something to do with the two suspects who escaped yesterday, because if so... "

"No, no," his boss interrupted him. "Those two have nothing to do with this. Others will take care of it, people from the first ring or something like that... they have nothing to do with us."

While Erik digested this new information, Hoffman straightened in his chair, leaning toward him: "I have analysed all the latest operations we made in the third ring. With each of them we had some sort of encounter with the rebels... It's as if every time they knew where we would strike," he said, handing Erik a dossier.

Erik quickly flipped through it, and to his surprise he realized there were other coincidences he hadn't thought of. Hoffman could very well be an insufferable dandy, but it seemed that behind that pompous facade he was hiding a more analytical mind than Erik had initially given him credit for.

"Do you have any idea who could... where, uh, could the information leakage come from?" he asked.

"Oh, Erik, I'm not accusing you, don't worry," Hoffman hastened to clarify. "Look, Persson... I mentioned this to you because I know you're a person I can trust completely. Geez, everybody knows that there is no one else who is as committed to stopping those damn infected as you are! I know that this conversation will remain between us. However..." Hoffman went on with a dramatic sigh, "How long have you known Zoe Hernandez?"

The question left Erik speechless.

Among all the people he had considered as a possible spy, he never thought it could be Zoe.

"A year... a year and a half... why?"

"Well, the encounters with the rebels during our operations began a few months after her arrival. That is very suspicious, don't you think?"

Erik shrugged, not knowing what to say.

"And then... she might be a decent officer, or at least so it seems, but," here Hoffman made a grimace, "she's still PIGS, isn't' she? Better not to trust those folks."

PIGS was the derogatory nickname that indicated the citizens of Europa whose ancestry came from Mediterranean countries: Portugal, Italy, Greece and Spain.

They were a minority and stereotypes labelled them as noisy, dirty and poorly organized. Erik thought that was a pile of rubbish, prejudices that were handed down from centuries ago, but people like Hoffman still looked down on those who did not have a French, German, Nordic or Anglo-Saxon surname.

"So, what do you think?" Hoffman pressed him.

Erik felt confused: "Honestly I don't know. Hernandez has always seemed a very good officer and an honest person to me. I would be really surprised if I found out she has anything to do with the rebels," he answered.

Hoffman appeared disappointed: "Well, I leave the file with you. Maybe you should take it home; do not leave it lying around on your desk. And don't show it to anyone. Meanwhile, think about what I told you, and let me know if you notice any suspicious behaviour."

Erik nodded and, a moment later, found himself ushered out of Hoffman's office.

He went back to his desk in a trance. He could not believe that Zoe was the mole.

She was the person who had made him suspect the presence of an infiltrator in the first place! Why would she do that if she was the spy? Unless it was some astute ploy to confuse him, perhaps anticipating that Hoffman would mark her as a suspect.

Yet it seemed incredible... Hernandez was the only person who really tried to capture the two suspects who were on the loose, while Hoffman did nothing about it except give out nebulous and dubious directions.

What if Hoffman initiated this discussion on purpose to divert attention from himself and at the same time make Hernandez seem less credible?

"What did the boss say?" Zoe Hernandez asked when she saw Erik coming back.

For a moment Erik toyed with the idea of telling her the truth, but then changed his mind.

He hunched his shoulders: "Um, nothing special. He just showed me some reports about how efficient we are and how we should all strive for more."

Hernandez rolled her eyes: "Go figure! Anyway, I have good news."

"Really? What?"

Zoe turned the screen in his direction to show him two images: one was that of a young woman, about twenty-five years old, who pulled up the hood of a sweatshirt that had momentarily slipped down, probably due to the rush of air caused by an arriving train. The other was an older woman who had taken off her hat for a moment to arrange her hair. Both were on the same platform, though each had a wagon with a different number next to her.

Hernandez could not suppress a smile: "Got them... they took a train to the sixth ring."

Chapter 5

Sophie didn't wake up before it was already late in the evening.

When Emma had suggested that they should rest for a while, she thought she would never be able to get to sleep, after all the events of that day. Instead, a few moments after her head touched the pillow, she fell into a deep, albeit distressed sleep.

She had dreamt that a police team surrounded the hotel and broke into their room; when she tried to escape, one of them took off his helmet, revealing the muzzle of a dragon underneath. His poisonous jaws opened and reached for her face, and she woke up abruptly.

She heard a gentle and regular sound that seemed familiar.

Emma was sitting on the bed, already awake, and was knitting. A long red woollen thread was stretched from her knitting-needles to her purse.

Sophie felt a pang: for a moment she thought she had seen her grandmother. Grandma used to knit all the time as well.

The quiet clicking sound of the knitting-needles was strangely comforting.

"Are you awake?" Mrs Lemaire asked.

Sophie sat up, pushing a strand of hair away from her face: "Yes... I never imagined I would be so tired."

"It's only natural," Emma nodded.

Sophie looked at the time on the television screen: nine p.m.

Usually at this time she would be at home, probably sitting on the bed just like she was now. Only it would be in the quiet of her home, with nothing more serious to worry about than what was left in the fridge or what occurred with some patient that day; instead, she was staying in a hotel room with a perfect stranger.

She watched the old lady knitting, wondering if Emma felt as disoriented as herself.

"Look, uh, Mrs. Lemaire," she began.

"Oh, you can call me Emma," the old lady replied.

"Yes... Emma. I was saying.... is there someone waiting for you at home?"

Emma looked a little surprised: "For me? No... just... well... a cat, to tell the truth."

"A cat?" Sophie repeated.

She had never met anyone who kept a pet without the intention of eating it. Having a cat sounded a bit like a waste of resources, to be honest.

"Yes. His name is Fuzzi," Emma replied, apologetically. "I know what you're thinking. Who can afford to waste food on a cat? But I am old, and my food distribution ration is far too much. And then Fuzzi doesn't need much at all, he hunts mice, he's very good. I don't have to worry about him," she sighed. "He does very well on his own, Fuzzi. But I know he still needs me... When I'm not with him I'm always afraid that someone might hurt him."

"I'm sure he'll be fine," Sophie assured her.

Most likely the cat was in a casserole by now; she didn't know anyone who would see a stray cat and pass on the opportunity.

"Do you have kids?" she asked to change the subject.

Emma shrugged: "I used to," she said, in a low voice.

Sophie didn't know what to say. "I'm sorry," she offered.

The older woman shook her head, as if to chase away the ghosts: "Oh, it was so long ago. A lifetime ago. At the beginning of the plague."

"My family too," Sophie said bitterly. "The first wave."

Emma nodded: "The worst, so far. People died in the streets, there was no control. Nobody knew yet how long the incubation period lasts or how the infection is transmitted," she sighed. "Such terrible times."

And they might come back, Sophie thought.

Unless Emma's blood was really the key to the vaccine. The thought brought back a wave of anxiety; why was the police hunting them? Why had they arrested Amanda? They should have been on their side, do everything to keep them safe. Why were they accused of being infected instead?

Part of her hated Amanda and Emma for putting her in that situation.

Almost ashamed of herself, she wondered if she might just opt out.

It was a horrible thought, unfair and treacherous, but Sophie could not help wondering what would happen if she turned herself in to the medical police... perhaps bringing the old lady with her...

"I'm sorry I had you dragged into this mess," Emma said, as if she could read her mind. "I know that if you had any choice..."

"No, I..." Sophie began, blushing.

"No, dear, I mean it," Emma interrupted. "No need to apologize. Nobody wants to send their life spinning off kilter just to help a stranger. I'm really sorry that it happened to you. You seem like a nice girl, one that doesn't look for trouble. Thank you so much for not leaving me alone."

"Um, yeah," Sophie replied, uncomfortable. "No problem."

The evening and then the night passed.

Sophie spent a few hours in a deep sleep, full of nightmares, but for most of the time she stayed awake staring at the peeling walls of the room.

Emma occasionally tried to start a conversation, asking about her life, her work, and the presence or lack of a significant other. But Sophie didn't want either to talk or to think about her life in general. She just wanted to be left alone to indulge her anxiety.

The next morning, however, they had to face a new problem: they were hungry.

Sophie realized she had not eaten anything since breakfast the day before.

Until this moment fear and adrenaline had driven away the hunger pangs, but now she realized that they needed food.

Obviously, going to the food distribution was out of the question: the medical police would have identified them in no time. Theoretically, the sale of food outside the distribution was illegal, but Sophie knew that many people broke the law fairly regularly in this regard. She had even done it herself, on occasion.

She tried to recall the last time she'd bought food at the black market: it must have been a couple of years earlier, when her neighbour had sold her a box of apples for ten credits.

It happened by chance, because she incidentally passed in front of his apartment while he and his family were carrying the boxes up the stairs. She had no idea where he had got them. In fact, she had not the faintest idea how, or whom, she might ask where to buy any food now. Talking to someone who she knew and mentioning that she would gladly buy some fruit if they had any extra was one thing... attempting to do it on the streets, in the midst of perfect strangers, was quite another.

She supposed that the guy at the reception desk could give them directions, but she preferred not to attract his attention any further.

She decided to venture out by herself: two people walking around would attract attention, since their identikit had been circulated together, and she feared that Emma alone would get lost.

She took a few ten credits notes and went outside. The morning air was cool and humid, and only at that moment did Sophie realize than she had missed the outdoors while she was locked in a room with Emma.

She pulled up the sweatshirt hood to hide her face and started walking around the block. It was an anonymous district, identical to thousands of others in the city, maybe a little more neglected and dilapidated than the fifth ring one in which she lived.

She passed a food distribution centre and felt her stomach rumble. What was she supposed to do? She definitely couldn't just stop some random stranger on the street and ask them to sell her food.

She passed by offices, medical centres, several small shops of electronic equipment or hardware. In the window of one of these she noticed a second-hand cultivation lamp for only a few credits. *Too late*, she thought bitterly.

And suddenly she saw a medical police station, with two officers in front of it. Instinctively she ducked into an alley to her right.

She noticed a man who was putting garbage in a can. He was wearing a stained tank top and cotton trousers.

Sophie looked around: the alley was almost deserted, except for a little girl, perhaps eleven years old, playing with a ball. This could be an opportunity.

"Good morning," Sophie greeted the man.

He looked at her blankly: "Hi."

"I was wondering if... um... if you could give me some information," she began, trying not to appear nervous and failing miserably.

He looked at her with a shrug, which she interpreted as a tacit approval.

"You see... well, it happened that... it's so stupid, ha-ha ..." she emitted a forced chuckle, "I happen to be away from home on a business trip for some days, and... I realized that I left my food card at home. How careless of me!"

The guy kept staring inexpressively.

"So I was wondering if... well, if you knew where I might buy food around here... for now. Only until I get home. Where I can use my food card again," she smiled encouragingly.

The man took a threatening step towards her and Sophie's smile froze on her lips.

"I'm not doing anything illegal, you know? No, nothing, you have no evidence against me!"

"No, of course not, I was just... "

He grabbed her by the collar of her sweatshirt: "So you can just tell your little friends from the tax inspection to stop being a pain in my ass. The next officer that they send, I'll cut their throat, you know?"

Sophie broke free and stepped back: "Listen, I assure you I'm not...
"

"And that's my last word, if you know what I mean."

Having said that, the man went back inside, slamming the door behind him.

Damn, Sophie thought. Maybe this wasn't the best way to approach this.

She put her hands in her pockets and began walking toward the end of the alley. She didn't have the faintest idea of what to do next.

"Hey, you!" a voice called her out.

Sophie gave a start, realizing it was the girl with the ball. She had forgotten all about her.

"Hi," she replied, more out of habit than from any real interest.

The girl had long, unkempt hair, and looked at her with open curiosity.

"You don't sound like a tax inspection officer," she stated.

"That would be because I'm not," Sophie said. "It just happened that... "

The girl laughed scornfully: "Yes, of course, you just..." here her tone became rather cynical, "...forgot your food card"

"That's what happened," said Sophie, defensively.

The girl rolled her eyes. "No one is stupid enough to forget their food card."

"Well I happened to be that stupid!" Sophie insisted.

The girl laughed again, and this time she seemed genuinely amused. "Well said!"

"How do you know that I'm not a tax inspection officer?" Sophie asked, mostly because she didn't know what to say.

"They are much smarter than you," the girl said, bouncing the ball and catching it.

Sophie was shocked by this lack of manners and turned to leave. Certainly, staying to argue was not worth the effort.

"Wait, where are you going?" the girl called out. "Didn't you want to buy food?"

Sophie stopped: "Who would I buy it from?"

The girl shifted her weight from one foot to another: "From me."

"Yeah, right," Sophie said. The girl looked like she didn't even have enough food for herself.

"Why not? Who else were you going to ask?"

"Um..." Sophie was confused. "I don't know, but... "

"Oh, come on. I'll get you a day's ration. For advance payment," the girl insisted.

"How much?"

"How much you got?"

Sophie frowned: "Wait, it doesn't work like that."

The little girl rolled her eyes: "Fine, fine..." she sounded bored. "Shall we say, fifty credits?"

"That's robbery!" Sophie protested. At the food distribution, a daily ration didn't cost more than five or six credits.

The girl merely shrugged. Sophie pulled the bills out of her pocket: "Besides, I need two rations and I only have sixty credits."

The little girl snatched the notes from her hand. "Perfect, thank you. See you in an hour," she said, counting the money.

"Hey, wait, how do I know that you won't just run away with the cash?"

"I'm not going to run away, trust me," the girl assured her. "Where shall we meet?"

"My hotel is just down the street, on the corner of..." Sophie began.

"What, and you tell me that too?" the girl snorted. "You just can't take care of yourself, can you? Look, let's meet here in an hour, if you manage to get here."

"Of course I'll manage!" Sophie said, exasperated.

"Fine."

"Fine!"

The girl walked away, leaving Sophie very frustrated.

She doubted she would meet her again. Most likely she had just wasted sixty credits for nothing. And she still had no idea where to get food.

It didn't seem prudent to return to the hotel and then go out again, so Sophie decided to spend the next hour walking down the streets. She noticed, here and there, the identikit of the General plastered on the walls and, despite the fact that the posters seemed very old and nobody spared them a look, she dropped the hood lower over her face.

Maybe her own identikit was now hanging on a wall somewhere.

On occasions she was tempted to stop someone and ask where she could buy some black-market food, but the wary expressions of the people around her made her hesitate every time. She continued to wander aimlessly until, an hour later, she found herself really tired and numb. Her hands and feet were frozen, the fabric of her sweatshirt was soaked with damp, and to make matters worse she was feeling the pangs of hunger more strongly than before.

She went back to the alley where she had met the girl, but she was nowhere to be found.

Perfect, Sophie thought bitterly, *how predictable.*

She waited there for about half hour, walking back and forth, but nobody came. *I might as well say goodbye to those sixty credits*, she thought.

Eventually she was so cold that she decided to go back to the hotel. When she was about to turn up the hotel steps, she got the feeling that she was being watched. She was walking with her head down, trying to attract as little attention as possible, when that odd feeling, like a tickle at the base of the neck, made her look up, and her attention was drawn by a familiar tuft of blonde hair.

It was Lukas, right across the road.

It all happened very quickly: their glances met before she could turn around, and she saw his eyes dilate in surprise.

Instinctively she turned around, plunged down an alley at random, and started running, her heart pounding painfully in her chest. Her side hurt and she was almost out of breath, but she couldn't stop.

She turned to a main road and saw that many people were watching her. Trying to feign calmness, she slowed her pace, then ducked into another alley and began to run once more.

Would Lukas follow her? Would he call the medical police?

Had he understood that she was about to enter the hotel? Would he talk to the owner? Would they connect her to Emma?

Lukas lived in the sixth ring, she knew it. She cursed herself for not having thought about it before. She looked back, still walking on: there didn't seem to be anyone behind her. Was someone following? Would she find a police patrol at the next corner?

Suddenly, she bumped against someone and fell to the ground.

"Hey, what's wrong with you?!"

It was the girl she had met before: Sophie noticed that she was holding a bag.

"Why were you running like that?" she asked.

Sophie stood up and dusted off her clothes: "I was in a hurry," she murmured.

"Look, if you're running away from someone, going like that is the best way to attract attention," the girl informed her.

"I'm not running away from anyone! What nonsense."

"Yeah, right. I could tell that right away."

"Well, I'm not."

"Yes, you are!"

Sophie refrained from emitting a frustrated snarl. There was something about that girl that made her argue as if she was an eleven-year-old herself.

"I brought the stuff anyway," the girl said.

"Stuff? What are you, a drug dealer?"

"I brought you," the girl raised her voice, "THE FOOD YOU WANTED ME TO ILLEGALLY SELL YOU!"

Sophie shuddered: "Shut up! Are you out of your mind?"

The girl gave an indifferent shrug: "You can scream all you want, no one will listen. If you go around like you do, like you have something to hide, everyone will begin to wonder. It doesn't take a genius to figure that out."

"Would you please stop telling me I'm stupid?" Sophie protested.

"You kind of are," the girl replied, matter-of-factly. "You don't know anything. I could get away with your money and you wouldn't ever find me. Who pays in advance with no guarantees? No one is that dumb."

That much is probably true, Sophie reflected.

"Look, it's a bit of a new situation for me," she admitted. "By the way, do we really have to stay here in the middle of the road? You know, I wouldn't want to stand out with the bags and everything... "

"Why, because perchance you're running away from someone?" the girl teased her.

"No, of course, it's just... "

"Come on, let's go."

She led Sophie behind the corner of a house in a small deserted street: then she bent down and lifted the lid of a manhole.

"After you," she said, indicating the tunnel.

"I'm not going in there!" Sophie exclaimed. "Where does this lead, to the sewers? Eww, that's gross."

The girl snorted: "See that you don't know anything? It doesn't lead to the sewers, it's only a door."

"A door where?"

"To the city under the city."

"You mean to the subway tunnels?" Sophie asked, horrified.

"Yes, of course, to the subway, where else would you want to go?"

"But... it's a dangerous place," Sophie said.

One heard all kinds of things about the subway tunnels: people who had got in and never found their way out, people who had been found with their throat cut, or eaten alive by sewer rats, or were infected...

"Not more dangerous than the city above," the girl assured her. "Look, I'm going. You do whatever you want."

Having said that, she slipped into the manhole and began to descend down a narrow iron staircase, very similar to the one Sophie had used to exit the tunnel hidden behind Amanda's office.

Sophie looked into the manhole, uncertain: there was the deeply rooted fear of the underground city, and some primal instinct that suggested not to squeeze into that unpredictable and dark place; on the other hand, she could not return to the hotel to Emma, at least not yet.

Perhaps Lukas and the medical police were after her, and she was cold and hungry. Indeed, it was her insistently rumbling stomach that made the decision for her, because the girl was carrying the bag where the food was supposed to be.

So, cursing herself and muttering in a low voice, Sophie lowered herself into the hole in the asphalt and she began to climb down.

"Put the lid back on!" the girl called from below.

Sophie dragged the heavy iron lid over the manhole and began to descend, now plunged into complete darkness.

Chapter 6

Erik poured the oatmeal into his cup, topping it with soy milk. He thought it tasted like pressed cardboard. According to some people, soy milk was supposed to be indistinguishable from cow's milk's, but Erik didn't buy that. That soy stuff had nothing to do with the milk he remembered from his childhood.

Not that he had much choice, anyway: with rationing, real milk was difficult to find, and very expensive. Erik already spent more than he should on the cigarettes he bought secretly from a neighbour, who in his turn got them from God knows where. And those little tubes of tobacco became more and more expensive by the month... but Erik had so few guilty pleasures in his life that he just couldn't bring himself to give up that small daily satisfaction.

"You look worried," Thea's voice startled him. "What's going on?"

Erik looked into his wife's eyes, which were big, honest, and had a look tainted with concern.

"Um..." he started.

He remembered that there had been a time, before Maja and Peter were born, when and Thea did nothing but talk.

They had differing opinions about virtually any subject, but he liked that.

When the medical police had been created, she tried to talk him out of joining it. She did not approve of it. According to her, the medical police was a dictatorial government measure which Erik should not back up. But the pay was better there, and there were career opportunities... and then when Maja needed medical care for that her asthma problem, it didn't seem like he had any real choice.

And although in the end, his enlisting with the medical police had been a mutual decision – sort of - Erik still felt that this was when a new detachment began to emerge between him and his wife.

The world around them had changed... they didn't have the luxury to make choices anymore.

The plague had changed everything: it had divided healthy people from the infected, loyal citizens from the rebels, the living from the dead.

Erik and Thea didn't have anything to discuss anymore. All the decisions had already been taken for them.

Erik wasn't sure Thea could really understand his work and his life: the fact that for years he had lived with a never-ending mission, with that feeling of danger that never quite disappeared.

At the same time, he could no longer bring himself to be interested in the anecdotes she told him about her patients. All their problems seemed so silly... what did they know of real trouble? About being, every single day, just one step away from infection and death? Yet he missed the relationship he used to have with Thea: her observations, her intelligence, her sense of humour.

He wished he could confide in her again... but he didn't know where to start.

"I had some problems at the office," he said at last.

"Oh, I'm sorry, dear," she said, placing a hand on his shoulder. "I'm sure it will all work out. By the way, I hope you make it for dinner tomorrow night."

"Why?"

"Maja is coming! And she's bringing a *friend*," Thea added significantly. "I wonder what sort of a young man he is. Maja never says anything about what she does at work, about the courses, if she has friends, how she likes it... "

Erik nodded: their daughter had always been reserved, and this became even more pronounced when she moved out. Or maybe she simply felt she could no longer talk to them? It was a sad thought.

After breakfast Erik went to the station to catch the train.

While he was traveling toward the third ring, he thought about the events of the last days.

He and Hernandez had searched Sophie Weber's apartment, but predictably found no clue as to where she might be at the moment.

As to the other suspect, Emma Lemaire, they had had some difficulty finding her address; evidently Hoffman restricted access to the police search system, since many data appeared encrypted.

Hernandez was still working on it.

She had started to suggest, very cautiously, that maybe Hoffman was making a deliberate obstruction, but Erik did not comment.

In any case Zoe had found, in a roundabout way, the number of the lab technician, Lukas Bonnet.

They had looked for him at his address twice the day before but did not find him. A quick search of his apartment revealed very few personal belongings and nothing that would help them in their search.

It looked like another dead end, until it turned out that, coincidentally, Lara Meyer knew Lukas's mother, and in less than no time she got them his mobile number.

They summoned Bonnet to the police headquarters, and he had assured them that he would show up that morning.

"Don't scare him, guys," Lara Meyer had said, "He's a nice boy."

When Erik arrived at the office, Hernandez told him that Bonnet was already in the questioning room downstairs. Erik noticed that she had chosen a room as far away from Hoffman's office as she could.

He didn't really know what to think of this situation: both Hoffman and Hernandez seemed to suspect one another, and Erik could not tell which of them was in good faith, or even if they were not both lying.

In the meantime, he decided to continue helping Zoe Hernandez in the search for the two suspects, primarily because, despite everything, his partner seemed sincere, and it was much easier to trust her than slimy Hoffman.

Moreover, the spy could also be a third party that neither of them suspected. He also considered it his duty to try everything possible to stop the infection, even if it meant disobeying his superior.

Lukas Bonnet was a young man who looked between twenty-five and thirty years old. He seemed uncertain as to why he was summoned to the headquarters.

Nothing particularly interesting emerged from the interview with him: yes, he had worked for Amanda Solarin for about a year, no, he did not know Sophie Weber very well because they had never spent time together outside work hours, yes, he had been screened for the plague that very morning and he was clean.

"So, you really don't know why Sophie Weber decided to flee from the authorities?" Hernandez asked.

Bonnet looked at Zoe, wide-eyed: "I don't know... I think... maybe she was scared by the arrest and the blood, and now she's still on the run, terrified..."

Erik raised an eyebrow: could the guy really be that naïve? After about half an hour, he realized that Zoe's questions had become more relaxed, a lot less like an interrogation. She seemed to be smiling more often than she normally did. Maybe she liked this Bonnet guy.

It wasn't impossible: he was around the same age as her, and looked like a decent guy, plus there were his good looks.

Actually, the young man appeared completely innocent... maybe even too innocent. His answers seemed really too naive to be true. Erik wondered whether the benign facade might actually be a clever strategy.

When Bonnet left, Erik felt slightly disappointed: talking to him had led them nowhere.

"That was a bit of a waste of time, wasn't it?" he said when the lab technician was gone.

Zoe looked at him: "Um, I wouldn't say so."

"Right, because you have a crush on that Lukas," Erik goaded her. "I wouldn't think someone like that could be your type."

His partner merely shrugged: "He would be anyone's type," the shadow of a smile crossed her face. "Besides, that's rich coming from you, given how you get all slack-jawed when you look at Lara."

Erik blushed: "Slack-jawed?" he repeated, in a wounded tone.

"Anyway, in the midst of all his nonsense, he also said something interesting."

"What?"

"He said that he had always made regular exams because the lab also kept infected blood for research purposes. Solarin studied the disease and its possible treatments, in addition to her regular medical practice. Perhaps the rebels were so determined not to let us take her because she found something they needed."

Now that Zoe pointed this out, Erik was surprised not to have made the connection earlier.

"... or maybe something they wanted to disappear," he added.

Back in the office, Erik began to search for information on Amanda Solarin.

He noticed with dismay that many of the data appeared encrypted; evidently Hoffman was going on with his policy of data security, hoping not to give any more important information to the alleged mole. Every request of the information database now had to be approved by

Hoffman himself, which of course slowed down the work and annoyed the other officers.

Janssen was particularly angry: Erik saw him several times furiously contacting Hoffman's office to demand explanations.

"I've been working here for ten years, what is this nonsense that I can't browse the archive data anymore?"

Janssen was terrible when it came to on-field missions, but on the other hand he was great at finding all sorts of information online. Denying him access to database crosschecks was depriving him of the possibility to do his job.

Laurent and Meyer, however, had a more philosophical approach: "He wants to pay us to fill out forms and wait around the hot drinks machine? All right, let him," they merely said with a shrug.

Erik wished he could be as indifferent as those two, but he couldn't. This was partly due to the fact that Hernandez seemed even more determined to find the two missing suspects. She was feverishly staring at the screen, which was flickering with the images of the surveillance cameras in the sixth ring. Deep dark circles appeared under her bloodshot eyes.

"Zoe, did you go to bed at all last night?" he asked.

"Sure."

"At what time?"

She shrugged: "Um, I don't remember. Maybe I stayed in the office a little longer than usual."

'A little longer' probably meant she had gone home around two a.m to catch a few short hours of sleep. Erik knew what it was like: once upon a time he would have done the same.

But now everything was more complicated, more restrictive: the family waiting for him at home, most of all, but also his body, his energy. When he happened to spend a sleepless night these days he paid its consequences for the rest of the week.

Even if he could not access the police records, Erik still did a search on Amanda Solarin on the internet, using the data accessible to everyone.

He discovered that twenty years earlier Solarin had published several studies and articles on viral diseases: some of them were still being used in specialized research.

Apparently, she had been a highly-esteemed scientist. At some point, however, it seemed that her career had been cut short. After a few years of intense activity, she apparently stopped all academic work. After a long period of obscurity, she reappeared in the telephone directories, with her current medical centre, only a few years earlier.

Not being able to access the police database was really frustrating: it contained a lot of information about all citizens, including their place residence, all their activities and, if the researcher had the patience to dig deep (something in which Janssen would have been very good), even their diets per the food distribution credits.

As far as Erik could gauge, the measures passed by Hoffman were a stupid palliative that slowed down the work of the officers but would never do anything to stop the rebels.

The lizard men did have their means of access to information, even if no one knew what they were: Erik knew, though, that access to the archives had always been one of the rebels' first priorities.

He remembered an episode from a few years earlier - it might have been the only time he felt he may not make it through alive.

They had caught the rebels, the infected, looking for something in the police archives, in the medical research section. It was a very special and restricted archive, whose data could be accessed only through certain strictly surveyed terminals.

No one knew how they managed not only to enter, but even to discover the existence of the archive and figure out how to access the information.

Erik had been part of the team that was sent to capture the rebels and arrest them.

It was a nightmare: the rebels did not only seem to know that the police were coming, but they had set them a trap. And the way they had escaped... Erik did not consider himself an emotional person, but memories of that incident still made him feel a jolt in his stomach.

They had a dragon with them: not one of the largest, he found out later, as they had managed to hide it in a big van, but still large enough to completely devastate the neighbourhood where the medical police headquarters were.

The rebels themselves were no less fierce and uncontrollable than the creature.

He saw one of them shoot in cold blood an officer who attempted to stop him. Lang, the man's name was.

Erik remembered him well: a good bloke, and a very experienced agent. Just a little too slow in pulling the trigger...

He remembered that moment like it was yesterday: how the infected made him believe that he was about to surrender and be ready to cooperate, and then pulled out another weapon and shot Lang straight through his forehead.

Many of those infected had an almost human form, apart from the scales, but not that one: Erik remembered his deformed body, the grotesque way in which he walked... but above all he remembered the look of perfect indifference with which he had ended Lang's life.

There was nothing human in that stare.

He would probably have killed Erik, too: at that time he was on the ground, with an injury to his leg, weak and vulnerable; but above all so shocked that he would hardly have been able to react in time.

At that moment, though, there was some diversion: an explosion perhaps, or maybe it was their dragon that set some house on fire... Erik didn't remember the details very well.

He only knew that one moment he was staring into the cold and merciless eyes of that monstrous being, and the next second he was being rescued by his colleagues.

Any doubts he might have had as to the necessity of exterminating all the infected ended that day.

Chapter 7

It took a while for Sophie's eyes to get used to the darkness. After a few minutes she could see a dim light, not far from the iron stairs.

She heard the girl jumping off the ladder, and soon found herself at the end of it.

"Where are we?"

"Not far from Karlsruhe station."

Sophie thought back to Amanda's words and the appointment with Jamie.

"Are we far from Stuttgart station?" she asked.

"You have to take the train to the seventh ring, it's just a couple of stops."

The source of the light turned out to be a crack under a thick metal door. The girl turned the handle and, with a great creak, the door opened up.

On the other side there was a long corridor with walls covered in white and yellow plastic panels. The floor consisted of old grey tiles. The narrow space was illuminated by electric light coming from the ceiling panels, but many of those were broken or emitting a flashing, flickering light, making the place look spooky.

Sophie looked around and noticed a pile of rags on the floor. A more attentive inspection revealed it to be a sleeping man.

"Come with me," the girl said, "I know a place where we can go."

Sophie followed her down the hall, which widened until it became a large, crowded room. There were men and women, children and elderly people: some were not very different from the people she met every day, while others seemed to belong to a completely different race. Most wore threadbare, ill-assorted clothes, composed of several layers to ward off the cold.

There were people walking in a hurry, and others that were sitting or even lying down on the ground. They all seemed to need a good shower; many had long hair and long beards, prematurely wrinkled skin, rotten teeth.

In the corners of the room some had laid out sheets, on which various merchandise was exhibited. *Food*, Sophie noticed. The distinct smell of meat was enough to make her hunger return in full force. She made to approach, but the girl yanked her arm: "This way!"

Sophie hastened to follow, as it would be very easy to get lost in the middle of the crowd. She wondered how many victims an infected could have made in a mere few hours down here, in the midst of all those people and without any kind of medical control.

A pale man who looked like he had never seen sunlight passed by Sophie, staring in front of him transfixed and, bumping into her shoulder. She shuddered.

The child led her across the room, then into another, less crowded corridor. Finally, she opened a door hidden between the panels: "Here," she said.

Sophie found herself in what had probably been a closet of some sort once, perhaps for electrical panels. Someone had pulled in two ripped seats from an old train, along with other scattered objects: a pile of clothes, dishes, a pot on a gas stove.

"So, you live here?" Sophie asked.

The girl rolled her eyes: "Of course not. This is just a place to hang out sometimes."

"What's your name, by the way?"

She brushed a dirty strand of hair from her eyes: "Gitte, and yours?"

"Sophie. Now, can you give me what I paid for, please?"

"Oh, yes!" Gitte said, handing her the plastic bag. Sophie pulled it open, finding two polystyrene boxes with the logo of the company that provided electricity.

These were two meals from their canteen, she understood. She opened a box and found it divided into three sections: rice and beans, salad and a dark loaf. Sophie wolfed it all down in a few minutes. Nothing had ever tasted so delicious.

"Easy, or you're going to choke," Gitte advised.

Once the first portion was gone, Sophie briefly considered the other container. No, she decided, she had to restrain herself. She had to go back to the hotel and take it to Emma, who has had nothing to eat for at least as long as she did; then they would go somewhere else.

That was, unless that the medical police had already traced them. She had no choice but to take the risk, though.

A part of her wanted to stay hidden in the old subway closet a little longer; it would have been so nice to stay there until all was forgotten: Emma, the plague, the vaccine, and her own connection to it all. She wondered how many other people in the underground city had followed a similar impulse.

"Gitte, were you born here? In the underground city?" she asked.

The girl shook her head: "No, my parents lived up above. My sister and I came here... after..."

"And where is your sister now?"

Gitte shrugged and said nothing.

Sophie didn't know what to say.

They stayed in silence for a moment, then Sophie stood up and shook the crumbs from her clothes. "Anyway, thanks a lot."

"You're welcome."

"Um, I think I'll go now."

She had no more excuses, she had to leave.

Listen..." Gitte said, "You have to stop paying in advance without haggling over the price. It's very strange. You'll end up robbed in half a day if you keep on like that."

Sophie thought about it, then nodded: "Thanks. You're probably right."

She snorted: "Of course I'm right."

It took Sophie a while to find her way to the trapdoor, and when she came out she found that she had used the wrong manhole and ended up a few blocks away. When she finally arrived at the hotel, the little bit of pleasant warmth she had managed to absorb during her visit to the subway was quite gone, leaving her even colder than before.

She entered warily and headed straight to the corridor. The guy behind the counter just looked at her curiously, but didn't say anything. Luckily, she managed to get to her room without further trouble.

When she opened the door, her heart skipped a beat as she scanned the room and didn't see Emma.

"Emma?" she asked, in rising panic.

Relieved, she saw the old lady come out of the bathroom and hurry toward her:

"Sophie! Oh, thank goodness you're back! I was so worried!"

Sophie handed her the bag with the polystyrene lunch box: "Here, this is what I found."

Emma looked confused: "What about you?"

"I've already eaten. Look, I met someone I know, and unfortunately I'm pretty sure he recognized me. We have to leave right away, possibly go to another ring."

Emma opened the package and began to eat greedily: "But... who...?" she enquired between mouthfuls.

"It's Lukas, the guy who works at the medical centre with me."

Worked, she corrected herself mentally.

Even when this whole horrendous business would be over, could she return to her life and her work as if nothing had happened? Now that she thought about it, it was unlikely that the centre would survive without Amanda.

Emma nodded: "Ah yes, I remember him - a nice young man, so polite."

"That's the one."

Sophie wondered if Lukas was more likely to try and help her or report her to the authorities. For the time being it seemed that no one had yet come to get them, but it was too early to reach any conclusions.

She noticed that Emma had emptied her lunch box and felt her stomach rumble again.

We will find something else soon, she told herself.

Maybe she could get back into the subway tunnels and investigate the origins of the grilled meat. It didn't *have* to be rats...

"Come on, let's go," she urged her companion.

It took Emma quite a while to collect her belongings and finally get moving.

Sophie tried to be patient (elderly people could be very slow, she reminded herself), but, given their situation, she was compelled to prod the old lady to get going.

"Wait... my knitting!" Emma said, stopping at the door for the umpteenth time. It was amazing how much stuff she had scattered around the room in just over twenty-four hours.

Finally, they managed to leave the room and get to the ground floor. Sophie had hoped to sneak out without attracting attention, but as they walked to the entrance door, the guy from the reception barred their way.

"Where are you going?" he asked.

His voice was flat, and Sophie failed to read his intentions, but she didn't like the determined look in his eyes.

"We're just going to..." she began, about to tell him that they were vacating the room, but Emma broke in:

"...to take a walk and get some fresh air," the old lady said. "We think we'll be back in a couple of hours."

Sophie was a bit confused but decided not to contradict her companion.

"Oh yeah?" the guy said. "Because it looks to me like you're leaving."

"Well, even if we were leaving, we paid in advance, so I don't see where the problem is," Sophie said, trying to swerve around him and get to the door. She wondered if he had seen their identikit somewhere and drawn his own conclusions, or spoken to Lukas, or warned by the police not to let them get away...

"The problem is that the price of the rooms increased since yesterday," he declared, pushing himself more firmly against the door. "Two hundred credits more. But I'm sure you can afford it."

"Well, you're wrong!" Emma replied with confidence.

The man took a step toward them, and in one fluid motion pulled out a small knife: "Well, suppose that now you give me your wallet, and I decide on the new tariff."

"You can't do that. I'll call the police," Sophie said, feigning an assurance she didn't really possess.

The guy grinned: "I don't think so. You know, I don't think you're on very good terms with the authorities."

He walked up to Sophie, bringing the edge of his knife dangerously close to her stomach. She felt his breath hit her nostrils, an unpleasant mixture of tobacco, onion and bad digestion.

"Come on, old fart," he said to Emma, "Get the money out."

The elderly woman paled: "All right, all right..." she stammered, pulling out her wallet from her bag and putting a handful of notes in his hands

The man pocketed them: "And now get out!" he told them.

Sophie and Emma hastened to leave.

Gitte was right, Sophie thought bitterly. They should have been more cautious. But now it was too late, they had no money, nor the faintest idea of where they could go.

"I'm sorry!" Emma said. She appeared thoroughly shaken by what had just happened.

"Don't apologize," Sophie replied wearily, "It was not your fault."

They walked away from the hotel, without knowing exactly where to go. The prospect of another next meal seemed even more distant now.

Suddenly she felt a hand on her shoulder and spun around, alarmed.

"Sophie," a familiar voice said.

"Lukas!" she exclaimed.

He looked worried but didn't show the sort of panic she would expect if he really believed they were infected.

Sophie didn't know what to do: it was useless to try to run, especially with Emma.

"I saw you yesterday, but you ran away," Lukas said.

"Ah... yes..." she replied, playing for time, "I must have mistaken you for someone else."

"What happened yesterday morning?" he asked, confused.

For a fleeting moment Sophie thought it was incredible that only a little more than one day had passed since she left the medical centre. The last thirty-six hours felt as long as her whole life.

"The police took Amanda, and you were gone," Lukas went on, "Then your photographs appeared everywhere, and they said that you were infected. But I know you're not, you were screened before you came to work! And I know that neither Lemaire nor Amanda are: I screened them myself. Now the medical centre is closed, and I have no job," he added, sounding plaintive.

"I'm sorry. I don't know exactly what happened," Sophie admitted.

"You know that the police are looking for you? They questioned me as well, but I didn't know anything. What have you done?"

"I don't know!" she could only repeat. "It's... it's all a big misunderstanding, OK? I think we should hide somewhere until everything comes clear."

Lukas nodded: "I understand. I think you should go home and stay inside for a while."

"Yes, but... to be honest, I don't know where to go. I cannot go home."

He stared at her, puzzled: "Why not?"

Sophie resisted the urge to roll her eyes: "Because that's the first place where the medical police would look for me," she explained.

"Ah, right, I didn't think of that," Lukas commented. "If it happened to me, I wouldn't have this problem. I just finished moving and haven't changed the documents yet. No one knows where I live! Cool, right?"

Sophie stared at him.

"Um, OK then, good luck! Stay in touch, alright?" Lukas gave her a friendly pat on the shoulder. "Goodbye, Madam Lemaire." he added.

He obviously had no intention of helping them.

Sophie knew she should be relieved even just because he didn't seem to believe the official version and didn't look like he was about to call the police, but she still felt slightly disappointed.

"Look, young man, I don't want to sound inappropriate," Emma interjected when Lukas had already almost turned to go away, "but Sophie and I are in trouble and we really need somewhere to stay. Could you let us stay at your place for a couple of days? Only until Thursday. We would be immensely grateful."

Lukas appeared surprised. As a matter of fact, he and Sophie had never been close enough to hang out together outside work hours.

"But yes, of course!" he said, regaling them with one of his dazzling smiles. "I just didn't think about it... "

Sophie realized that she had been holding her breath the whole time.

"It's not far from here, follow me!" Lukas told them, evidently brimming with enthusiasm.

The good news was that the apartment really wasn't far off. The bad news was that during their short walk they had to stop countless times to greet all the people who knew Lukas, which turned out to be quite a lot. A couple of times he even lingered to chat, and Sophie was pretty sure that at some point he was about to introduce them, but luckily stopped just in time.

Apparently, he found the notion of discretion hard to grasp.

When they finally stepped into his flat on the twenty-sixth floor, Sophie felt the weight of the day's fatigue crush her. Lukas' flat was very similar to hers, even though he didn't have the bathroom or the salad seedlings. But it was much more orderly than hers, and the furniture looked of better quality and a lot newer.

Besides, Lukas appeared to be very well-stocked on food supplies: after a portion of fish and potatoes and a cup of instant barley, Sophie felt much better, and Emma looked a lot sprightlier.

Sophie started to feel that maybe, just maybe, they would be alright.

Lukas chivalrously announced that he would leave the bed to Emma, so he and Sophie settled on the floor with blankets and pillows. Normally it would have been too early to go to sleep (it was only six p.m.), but Sophie felt exhausted. If she hadn't been so hungry, she would surely have fallen asleep while she ate. Her eyelids seemed increasingly heavy.

When she woke, the room was dark except for the bluish, intermittent light from the TV. Sophie realized she had fallen asleep on the floor in the middle of the room. Someone had covered her with a woollen chequered quilt while she was sleeping.

She yawned and ran a hand through her hair, finding it dishevelled and sweaty. When was the last time she took a shower?

Emma was asleep on the bed, as was demonstrated by her heavy and regular breathing. Lukas was sitting cross-legged on the floor, with his back to the bed, and watched TV with great concentration.

Sophie recognized the show, one of the many reality show where the protagonists had to survive in a hostile environment, a wasteland near the quarantined areas, eating grasshoppers and other crap the mere thought of which made her feel sick.

"Lukas," she whispered, careful not to wake Emma.

Lukas looked up at her: "Hello!" he smiled. "How are you?"

"Fine," she said, dully.

Actually, as her mind awakened from the deep sleep, she felt the now familiar pang of anxiety that clawed at stomach. She was still on the run from the medical police, together with an old, slightly scatter-brained lady, with no directions except a vague indication to meet a stranger two days hence.

Great. Just perfect, she thought bitterly.

"Look," Lukas said, pointing at the TV, "It's my favourite show, 'Beyond Europa'. Do you know it?"

Sophie got up and moved to sit next to him: "I have seen it a few times."

"In this episode the participants must build a hut during a tornado. It's said that they are very common in those places."

Images of people trying to fix shrub branches together, while a violent storm raged all around them, flickered on the screen. All the competitors were covered with mud and looked really miserable.

"Maybe next year you could sign up for it too." With his beautiful smile, Lukas would be the perfect candidate, a natural public favourite. "You could win and go live the good life in the first ring."

The grand prize of those shows was very lucrative - an exorbitant amount of credits and a new life in a luxurious villa in the first ring, so many people tried their fortune.

As far as she was concerned, however, Sophie did not want to get out of Europa under any circumstances.

Lukas was of the same opinion, actually: "No way!" he exclaimed. "Better you than me. I don't want to have to live off spiders for a month."

"Really? I thought they were your favourite food," she joked.

"Of course, but only city spiders. Like the one next to you."

Sophie gasped: "Where?!"

Lukas laughed, then lowered his voice so as not to disturb Emma: "Just kidding! You should have seen your face."

"I don't like spiders," she admitted "They have too many..." she shivered "legs."

He laughed again, as if she said something very funny.

"Ah, Sophie..." he said "I didn't know you were so much fun outside of work! How come we never went out for a beer or something?"

She shrugged: "Dunno. It just never happened, I guess."

Maybe she was not the kind of person who made friends very easily, she thought. When she was little, most of the people in her life were adults, Grandma and her friends for the post part. Sophie was used to having a lot of privacy and space, and even at school she had struggled to bond with her classmates.

When her grandmother was gone, Sophie had been catapulted into a completely foreign world, where the other children were everywhere, noisy, intrusive, ready to make off with her lunch or the few belongings she had brought from home.

It had been a shock.

Then, the few people with whom she managed to establish some kind of relationship (the kind girl who had the bed next to her in the dorm or the laconic canteen operator who allowed her to hide in the kitchen when she was chased by a gang of children) always disappeared, transferred to other facilities or perhaps gone to meet a worse fate, when the plague raged in the streets.

Beyond the mandatory work interactions, furthermore, it was easy to be alone in Europa: the social gathering places were few and tightly controlled by the institutions.

Gradually, the habit had become routine, and breaking it was increasingly difficult.

The person she liked best was Amanda and... thinking about her, Sophie felt a lump rise in her throat again.

Once again wondered if Amanda was still alive, and once again she was too scared to give herself an honest answer.

"Did you see how they took Amanda away?" she asked Lukas.

He didn't say anything for a while. "Yes," he answered at last, "It wasn't nice to look at."

"Do you think...?"

Lukas sighed: "I don't know," he admitted. "Listen, Sophie... why do you keep running away?" he asked.

She stiffened: "What kind of question is that? You saw..."

"Yes, I know, but... well, you know how it works with the police, don't you? Those who are sent out on the raids are fanatics, people who are used to kick doors down."

Lukas turned and looked into her eyes: "I know a person, a family friend. She's in the medical police but she is not.... no, wait, let me speak!" he exclaimed, when Sophie began to shake her head.

"Lukas, no!" she exclaimed, standing up. "You don't understand... you ... You weren't there..."

"I saw what Amanda looked like when they took her away."

"There! How can you still want to have anything to do with those people?!"

"Because this is bigger than me, you and Mrs. Lemaire put together! If we talked to a reasonable person, someone trustworthy..."

"There are no trustworthy people!" Sophie snapped, in a louder voice than she intended.

Lukas said nothing for a moment, then threw up his hands in surrender: "I'm sorry! It was just an idea. Please, come back and sit."

She sat down on the floor again. They remained silent for a while.

The TV station broadcasted an interview with President Hartmann, in which he spoke of the efforts made by the police to contain the possible new cases of the plague.

"The episode is over. Want to watch another?" Lukas proposed.

"No... I think I'm going to sleep," she muttered.

She wasn't really that sleepy, but she didn't feel like staying there with him any longer.

"Ok. Good night," he said.

Sophie lay awake for a long time, watching the TV lights reflected in Lukas' eyes.

Chapter 8

"You said you would sleep," Erik said wearily.

"I know, I know," Zoe replied, "I did sleep, I swear!... for a reasonable length of time," she assured.

Erik sighed: though she was older (not by too much, however, now that he thought about it), Zoe reminded him very much of his kids.

Finding Zoe at all hours in front of the computer did remind him of how he would wake up at night to go to the bathroom and find the light on in Maja's room: sometimes she was still awake reading, otherwise she was asleep with a book in her hands.

"You must sleep, Maja, you'll have enough time to read tomorrow," he would tell her.

"But Dad," she would retort, "I need to know how it ends!"

Zoe's determination to find the infectors was very similar to Maja's desire to know how the story ends.

Then it occurred to him that maybe he misunderstands her; maybe it is not simple stubbornness. Hernandez could have personal reasons to make absolutely sure there were no more waves of the epidemic.

After all, almost every family had suffered losses in the former years.

"Zoe," he asked her, "Have you lost someone to the plague?"

She raised her eyes from the screen, surprised.

It had been an abrupt question, so uncalled for and unexpected... he should have thought before speaking. The only excuse Erik had was that he had run out of cigarettes and when he knocked on his neighbour's door he hadn't found anyone.

He always said that he could quit smoking whenever he wanted to but doing without his morning cigarette threw him off balance.

"Um... didn't everyone lose someone?" Zoe finally answered, then went back to staring at her screen.

Erik waited for a moment, then realized Zoe would not elaborate.

"Who was...?"

"To tell the truth, I'd rather not talk about it," she cut across him.

"I'm sorry, I didn't mean to pry."

"That's OK," she said, smiling to show him that she was not angry, "Maybe we can talk about it some other time."

The fact that Hernandez refused to talk about her personal history surprised Erik: usually she was so talkative and ready to share anecdotes from her daily life. However, at that moment he realized that, although he knew all about her adventures with the maintenance of the boiler in her apartment or the recurring issues of her food card, he knew very little about her private life.

"So..." Erik spoke again, more to change topic than for any other reason , "Found anything new?"

"Actually, I have," Hernandez replied, instantly switching to the practical tone that characterized her work interactions, "Take a look."

Erik moved so he would be able to see the screen of her computer, where the image a grainy grey figure was shown; he could only make out that the person was wearing a hooded sweatshirt.

"What do you think about it?"

"Dunno," he admitted, "It could be anybody."

"Wait, look here now," Hernandez pulled out a blown-up photo from a pile of papers on her desk: it clearly showed one of the two fugitives.

"This is Weber in the video of the station in the third ring. See? The sweater is definitely the same... see the raised seams on the pockets, and the print on the shoulder? She's even wearing the same trousers and her height is more or less the same. Even the posture is recognizable... look how she bends the shoulders forward, as if to be noticed as little as possible. I think it's her, I'm sure!" she exclaimed.

"Where did you get this?"

"The security camera of a medical police station in the sixth ring. We should send someone to that area. Which, of course, means that we must go there ourselves," she added with a sarcastic grimace. "It is unfortunate that there are so few cameras in that area," Zoe mused.

Erik threw a disconsolate look at the pile of dossiers that had accumulated on his desk. Lately he had been neglecting his routine work a little to follow the tracks of the two fugitives... soon he would have to pay the price for that.

He considered whether to stop by that night to take care of the paperwork, but then he remembered that Maja was coming over for dinner.

"Maybe we can go and take a look this afternoon," he said eventually.

Catching up with the paperwork would have to wait for another day.

In the afternoon Erik and Zoe took the train to the sixth ring, dressed in civilian clothes. Under their clothes, however, they were wearing very thin protective suits, and they took the thinnest gloves and face masks with them.

Taking a car would have been more convenient, but they wouldn't know how to justify it to Hoffman.

Erik watched the city whiz by outside the train window: the transition from the third to the sixth ring was especially sad to observe. The farther away from the centre they got, the bleaker and more degraded the landscape became: the buildings were dilapidated, the streets dirty, with heaps of garbage overflowing from trash cans.

The contrast with the first and second ring and their carefully restored historical buildings was even more striking.

Here one would see no historical houses or gardens enclosed by wrought iron gates; there were only high-rise condominium buildings and an industrial plant now and then.

Erik knew he was privileged to live in his quiet residential neighbourhood in the fourth ring. It wasn't as luxurious as the innermost rings, but it was still built on a human scale, the last outpost before the most degraded areas.

The vast majority of people in Europa, however, lived and worked in the outer rings.

The idea of an epidemic spread in those overcrowded condos was simply terrifying.

Next to him, Hernandez fiddled incessantly with her handheld computer, seemingly indifferent to the changes in the landscape around her.

"Zoe, which area do you live in?" Erik asked.

"Fifth ring, north side, why?"

He shrugged: "Just curious."

Perhaps the fifth ring was not so bad, he thought, there were liveable areas there too. If one wasn't too picky about urban decor…

Meanwhile, the train had arrived at their station.

As he stepped out, Erik wrinkled his nose: the outer rings even had a distinctive smell of their own, a mixture of trash, illegal spicy food and humidity.

First they went to the local medical police station, where Hernandez showed their colleagues the images of the suspects she had found on the surveillance videos.

Unfortunately, none of the officers seemed to remember seeing the hooded young woman.

After leaving several copies of the photographs at the police station, and asking the officers to send for them if there were any news, Erik and Zoe decided to take a survey of the area.

"Where do you think they could hide?" Zoe asked, thoughtful.

Erik thought about it: "Well, it depends. There are two possibilities: either they are in contact with the rebels, and in this case they could be literally anywhere - those creatures know how to hide - or they are on their own. Here's what I think: if they had been picked up by the rebels, they wouldn't accidentally show up in front of surveillance cameras. They wouldn't appear at all: the rebels would make them vanish, as happened with all the other infected they managed to free."

"So, you think they are still somewhere around here, frightened and pretty helpless?"

"I think so."

Zoe bit her lower lip, brooding. "But why?" she finally asked. "Why didn't they try to contact the rebels? Assuming they are now basically the same as the lizard-men... why didn't they look for protection?"

Erik shrugged: "Maybe they don't know how to reach the rebels. Or maybe they don't know for sure they have the plague, and they want to wait out the incubation period and see what happens."

"Or maybe they are too scared, and they prefer to face the disease on their own than associate with those creatures," Hernandez mused.

Erik thought about the infected that killed Lang, his ravaged face, his hollow eyes. "That's definitely possible," he confirmed.

Instinctively he patted his pockets in search of his cigarettes, then remembered that he had none left.

Damn. Although, now that he thought about it, maybe it would be easier to find some in this area.

"I don't get how you can smoke that crap," Hernandez observed, noticing his survey of his pockets, "It's so unhealthy, everybody's known this since the twentieth century or so."

"What can I say?" Erik sighed. "Everyone has their vices. Janssen plays those stupid online games, Laurent occasionally drinks one glass too many, and I have my cigarettes."

"I wonder what Hoffman's vice is," Zoe muttered. "Espionage?"

Erik avoided her eye, trying to think of a way to change the subject. He preferred not to take sides in this inner feud, at least until he had come to any conclusion.

Erik noticed that their walk had taken them to a street with a number of cheap hotels, the kind of place that would rent rooms by the hour to those who engaged in the most ancient trade of all: prostitution.

"Look, how about we check in some of these places, ask if any two women who looked like Weber and Lemaire took or tried to take a room?" he suggested to Hernandez, more to divert her thoughts from Hoffman than out of real hope to find the women. This was like looking for a needle in a haystack, but in fact those hotels, from a fugitive's point of view, had the great advantage of not demanding documents or asking too many questions.

"Let's split up, it'll go quicker this way," Zoe proposed.

Erik started with the hotels on the right side of the road, showing the photos of the two wanted women to the people at the front desk.

No one had seen them.

All the entrance halls were much the same: cold, impersonal, and rather dirty.

The people occupying them had an ugly, mean air, it seemed to Erik, but that was probably only their uncooperative attitude.

They were not very willing to talk to the police, probably because all their affairs were conducted among people with a less than immaculate criminal record.

Erik wondered if the hotel workers would mention seeing the suspects at all, even if they had been there, but ultimately he decided they probably would: the fear of the plague was stronger than the reluctance of having anything to do with the law.

Not that Zoe and Erik mentioned that the two women were infected - they did not want to cause panic - but when a citizen saw a medical police badge, they could usually put two and two together.

Erik questioned every hotel receptionist on his side of the street, with zero results. He stood waiting for Zoe on the street corner. When she emerged from one of the buildings (one of the ugliest and filthiest), she motioned to him to come inside.

The man at the reception, who vaguely reminded Erik of a rat, claimed to have seen the two women.

"They left yesterday, they stayed for one night," he said.

"And do you know where they were headed to?"

He shrugged: "I don't know. They wanted to stay longer but had… er… cash problems."

They tried to obtain more information from him and scoured the room where the two had reportedly stayed but found nothing.

Once they were out, Zoe remarked: "The fact that they stopped here and are short of funds confirms your theory that they are not in contact with the rebels."

"Exactly," Erik nodded. "So they can't have gone too far without leaving traces," he concluded.

When they returned to the headquarters, they encountered a familiar figure outside Lara Meyer's door.

"Lukas Bonnet!" Zoe exclaimed. "What are you doing here? Have you been called for another interrogation?"

The young man smiled: "No, no, nothing like that. I just stopped by to say hi to Lara. She helped me find a job, and I passed by to thank her."

Hernandez's face relaxed: "I see."

Erik returned to his desk and observed the rest of their conversation from afar.

Zoe sure seemed to smile a lot in the young man's presence, and Erik noticed that she placed her hand on his arm. He wondered if they would ever see each other again outside of this bizarre investigation.

Maybe they would.

It was a comforting thought, that people's lives would go ahead despite all the horrible things like the plague and the terror acts of the rebels that were happening around them.

Suddenly, he remembered he had to go home to meet Maja… actually, he was already late. After a last guilty look at the growing stack of files accumulated on his desk, he picked up his coat and headed home.

When Erik arrived at his apartment, everyone was already at the table which, he noticed, was laid out with more care than usual.

"At last!" Thea whispered, greeting him. "What happened?"

"I'm sorry, I was held up in the office..."

"Come on, your dinner has gone cold ages ago."

"Hey, Dad." a different voice greeted him.

"Maja! How are you?"

She shrugged: "Fine."

Since his daughter left home, every time he saw her, she looked different. More and more beautiful, but above all more and more grown up: a mixture of self-confidence and preoccupation.

How had his little girl grown so much in such a short time? Surely a year ago she was still a child...

Peter, meanwhile, was fumbling as usual with his handheld computer, which emitted a frequency of shrill sounds probably belonging to a videogame.

"Hello, Peter. Could you put that thing away please?"

His son rolled his eyes but put the device on the table: "Well, I had to wait for you."

It was then that Erik noticed the stranger at their table: it was a young man around Maja's age. He looked tall even when he was sitting; he had very dark eyes and a smile that appeared vaguely fake.

"Marc Werner, nice to meet you," he said, standing up and shaking his hand. "Maja and I are in the same class."

As the conversation passed in the direction of the courses, examinations and teachers, Erik was distracted by the urge, probably a professional quirk, to study the young man in front of him.

There was something about him that didn't seem quite right: every movement was too controlled, too studied, his smiles too bright.

Erik wondered what this Marc might be hiding, and then, immediately, he inwardly smiled at his own paranoia. Marc was probably just a guy trying to make a good impression on the family of the girl he liked.

He had to try and keep under control his tendency to investigate even where there was nothing to discover, Erik decided.

While he had been distracted by his thoughts, Thea had begun to talk about a patient of hers who was convinced that her sister was still alive, somewhere outside Europa.

The woman had left many years ago for research in the quarantined areas, and she never came back. The woman, however, claimed that she had received a letter from her. Most likely she had fabricated it on her own, in her self-delusion, Thea explained.

"Where did she say it came from?" Marc asked.

"Oh, I don't remember... from one of the countries destroyed by nuclear war, Italy, or Greece perhaps."

"The most incredible part is not only that she believes her sister survived, but that there is mail service in those ravaged lands," Maja smiled. "It is said that it wasn't much to begin with, even before the war".

Marc smiled as well: "You know what they say about PIGS. A nuclear disaster must have been an improvement for their services."

"I don't remember how she explained that... ah, yes, she says that the letter passed from hand to hand, something like that," Thea said, shaking her head disconsolately. "I wish I could avoid giving her drugs but... well, I don't really know how to help her come out of this delusion."

"What if it's true?" Peter asked unexpectedly.

"What?"

"You know, that her sister is alive and that she wrote to her. Maybe there are people still alive in Greece, and they have a mail service. Perhaps we aren't being told the truth."

Erik smiled indulgently: "You read too many adventure books."

"Actually, I was the one who liked those," Maja contradicted him. "Peter is probably confusing this story with the plot of some videogame."

Thea laughed while Peter glanced at Maja, looking offended.

"Well, who knows, maybe there are survivors," Marc chimed in. "After all, it's been years since someone ventured that far."

Peter nodded, sitting a bit straighter on his chair: "Yes, exactly."

Erik rolled his eyes involuntarily. Marc was really trying hard to ingratiate himself with them all, even defending Peter's outlandish theories.

What a show-off, he thought.

At that moment, the handheld in the pocket of his pants vibrated. Zoe Hernandez, he read on the display.

Thea looked at him disapprovingly.

"I'm sorry, I have to get this, it may be urgent," he explained. "Hello?"

"Erik," Zoe's voice seemed anxious, "I know where the suspects are."

"What? Where?"

"I'll give you the address," Zoe dictated a sixth ring address, which Erik wrote on a napkin, under a very annoyed look from his wife.

"Wait, it's too far to go by train – it'll take too much time."

"I'll pick you up. I've already called two other cars."

"Zoe, are you sure...?"

"I am totally sure! I'll be at your place in two minutes."

"Ok," Erik finished the call. "I'm sorry," he told his family, "I really have to go."

He hoped that Hernandez wasn't wrong, or they would be in big trouble.

Chapter 9

The day after the arrival of Sophie and Emma, Lukas announced that he should go and ask a friend if they had news about job offers, and therefore he had to go out.

"There's a lot of stuff to eat in the fridge and on the shelves. Make yourselves at home," he offered generously.

"I'm leaving the keys here," he informed them, hanging the key ring on a hook by the door. "The inside handle is broken, and you can't open the door without the keys, so if I took them with me you could not even get out to go to the bathroom."

"Thanks."

"Don't lose them, please!"

Maybe because of the strong emotions of the last days, or the anxiety of not being sure of how they would get their next meal, but Sophie felt hungry like a wolf.

Still she tried not to overstuff herself and empty poor Lukas' pantry.

Emma settled in a chair and began to knit: "I hope that the wool I brought will be enough to finish this. Now I'm almost done."

"What are you knitting?" Sophie asked, a little out of curiosity, but mostly to make some conversation.

The cup of powdered barley in her hands emitted a comforting scent and a feeling of warmth. Being in Lukas' house felt safer than staying in that dirty hotel, perhaps because his apartment was so similar to hers that she could almost pretend she was still at home and that nothing had happened. Or maybe it was because Lukas was, at the very least, someone familiar.

But even so, she could not get rid of the discomfort brought on by the conversation of the night before.

"It's a sweater," Emma explained, showing her various knitted parts. "I have already made the front and sleeves, now I just have to finish the back."

Sophie was reminded of her grandmother: she, too, had left many unfinished pieces of knitting.

After her grandmother's death, she found a few incomplete knitting projects that she didn't have the heart to throw away, though she had no skills, time or inclination to finish the job either. When she found those misshapen woolly objects, she sat staring at them for hours: they still had that characteristic smell of wool and detergent that she associated with her grandmother; it made her absence more palpable than ever.

She still used to take them out and look at them sometimes.

"How long have you been working on it?" she asked.

"Oh... a couple of months," Emma replied. "I thought a nice sweater would have been just right for this weather."

"Yeah," Sophie looked at her knitting, thoughtful.

Emma most likely didn't have a great life either.

Sophie assumed that she must have seen the sights of the Great War, the plague that had taken her children away and who knows what else... and now this.

"We will find some more wool somehow," she promised at last.

She didn't feel like she could make promises for the rest, but some yarn could not be that difficult to obtain. At least it was something.

"Thank you," Emma said.

"Who do you think this Jamie is?" Emma asked after a while.

"I don't know. Someone who will help us, I hope."

Sophie actually gave very little thought as to what would happen when they'd finally find Jamie. He would solve everything, she told herself. Emma would be taken somewhere safe, and Sophie would return to her old life.

Doubting that this would actually happen was unthinkable.

Lukas returned that afternoon, with a new position in another laboratory, where he would start the week after. Sophie was stunned, because unemployment was still very high, and changing jobs was never easy: finding a new job when the old one was lost was not impossible, but it usually took several months. In response to her inquiries, Lukas merely shrugged and explained that his friend in the medical police had tipped him off about a lab where a new technician was needed.

"Lara Meyer. A really nice person, she has helped me so much."

Sophie strained to display a natural-looking smile as she shifted her weight nervously from foot to foot. She wondered if Lukas would feel compelled to return the favour he just received... for example by telling his dear cop friend where two suspects on the run were hiding...

She shook her head, trying to chase away that unfair thought. After all, so far Lukas' presence has turned out to be a blessing. He had brought a cake to celebrate, something soft and spongy, in a bright, unnatural, pink hue, strawberry flavoured.

"I love strawberry. It's my favourite!" Sophie said, helping herself to a second slice just to lighten up the atmosphere.

Emma chuckled sceptically: "This is not the true flavour of strawberries," she stated. "Oh, don't get me wrong, the cake is delicious," she added, turning to Lukas, "but this is not what fresh strawberries taste like."

"So what do they taste like?" Lukas asked.

Emma thought about it: "Um... they're not as sweet," she seemed to struggle to find the words. "They taste fresher, more... how shall I say... vegetable-like."

Sophie and Lukas looked at each other, perplexed. Described like that, it didn't sound very tempting.

"They're very good, I assure you," Emma insisted.

"Yeah, sure... I imagine," Sophie said, not quite convinced.

In the distance, she heard the familiar sound of police sirens. It was a very common sound in the city, and in the past Sophie usually didn't even pay attention to it. Now, though, she felt an icy chill down her back when she realized that they were very close... too close.

She moved over to the window and saw that several cars had stopped below their apartment building: one, two... a third was coming.

"What's going on?" Emma asked, worried.

For a moment Sophie could not answer.

"They are coming for us. How did they find us?"

Sophie felt a heavy weight pressing down on her chest, obstructing her breath.

"It's the medical police," Lukas said, puzzled. "But how...?"

"Have you talked to anyone?" Sophie interrupted him.

"No I... of course not," he protested.

He looked sincere but...

"Not even with your dear friend, Officer Meyer?"

Emma seemed confused: "Who is Officer Meyer?"

"A family friend, nothing else! I haven't said anything!" Lukas insisted.

"Who else could know?" Emma said sharply.

Feverishly, Sophie began looking for a way out. The police was still on the ground floor and they were on the twenty-sixth: if they managed to get out before the cops arrived...

It felt like oxygen could not reach her lungs, and every breath was painful.

"We need to get out of here," she wheezed.

Lukas sounded desperate: "Where should we go?"

"You can stay here. Emma," she said, turning to the old lady, "Let's get going."

Sophie dressed in a hurry, putting on all her possessions: shoes, sweater, sweatshirt...

Her fingers were shaking to the point that it was difficult to tie her shoes.

Everything around her seemed to move too slowly: why didn't Emma at least try to hurry up? Didn't she understand how important it was to leave as soon as possible?

"Wait," Lukas said, "Why are you in such a rush? Maybe they're not even here for you... maybe it's all a misunderstanding..."

Sophie felt cold again, as if a block of ice was slipping down her spine. Without bothering to answer, she slowly moved back towards the kitchen and opened the cutlery drawer. Her fingers blindly brushed the contents, then closed around the object she was looking for.

"Lukas," she said, trying to keep her voice steady, "we're leaving now."

He was right in front of the door, as if to keep them from leaving. By the expression on Emma's face Sophie knew that she had realized it too.

"Wait," Lukas repeated, "You can't just disappear like that... maybe that's not necessary."

He had a bewildered expression, and Sophie wondered for the first time if his whole personality had always been a sham. Was he really as naïve as he appeared to be?

The tightness in her chest grew stronger.

"Step aside and none of us will get hurt," she said.

She had intended to use a firm and resolute tone, but her voice came out shaky.

Lukas took a step toward her and grabbed her arm: "Sophie, no..."

It all happened very suddenly: she let out a cry, and her hand slashed out before her brain could process the action. Sophie raised the knife she had taken from the drawer and hit Lukas blindly. He screamed as a blood spurt gushed from his hand, staining the front of Sophie's sweater. The knife had sliced through the back of his hand, the tip coming out of his palm.

Sophie stared at it, feeling shocked and horrified.

"Sophie!" called Emma, "We must leave now."

While Lukas was writhing in pain, Sophie pulled away and reached for the door.

Her heart was pounding in her throat, but the fresh air of the corridor gave her a small, momentary relief.

Once she had let Emma out, she grabbed the keys from the hook on which they hung, closed the door behind them and turned the lock three times.

That would stop him for a while.

She took a look around: the elevator was stuck, and from a sound of hurried steps came from the stairwell. How would they get out?

Meanwhile, she heard Lukas beating frantically against the door.

"Sophie," Emma said, pointing to the window in the corridor, "The emergency stairs..."

Of course, Sophie thought, that was probably their only chance. All the buildings in Europa were supposed to have, by law, a network of external stairs, which were very useful in case of a fire. The hundreds of people who usually occupied a single apartment building could not all go through the main stairs without getting jammed.

In theory, at least half of the apartments (the chosen ones were marked on the emergency evacuation plan) would have to be able to get out through the emergency stairs.

That, however, was the theory: the buildings had often a set of external stairs, but their steps were so narrow that they could barely be used by one person at a time.

The idea of a crowd of people getting out through them was simply ridiculous.

The building where Lukas lived was unfortunately was one of those, Sophie discovered as she looked out of the window. There was no other way, though: she climbed over the railing and landed on the metal stairs. They were quite steep, sure, and at that height the gusts of wind made her lose her balance a little, but she could handle it.

For Emma, though, things didn't go as smoothly: getting her to climb over the window sill was very laborious, but the descent was virtually impossible. She was dizzy for the height, and it was very difficult for her to keep her balance on the narrow stairs, with only a discontinuous handrail to support her; but what gave her the finishing blow was the wind. The gusts made her stop every few seconds, and when they finally reached the floor beneath, the twenty-fifth, Sophie realized that they could not continue at that pace for twenty-four floors more.

"We get back in!" she shouted, trying to make herself heard above the howling wind.

Emma looked up at her, terrified: "What?"

"We go back inside from that window!"

Sophie knew from her expression that, though Emma was relieved, she was also wondering how they were going to get out.

Climbing the window to get back in was much easier than getting out.

"And now," Emma asked, panting with fatigue, "how do we escape?"

Sophie looked around: the steps from the stairwell sounded closer and closer.

A door opened: a middle-aged man with a tartan jacket flashed them a puzzled look, then kept walking down the corridor.

Sophie looked in the direction of the lift and had a flash of inspiration. "We'll take the stairs," she announced.

"But they will see us," Emma objected.

Sophie nodded: "Yes, but we won't be the only ones they see."

She approached the fire alarm, which was protected by a transparent box. In case of emergency break glass, it read.

Well, this was definitely an emergency, she decided: she took off her shoe and used it to break the glass. Then she pulled down the alarm handle with all her might.

For a brief moment nothing happened. Maybe it's broken, Sophie thought, full of anguish.

After a moment the siren sounded above their heads, intense and deafening as if it was hammering inside Sophie's eardrums, and flashing red lights turned on down the aisle. A few moments later, the doors of all the apartments were thrown open: a flood of people poured into the corridor and headed for the stairs. Some were calm, others looked concerned, many visibly terrified.

Sophie and Emma watched, open-mouthed, as more and more people swarmed from the upper floors to the lower ones, all elbowing their way towards the exit.

"How many people are there in this building?" Sophie asked no one in particular.

She felt someone push her from behind. "Move on! What are you standing there for? There's a fire!"

They had to move, but it was impossible to prevent the crowd from separating them.

"See you outside, across the street!" she yelled to Emma.

A few seconds later she could no longer see her. She hoped the old lady had heard.

The stream of people continued to pour down the stairs: twenty-third floor, twentieth, fifteenth...

When she was on the tenth floor a policeman passed close to her; he was still trying in vain to climb up the stairs. Sophie could see him well: he was very tall and sturdy, with light blond hair cut very short.

When he looked in her direction, she looked away, towards the floor. Not that it was necessary: the officer was too busy trying to keep his balance to notice her presence.

She wondered what would happen when the medical police raided Lukas' apartment, finding him alone and wounded. Thinking back of how she stabbed her former colleague, she felt a mixture of anxiety and guilt; what if he really hadn't reported them?

She wondered if he would ever manage to use his hand properly again.

Now that the moment of panic had passed, she felt a little ridiculous. Maybe she should have stopped to think before attacking him?

She shook her head to chase away those thoughts. This was not the time to let doubts torment her.

The crowd kept growing thicker, and now Sophie felt crushed: the smell of the people was harsh and pungent, at times even nauseatingly sweet. She couldn't wait to get out of there.

When she finally felt the cold evening air on her face, she breathed a sigh of relief.

She ran across the street when the crowd dissipated enough to let her break free, but she couldn't see Emma anywhere.

Sophie looked around, searching for her companion, then, increasingly concerned, she ran from one side of the building to another.

"Emma! Emma!" she kept calling, but there seemed to be no trace of the old woman.

"Excuse me, have you seen a lady, about seventy years old, in a grey raincoat?" she asked some of the people evacuated from the building.

They all shook their heads, until some guy said: "You mean like that one?" and pointed to a crossroad where Emma was standing, looking lost.

"There you are!" she exclaimed with relief. Emma, too, seemed comforted by seeing her.

"Hey!" exclaimed a guy with a tartan jacket, pointing at them.

Sophie had the impression of having seen him before... ah yes! They had crossed him in the hallway not long before.

"I saw your identikit in the office," he said, "you are the two infected that the police is looking for!"

"Oh no", Sophie thought.

Emma feigned offense: "Of course not, young man! I have nothing to do with any infected. How dare you?"

It was so convincing that for a moment even Sophie believed her.

But the man seemed confident: "Yes, you are! I thought I recognized you before, in front of my door, but now I'm certain."

Unfortunately, his shouting had attracted the attention of some other people, who now stared at them, some curious, some worried. Some promptly scuttled away, and Sophie had the distinct impression that they were going to warn the medical police.

It was better to leave as soon as possible.

"Emma, let's go," she ordered, taking the old lady by the arm and dragging her away.

"Where do you think you're going?" the man with the tartan jacket protested, following them. The others, thankfully, seemed reluctant to follow his example.

Sophie quickened her pace, forcing Emma to do the same. The old woman was panting, but they could not slow down.

"Someone stop them!" the guy screamed again.

Sophie left Emma and took a few steps toward him: "Let's say you're right. Let's say I'm infected," She raised an arm towards him, which made him leap backwards. "Do you want to be infected too? Really want to risk him?"

Sophie came even closer to him, trying to look as menacing as possible. Apparently it worked, because the man looked scarcely able to move with terror.

"Do you really want to be a hero?" she whispered, close to his ear.

He gave a gasp of fear and got away as quickly as he could.

"Come on, we have to get out of here as soon as possible!" Sophie said, pulling Emma by the hand.

They walked as fast as they could, not quite knowing here.

Behind her, Sophie heard footsteps and a siren getting closer.

They turned abruptly in an alley, and a medical police patrol car darted into the road they had just left.

"Others will come soon," Emma said, "They'll comb the whole area." She appeared pale and breathless.

Sophie tried to think, ignoring the pounding of her heart in her throat. She looked around frantically, looking for a way out. A train station, she thought. No, they will definitely put a patrol there. A bus, then...

Then she saw the manhole. This is crazy, she thought.

She didn't have the faintest idea where it would take them. She was not even sure it was an entrance to the Underground City, or a simple drain to the sewers.

But the footsteps were approaching, and the sirens sounded louder and louder, so they did not have much time to waste on doubts.

"Help me lift it up!" she told Emma.

Together they managed, with difficulty, to lift the lid of the manhole, which apparently hadn't been used for a long time.

Sophie kept the entrance open while Emma climbed down the metal stairs, then slipped down as well and closed the manhole above her. A moment later she heard the police siren and the sound of a car passing right over the metal lid.

"Just in time!" Emma commented. Her voice sounded increasingly fatigued.

"Shall we stop a moment to catch our breath?" Sophie proposed, and slid down to sit, leaning against the wall. The ground was cold, but at least it was dry.

All around them there was nothing but darkness, and an overpowering stench of the sewers. Instinct told Sophie to move on as soon as possible, but she was afraid that Emma would not make it.

After a few minutes, Emma stood up: "We should go now."

Sophie could not see her, but she thought the old lady sounded more resolute.

They started to walk along the tunnel, in the dark, holding on to the wall to follow the path. Next to them they could hear the stinky sewer water lapping, and squeaks that surely belonged to rats, a noise that made Sophie shudder.

Every time she felt something touching her, she twitched in fear.

Suddenly the tunnel split, and they decided to move away from the sewer along a narrow corridor, which appeared more likely to lead to the subway tunnels.

There was a thought that Sophie could not shake off. "Do you think it was Lukas who called the medical police?"

"Well," Emma said uncertainly, "who else could have done it?"

Sophie shrugged, even though she knew Emma couldn't see her gesture in the dark.

"I don't know. We're just... we don't even really know if they were actually there for us, do we? We just ran away. Maybe they were there for an entirely different reason. You know, they make these controls all the time in large buildings, especially in the most troublesome neighbourhoods..."

Emma stood in silence for a few moments. "Sophie..." she said eventually, "I know that you and Lukas were friends, but... have you ever thought that he was the only person apart from you and Amanda that had seen my tests?"

Sophie didn't answer. In fact, she had not thought about it. Or maybe she had, but she preferred not to believe it.

In her mind, Amanda's last words echoed: trust no one.

They walked for a long time, stopping occasionally to rest. In the complete darkness, Sophie began to lose track of time.

"Oh!" Emma exclaimed suddenly.

"What?"

"I think I stumbled on something... I felt it against my ankle..."

Sophie knelt and felt the ground blindly but found nothing. "Maybe it was just a piece of concrete," she said to reassure Emma.

"No, it was different... it felt different. "

"Maybe it was a mouse."

It was not a nice thought, but overall mice were the last thing to be afraid of at the moment.

They kept walking, for a timespan that Sophie could not quite gauge (ten minutes? An hour? Two hours?), until, suddenly, they heard muffled noises that sounded like footsteps and objects falling.

"What's going on?" Emma whispered.

"I don't..."

She could not finish the sentence, because something hit her shoulder.

Sophie screamed and heard a mocking laugh behind her.

"What is it?" Emma exclaimed, her voice cracking with fear.

"Who's there?"

There were murmurs all around - then, in the pitch blackness, someone lit a candle.

"Well, well, well... who do we have here?"

It was a very dim light, but after Sophie had been in the dark for so long, she had to squint.

She realized that the candle illuminated a group of three people.

They were evidently inhabitants of the Underground City: she could tell from their colourful, mismatched clothes that seemed to make her eyes water, as well as something else, more difficult to define. Perhaps their smell, which felt strange and spicy.

One of them was tall and well-built, with a shaved head and an ear covered with earrings; another was a woman who had long braided hair weaved with small items that Sophie could not identify, like pieces of coloured glass.

The third, the one who was holding the candle, was a skinny guy with a dirty tuft of hair that fell conspicuously on his face.

All of them wore spectacles held by a piece of elastic at the back of their heads. Sophie realized that those allowed them to see the in the dark. When they lit the candle, they took the spectacles off.

Sophie noticed that the guy who was holding the candle had eyes rimmed by a thick layer of black kohl. "What are you doing here?" he asked smugly.

Sophie wondered if there was a proper answer to that.

"We're trying to get to the Underground City," She replied at last.

The woman with the braided hair looked at them critically: "You don't look like people from around here. I think you look like two honest citizens of the city above, if you know what I mean."

The tall giggled as if it was a joke.

"What have you done to end up down here?"

"We had no money and no job. We do not know where else to go," Sophie said.

After all, it was part of the truth.

"Then I'm afraid you're going the wrong way," the boy with dirty hair informed them, "You're about to enter the territory of Korbinian, the Crow."

From his expression it seemed that he expected some kind of reaction, but the name meant absolutely nothing to Sophie. She looked at Emma and saw that her companion had the same uncertain expression.

"Um... so?" Sophie asked.

"So!" exclaimed the guy with the shaved head, "So you can't get in here without his permission."

"Otherwise?"

"Otherwise, you should go back to where you came from. Look for another entrance, one that brings you to a quieter area. This is not the place for you," the woman explained.

"We can't go back," Sophie said.

The three strangers looked at each other.

"Well, well, well. Sounds like you have a problem," said the boy with the candle. "You're not in trouble with the law, are you? Two respectable ladies like yourselves?"

Sophie sighed: "What if we are? I thought that the law didn't count down here."

"Not the law of Europa, no. But there are other laws."

"In any case, we don't want trouble with the police," the woman chimed in, "We wouldn't like them to follow you down here."

Sophie and Emma looked at each other. Sophie didn't really know what to do.

Too many people had seen them at Lukas' house. Besides, soon the police would find him if they had not already done so, and she would also be accused of attacking him.

And the very idea of walking the entire way back through the rat-infested sewer... Sophie shuddered.

"Please. We cannot go back!" Emma said, evidently coming to the same conclusion.

"Here you can't pass without Korbinian's say-so," the boy shook his head.

"And would you be kind enough to let us know how to get it?" Emma asked, her politeness much too formal under the circumstances.

"Oh, right," he said, pretending to think about it, "You must pay a toll. A mere formality, a no brainer. Three hundred credits each."

"But... you are thieves!" Emma gasped.

The three of them looked at each other, with falsely scandalized expression: "Thieves? Us?" the woman said.

"Absolutely not!"

"Just mere keepers. As the controllers on a train, nothing more."

"The price may seem a bit high," the boy admitted, "but once you are in our area no one can touch you."

"There is a truce," the tall man said solemnly, "Everyone respects it."

It seemed that the matter of the truce was taken quite seriously around there.

"We would gladly pay the price," Sophie assured, "But we're out of money. We were robbed in the hotel where we were staying."

The three of them shrugged, in an almost choral gesture.

"In that case... you know the way, I suppose," the boy said, pointing at the dark road from which they had arrived

"Good-bye!"

He theatrically bowed, then turned off the candle.

"No! Wait!" Sophie shouted.

The candle flared up again almost instantly.

"Oh, what happened? Have you magically found the stolen credits?"

"These miracles happen quite frequently," the woman said matter-of-factly.

"No, we don't have credits but..." Sophie began, feeling the pockets of her sweatshirt and looking for something, anything that might have some exchange value. Maybe she still had some coins somewhere? Her hand found the medicine packages that Amanda had given her. She pulled one out at random and waved it under the boy's nose.

They were strong sleeping pills. "Does this interest you?"

He took the box in his hand and examined it, then passed it to his companions, who greedily did the same.

From the gleam that flared up in their eyes, Sophie realized that the drugs had, after all, some value down here too.

"Where did you find this?" the tall man asked.

"I'm a doctor," Sophie explained, "I can find more."

Actually, she was not so sure she could get to sign prescriptions, but she had more pill boxes in her pockets and when they would be finished... well, she would do something.

The three strangers exchanged glances.

"All right, with this you can pay for your entrance," the boy said at last.

"And hers too," Sophie said, pointing at Emma.

She spoke defiantly, but anxiously held her breath until she obtained an answer:

"Alright, hers too!" the guy granted with a bored look.

Sophie struggled to hold back a sigh of relief.

Once they had pocketed the pills, the three led Emma and Sophie inside a maze of tunnels, until they found themselves in front of a metal door with a round handle, similar to those Sophie had seen on television, in the documentaries about the shipwrecks of boats and submarines.

"Martha, shouldn't we...?" the bald man reminded the woman.

"Ah, yes," she said, "Just another little formality," she added, pulling a tool from her pocket.

It was similar to the one used by the medical police for screening, but it looked older and more handcrafted.

"Your fingertip," she ordered.

She let a few drops of Sophie's blood touch the sensor, and its screen immediately turned green.

"Clean. Your turn," she said to Emma.

When the blood of the old woman touched the sensor, there was a quick flicker on the screen.

"What's wrong?" the boy asked.

"Nothing," Martha replied, irritated, "It's just this thing acting up as usual. What a heap!"

She gave the screen an unceremonious shake, and it became green.

"Perfect, you can get in."

The man with the shaved head turned the knob and opened the door.

"Have a nice stay," he said.

Sophie and Emma walked through the door, then heard it close again behind them.

Chapter 10

Only a few minutes after Hernandez had called, Erik was with her in the car speeding on the freeway towards the sixth ring.

"Now tell me why you're so sure you know where they are." He exclaimed as soon as he found himself in the car with her.

"You know this afternoon, when we found Lukas Bonnet at the headquarter?"

"Yes. Did he tell you where they are?"

Zoe grimaced: "Um... not exactly. I had the impression he was hiding something, I don't know... it was a feeling. So I stuck a microphone with a locator on the sleeve of his jacket... you know, one of those tiny things that Laurent uses too."

Erik remembered when, a few hours before, he had seen her confidentially touching Bonnet's arm.

Apparently, it hadn't been the loving banter he had imagined.

The incurable romantic in him was a little disappointed.

"It took a while to be able to get a decent reception, and I don't think I would have made it if Laurent hadn't helped me... in any case, in the end I could hear shreds of a conversation. There were definitely two women and they spoke of the police and Meyer... so I called the headquarter and asked for three cars to make an incursion."

"What about Hoffman?"

Now Hernandez looked distinctly uncomfortable: "Hoffman... I'm not sure he knows yet."

"What?" Erik gasped "Look, we could be in some serious trouble! If you're wrong..."

"I'm not wrong!" Hernandez insisted "It was them, I'm sure! When we'll arrest them, it won't matter if we had the authorization to proceed or not, and even Hoffman won't be able to do anything about it."

"And what did you say to other officers to get them to follow you?" Erik was seized with a sudden realization "You didn't tell them that Hoffman had already given his approval, did you?"

"Uh... maybe."

Erik rolled his eyes. He had the distinct feeling that the whole thing would have given him endless trouble.

Even if they would discover the most important terrorist cell in Europa and captured a dozen infected, Hoffman would never agree to be bypassed in that way.

He wondered in what mess he had thrown himself.

Erik had always been very scrupulous in respecting the rules, it was one of his points of honour: now, there was making unauthorized extra investigations... in fact, that could be categorized as an excess of scruples; but making three units believe that they had the authorization to proceed with an arrest, when this authorization had never been issued was a whole other matter.

But at that point they had no time to turn back: they had arrived at the address indicated by the locator, which was flashing increasingly and furiously.

"Do you know at what floor they are?" he asked.

"Unfortunately not," Hernandez said. "We should take the stairs and see where the signal intensifies".

Erik looked up and could not suppress a sigh of anguish: there must have been at least fifty floors. He could only hope that Bonnet lived in one of the first ten.

Once they entered the building, Erik took over the management of the operation.
Since he was there, he might as well do everything in his power to really stop the infected.

"You." he told one of the officers who followed him "Stop the elevators. You check the emergency exits." ordered to some others.

He glanced at their names listed on the breast pocket of their suits, but he didn't know any of them.

After arranging the officers in the usual scheme that he used during the arrests, he started climbing the stairs.

Around the fifteenth floor he began to feel fainted and wished he had stayed on the ground floor, leaving the action to the youngsters.

"Persson, are you all right?" Zoe asked. "You're very pale."

He opened his mouth to answer, but he felt short of breath.

Damned middle-age, he thought... *and damned cigarettes*.

An officer came up to hold him.

"I just need to... take a breath... "Erik gasped.

In that time, the fire alarm in the building began to ring.

"We should leave the building," the officer who was supporting Erik noticed.

Hernandez snorted: "If this is a real fire, I'll eat the suit. I'll keep going on!"

People began to swarm up the stairs, from all the doors of the apartments.

Understandably, in those crowded buildings the risk of fire was taken very seriously.

Thinking that there could be two infected in the crowd, infecting everyone with whom they came into contact...

Hernandez was making her way into the growing crowd that descended the flights of stairs: "Persson, if you don't feel... "

"Go ahead!" he shouted "I'll arrive later. And you." he added, addressing the other officer. "Keep climbing. I will join you as soon as I manage."

The other made a sign of assent and walked away.

Erik wanted to sit, but it was impossible: people continued to arrive, pushing him from both sides, with the sole purpose to get out of the building as soon as possible and escape the potential fire.

A few minutes later he was struggling to keep his balance: he tried to climb the stairs for a couple of floors, but he soon realized it was a futile effort.

So he decided to climb back down, and position himself near one of the exits.

If the two fugitives wanted to get out, they would necessarily pass there.

When he arrived downstairs, he realized it would be much more difficult than expected: the crowd was too big for only six officers to contain it.

When he exited the building, the sidewalk was littered with people looking towards the block of flats, trying to catch a glimpse of the fire from the windows.

Part of Erik wanted to remind them that staying under the building was almost as dangerous as staying inside, but the fire procedure required to disperse the crowd in the side streets, making the location of the two women impossible.

Even so, it was like looking for a needle in a haystack.

A man with a chequered coat ran to him: "You're looking for the two infected, right? The ones whose identikit was spread yesterday?" he asked urgently.

Erik, although he was still feeling weak for the sudden illness that caught him on the stairs, became immediately alert: "Yes, have you seen them?"

"They threatened me! One of them, the younger one... she's completely insane! She wanted to infect me, to kill me... "

"That's terrible, but where are they now?" Erik urged him.

"That way," the man said, pointing to one of the side alleys.

Erik saw, in the distance, two figures quickly moving away.

Instinctively, he ran behind them.

When he turned the corner, he felt short of breath and he realized he had a throbbing pain in the chest which seemed about to explode, his lungs burning.

He had no choice: he must stop.

He dropped on the sidewalk, next to a garbage can, and felt the suit looking for the transmitter.

He realized he had blurred vision. With his remaining strength, he called with the transmitter the two officers who were left to guard the exits and told them to get there.

He could not remember their names, but he hoped that they wouldn't mind.

Suddenly, he heard the sound of an approaching engine.

A car appeared at the opening of the street. It was quite an old car, a taxi whose display on the roof gave a busy signal.

There was something wrong though: taxis never travelled at that frantic speed, nor usually looked so massive...

The car was approaching fast, but not enough he couldn't see, for quick instant, the scales that crossed the face of the person on the driving seat.

They were rebels.

They want to reach the two women, he understood.

With his last strength, he stood up, picked up the garbage can next to him, and threw him against the car.

This was forced to divert to avoid it and skidded sideways.

The car stopped before crashing into the pavement (the rebel driving must have excellent reflexes, or at least good brakes, Erik thought), then backtracked to resume its run passing by the trash can.

He had to stop them... he couldn't allow them to get the two women on the run, or they too would be lost forever too.

In that moment, he heard the sound of the siren and a car arrived, driven by one of the two officers that he had left on the ground floor.

Roche, he read on his suit.

"Follow that car!" he shouted, climbing on the seat next to him.

Roche asked no questions, but he pushed the vehicle hot at the heels of the rebels.

When both cars turned the corner, there was no trace of the two women.

Even the rebels had to be puzzled as them, because the car seemed to slow down.

Then the trunk opened, and a volley of bullets hit the car's windshield in front of Erik.

Thankfully the glass was bulletproof, but the car skidded sideways, slowing heavily.

Erik drew his gun and leaned out the window, grateful for the helmet and the bullet-proof suit that fully protected his body.

He fired a few shots at the car, but the trunk was already closed.

Now that he could see it closely, he noticed that the taxi was completely armoured, which made him more like a tank than like a compact urban vehicle.

The car sped down the street, then turned right, turned and sped up again.

After a few minutes of chase, Erik found himself in front of the building from which they had come out, with the mass of people waiting in front of it.

"They won't dare..." Roche began, but obviously he was wrong.

The rebels were just going to drive through the crowd.

Luckily, when they heard the engine approaching, most of the people was fast enough to dodge sideways.

Erik saw a woman being thrown on the sidewalk, and a man being injured at his leg.

The infected are just like beasts, he thought.

"What should I do?" Roche asked.

After the passage of the rebels' car, people had again occupied the street, running towards the wounded to help them.

"Stop," Erik sighed.

He knew that if he stopped he would never be able to reach the rebels, but he didn't want to race at full speed into the crowd, unconcerned about those who would find themselves under his wheels.

In the distance, the rebels' car turned a corner and he disappeared, now impossible to reach.

His only consolation was that he was pretty sure that they, too, had failed finding the two fugitives.

Once the firefighters had arrived and had completed their inspection (noting that, as he suspected, there was no fire in progress), all inhabitants of the apartment building returned within their housing units.

Erik noticed Hernandez next to the ambulance.

"What's going on? Are you hurt?"

She shook her head: "I'm fine. But we found Bonnet locked in his apartment with a knife stuck in his right hand."

"What?!" Erik exclaimed "And how...?"

He felt in his pockets, in the vain search for a cigarette.

"Apparently the two fugitives broke into his house and attacked him."

Erik shivered: "Well, it is known that the infected can become very violent."

Zoe grimaced: "Um, yes, but this is only Bonnet's version and it doesn't hold water: there are dishes for three people on the table, and makeshift beds... not to mention what we heard with the transmitter's microphone. Clearly he was harbouring them."

"Let's arrest him then."

She bit her lower lip: "We could but... well, I don't know. There is something that I don't get in this story. We just tested his blood and he's clean. No contagion. How come that he spent two days in the company of two infected and hasn't caught anything? In addition, there is another thing that puzzles me: he has sworn to be sure that the two don't have the plague, because he had seen their tests the day before.

But if they haven't been infected, then why are they fleeing and why are even the rebels looking for them?"

"Yeah, that's weird..." Erik admitted "But would you really let Bonnet go? It is contrary to any law or procedure. He gave asylum to two rebels, my goodness!" he exclaimed.

"To tell the truth I did not think of just letting him just go. I think I could easily get him to cooperate. He's absolutely terrified of ending up in prison, and all in all I think it would be more useful to have him around, should Weber and Lemaire show up again, rather than let him rot in a cell."

Erik thought about it; Hernandez's proposal was very sensible, but such a decision should have been authorized by someone with a far higher rank than her.

It was not something that the two of them could decide...

"Have you spoken with Hoffman?" he asked.

Hernandez diverted her eyes.

"Zoe! We must warn him immediately! With everything that happened here today... "

"He already knows, don't worry about it," she interrupted him. "But I have to warn you... he's not happy."

She handed him the cell phone, where Erik saw a dozen missed calls from Hoffman and a series of angry messages asking where Hernandez was and what had got into her mind.

Erik ran a hand through his hair: it was a real disaster, the materialization of his fears when he became involved in that absurd investigation.

"Don't worry," Hernandez said. "I'll tell him that it was my initiative and that you, like the others, thought we had his permission."

"But that wouldn't be... "

"Look, I'm already in trouble, and it's better if it's only one of us, right? If I'll end up cleaning toilets at the headquarter, I would prefer that there was still someone in the team that I can trust."

Erik returned home very late that evening.

He had to go to the headquarter, fill a lot of forms, and try to explain the situation to the other officers who had been involved, who were understandably very upset.

Hernandez had been summoned for the next morning to Hoffman's office, who fortunately had decided to postpone the lecture, at least for that evening.

Erik had breathed a sigh of relief: he wouldn't have managed to deal with it in that moment.

When the adrenaline of the chase had dropped, he found himself exhausted.

He wanted nothing but letting himself fall on any horizontal surface and sleep; he felt too tired even to want a cigarette.

It was night when he opened the door of his flat.

He had a great need of a shower, but he was too tired, and he did not want to wake up the whole house; so he just got rid of the sweat-soaked clothes he was wearing and put on his pyjamas.

He would worry about making himself presentable the next day.

"Erik... are you all right?" Thea asked in a sleepy voice.

"Yes, yes... go back to sleep," he whispered in answer.

"What happened? Did you find other infected?"

"No, it was just a false alarm."

"I see. It's a pity you had to run away from the dinner. Maya was very disappointed."

Erik sighed: "I'm sorry too. Tell her to come again next week."

Hoffman would do anything to strip him of any responsibility, he reflected bitterly, and he was pretty sure that he would be able to come home for dinner for a while.

"Hmm, ok." she murmured, yawning, and Erik realized that she was about to slip back into sleep, "but I don't know if she will bring back her friend Marc. I hope so, though. He looks like a nice guy, right? So nice and polite."

"Um... yes... maybe he's just a little... I don't know how to say..."

The only word that he could think of at that moment was 'slimy', but he didn't want to sound like a killjoy.

"...dull."

Thea chuckled: "Dull. Sure."

"You know what I mean? I thought you also wanted Maya to hang out with people more... with more personality, you know".

She straightened the pillow under her head to make it more comfortable: "No one is ever enough for Maya in your opinion."

"You might be right," Erik smiled.

But it was not his fault if he thought his daughter was more brilliant and intelligent than all her friends.

Maybe it was the parental love that made him biased, but he was convinced he was right.

"She likes him, that's the important thing, right?"

"That's right," he confirmed.

Thea yawned and after some instant her breathing become slow and regular.

Erik believed that he would fall asleep as soon as he touched the pillow, but instead he rolled over in bed long, until he could see the daylight filtering through the blinds of the room.

When he finally managed to get to sleep, he dreamed of the infected with the cold eyes that had killed Lang years before, running away on the rebels' van, but when he turned to shoot him, he had Marc's face.

Chapter 11

Sophie had expected to discover another subway station with battered and impersonal-looking halls, or perhaps another crowded corridor. Nothing, however, had prepared her for what she found on the other side of the door.

She was in a very large room, composed of a central nave and a lower aisle separated by an arcade on each side.

The ceilings were very high, with pointed arches of grey stone. The walls were mostly nothing but pillars where large stained-glass windows were framed. Most of them were broken and ruined, but here and there Sophie could still recognize the drawings of human figures.

At one end of the great hall there was a large circular window with a shape that reminded Sophie of a daisy.

"We are in a cathedral," whispered Emma, who seemed just as impressed. "I have never imagined that they could be so.... majestic," she added quietly to herself.

"Why would anyone build a cathedral down here?" Sophie asked, puzzled.

Emma chuckled: "They didn't build it here. It is very ancient, and it was once at street level. Then the city had grown more and more, piling up centimetres of dirt, earth and asphalt each year... until, finally, the cathedral was buried entirely underground."

"Oh," Sophie said.

The central part was evidently used for transit, because it was travelled by many people in both directions. On the sides, in small areas with a much lower ceiling, there were encampments of people, even families, who seemed to live there.

There were mattresses, camping stoves, hammocks strung between one column and another.

In the middle of the passageway, like seemingly everywhere in the underground city, there were people selling something. Sophie noticed a woman offering colourful necklaces and bracelets made of glass, which most likely originated from the windows, and another that had polystyrene boxes very similar to those she had bought from Gitte. Though it only happened two days earlier, it seemed a lifetime ago.

"Fresh meals!" announced the seller. "From the canteen of the hydroelectric power plant... freshly cooked today! I'm ready to trade or sell, only three credits each!"

"What?!" Sophie exclaimed. Gitte had made her pay ten times as much.

That's why she had been so keen to help.

While she was engrossed in these thoughts, a woman approached them.

"Hello," she greeted them, extending a hand. "My name is Jeanne, what's yours?"

She had dark hair, and the excessively pale skin of those who did not go out much in the sun.

Sophie squeezed her hand: "I'm Sophie, and this is Emma."

Only then it occurred to her that perhaps she should have invented false names, but it was too late.

Jeanne nodded and smiled. She smiled a lot, as if she was genuinely happy to meet them, and she kept her eyes wide open, which gave one the impression that she was afraid of missing some important detail if she blinked.

"So, you're new? Do you plan on staying here a long time?"

"Not really," Emma replied immediately, "Only a couple of days."

Jeanne appeared surprised: "You paid the toll just so you could stay here a couple of days?"

Sophie shrugged: "Um, we were in trouble."

The woman nodded: "Yes, I suppose. Most of the people who are here came from a difficult situation... but I'm sure you'll like it around here! We are a close-knit community, like a big family. We are all brothers and sisters here!" she added enthusiastically.

Sophie had the immediate urge to get as far away as possible.

"Thank you," replied Emma, who smiled in a way that appeared a bit forced to Sophie, "This is really – "

"Oh!" Jeanne exclaimed, as if a thought had suddenly struck her. "Do you already know where you are going to stop for the night? No? But then you should definitely be my guests... come, come..."

Sophie and Emma attempted to come up with some excuse, but it was useless: Jeanne led them into one of the side alleys, where she had fixed her abode. Two children were playing on the floor; upon their arrival they waved casually.

"Claude and Marcel," Jeanne introduced them.

There was a large marble altar with the remains of a statue, which was used as a table and work surface, and comfortable-looking mattresses by its side.

"This was once a chapel of the cathedral," Jeanne explained, pointing to the middle of the destroyed monument, which, from what Sophie could see, seemed to represent a man kneeling in prayer.

"A sacred place, so full of... energy, magic! I bet you felt it too... it was the energy of this place that guided you here, wasn't it?"

Emma and Sophie exchanged a perplexed glance.

Someone had unceremoniously left a hat on the head of the statue, and next to it some food was simmering in a pot on an electric stove.

Jeanne stirred its contents with a plastic spoon: "It's almost ready," she announced. "You'll be staying for dinner, of course?"

To be honest, Sophie didn't really feel like staying with Jeanne, who seemed a bit mad; on the other hand, it was still a free meal, and the smell coming from the pot was far from repulsive.

While Jeanne's back was turned, Sophie looked at Emma, then pointed to the pot with her eyes; her companion seemed to understand, because she politely replied: "Of course, we'd love to."

"We must go and fetch some water. Come along, follow me," Jeanne announced.

She led Sophie and Emma to what had once been the main door of the cathedral. She opened a small door within the large wooden door (which was very rotten and ruined, but still allowed one to discern the original carvings) and brought them out of the cathedral.

"Over here we have bathrooms and drinking fountains. You know, we are connected to the city water supply."

"That's amazing," Emma commented.

Jeanne smiled proudly: "We did the same about electricity. This way we have everything we need."

At the end of the tunnel they found what might have been the old toilets of a subway station. At the centre of the room there were a number of fountains where people lined up to collect water. All around, there were bathrooms divided into cubicles.

In another corner there were basins where others were washing the dishes. There was also a girl brushing her very long hair.

Sophie noticed that the people who lived in the cathedral actually seemed a lot cleaner than those she had seen in the subway hall she visited with Gitte.

Indeed, since these people had a more or less unlimited supply of hot and drinking water, there was no reason why they should be dirtier than her or anyone else.

Once they had filled a jug, Jeanne shut the tap very carefully, taking care to make the two full turns of the knob.

"You must be very careful, you know," she explained. "The connection to the water pipes is very delicate. During certain times of the day the water pressure grows stronger, and if the taps are not all tightly closed they risk blowing up. It happened a few years ago," Jeanne winced. "A disaster. We almost had to leave, all of us."

Sophie watched the taps with suspicion, then walked back to the cathedral.

Once they came back, Jeanne turned off the stove and began to fill the plates with servings of a juicy dish that smelled as inviting as it was foreign.

Claude and Marcel began quietly eating, always whispering among themselves. They seemed used to being surrounded by strangers.

Sophie pushed the contents of her plate around for a while, and finally asked: "It really looks fantastic but... um, what is it?"

"Oh, it's a pork and cabbage stew. You don't like it?" Jeanne asked, worried.

"No, I mean... yes... I think..."

Actually, the sight of it made her slightly sick. It did not resemble in the least anything she had ever found in the tins of the food distribution. However, since Jeanne continued to stare, she took a bite and stuck the fork in her mouth with feigned enthusiasm which, to her surprise, turned into real enjoyment as she discovered the stew to be flavourful and spicy. It was a completely unknown taste, but very pleasant.

In a few minutes she had cleared off all that was on her plate, and Jeanne served her a second helping.

"It's very good indeed. But where did you find the meat?" Emma asked. "It's been a while since I saw any pork, at least in the city above."

Jeanne shrugged: "I bartered it with Joseph over there when I fixed his stove. Hey, Jo!" she called loudly.

An old man in a hat, who was intently plucking a chicken on the other side of the room, nodded in greeting.

"They like the meat you brought!" Jeanne informed him, shouting.

Joseph smiled and took off his hat for a moment, then returned to the chicken.

"We prefer barter to the credit system," Jeanne explained in an eager tone. "It's much more socially correct."

"Ah," Sophie commented, without really knowing what to say.

"This way the value of a person is not defined by their material wealth, but by their real abilities," Jeanne continued, then launched into a long speech about how the credit system was the root of poverty and hardship in the outer rings of the city.

Sophie listened to her at first, but after a few minutes her mind began to wander: she had a full stomach, pleasant warmth came from a stove in the corner, and she realized she's going to drift off to sleep any moment.

Would it be very rude to ask permission to take a nap?

The arrival of the boy – the one with heavily made up eyes and dirty hair who had admitted them to this strange place - startled her from her thoughts.

"You two," he said, gesturing at Sophie and Emma, "Korbinian says he wants to see you."

"Now, Alois?" Jeanne objected. "We are just having dinner."

Alois shrugged: "Thus saith the boss."

Sophie and Emma got up and followed him to the end of the central hall, where a large decorated wooden panel separated the main room from a smaller, semi-circular area. The panel didn't go all the way up to the dome high above their heads, so pieces of fabric had been stretched above in lieu of a ceiling.

The room was bigger than it looked from the outside, and there were several people talking in small groups. Sophie recognized the girl and the bald guy who were with Alois in the tunnels. There were also a table, chairs, and other furniture collected in an apparently casual way.

At the back of the room, on a carved chair that might once have been part of the cathedral, sat Korbinian.

Sophie knew at once that it was him because everyone looked at him for approval, falling silent whenever he spoke.

His hair was too long, dyed an unnatural pitch black, and he wore makeup on his eyes. Sophie realized that the young Alois was probably trying to imitate the leader: but while the eye makeup was a little ridiculous on the boy, it somehow suited Korbinian.

He was sprawled on the chair, almost lying down, looking quite at his ease. When he saw Alois, he gave a rather indifferent nod, motioning the boy to come closer.

"So, these are our new guests?" Korbinian asked. He didn't sound very enthusiastic, to tell the truth.

"Yes," the boy said, "They arrived a few hours ago."

"Have you already told them of our…ah… financial policy?"

"Not yet," Alois admitted, "But I think Jeanne said something about it."

Korbinian smiled, a bit condescendingly: "Ah yes, Jeanne is always very enthusiastic when it comes to welcoming the newbies," he said, standing up. "The thing is very simple: you can go where you want, you can go out, go around the underground city or the city above if you feel like it, but every time you come back you will have to pay the entrance fee. Otherwise you can join the common fund and give us all your credits."

Emma snorted in irritation: evidently, she didn't like the idea much.

"Oh, I know what you're thinking," Korbinian continued, "But here you won't really need them. We don't let people starve. We will give you a bed, and if you don't have food you can come here twice a day and we will give it to you for free. Or you can exchange something or do some work for us. For example, what did you do before you came here?" he asked, addressing Sophie.

"I was a doctor," she replied, slightly reluctant.

She did not like the idea of giving them too many personal details, but she had already told this, so it didn't make much difference.

Korbinian's eyes sparkled with interest: "Really? A doctor? Well, wouldn't it be convenient to have one around here?" he gave a look to the other guys next to him. "At times our – ah - business involves some risk. It wouldn't hurt to have someone who knows how to patch us up, am I right?"

A couple of people in the room laughed. Sophie had the distinct impression that the business which Korbinian was referring to was not strictly legal.

"Not to mention the fact that old Edmund would be happy to have someone to talk to about his research."

"Research?" Sophie asked, intrigued despite herself. "What kind of research?" Korbinian gestured vaguely with his hand: "Something about the plague. He's supposed to be a medical researcher, some kind of scientist... He can't even put a plaster on, anyway," he pointed out with a grin. "He has been working on it for years, sometimes he says he has made progress, but... well, you'll see."

"Thank you very much, but we have to leave tomorrow," Emma said resolutely.

Korbinian stared at her, slightly surprised, since it was the first time she spoke in front of him. "You may want to think about it some more," he offered gently.

"Actually..."

"We'll think about it," Sophie interrupted. There was no need to argue just then.

"In any case, the police never broke in here, right? Even the medical police?"

Everyone laughed.

Sophie felt her cheeks growing hot.

"Police doesn't hang out round here," Korbinian confirmed, shaking his head. It seemed that the very thought amused him.

"Have you already found an accommodation for the night?" Alois asked.

Emma nodded. "Jeanne offered to host us."

"Ah, Jeanne," Korbinian exclaimed. "What would we do without her? Good then, goodbye."

Korbinian went back to his business, whatever it was, and Alois escorted them outside.

Sophie and Emma walked back to the area where Jeanne lived (it seemed improper to speak of it as 'her house').

"I don't like this place," Emma said, clutching her coat, "It makes me shiver. These people are criminals."

Sophie shrugged: "I don't know. I mean, yes, Korbinian and the others in there definitely are..." she stopped short, noticing Emma's shocked expression. "But the people who live here look normal enough. And after all they seem to be doing fine, right?"

Emma shook her head: "The earlier we leave, the better".

As soon as they got to Jeanne's, one of the kids (Claude, probably) ran breathlessly toward them: "Which of you is the doctor?" he asked.

"That's me," Sophie answered. "What...?"

Claude took her hand: "Come on, Edmund wants to see you!"

Edmund... The name was familiar. Ah yes, he was the one who was doing some research on the plague, she remembered. That could be interesting.

"Ok, let's go."

Emma made as if to follow them, but at that moment Jeanne came: she asked the old lady to wait there and offered her a cup of tea, so only Sophie walked away with Claude.

The child led Sophie out of the cathedral (from a different door than the one through which they had entered), then through a network of tunnels up to a metallic door.

"Here we are, see you later!" Claude told her and ran away before Sophie could ask him how to get back.

She knocked on the door but received no answer. After knocking again and waiting for a few minutes, she decided to try and enter. She pushed the handle and the door opened, but she had to struggle a bit, because it was old and rusted.

She entered a long room similar to a corridor, badly lit, apparently full of shelves. The shelves were packed with binders which in turn were overflowing with sheets. Sophie ran her eyes over them, noticing that they were all classified with some incomprehensible codes.

"Hello?" she called. Still no answer.

She kept walking towards the back of the room. After a while, she saw the pale light of a lamp. "Hello?" she repeated.

"Yes, yes, come in," a voice answered.

Sophie came over to the back of the room, where a rudimentary laboratory had been set up. She couldn't help but mentally compare it with Amanda's office at the medical centre, where everything was always sterile, clean and immaculate.

Here, in contrast, chaos reigned: wherever she looked she saw crumpled sheets haphazardly thrown upon the shelves, test tubes filled with something that looked like blood (which, in fact, it probably was), piles of dust in the corners, open boxes full of unused equipment.

Almost hidden behind a desk, there was an old man who stood to greet her, warmly smiling at her. His little remaining white hair was combed back. His bright blue eyes sparkled behind very thick lenses, and he wore corduroy pants with suspenders. He looked like a grandfather from a school book.

"So you're a doctor, are you? Please, come on and sit down," he welcomed her, gesturing towards a chair; noticing that the seat was full of papers, he hurried to clear it.

"What brings you here?" he asked with genuine interest.

"Claude told me you wanted to see me," Sophie explained, perplexed.

"Ah, yes! That's right," he admitted, scratching his head thoughtfully. "Dear, what happened to my manners?" he added after a moment. "Let me introduce myself first: my name is Edmund Harris and I am, or rather was, a researcher at the Sorbonne University until a few years ago."

"Oh!" Sophie exclaimed, impressed. "Wow. I mean, wow. And then what happened?" Edmund grimaced: "An odious conspiracy... envy from my colleagues, pure envy..." his voice was lost in an indistinct mumbling. "However, you know how life goes... I found myself here."

"I understand," Sophie said, though she wasn't really sure she did. Then, since the old man kept muttering something unintelligible about a colleague who had always wanted his professorship, she added: "Korbinian told me you're working on some kind of medical research."

Edmund's eyes lit up with pure joy: "Yes, that's correct! I spent half my life on this project... my goal is to cure the dragon plague. Does this interest you?"

Sophie felt her heart pounding: "Actually, yes... a little."

"Then you should definitely read my notes!" the old professor exclaimed enthusiastically. She had to smile - his exuberance was contagious.

After having rummaged a bit in the mess on the desk, Harris handed her a huge binder full of pages stuck at messy angles.

"Go on, read it!" he urged her. "I'm sure you will find it very interesting."

Sophie began leafing through the contents of the binder: it was all piled up in a very disorderly manner, but from what she could understand it contained the results of the interaction between infected blood and other substances that could potentially provide a cure. From what she could see, though in some instances the antibodies had reacted in an interesting way, Edmund hadn't been able to find a cure yet.

"I wanted to do more experiments, but as you know the plague does not affect other mammals except humans... fascinating, isn't it?"

"Yes," confirmed Sophie, though naturally she already knew it, and kept leafing through. She noticed that Edmund Harris had done tests with antiviral compounds similar to those she had been working on with Amanda, but the results looked very different. When she asked him about this, Edmund launched into a long explanation, describing the various stages of his experiments. A heated discussion arose, and soon Sophie lost track of time.

Finally having someone to talk to about a subject that was close to her heart was like a breath of fresh air, something she had lacked in the past days. And it was evident that, despite his dreamy air and disorganized work space, Edmund Harris knew what he was talking about. Considering that the documents she had been leafing through were only the conclusions of Edmund experiments, the bulk of his research was impressive.

There was, however, a detail that didn't quite add up.

"Excuse me, Professor Harris, but how did you get all this infected blood on which to experiment? It is very difficult to obtain it from the medical police, and I don't think that the black market would..."

"Korbinian saw to that," explained Edmund. "Do you want to see it?"

"What, the blood? I don't think I..."

"Ah no, something better!" he said, winking at her.

Sophie followed him through a door concealed by shelves, through a dark tunnel toward a door secured with many locks.

"There are not many people who have seen what I'm about to show you," Edmund announced, fiddling with a bunch of keys he kept on his belt and opening the locks one after another. "I must ask you not to tell anyone... I think most people would feel, let's say... uncomfortable, knowing what I'm hiding here."

Sophie felt an icy chill creep down your spine: "Sure."

Edmund finally removed the last lock and turned on the light.

The room seemed empty, except for a table with a display of rubber gloves, syringes, scalpels, and other standard medical equipment. One side of the room was made primarily of a glass wall that extended from about one meter above the floor almost to the ceiling, with a small, battered-looking computer monitor in front of it. Sophie noticed a large refrigerator in the corner and guessed that the blood was stored there.

It had to be a rather impressive reserve, and if anyone felt nervous about so much infected blood nearby, she certainly couldn't blame them.

But to her surprise, Edmund approached the window and lit another light. The room on the other side of the glass became illuminated. Sophie got closer and finally realized what Edmund meant.

It was a very small room, little more than a cubicle containing a bed, monitors and other equipment for the surveillance of vital functions.

Stretched on the bed, wearing a gown similar to the ones used in hospitals, but much more ragged and dirtier, there was a human figure.

He was, or rather, had once been a man; he was skeletal, so that Sophie could see the skin stretched tightly over the bones of his arms and legs. His hair, thinning on top of the head, was so fair that it seemed white, and even his skin was grey like a corpse's. Only the steady rise and fall of his chest indicated that he was still alive.

He was pinned to the bed by narrow straps holding down his wrists and ankles.

The most chilling of it, though, were the scales: pale green but unmistakable, they covered his face all the way down to his neck, disappearing under the gown.

"But it's... it's..." Sophie stammered, paralyzed by horror.

"Oh, don't worry, it's sedated. We almost always keep it this way, it's much safer," said Edmund matter-of-factly.

"How long have you -"

"We captured it several years ago... I would say at least six or seven... before that, Korbinian and the others provided me with samples of blood, but it was not the same. You must know that it is best to use fresh blood, because within a few hours it has completely different properties..."

Sophie could not tear her eyes from the figure on the bed. She moved closer to the glass.

"At first, we kept it in the room and tried to give it food and water through a small door, but it didn't work. It was too violent. It wanted to get out and tried to attack me once. Said it wanted to go home... go figure. It even seemed rational at times, but..." Edmund sighed. "Well, it ended up betraying our trust once too often. So, we started with the straps, and then went on to use sedatives."

The man (could he still be called that?) on the bed gave a start, and Sophie recoiled.

"Oh, don't be afraid, it's just dreaming!" Edmund laughed. "It happens all the time."

The creature's eyes were moving rapidly under the eyelids. Sophie wondered what he could be dreaming.

"It is, quite fascinating isn't it? A living specimen has been a boon for my research... I made a huge leap forward!"

Sophie looked at the old professor, and suddenly saw something sick in his enthusiasm; the light in his eyes looked more fanatical than reassuring.

"I think I should go now," she murmured.

"Of course, of course, we've been down here quite a while, haven't we?"

Edmund took her back to his lab, and from there to the entrance of the cathedral, chatting amiably and asking questions about her work the whole time.

By the time Sophie reached Jeanne's place, the feeling of unease she had been unable to shake off since seeing the infected man had almost entirely disappeared, and she ended up wondering if she hadn't overreacted.

She accepted a cup of tea from Jeanne and played cards with her, Emma, Claude and Marcel. The latter, despite being the youngest, was also by far the best player, and won almost all the games.

"Good thing we're not betting money," Emma said with an indulgent smile.

When Sophie's eyelids grew heavy, and Claude and Marcel had dozed off under the table, it was clearly time to go to sleep. Jeanne pulled some mattresses out of a large box and offered them to the guests.

Sophie and Emma made a last trip to the bathroom before settling down to sleep. Most of the cathedral was already asleep, and she could hear a faint snoring issuing from various corners.

"Tomorrow we must wake up early if we want to get to Stuttgart by seven p.m. We ended up a little off track," Emma said when they were alone in the bathrooms.

Sophie nodded. "We'll leave as soon as we wake up. I thought I might borrow some men's clothes and keep my face covered. They are looking for two women alone, after all."

"Good idea."

Sophie took a deep breath: "It's not that bad here, is it?"

Emma was silent for a moment, thinking about it. "I find this place terrifying," she admitted. "But Jeanne is nice, and we had a nice evening."

Sophie nodded. "I wonder if we should go to meet that Jamie tomorrow."

Emma frowned: "What do you mean?"

"Um, I was just thinking about it before, "Sophie sighed, running a hand through her hair and noticing absently how tangled it was. "What do we know about him, anyway? Nothing, except that Amanda told us to go meet him. And that isn't much, is it?"

"That's true," Emma said.

"And then... we don't even know if he is still alive, if he knows that we're looking for him... and we have to cross half of Europa to get to the right place on time…"

"I know, it's just that…" Emma spread her hands, "What other options do we have? We cannot run away forever."

"No, certainly not! But if we stay here, we won't have to run away. We could live quietly, and the medical police wouldn't bother us."

"It's true, we could stay here. But..." Emma sighed. "Do you really want to spend all your life in the dark, cooped down here? I get a little anxious at the idea," she admitted.

Sophie knew her companion was right. Living conditions in the underground city were far from ideal. However, who could guarantee that what Jamie had to offer was not something similar, or even worse?

There was also another concern that gnawed at Sophie, although she was not very keen to talk about it: what if Jamie and his men, whoever they were, took Emma and locked her up in a laboratory as Edmund had done with his 'specimen'?

If she had to deal with just one mad scientist like Edmund Harris, Sophie was pretty sure she could persuade him to leave Emma alone, and ask her for a blood sample only when necessary. But would she be able to stand up to many potentially aggressive strangers?

That night, while she tossed and turned on Jeanne's soft but slightly foul-smelling mattress, Sophie reflected for a long time on what she had seen. Keeping a man (or rather, a creature) captive that way seemed cruel, inhuman, but if it was the only way to find a cure and save countless lives, maybe it was worth it? She wondered if it was not, in fact, the most sensible solution and even the most compassionate one: after all, Edmund's prisoner didn't seem to suffer, and his sacrifice could change the world.

Part of her, however, shuddered at the idea of anyone kept alive in those conditions without even being granted the liberation of death. What if Edmund had treated Emma the same way - to save humanity, of course?

Sophie shivered. No, it didn't make sense: Emma was a human being, she just had... some abnormal markers in her blood.

She was not an infected.

Sophie tossed and turned for a long time before falling into a light and restless sleep, disturbed by the occasional sound of footsteps and the snoring of the people around her.

Chapter 12

When Erik returned to the headquarters the next morning, he noticed that Hernandez was in Hoffman's office. The boss appeared very upset.

From what he could see, Zoe was listening to Hoffman's long tirade without reacting.

It was a good tactic, he thought: it was best to let people like Hoffman blow off steam.

He had received a message, also addressed to Roche and the other officers who were involved the night before, ordering him to report to Hoffman that morning at about ten o'clock, and he had received a copy of the procedure of arrest preparation. Upon the whole, he knew he had got by with little damage.

This made him feel very guilty: it was true that the attempted arrest of the two fugitives had been Hernandez's initiative, but it did not seem right to pretend to be completely ignorant of the whole investigation. He had been an accomplice, transgressing Hoffman's orders, and he was prepared to take his own share of responsibility. Hernandez, however, had been immovable.

Erik admired her for her tenacity... once again, he wondered why she was so determined to discover the truth. Simple work ethics?

He didn't find this believable: of course, for some this would be a sufficient motive, but in his experience Erik found that idealists and workaholics were an absolute minority compared to those who engaged in what they were doing with completely different motivations, ranging from the desire to forget some personal trouble, to climbing the career ladder or the need for money.

He hadn't been able to frame Zoe Hernandez's motivation yet.

Now that he thought about it, other disturbing details began to emerge in his mind.

The night before had been too agitated, too full of events to digest all at once; when he got home, he only managed to fall exhausted into bed, with the sole desire not to think about anything.

But now he was struck by a question he couldn't figure out: how did the rebels know that the two fugitives were there?

Apart from the suspects themselves, and Bonnet, who was hosting them, only Hernandez knew of them, because she had heard it in the microphone that she had placed on the young man.

Erik couldn't imagine Bonnet having any collusion with the rebels: besides, they had arrived slightly later than the police. If the young man wanted to hand the two fugitives to the rebels, he would have had plenty of time to do it before.

The rebels arriving at the same time as the police was a coincidence too great to believe. Which left the possibility of the mole inside the police forces.

Despite some confusion, Erik began to realize that Hoffman's suspicions were not entirely unfounded. Hernandez was the only person (apart from himself, of course) that knew of the impending arrest. Unless the informant was Roche or one of the others... no, he did not believe it could be one of them. They were only officers who happened to be on duty; they seldom performed arrests of rebels or infected. Their usual job consisted of performing routine screening on public transport and at checkpoints. Erik even doubted that they knew the details of the mission when they were called to action.

But then why had Hernandez set up that disastrous arrest operation, if its purpose was to warn the rebels and let them get away with the two fugitives? It would have been much simpler to pass them the information and not say anything to anyone else in the police. Not to mention the doubts that Zoe had expressed the previous evening, her suspicion that the two fugitives, in fact, were not infected at all.

Erik sighed: nothing in this story made sense. As he stared at Zoe Hernandez's profile through Hoffman's office glass wall, though, he wondered who she really was.

When Hoffman had finished with Hernandez, she left the office with a rather dejected look.

"Your turn - he told me to tell you to go in," she informed him.

"What did he say?" Erik asked.

She frowned: "I'll tell you later."

Erik walked into Hoffman's office, closing the door behind him. Hoffman sat at his desk, ostensibly studying a document he was holding.

Erik made himself comfortable in his chair, expecting the usual silent treatment that preceded every conversation with his superior.

"Persson, Persson..." Hoffman said wearily, after a studied pause of a few minutes. "What have you done last night, huh?"

"Well," Erik began, "I received an emergency call at about eight in the evening, and..."

Hoffman stopped him, raising his hand: "Wait, wait... listen to me before speaking." He let out a dramatic sigh: "You see, when I put you and Hernandez on the same team, I hoped that you would be able to set a good example for her, leading her to moderate her reckless actions. And I'll tell you, until last night I was pretty convinced it was a good choice. And then, guess what? I was at home, with my family, having my dinner in peace, when I found out..."

Erik continued to observe the feigned concern of his boss, and his mind began to wonder. With much sentiment, Hoffman described his surprise and anger of the previous day, and for a long time Erik had to listen to Hoffman berating him for his inability to be a good mentor for anyone who was paired with him.

"But now, be honest, please: why didn't you verify that the operation had really been authorized? Didn't it seem strange to receive such an urgent call for an investigation that you hadn't even followed?" Hoffman finally asked, exasperated.

Erik hesitated: if he told the truth he would certainly provoke Hoffman to execute some disciplinary measures. On the other hand, he was still reluctant to leave all the blame to Hernandez.

"I don't know," he finally said. "You know how I feel about the infected: the idea that there out there, roaming free..." he shook his head. "When we talk about these things, for me it is a priority to make sure that citizens are safe. Everything else, authorizations, hierarchy, bureaucracy... when rubber hits the road, all the rest goes into the background. It's my weakness, I realize it. I know it's not an excuse..."

This seemed a fair compromise between keeping Zoe's secret and telling the truth: after all, that was the motivation that had led him to help her in the first place.

Hoffman sat, apparently exhausted by his monologue. "I know," he finally admitted, "That's why I am convinced that you were in good faith."

Erik breathed a sigh of relief, realizing at that moment that he had actually been worried about the outcome of the conversation.

"For your information," Hoffman continued, "I'm not going to take any disciplinary action against you. However, I think you would do better in another department for a while. Maybe the stress of all these field actions, all those arrests is beginning to take its toll on you. After all, you are no longer a kid, am I right?"

Erik clenched his fists in anger: it was all a bunch of nonsense, and Hoffman knew it. Removing him from his department was simply a punishment for not having referred to him as an authority. However, he merely gave him an evasive nod.

He wouldn't give Hoffman the satisfaction of seeing how upset he was.

"Some time in a quieter department will do you good; a little less action and some routine chores will make you feel much better. Here," he went on, extracting a file from his desk drawer and handing it to Erik. "Here you will find all the information about your new position. Take the time to go through it and let me know if you have any questions. You can collect your things from the office now, and next week you will present from your new superior."

Erik nodded, trying to maintain an impassive façade as much as he could, then left the office and went to his desk. Zoe looked at him hesitantly, as if she did not know whether it was the right time to speak.

For a moment, Erik was seized by a violent grudge against her: if she hadn't dragged him into that unauthorized investigation… if he hadn't listened to her…

"Erik, I'm so sorry," she said eventually.

He shrugged. The anger bubble deflated as fast as it had appeared.

Hernandez hadn't forced him to do anything; those were his choices that got him dragged into this mess. "That's OK," he said. "We knew this could happen when we decided to go on with the investigation. That's how it goes."

"I've been suspended for two weeks," she informed him.

Only then did Erik realize that she was gathering some items in a cardboard box.

"And then I'll have to go through some kind of internal trial," she shook her head, visibly distraught. "Hopefully they'll reinstate... otherwise I'll have to look for something else."

Erik could not hide his surprise: it was a very serious punishment. He hadn't expected Hoffman to be so strict. In comparison, he realized that he experienced an absolutely privileged treatment.

"What about you?" Hernandez asked.

"I've been transferred," he told her, realizing only then that he hadn't even checked where he would end up.

He opened the file and read the header: "Pre-emptive custody hospital."

Chapter 13

The next morning, they woke up very early. The great cathedral was still immersed in shadow, and almost everyone was asleep.

Jeanne heated their water in the pitcher she had filled the night before and offered them coffee (the instant kind, not as strong as the one Sophie had been drinking with Amanda and Lukas centuries ago, but with a definitely more intense flavour than the beverages she was used to) and homemade cookies, very hard and sweet.

"Jeanne," Sophie asked, "Do you know where I could find some men's clothes? I'm trying not to... um, attract attention," she added, seeing Jeanne's perplexed expression.

"I'll ask around," Jeanne replied, obviously not entirely convinced.

Indeed, it was not much of an excuse, Sophie thought later. There was no reason why she should draw more attention than a man... of course, if one dismissed the small detail of her being a fugitive whose picture had been spread throughout the city. But she didn't really feel like explaining that to Jeanne.

She plunged a biscuit in her coffee, hoping it would soften a bit, then chewed it slowly. She had to admit she was a little sorry to leave the tranquillity and the relative safety that the cathedral offered. She wondered if she should try to discuss it with Emma again.

While Sophie reflected, she heard excited voices coming from the exit of the cathedral leading towards the bathrooms: Joseph, the man Jeanne had introduced her to a few hours earlier, arrived out of breath, and began to pull frantically at a rope near the door. The rope tugged on a bell with a shrill and high-pitched sound.

"Alarm!" Joseph yelled. "Flooding in the bathrooms! Flood!"

The cathedral, which had been immersed in a drowsy stupor until then, became animated at once. People started running frantically, trying to collect seemingly random objects.

When Sophie turned around to ask Jeanne for explanations on what to do, she saw that she and the boys had already disappeared. Emma seemed find her senses before she did: "Sophie, we must get out of here!" she urged, worried.

Sophie looked around. The nearest exit was the one to the bathrooms, but it was unavailable, because it had been barred; many people were already isolating it with plastic objects, probably to contain the water outflow.

Sophie remembered the passage she had used to get to Edmund's lab: "This way."

They made their way among the people that were running towards the back of the cathedral. Though clearly afraid, they seemed to know what to do.

They had almost reached the exit when a hand rested on Sophie's shoulder: "Where do you think you're going?"

She turned around, finding herself in front of Alois' unfriendly face, surrounded by a small angry-looking crowd. Unnerved, she noted that Korbinian stood behind him.

Jeanne followed them, pointing her finger: "It was them, I'm sure! They were the last to go to the bathroom!"

"What? No!" Sophie protested. "It wasn't us! We were very careful!"

"They insisted on going alone!" Jeanne continued, furious. "I should have realized they were planning something!"

"We aren't planning anything!" Emma said in an anguished voice. "How can you believe it was us? It must have been an accident."

"Yes, that's right!" Jeanne said with a sarcastic high-pitched laugh. "I'm sure it was all just a coincidence – "

"Silence," Korbinian ordered, raising a hand in Jeanne's direction. "The circumstances are very suspicious," he told Sophie and Emma. "As you understand, we cannot let you go. You will be judged by the people of this community, and they will decide..."

"We had nothing to do with the flood!" Sophie insisted. "And we have to leave anyway."

Korbinian stepped forward, and Sophie realized how threatening he looked: "No one here runs away without facing the consequences of their actions."

At that moment the door that they had tried to reach opened and Edmund came out.

The old scientist was completely drenched from head to foot and seemed in the middle of a panic attack. He went straight at Korbinian, grabbing his arm.

"The power!" he murmured. "The power went out last night... the water... the pipes..."

"We know, Edmund," Korbinian cut him short. "Now, if you will head with the others towards the emergency exits..."

"No!" the old scientist cried feverishly. "You don't understand! Without power, the surveillance and control system don't work..."

Sophie clasped her hand over her mouth, realizing what Edmund meant: "Oh no..."

"It's awake! The infected is awake! He got up tonight and... I have no idea where he is," Edmund concluded desperately.

Meanwhile people around them were processing the news.

"What do you mean, infected?"

"An infected? Down here?"

"Korbinian, what...?"

In a few seconds, panic exploded: people who were heading towards the exits in an orderly fashion began to run away like mad, terrified to find an infected in the tunnels. Many clumped around Edmund and Korbinian, asking for explanations or, mostly, railing at them. It didn't take Jeanne very long to switch the flow of her indignation from Sophie and Emma to Korbinian. In the general chaos, no one seemed to pay much attention to the two women.

Emma approached Sophie: "Let's go, come on!" she whispered in her ear, indicating the tunnel where Edmund had entered.

"But... the infected...?"

"There is no time!" she insisted.

They slipped into the tunnel and closed the door behind them.

The hallway was dark, lit only intermittently by greenish flickering lights turning on and off unpredictably. Sophie walked as fast as she could to get away from the cathedral, while Emma was trying her best to keep up. At one point they stopped so that the old lady could catch her breath.

I don't even know why we are in such a hurry, Sophie thought: they didn't really know where they were going, they were just running off in an unknown direction. For all she knew, there might not even be an exit where they were heading. They might be throwing themselves straight into the arms of the infected... on the other hand, however, they could not possibly go back. They had to try to get out and reach Stuttgart at any cost.

"Where are we?" Emma asked shakily.

"I don't know."

The flickering light barely allowed Sophie to see the concrete floor. Looking more closely, she noticed that it looked pretty beaten: there was no dust in the central area, and the surface looked old and battered. If one looked hard while the light bulb momentarily switched on, it was possible to see the metal door of Edmund's laboratory not far away. Other tunnels extended to the left and right of the door.

"We have to choose one way," Sophie told Emma.

The old lady thought about it: "I think I remember that the emergency exits were at the bottom of the cathedral - therefore, roughly to the right."

Sophie nodded: "But if we go there, we risk running into all the others again."

"That's still better than drowning or wandering aimlessly down here for days!"

"You're right."

They resumed their journey and walked down the tunnel on the right.

"What do you think could have happened to the taps?" Emma asked suddenly.

"Dunno. Maybe some of the children got up to go to the bathroom and did not close the tap very carefully."

To be honest, Sophie had not thought much about it, assuming it had been an accident.

"Isn't it a bit strange that it happened during the one night we spent there?"

Sophie looked confused: "What do you mean?"

"Oh, I don't know, it's just..." Emma snorted. "Since the start of this whole horrible business I've had the impression that there is someone or something that works against us... The police coming for us, then the incident here..." the old lady shook her head. "I do not know what I'm trying to say. It's just a bad feeling about it all."

Sophie had to admit that Emma had a point: there was something strange about the proceedings. But who could be following them? The police? That didn't make sense, they would just arrest them. Who could be trying to expose them? Only two days ago, she was certain that Lukas had betrayed them. But what if Lukas was part of a bigger picture?

A noise at the bottom of the tunnel made her twitch.

"What was that?"

"I don't know," Emma whispered.

There was silence at the bottom of the tunnel. Then another noise, perhaps a step, startled her again.

Sophie cleared her throat: "Who is there?"

"No, please, don't make any noise... don't draw attention to us!" Emma murmured. "Maybe it's just someone looking for the exit like we are!"

"What if it's someone who's looking for us?"

The noise repeated, again and again: those were footsteps, Sophie decided, slow and shuffling.

"Who's that?" Sophie said.

A gasp was heard from the bottom of the tunnel, and little by little, in the flashing light, Sophie could see a figure. It was hunched and moved uncertainly and...

When she saw the stranger's face, she froze.

"No..." she whispered.

"What's going on?" Emma asked. "Who is it?"

It was the infected that Edmund had held captive for so long.

He still had tubes attached to his arms, and looked confused, but moved with increasing confidence. He raised an arm in their direction and gave an uncertain sound, as if he didn't remember more articulate words.

Finally, Sophie shook herself: "We have to go, go, go!" she urged Emma, pulling her arm. She threw herself down the corridor, running as fast as she could, until she realized that the old lady was left behind.

"Come on, we have to go, damn it!"

"I... I don't think I can keep up..." Emma panted.

"You must!"

Sophie pulled her up again, trying to make her move more quickly: she couldn't stay behind. The infected was chasing them, perhaps more out of instinct than for any real purpose: horrified, Sophie realized that he was picking up speed. His muscles were weak and atrophied, but they could compete with Emma's old and tired legs.

"Come on, let's go... please, Emma, hurry up, please..."

Sophie ran a few metres further, then heard a chilling sound behind her.

Emma had fallen.

In a single instant, the infected grabbed her leg. His scaly hands were pale and thin, but Emma, apparently, was unable to shake him off. Sophie saw her hitting him on the hands, the face, the legs. She watched the scene frozen, wide-eyed.

He's infecting her, was all she could think. *She's been infected.*

"Sophie!" Emma shouted.

The words rang empty in her head. Her instinct told her to run away, but she could not move.

"Help! Sophie!" Emma repeated.

Something snapped in her mind: without knowing what she was doing, Sophie ran towards the infected and kicked him with all her strength, hitting him in the shoulder.

The creature fell back to the ground, muttering something incoherently.

"Let's go," she told Emma. "Up, come on!"

She helped the old lady up and pulled her along, down the tunnel and as far as possible from the infected.

To tell the truth, the creature did not seem to want to chase them: he just sat on the floor, exhausted, looking at his hands with a confused look.

Sophie kept walking and dragging the old lady along, trying with all her might not to think about what the contact with her involved.

A little later, they found themselves in front of another metal door, similar to that of Edmund's lab. The tunnel had no other branches, so there were only two options: to go forward, through the door, or to go back.

"What shall we do?" Emma asked, panting with fatigue.

Sophie did not like the idea of opening that door and maybe finding herself in front of Korbinian and Jeanne, or worse; on the other hand, the idea of having to go back and face that creature again...

"We go forward," she decided, and turned the metal wheel that kept the door shut.

As the mechanism snapped and she pulled the metal door back, a jet of water gushed forward. Sophie just barely managed to keep her hold on to the handle, while Emma was thrown against the wall.

"Are you okay?" Sophie shouted.

Emma just nodded wearily.

"I think we're close the bathrooms - the exit should not be far," Sophie said.

"I thought the emergency exits were on the other side!"

"Not the emergency exit - the road from which we came, it must be flooded now."

Once the gush of water ran out, Emma stood up and began limping along the new tunnel. The water came up to their knees and every step was a struggle, so they remained silent for most of the time, saving their strength.

Sophie walked slowly, focusing on each step to keep away the thought of the fate that probably awaited her: Emma had to be infected; the man had touched her bare skin. And then she had taken her by the wrist and...

"Look, we got to the bathrooms," Emma pointed after a while.

"Yeah, that's right."

The water pressure had done a lot of damage, and some of the taps were torn off. From that point on the tunnel became increasingly flooded: sometimes the water level was so high that she had to walk on tiptoe to keep her head above water.

Turning around, Sophie saw Emma effortlessly swimming, making slow circular movements with her arms. But Sophie had never learned to swim, so she had to settle for walking.

They continued this way for what seemed to be a very long time. Finally, however, they arrived at a manhole surrounded by streaks of light, which evidently led outside.

"Sophie, before we leave, I just wanted to tell you..." Emma took a deep breath. "Thank you for what you have done for me, for the risk you took. I don't really know how to thank you. If I consider what you risked..."

Sophie gestured for her to stop. She didn't really feel comfortable hearing this.

"It doesn't matter. What's done is done. Now we must only think of getting out," she said. "I don't know how we're going to catch a train if we cannot pass through the medical checkpoints."

Emma looked confused: "Why shouldn't we?"

Sophie blinked. How could she not understand?

"Sophie... I'm immune, you know. I cannot be infected again."

"What...?"

"I already had the plague once. That is precisely the reason why we have to find this Jamie in the first place, remember?"

It was as if a boulder had been lifted from Sophie's chest. Of course. Emma could not be infected - how could she forget it? And if the contact with the infected could have no effect on her, Sophie was safe.

Suddenly she had a great desire to laugh, or perhaps to cry.

The journey to Stuttgart passed very quickly, in a sort of confused fog.

When they went out in the street, completely soaked, tired and chilled to the bone, the first thing Sophie did was walk to the first medical centre they found and sell the last pack of medicines Amanda had left her. They were painkillers, and she knew that no medical centre of the city would refuse to buy them, legally or not.

With the sum she obtained she bought some third or fourth-hand clothes for her and Emma, scissors, two packages of hair dye and two tickets to Stuttgart. They changed in a public restroom, then she dyed Emma's hair brown. As for her own hair, she cut her curls short and dyed it jet black, then pulled on the men's clothes she had bought.

When she looked in the mirror, she saw an unfamiliar face which not only didn't look at all like the girl in the mug shots, but nothing like herself either.

It was a much thinner, tenser, older face. She looked neither like a woman nor like a man; she was a shadow, an invisible figure, like those she had seen crowding the old subway when she had descended there the first time with Gitte.

In a few days, she had become one of them. Emma looked different with darker hair, too, but that actually suited her. She even looked younger. Her skin was much prettier and smoother than Sophie had assessed the first time she had seen her.

The train ride was fast and passed without a hitch: they passed all blood tests without problems and came to Stuttgart a little early.

Finding the entrance to the old metro station was not difficult, because at that time many people were returning to the underground city: they only had to follow them.

They milled around the hall for a while, wondering how they were going to find Jamie or recognize him, until Emma proposed to head for the tracks.

"You could also go away at this point," Emma suggested gently. "I don't know anything about these people... if they are dangerous or..."

Sophie shook her head: "We've come this far together. I'm not going to leave you now."

Emma smiled and squeezed her arm gratefully.

The area was dark and deserted.

"Hello?" Sophie asked. "Jamie…?"

She heard a noise behind her, and saw a tall figure emerge from the darkness.

"Who are you?" a deep male voice asked.

"My name is Sophie Weber. I used to work with Amanda Solarin," she explained.

She was unable to keep her voice from shaking. Next to her, Emma seemed frozen.

In the shadows, she could see other people, three, four, maybe more.

"Ah yes, Amanda told me about you. Has she told you the password?"

"Saint George," she said, with confidence.

The figure stepped forward: he was a man in his forties with a hooded jacket, and Sophie knew immediately who he had to be. His dark-skinned face was so similar to her friend's that it made her feel a twinge of pain: the same face, the same nose, the same shape of the eyes.

Like Amanda, he was tall, athletic-built, and even what she saw of his hair was the same shade of grey.

"You are Amanda's brother!" she exclaimed.

The man smiled sadly: "Her twin, in fact. James Solarin," he confirmed. "Is this Emma Lemaire? The woman who recovered from the dragon plague?" he asked, pointing at Emma.

Sophie hesitated, but it was Emma who answered: "It's me."

"Good."

James Solarin stepped forward, leaving the shadows. At that moment Sophie saw what he was attempting to cover with his hood: the unnatural shade of his eyes, the scales running down his cheeks and neck.

"You are... you're..."

"Calm down."

"No!" she cried out. "I... Why have you brought us here?"

She looked around, trying to find the exit: the hall, crowded with people, was not far. "Sophie, what's happening?" Emma asked, apparently not understanding what was going on.

We must leave, Sophie thought frantically, *get as far away as possible.*

From the corner of her eye, she saw that the people who accompanied James Solarin were moving towards her as well: they were all infected, all covered with scales, every one of them...

She made to bolt towards the hall, but two of them were faster: one grabbed her arm, the other held Emma by the shoulder, restraining her.

"Don't touch me!" Sophie screamed at the contact, though the hands that touched her were covered with plastic gloves.

"Help! Somebody, help!!!"

The woman next to James looked worried: "She's making too much noise, she'll draw attention."

"What do we do?" asked another.

Sophie continued to shout: "Help! Somebody help us, please!"

James Solarin thought about it: "We'll take her too," he decided.

"No!" Sophie shouted, trying to wriggle out. "You can't do that!"

"Sophie!" Emma's voice was the last thing that Sophie could make out before someone pulled up her sleeve and plunged a syringe in her arm.

Then everything went dark.

END OF PART ONE

SECOND PART

Chapter 14

Sophie opened her eyes. Or rather, she tried to open her eyes, but her eyelids were heavy and seemed to be glued together. She wondered how long she had slept.

When she managed to pry her eyelids open, she was momentarily blinded by the light. She had a headache, a dull pain that radiated from the base of her neck to her temples.

When she became accustomed to the light, she looked around. She was in a small room with battered, old-fashioned furniture. The bed where she lay appeared to be made of wood, and there were woollen blankets on it.

The pale yellow paint on the walls was peeling and criss-crossed by many cracks.

One side of the room was occupied by a fireplace with a burning fire, in which Sophie, amazed, noticed pieces of real wood.

It was very hot, but the room remained damp and she could feel a slight layer of condensation on her pillow.

Where the hell was she? And what had happened to Emma?

Clear, cold light filtered in through the little window, but the glass was too tarnished to look outside. Sophie threw back the covers, noting that she was still fully clothed, and cautiously put her feet on the floor.

Her boots, the only garment she wasn't wearing, were at the bottom of the bed, so she put them on.

When she tried to take a few steps, though, she realized that her legs would not hold her weight, and before she could grab the back of the chair next to the bed, she fell sprawling on the dusty tiles.

Oh, shit.

She had to get out of there as soon as possible and figure out where she was.

Grasping at any surfaces she found at hand, she reached the door, opened it and found herself on a small landing, with a flight of stairs leading down.

The room below was considerably colder. She noticed that even the handrail, as well as most of the furniture, was made of wood, which seemed rather unusual, as all the furniture she had seen in her life was made of plastic or metal. Now, however, was not the right time to focus on these details.

She heard sounds from below, so she stepped down the stairs as quietly as possible.

The entrance door was right in front of her; when she got to the bottom of the stairs she took a deep breath, then lunged at it.

She just had the time to hear a voice exclaiming: "Hey, where you going?" before she opened the door (which, fortunately, was not locked) and ran out. What she saw left her speechless.

In front of her there was a vast green lawn descending towards a rocky slope. And beyond it, she saw a mass of grey water, which loomed threatening and boundless.

The sea, she thought, *that must be the sea*.

She had never seen it before, of course. She had never been out of Europa.

However, the sea that was shown on television or described in books was nothing like that; it always looked blue, crystalline, and associated with clear skies and warm sunshine - the kind of landscape that made her want to take off all her clothes and run to the shore. The monstrosity that now stretched in front of her was the colour of lead and did not seem inviting at all.

A cold and bitter wind came from the sea, along with a penetrating, unfamiliar odour, something wild and rotting.

It was cold, she noticed; much colder than she had ever felt in her life.

"Sophie," said a quiet voice behind her.

She spun around: it was James Solarin. He wore nothing but trousers and a light shirt but didn't look cold.

On his arms she could see the dark lines of the scales. He was wearing plastic gloves.

"Stay away from me!" she said, taking a step back.

She looked around for something to defend herself with, found a stone a little larger than her fist and bent to pick it up.

"Sophie," James repeated, "Please calm down. Let's go back into the house."

"No! I have to... Emma..." she began.

Once more, she felt the weakness that had seized her when she woke. Her head was spinning.

"Emma's fine. She is in a house not far from here. Later, if you want, you can go to visit her, but first there are some things I need to explain. Let's go back inside, please," he added. "It's too cold for you here, and you have nowhere to go."

"You want to infect me!" she accused him, her voice shaking with agitation. "You want to make me one of you, you want to…"

James sighed: "No one wants to infect you. On the contrary, I assure you that we have taken every precaution to keep you safe. You have not been in contact with anyone. You're as healthy as you were four days ago."

"Four days?" she repeated. "I have been sedated for four days?"

"For your own safety."

There was a long pause in which Sophie weighed her options. She didn't know where she was, but it certainly was many kilometres away from home; she didn't know where Emma was or how to reach her. In addition, it was starting to get really cold, and she really needed to sit down for a while.

Not that she liked the idea of trusting one of those beings... but what else could she do?

"Fine," she said at last.

James headed to the door, opening it for her. Sophie was careful to keep as much distance between them as she could while she passed in.

"You can leave it here, you know. That stone, I mean. In the kitchen there are knives, cleavers, everything you can wish for," James suggested.

His expression was deadly serious, and Sophie could not tell if he was joking.

"I'd rather keep it, thanks."

"As you wish."

Sophie followed James into the kitchen: this room, unlike the one in which she had awakened, seemed routinely used, and was clean and organised.

All the furniture here was very old and seemed to date back to hundreds of years ago: the table was made of plastic, Sophie noticed, but the stoves were made of wood and heavy, dark metal. She had only read about such things in books and saw them in some films set before the Great War.

The kitchen, like the darker the room upstairs, was illuminated by candles, Sophie noticed with some confusion.

"No electricity," James explained, following her gaze.

Sophie frowned: "How is it possible?"

"Well, to be honest we have generators, but we normally use them only for the equipment we cannot do without. For the rest, we have to make do the old way."

"And how do you heat water for showers?"

James laughed, sitting down at the table: "We have them cold."

Sophie stared and shivered, clutching at her sweater. She sat down too, careful to keep the length of the table between them. She felt a little stupid holding the stone, but she didn't know where to put it. She ended up leaving it on the table.

"But that's hardly a problem for us," James added. "You know, we survivors have a higher tolerance to heat and cold than we had before being infected. We believe it is a trait inherited from dragons."

"Oh," she said uneasily.

She wanted to ask him some questions about his condition but didn't feel safe enough around him. James seemed quiet and reasonable, but he was still an infected, and as such could become aggressive at any moment. It was well known: there was no information booklet which didn't mention that.

"By the way, are you warm enough?" James asked. "It's difficult for me to gauge what's the right temperature for you. Amanda always makes fun of me for this."

"I'm fine."

"Do you want a cup of tea?"

She looked uncertain, wondering if it was safe to eat their food. She could not deny, though, that she was hungry, and the idea of drinking something hot was very tempting.

"Yes, please."

Now that she could take a good look at James, who was fiddling with the stove and the kettle, she could see that, though he looked very much like his sister, they were not as much alike as she had thought at first sight: James was much taller, massive, and his features were blunter.

She wondered if he knew about what happened in the lab the week before, on the day when her personal nightmare had begun. If he didn't, she believed it was her duty to inform him. It was right. Whatever he might be, he was still Amanda's brother.

Who knew how he would react, though? The emotions of the infected were probably different from those of normal people. Would they be more uncontrolled? Or maybe, on the contrary, the disease made them unattached, so the news would not trouble him much?

"Look," she began, "I must tell you something about Amanda. It's that... the day when the medical police tried to take Emma, Amanda couldn't escape with us... so..." Sophie took a breath, "I think she might..."

"Sophie, I know what you're trying to tell me, but wait," James interrupted her. "We have received news. As far as we know, Amanda is alive."

Sophie's heart skipped a beat: Amanda, alive? She had completely lost hope, and now, after all this time...

"Where? Is she here? What about her wounds? Can I see her?"

"Wait, wait..." he said, putting a steaming cup of tea and a container of sugar on the table, and pulling out a bottle of milk from an ice-filled container. "Unfortunately she's not here. She was arrested by the medical police and she's now in a prison for the infected."

Sophie picked up the cup, but the excitement made her replace it back on the table, dropping a few specks of tea on its surface: "Oh... but... now they know that she's not infected, they must know!"

"Of course they do," James nodded, "but that's not why she was arrested in the first place. The real reason is that, somehow, the government learned that Amanda works with us survivors."

For an instant, Sophie was too shocked to speak.

"Amanda... with you?!" she finally stammered, incredulous.

James nodded: "For many years. Since I was infected."

Sophie remained silent for a few moments, trying to assimilate this new information. All that time her mentor and dear (and actually only) friend had been involved with a criminal organization of semi-human creatures that everyone knew to be dangerous and violent. The government of Europa knew it, and they had arrested her.

"You aren't drinking your tea," James reminded her.

Sophie took a sip, burning her tongue. There were many things she wanted to ask, but she didn't know where to start. From the beginning, she decided.

"When did that happen?" Sophie asked. "When were you infected?"

"Twenty years ago, more or less," James said.

Sophie continued to look at him with a questioning expression.

"Ah, you want the whole story? Fair enough," he began, leaning back in his chair. "We had finished our studies a few years ago by that time. I had a degree in energy engineering and won a doctorate scholarship to research safe travel in quarantined areas; Amanda worked in the hospital of the second ring, in the Department of Infectious Diseases, and everyone was sure that she would become one of the youngest Head Physicians in Europa. In those days no one talked much about the plague, because there had been relatively few cases, at least compared to the epidemic that happened later, and top authorities had kept it all quiet.

It is ironic indeed that I was the one who got sick and not she, considering that she spent all her days in the hospital, but..." he grinned mirthlessly. "Well, that's what happened. We didn't meet very often, because I lived in the dorms, while Amanda lived near the hospital. One day I came home feeling very weak, and during the night I had the worst fever of my life. In my delirium, I did not think of calling the university doctor, but dialled the only number I knew by heart - my sister's. Amanda rushed to me at once, and immediately recognized the disease. In her circle its existence had been known for a while. A while ago, she told me then, a law had been enacted, requiring every doctor to go to the authorities whenever they found someone with DH16N10."

"But she didn't do it."

"No," James confirmed, "She didn't. And this choice changed her life."

Sophie frowned and took another sip of tea: it tasted good, although it was much stronger than what she was used to drink.

"Why didn't she call someone? You could die," she objected.

"Yes, that's true. But a few months before that, she had diagnosed a case of the plague and called the medical police, which back then was called 'infectious diseases containment unit' or something like that. She didn't like what she saw. Well, now you know their modus operandi too. Later, she had asked news of the patient, but no one had any answers. She went to his house - his family had tried to get information, but..." James sighed, "Nothing. It was as if the man had disappeared off the face of the earth. Amanda realized there was something wrong with the way they worked."

"How come you survived when so many others died?"

He shrugged. "I don't know. No one knows. We tried for many years to figure out who was the most likely to survive: men or women, whites, blacks, Asians, young or old, but we never came to a conclusion. Apart from the fact that, unfortunately, infected children rarely make it through." A shadow passed over his face. "Anyway, I only remember that I had a fever for days, and then the pustules... and damn, those did hurt!"

Sophie shuddered.

"Amanda stayed with me the whole time. She had heard that the latex and plastic would probably stop the infection and took every precaution not to get sick too.

After some time, a week, I think, the pustules began to burst, and the scales emerged.

I spent days between life and death... until, after a particularly difficult night, I woke up. The fever was down, and I... I was like this."

"And then what happened?" Sophie asked; almost despite himself, she was intrigued by the story.

"At first I never left the house... it was too dangerous. I sent an email to the university, inventing a story that I had decided to join a research expedition in the quarantined areas. After a few months the epidemic broke out, and all the infected were sought as criminals. At that point, however, there were so many victims that when nobody heard from me anymore, they just assumed I was dead. "

"What about Amanda?"

He ran a hand through his short grey hair: "Amanda... I guess you could say she paid for her choice for the rest of her life."

"What do you mean?"

"She took care of me. She helped me recover, she sheltered me. At first, I could not accept my new condition; I spent almost all the time vegetating in the bed... it was a, um, difficult time for me."

Sophie finished her tea and wrapped her hands around the cup, which was still warm. She tried to imagine what she would do in his place. Yes, she could understand his being depressed.

"Amanda began investigating to find out what had happened to the other survivors. After some time, she was forced to leave her job, because the long shifts at the hospital did not allow her to seek other rebels or make sure I was okay. Our parents had died years before, and had left us a considerable fortune, which dissipated slowly over the years. It was only after Amanda found Cain and this place that she gathered her last savings to buy the medical centre where you used to work."

James made a long, thoughtful pause. "You know, she never married, never had... close friends, or personal relationships with anyone for years. She could not risk anyone, even the most trustworthy person, to find out about me. Of course, she said she was never able to stomach many people..." here Sophie smiled, because it was exactly the kind of thing that Amanda could have said. "But I always knew it was because of me."

Yes, Amanda had always been a loner, but Sophie had never imagined she could hide a secret like this: she had simply assumed that her colleague, much like herself, was not very inclined to socialize.

"She has often talked about you, you know," James said unexpectedly.

"Really?"

"Yes. She said that you are bright, smarter than you think, but lack a little courage."

Sophie raised her eyebrows: "Courage for what?"

James shrugged: "I don't know. To fight for what you want. Or maybe to decide what you want out of life."

"I'm not sure. After all, I got here, right?" She retorted.

She had never considered herself a particularly brave or determined person, but the remark annoyed her. She had her own problems too, but she managed to carve out a calm and safe existence for herself. How many could say the same? How many ended up living out their life in the slums of the underground tunnels?

"Yes, you did," James agreed, looking at her with a mixture of curiosity and amusement. "Anything else you want to know?"

Sophie straightened up, leaning against the back of the chair: "Yes, actually I do. What happens now? When can I get back home?"

James looked away: "Um, this is an open question, to tell the truth."

"What do you mean?"

He cleared his throat: "Sophie... this is the first time we've met, but Amanda has told me quite a bit about you. I know you wouldn't do anything to put us in danger. I know that if we gave you a chance to leave you would go back to living a quiet life as you always have."

"Except that I can't, can I? Now I'm a fugitive. Is that what you want to tell me?"

"Not just that. There is, indeed, the problem of your identity, which is now compromised, but I don't think it would be difficult to give you false papers and a new identity in another part of Europa, where no one knows you. No, this problem can be easily overcome," James sighed. "I mean that some of the people here... well, they think it would not be safe to send you back home now. They think that you would expose us to the medical police."

"That's ridiculous!" Sophie snapped. "I would never do that! I don't like those people any more than you do!"

She had never really cared for the medical police, but after she saw how they arrested Amanda, and spent the past few days hiding from them, she had very little desire to deal with them.

"You can't keep me here forever!" she exclaimed, rising from her chair. "I... I cannot stay here... with you." The idea of being surrounded by those creatures, not even entirely human, terrified her. "I mean, it's dangerous, you will end up infecting me!"

"Not forever!" James assured her. "Absolutely not... just... let's say, for a while, so that you can better understand our problem and see for yourself that we don't want to infect and exterminate all the world."

He stared into her eyes. He had a sincere and penetrating gaze, just like his sister.

"Because this is what you think of us, right?"

Sophie averted her eyes: "I don't know anything about you. But it doesn't sound safe to live in a place where anyone, at the slightest contact, could infect me with a deadly disease."

"There are precautions you can take. You can wear clothes of materials that don't transmit the infection and be careful to always cover your hands and arms."

"What about Emma? What will happen to her?"

"You realize that all you did was meant to bring her here, don't you? We need her cooperation, and her blood, and the best thing would be for her to stay on the island with us."

"What island?" she demanded. "On what island are we?"

James half-smiled, perhaps to lighten the tension: "You know I can't tell you."

"Who doesn't trust me?" Sophie asked, defiantly, with a courage that she never knew she had. "Who wants to keep me here? Who is your boss?"

James made a long pause before answering.

When he finally spoke, his voice sounded cautious, as if this was a delicate subject: "I do not like the term 'boss', but... yes, there are some people who... shall we say... have more influence than others. Those who people listen to, because they have been infected a long time ago and helped the others. Among them, in particular, there is a man named Cain that has long held a certain authority."

Cain. It was the second time in a few minutes that Sophie heard this name.

"It is him that I have to talk to, then?" she asked.

James nodded: "Well, yes, if you want to plead your cause, you might as well go directly to him."

Sophie took a step towards the door: "Then let's go immediately."

"We can't go now. Cain is in the city, I think he will come back next week."

Damn, Sophie thought.

"In the meantime, however, I can take you to see Emma."

That was a good idea, and Sophie nodded: "Okay."

"First, though, you'll want to get changed. In the room where you slept there is a basket of clothes made of safe materials which block the transmission of the disease. I don't believe anyone would touch you, but you'd better be careful. I hope there's something in your size."

"Fair enough," Sophie said, walking toward the stairs.

"Ah, do dress warmly. I think you're not accustomed to the climate around here."

The basket turned out to be a container made of twigs which contained a hodgepodge of clothing of every shape and size, but all much too large for Sophie.

Eventually she chose what looked like nylon stockings, trousers with an elastic waistband and a synthetic shirt with a high collar, over which she threw a fleece sweatshirt and a hooded jacket. She had to roll up all the cuffs many times over.

Everything had a faint damp smell.

She washed as best she could with the cold water in the sink. She wanted to wash her hair, but it was too cold; however, she was glad to have it cut so short, because having long dirty strands stuck on her face would have been unbearable.

Sophie thought she had to obtain a change of underwear, or at least find a way to wash what she was wearing. She shuddered at the thought of having to wash all the clothes by hand in that cold water.

She also found a box of latex gloves, and she slipped a pair on. Since there were no shoes of a size even close to hers, she put on her boots again. They seemed to be made of plastic, so she supposed they were alright.

When she went downstairs, she found James waiting for her, with a small white object in his hand. "Here," He said, handing it to her "For you."

Sophie saw that it was a mask similar to the ones used during surgery, with added flaps to cover her cheeks.

"I think it's very unlikely that someone will touch your face, but I imagined it could make you feel safer," James explained.

"Thank you," she said, putting it on.

When they went out, Sophie was again hit by a burst of gelid wind. Despite the many layers of clothing she wore, she could not help but shudder, and was happy to have her face covered from the pangs of cold.

The island had to be much further north than Europa... maybe in the Northern Sea?

She had only a very vague memory of maps hung in school classrooms. After all, what was the point of studying geography? There was nowhere to go outside the city, not since the nuclear bombs...

A horrible thought struck her suddenly and she froze.

"We are in the quarantined areas!" she exclaimed. "But... we cannot stay... it's dangerous here, the radiation..."

James shook his head: "Sophie, no, we're safe..."

"How can we be safe? Everything is contaminated!"

"The level of radiation is not dangerous for..." he began, but Sophie would not let him continue. What kind of nightmare had she ended up in? There was the constant threat of a deadly disease, and now this! She breathed with difficulty through the fabric of the mask.

"You mean to tell me that radiation can't hurt you because you are abnormally resistant? Well, good for you, but I'm just a normal human being and..."

"As I was saying," James interrupted, raising his voice for the first time, "Here, like in most of the so-called 'quarantined areas', the level of radiation is no higher than in any corner of Europa."

"That's not possible," Sophie declared.

James Solarin rolled his eyes: "Sure, because you are an expert on radiation, right? You know everything about nuclear energy, don't you? You've spent a lifetime studying the energy policy of Europa, haven't you?"

Sophie opened her mouth, then closed it again. Everyone knew that the quarantined areas were contaminated. Everyone. That was the reason why they were quarantined.

She folded her arms across her chest.

"Sorry if I was brusque," James said after a moment. "I'm afraid I'm a bit touchy on the subject. In a sense you are right: these territories have been subjected to radiation. The fact is that the area of Europa is contaminated as well. So, it makes little sense to speak of quarantined areas. This is our world now, and we have no other place to live."

He started walking again, and Sophie could not help but follow him, trying to process what she had just heard. Could she believe him? Were there really no contaminated territories, but rather the whole of Europa was contaminated?

How could it be possible that no one knew? Why, instead, was everyone convinced of the contrary? Assuming that what James told her was true in the first place, of course.

Sophie reminded herself that James, despite looking like a quiet and reasonable person, was not really *a person*. He was one of them. One of the infected. She had to remember to take anything he told her with a grain of salt.

In the meantime, they had arrived at the edge of a small ruined town.

Most of the houses, which seemed to date back to the great expansion of the twentieth century, were abandoned and exhibited conspicuous holes in the roof, or trees and shrubs that grew through their windows.

Delving deeper towards the centre, however, some signs of habitation could be seen: the road was clean, free of debris or abandoned objects; some of the houses had intact doors and repaired windows through which she could see curtains. Some of the facades had even been repainted.

Sophie observed that it was mainly one-storey houses that had been renovated, while the condominiums continued to lie abandoned. Some of the houses had small plants growing in flower beds in front of the door, and she noticed the crops in the gardens were sheltered from the cold by a few cloth sheets. There were even some flowers on a sill.

Finally, after about ten minutes of walking through the town, Sophie began to notice some inhabitants. From afar they might have passed for normal people, although most wore light clothing despite the piercing cold.

Getting closer, Sophie saw a young woman pushing a cart, looking at her curiously.

She was wearing a tank top that left her shoulders bare, and Sophie noticed the scales that streamed down her arms, joining those on the neck and drawing elaborate spirals on her shoulders.

She averted her eyes, uncomfortable, and the woman laughed scornfully.

"Hey Jamie!" she called. "You brought another?"

A crowd of people had stopped to stare at her. Sophie was glad no one could see her blush under the mask.

"How long do you think this one will last?" the young woman asked.

Someone in the small crowd laughed.

"Leave us alone, Nadia," James said, more exasperated than angry, continuing to walk.

"Is she perhaps another one who wants to find the vaccine? So no one can become a monster like us?" Nadia called after them.

Sophie was shivering, and this time not from the cold. If one of them should ever attack her, she would have no way of defending herself. Just a single touch and...

"Don't worry about Nadia," James said, interrupting the flow of her thoughts. "She's not a bad person, she's just..." he shrugged. "Let's say that it's not only the uninfected who don't trust us. There is some animosity on both sides."

"Has Amanda ever been here?" Sophie asked.

James nodded: "Yes, of course, she has been here many times in the past, and she has stayed for a while."

Sophie wanted to learn more, but James arrived at a house with the façade painted in pale yellow and knocked on the door.

They were greeted by an elderly lady, around Emma's age, Sophie guessed, but there the resemblance ended. Unlike her friend, whose innate sweetness Sophie learned to appreciate, the woman in front of her had a hard, scrutinizing look.

"Is she here?" she finally asked James.

James didn't have time to answer, because Emma appeared on the threshold and stared at Sophie.

"Sophie, is it really you?"

"Yes, that's me under all these layers!" Sophie smiled, although her face was invisible. She also realized for the first time that her voice sounded muffled. She was happy to see that Emma seemed fine, although her friend did look slightly lost.

The woman with the stern look ushered her into the house, which was arranged more or less like James'. Emma led Sophie into the room where she had stayed during the last two days, and there they could speak alone for a while.

Being able to remove the mask was a relief. Outside its warmth was almost comforting, but inside the house it was oppressive.

Sophie discovered that while she had been unconscious, they were brought to the coast by an old train that used the abandoned tracks of the subway.

A sensor had been passed over their bodies to make sure that they carried no radios or bugs, but none were found. Later they spent many hours on a boat, an experience that Emma would have preferred to avoid.

"I was sick to my stomach! I almost wished I had been sedated too."

The morning after, they had arrived on the island. Emma had spent three days inside the house, being too scared to go out.

"But you can't be infected," Sophie objected, perplexed.

"No, but who can predict how those creatures think?" Emma appeared downcast. "I miss Fuzzi. I wish he was here with me."

It took Sophie a moment to realize that she was referring to her cat.

"You may ask someone to pick him up. I think they go to the city regularly enough," she suggested.

Emma shook her head: "No, no... that's impossible, who could track him down after all this time..."

Sophie put a hand on her arm: "Maybe there are other cats out there."

"Go figure!" Emma snorted. "They have probably eaten them all."

"Which reminds me..." Sophie interjected, struck by a sudden thought, "How does it work here with the food distribution? We have no money - what can we do?"

In fact, she was beginning to feel a little peckish. Even the idea of a cat stew was beginning not to sound that bad.

"Oh, don't worry," said the old woman, "This isn't a problem. They have a lot of food here."

"Really?" Sophie frowned. "How do they get it?"

"I don't know," Emma shrugged. "I heard someone mention farms, and perhaps they have fields too. But it's so cold, how can anything grow here?"

"Maybe they have farming lamps," Sophie suggested, thinking of the lettuce seedlings in her apartment. She wondered what had become of them. "Even though James said they don't have much electricity."

"In any case," Emma concluded, "it's not that hard to find something to eat. And Britt has a full pantry, too."

Sophie understood she was referring to the hard-eyed old lady. "Oh, good," she commented. In all this nightmarish situation, this was one bit of welcome news.

"That lady, Britt," Sophie began cautiously, "has she treated you well? Has she been nice to you?"

Emma shrugged: "Yes, yes, she was very hospitable... I mean, I wouldn't go as far as calling her 'nice'..." she added, rolling her eyes.

Sophie could not restrain a chuckle. No, she definitely didn't look nice.

In any case, despite the many upheavals that she had gone through, it seemed that Emma was doing pretty good, which was a comforting thought. She couldn't, however, persuade her to get out of the house.

After a while James knocked on the door of the room, announcing that there were a couple of other things he wanted to show her that day.

Since Emma didn't want to venture out, James and Sophie walked out alone again.

"Where are we going?" she asked.

"You'll see."

The building where James led her was large, built on just one floor. In front of it there was a large open space that had once been paved but was now largely conquered by weeds growing between the cracks.

At the bottom of the entrance hall there was a counter, and battered signs saying "radiology", "orthopaedic" and "oncology" still hung on the walls.

"It was a hospital," Sophie understood.

It no longer had that characteristic smell of hospitals, a mixture of medicine, detergent, and overcooked food. She knew many people hated that smell, but she never minded it. To her, it smelled like hope.

In that place, however, there was no hope left, and the only smells were of humidity and vegetation that had slipped in from the roof, windows, and even from the floor.

James nodded: "It still is."

Sophie raised her eyebrows: "Who works here, then?"

"Amanda, when she is here."

"Ah, OK," she said distractedly. A large hospital for a single doctor who was now prisoner and might be hovering between life and death.

She didn't understand why James had brought her here. Perhaps he hoped she would volunteer to help out? Don't hold your breath, she thought.

"It is not the hospital itself that I wanted to show you," he said. "Follow me."

James guided her toward the end of the hall room. When he opened the door, she found a small tidy room, an office. There was a desk with an old-fashioned laptop, a library full of binders and notebooks, some pictures on the walls. It looked lived in, as if someone had worked there for a very long time. It only took her one look at the handwriting in the notebooks to understand who they belonged to.

"Amanda worked here," she said.

"Correct," James Solarin confirmed, sitting on the chair behind the desk. "In fact, the research that Amanda made in broad daylight, so to speak, in her medical centre, was only a small fraction of all her activities. She had access to me and my blood for many years and has worked here for a long time to find a vaccine."

"But she didn't find it," Sophie objected.

"Not yet," James granted, "but now that we have Emma... she is the key, she and her antibodies. It is a miracle."

Sophie shrugged. Of course, Emma's blood was very important, and it was the reason why she was there. However, now that she knew her better it was difficult to speak of her as a guinea pig... like that man imprisoned underground by Edmund.

She shuddered, thinking of those tunnels – it might have been the cold, or perhaps something completely different.

"Shame that Amanda is not here," a sudden thought struck her. "Are you trying to set her free? You said you have news... so maybe there are infiltrated people who could..."

The phrase died in her throat because she did not know exactly what these people might do. Would they really save Amanda? Or would they simply put her in danger and kill many other people as they often did?

James' jaw stiffened: "We are doing everything we can. Do you think I could stay here, doing nothing, if I didn't know that others are working to free her?" his gaze became hard. "Do you think I don't care about my own sister, my twin?"

"No, of course not," Sophie said quickly, "I know you... you... I just wanted to know, that's all," her voice was reduced to a faint murmur.

James looked away and stared at the scenery outside the window for a moment that seemed very long to Sophie.

"We have... people in the city, people who work with us. Like Amanda did," he said at last. "As I said, they are doing everything they can. If she were to run away, they would be the first suspected; covers that we have spent many years building would be lost... it's not an easy decision."

Sophie said nothing. She wanted to express her solidarity but was too afraid to make him angry again.

"Anyway," James continued, "the reason I brought you here is that you know Amanda's job very well. I was hoping that you might want to continue her research, here."

Sophie was speechless. It was not what she expected.

"But... but... I'm not... Amanda was the one that led the actual search. I would just... uh, give her a hand."

He frowned: "My sister described your participation in different terms."

Sophie looked around frantically. What a situation... of course she had no intention of accepting the offer, but she wouldn't risk upsetting James again.

If she began that job, who knows when she would return to the city?

"I... well, do I have to give an answer right now?" she asked desperately.

James shook his head, appearing perfectly reasonable again: "No, of course not. You can have all the time you want to think about it."

"OK. I will," she promised.

Chapter 15

Erik showed up on his new job on Monday morning, a little early.

The job was in the tenth ring, and he had left with plenty of time to spare, but the trip was shorter than he had expected.

Staring at the façade of the anonymous building, he could not restrain a sigh. He couldn't believe that, after all these years of service, Hoffman could move him to such a position.

He had said goodbye to his colleagues on Friday afternoon: they were all very nice, some even visibly moved despite doing their best to play down the episode. None had mentioned the conspicuous absence of Hernandez, who had quietly gone away the week before.

"It's just a 'see you later', isn't it?" Meyer said. "You just keep it quiet for a while, and in a few months, you'll be back with us."

Erik felt much more melancholy than he had imagined he would as he said goodbye to Lara Meyer: after all, she had been a constant presence in his life for more than ten years, with her intelligence, her humour, her beauty…

"Yeah, sure," he nodded half-heartedly, doing his best to appear confident. He hardly believed that Hoffman would reintegrate him into the investigation unit. He was sure that he would be a jailer for the rest of his career.

He extracted some loose tobacco and rolling paper from his pocket and rolled a cigarette. He really needed it. His neighbour had said he was no longer able to find the ready-made cigarettes, so he sold the bulk ingredients.

Smoking that way was much more laborious: he missed the instinctive gesture of pulling out the package and putting a cigarette to his lips. On the positive side, however, he smoked much less and the tobacco lasted much longer.

He took a deep breath, noticing the slightly spicier taste than the one of traditional cigarettes, and delaying for a few minutes the inevitable entrance to that depressing-looking hospital.

Thea had done her best to show him her support. She had even taken it *too* well, Erik thought, unable to repress a touch of annoyance.

"I actually feel kind of relieved," she had said. "All those arrests, those chases… you are not twenty years old anymore."

Erik shrugged: "I guess I'm not," he admitted. That had more or less put an end to the conversation. But how could he explain the anguish he felt at the idea of being pushed aside?

There was much more than work to his life, of course; and yet he could not deny that being a cop was part of him, of his identity, a source of pride... sure, technically he was still part of the medical police, and he had maintained his rank as well as his salary... but who was he fooling? Working in a custody hospital was little more than being a watchdog for the infected about to be eliminated.

He could remain outside no longer, or he'd be late. He inhaled the last puffs of smoke, threw the butt into a trash can and walked toward the entrance door.

A guard asked him for his documents, took his fingerprints, checked that he was not infected by taking a drop of blood from his fingertip and dropping it on a sensor, made a scan of his retina and finally handed him an access badge.

Erik noticed the bulletproof doors and the retractable shutters, which meant that the building could be shut off completely at a moment's notice.

The guard led him through long corridors, many of which were interspersed by armoured doors that opened only with a badge and a retinal scan.

"Are you the new guy?" the guard asked him suddenly. He was a very tall and burly man with a curiously childish face.

Erik nodded. "Persson," he introduced himself, shaking hands.

"Martin Nagy," the other said. "They said that you were on an operational team and they transferred you here from the headquarters. Is that true?"

"Yeah," Erik confirmed, unable to hide his bitterness.

Nagy laughed: "Well, you must have fucked up big time, eh?"

For a moment Erik was tempted to tell him to go to hell but realized that the remark was probably not made to poke fun at him.

"Pretty big time, yeah," he admitted.

That made his new colleague laugh even more: "Ah, I thought so. Half the guards are here because they stepped on the wrong feet. But don't worry: it might not be the most exciting job in the world, but it's quiet and we rarely get superiors coming here to bother us. That's already something, am I right?"

Erik felt, if anything, even more mortified, but he tried not to show it, exhibiting a drawn smile.

The structure he was in was called a 'hospital' because according to the law they could not arrest someone on the suspicion of having contracted a disease; of course, there was no trial for such a crime. In reality, though, the custody hospital was a prison for the ones infected with the plague.

There were not many doctors or nurses, surgery wards or visiting rooms: on other hand, the place abounded with cells and armed guards. Erik had the distinct impression that this was the most depressing work place he could think of: he would be locked up all day to guard the infected, waiting for the inevitable conclusion. To think that he had worked all his life to get to this... he clenched his hands into fists, trying to control his frustration.

This was his job now, and he better get used to it.

In the meantime, they had arrived at the director's office: the sign on the door announced that her name was Eileen Murray. She turned out to be a woman in her sixties, very thin and petite, with exceptionally thick glasses, and welcomed him coldly.

"Please, sit down."

Erik sat down at his desk, while Murray took off her glasses with studied slowness.

Please, Erik thought, not another Hoffman...

"I'll get straight to the point, Persson," she said instead, leaning toward him. "I read your resume and I know you've probably been sent here to get you out of someone's way. I don't care why they decided to move you away from the headquarters. You probably regard this as a kind of punishment: it maybe so. In any case, from the moment you join the hospital staff, I expect you to take up your new post as seriously as you would face an investigation and arrest operation. We had too many agents arriving here in the past, thinking that they were here on vacation. It isn't so: the work here is as hard and challenging as in any other place. Of course, I cannot promise you great excitement or," here she grimaced, annoyed, "any award... but I still think it is a very important job. Perhaps you thought that removing an infected from the streets was the culmination of the work done by the medical police... "

Erik shook his head: "No, of course not..."

Actually, to be honest, he never thought of what happened to the people he had arrested. Obviously, there was no trial for having a disease, so... well, he had always assumed that someone would take care of it. Apparently, now that someone was him.

"I'm glad to hear it," Murray said, "because you'll find that it is actually just the beginning. If we want to permanently eradicate the plague, the solution is not just to withdraw all the infected but try to prevent the spread of infection. And that means also eliminating the scourge of the rebels... and the work that we carry on here is vital to learn more about them and try to stop them."

Erik nodded, trying to look interested. He realized no one likes to think that their work is just plain depressing, so he tried not to show his true feelings about the handling of arrested infected.

"I have just one last recommendation, which I beg you to bear in mind. The medical police function here as guards: your job, therefore, is to ensure that no one enters or goes without authorization."

Erik involuntarily raised his eyebrows: yeah, I had gathered as much.

"That means," Murray continued, "that any kind of familiarity with patients is to be avoided. I know it might often seem that we spend more time with them than with anyone else in our lives, but we must remember the barrier that separates us from them: the physical and mental health which we possess, and those people do not."

"Of course." he nodded. She surely didn't need to point out something so obvious.

"Keep it in mind, Persson," agent Murray said, leaning back in her chair.

Erik understood that the interview was over.

"Now you can go pick up your uniform and meet your new colleagues. Nagy will show you the way."

They shook hands, then Erik followed his burly colleague. That day he received a locker and some work wear consisting of shoes and ordinance trousers, plus a shirt and a bullet-proof vest with the symbol of the medical police and the hospital's name.

When he looked in the mirror, he felt humiliated: it had been years since he was required to wear that uniform. Apart from the protective suit that he used during the arrests, he had worn his civilian clothes to work for decades.

His colleagues, all wearing identical uniform, were almost all officers close to retirement, plus some rookie without much hope for a career. Erik wondered what had gone wrong in their life to get them to such a sad place.

He introduced himself and shook many hands, but at the end of the day the names were jumbled together in an undefined mass.

He experienced another depressing moment when it came to the organization of the shifts: a colleague handed him a chart showing the hours in which he had to show up.

Twice a month he had the night shift.

During all the years he had spent at the headquarters he always worked during office hours, and even then the time management was flexible depending on the work necessities.

Nagy smiled sympathetically: "The night shift is not so bad. Very quiet. After a couple of months you get used to it."

Erik tried not to appear too dejected: "Ah yes, I am no stranger to sleepless nights. I've done the night shift some years ago." *More than twenty-five*, he thought, *but who's counting.*

"I have a friend who brings me coffee. I'll offer you a cup," Nagy promised.

Erik thanked him.

At least there will be coffee, he thought.

Later that day, Nagy led Erik on a guided tour of the structure.

The first part of the building hosted the administration department: an office as far away as possible from the cells where the prisoners were kept, and a large archive, with both paper and digital files. About fifty people worked there, all government employees.

"I thought the hospital was run by the medical police," Erik said, surprised.

"It is," Nagy confirmed, "but this office handles the data we gather. Some kind of outsourcing, I suppose."

Erik did not know why, but it seemed vaguely wrong. This data belonged to the police; it didn't seem correct that citizens would handle it. But why should he care? Now all he had to do was put on his uniform, show up for shifts, and avoid asking the wrong questions.

After the administration department he was shown the infirmary, the kitchen, the police canteen, some interrogation rooms and various service rooms.

"And now the best part," Nagy announced, "I'll take you to see some cells."

The inmates' cells, in fact, formed the bulk of the hospital. Erik repressed a shudder when he realized they were heading there: rationally he knew that much of his work would be carried out in close contact with the infected, but the idea of entering that place caused him a strong feeling of unease.

Better deal with it right away, he thought; he was sure that after a few weeks he wouldn't even think about it anymore.

The hospital area used for the confinement of the infected was divided from the main body by a series of armoured doors. To access that area, his colleague led him through some flights of moving stairs, then down a lift. When the doors opened, he realized he was underground.

The controls were much more intensive there: Erik's badge got checked several times and on a couple of occasions he also had to do the retinal scan again.

Nagy seemed accustomed to these procedures: "I know, it seems really tedious at the beginning," he commented.

When the last of the armoured door had closed behind him, Erik found himself in a corridor whose left side was occupied by a series of cells. There were no bars, but the doors were transparent.

"So, this is pod one... come on, come on..." Nagy urged him. "There's nothing to be afraid of. These are as safe as the armoured ones," He said, knocking on the doors of a cell.

Inside, a figure was lying on a cot in the shadows. When Nagy touched the door, the figure moved, and Erik saw that it was a man with his face covered in greyish scales.

Instinctively, he took a backward step.

His colleague laughed: "That's OK, Persson... It's just Bob. Hey, Bob, how are we doing today?"

The infected stretched, bored: "Do you have a cigarette, Marty?"

Martin Nagy looked at Erik and chuckled uneasily: "Heh heh... never mind, let's move on..."

Erik continued walking down the hall, looking with suspicion at the inmates in the cells. There were both men and women, of all ages. They all looked very quiet: some slept, others read or just stared at the void. Most ignored them, but some acknowledged Nagy's presence with a vague greeting gesture.

"When you are on duty you have to check that there are no problems, but let me tell you, they are very rare. The trickiest part is handing out the meals, because some detainees have fun scaring the new attendants. Don't worry, though, the trays pass through these drawers, see? No one ever comes into contact with the infected, everything is designed for it. They have their toilet and a sink in the cell, and there's a shower too… normally they don't get out a lot."

"Are they... um... out of control as they say?"

The guard looked at him, amazed: "Out of control? No, not really… well, alright, there are some difficult characters, especially in pod six… but most detainees don't give us too much trouble. Besides, you know…" here he lowered his voice, "it's not like they have great prospects, if you know what I mean."

Erik nodded: he already learned, to his surprise, that infected were kept in detention for several months, even years, before execution. He had always been of the opinion that they should be terminated at once.

"Yeah, poor devils…" Nagy sighed. "Come, let's go out, I'm not going to talk about these things here."

When Erik went back to the guards' common room, he sat down to gather his thoughts. The situation he found in the cells had surprised him; admittedly, he hadn't known what to expect... possibly infected throwing fits, hurling themselves against the bars while the guards kept them at a distance with tasers.

That was probably a little naïve of him.

The medical police had various options to keep the infected subdued and harmless, for example by putting sedatives in their daily rations. He decided to ask Murray about this, if he had the occasion… if not for professional duty, at least out of curiosity.

Chapter 16

In the following days, Sophie tried as best she could to get used to the island and its inhabitants. When she got up in the morning, she heated on the stove all the water she could carry and washed herself with that; then she wore all the protective clothing she could find and went downstairs to have breakfast. An undoubtedly positive side of her enforced stay on the island was the abundance of food. The islanders were few and the food was more than enough to feed them.

As far as she could tell, there were about two thousand survivors, about the same as half of a fifth ring apartment building.

The islanders raised cattle and sheep that took advantage of the wide open pasture. Cereals, on the other hand, were mostly imported, because the climate was too harsh for extensive cultivation: every week two large boats went to the city and brought all the food that the islanders needed. Sophie, to be honest, didn't quite understand whether the food was paid for or simply stolen. In any case, the system seemed to work.

The loads contained not only the usual food distribution staples (beans, rice, canned goods), but also exotic foods, fresh fruits and vegetables, chocolate, coffee, tea. This gave Sophie many doubts. If that food could be bought (or systematically stolen without consequences), why did the city had to submit to food rations? Where did all that stuff come from? And where did it go, apart from this remote island?

James often cooked eggs with butter for breakfast, and the scent filled the house.

Every time Sophie wondered how it was possible to have such a wide choice of food and if it was unhealthy to eat such greasy, heavy foods for breakfast, and then decided, every time, that she didn't care. It was all just too delicious to resist. She had never eaten anything like that. She probably wolfed down, at breakfast alone, her usual daily ration in protein and calories.

During the day she walked around the island, taking along something to nibble; when she came home at the end of the day, she ate the evening meal with James.

This, too, had little to do with the dinners she was used to: in a few days she had tasted more foods than she had eaten in her whole life.

Sophie had to admit that James, despite a few bursts of bad temper, was a very thoughtful host. After a while she almost grew accustomed to his alarming features; now it was easier not to be distracted by the scales running down his skin.

If he had not been one of those twisted creatures, she would have considered him very good company: he was educated, intelligent and, last but not least at that moment, a great cook. He didn't have Amanda's caustic humour, but Sophie thought there was something similar in the two siblings' way of thinking.

She didn't see much of the other plague survivors. One of the most surprising aspects of life on the island was how much space they had at their disposal. From what she understood, the island had an area of about five square kilometres... a disproportionate space for a couple thousand people, who were furthermore almost all concentrated in the town near the coast. Sophie could walk for hours, meeting no living creatures but a few sheep.

The streets were old and dilapidated, the asphalt cracked and overgrown with weeds, but still well distinguishable. At the beginning the feeling made her dizzy. There was just too much.... emptiness. She could not remember a time in her life when she was not surrounded by other people.

Even when she was in her apartment, she would only have to go out and walk a single step to knock on the nearest door. In fact, only a thin layer of metallic wall separated her from her neighbours. Any moment she could hear their voices; now that she thought about it, they slept only a few millimetres from her... and these were people with whom she had never spoken in her life.

On the island, on the other hand, one of the most disconcerting sensations was the silence around her. After a few minutes of listening, however, she observed that what had sounded like silence actually was far from it. The island was full of noises, though completely different from those she was used to: the roar of the waves on the beach, strange rustlings in the meadows, even the vaguely disturbing predatory calls of the birds in the trees. This unknown place attracted and repulsed her at the same time.

An aspect of solitude she was very fond of was the chance to safely take off the mask and plastic gloves. The climate of the island was much colder than she was used to, but when the sun shone it was nice to feel its warmth on her face.

At first, she was sorry that Emma was so terrified at the idea of setting foot outside Britt's house, but then she discovered that she loved solitude so much that if the old lady had offered to accompany her, perhaps she would have been a bit disappointed.

"Have you thought about the research thing?" James asked one morning.

Sophie was busy eating a big slice of toast with butter and jam, and for a moment the morsel she was about to swallow nearly choked her. Actually, she had not thought about James' offer at all. It was very convenient to delay the decision, and after a while she almost convinced herself that if she stopped thinking about it, the problem would solve itself. It had worked perfectly until that day.

"Ah... er..." she began, spitting out bread crumbs. "I've thought about it... a little..."

James raised an eyebrow: "And what did you decide?"

Sophie shrugged: "Um... I'm still not entirely sure... but... well, maybe I should think about it a little longer."

He slowly nodded: "I understand. Obviously I wouldn't want to put you under pressure, since you're basically forced to stay here, it's just that..." he ran a hand through his short grey hair, "I think it would be really nice if you at least agreed to try... you know, it would give you something to do... "

Sophie swallowed the mouthful of bread and jam: "Yes... I promise I will think about it, OK?"

"Of course." His smile was a little strained.

Sophie did not know what to say, so as soon as she could she got out of the house and walked into the meadows within the island. The air was, if not exactly hot, pleasantly warm, at least in the sun; she took off her mask and gloves, and after a while she proceeded to let go of her anorak. She was still wearing a sweatshirt underneath, made of anti-infection synthetic material, so she felt relatively safe.

While she walked, she reflected on James' words. All in all, she thought, she could have a look at that material. What did she have to lose? If she didn't manage to get any results, no one could blame her.

On the other hand, she was afraid that this could delay her return to normal life even further. To tell the truth, in a mere few days so many things had happened to her, that she was beginning to wonder if it would be so easy to just go back to her old life.

She would need new documents and a new job. It would be odd to think of herself under another name.

While she was engrossed in these thoughts, she found herself walking in a direction she had never taken before. The landscape was much the same all around: meadows interspersed with low walls, a few trees, a lot of sheep.

Sophie realized she was close to a dilapidated shack, from which a half-familiar figure was coming out. It was the girl who had called after her when she had gone to see Emma for the first time; she recognized the curly hair and the spirals of scales that criss-crossed her shoulders. *Nadia*, she remembered.

"What are you doing here?" she asked abruptly.

"I... I was just... I was..." Sophie stammered, taken aback.

Another figure stepped out of the shack, a girl with very long blond hair. This one just looked at her in surprise. Sophie wished she had not taken off her gloves and mask.

Nadia was striding towards her and she felt completely defenceless.

"Come on, leave her alone," the blonde girl urged. "She was just taking a walk."

"Yes," Sophie confirmed desperately. "I was only walking. I think I've taken the wrong way... I'll leave, ok?"

"Are you looking for information? Why are you still here on the island?" Nadia continued to ask, getting closer and closer with a threatening look.

"James... he said I can't leave... I wish I could, I swear..." Sophie replied, now in panic.

"If they aren't letting you go it's because someone doesn't trust you."

Nadia was now less than a step away from her.

Sophie noticed with horror that there was something about her eyes: their colour was unnaturally metallic, and even the pupils seemed slightly vertical, like a reptile's.

She remembered a medical police poster she had seen at a train station: "In case of an encounter with an infected, please note that they can become very aggressive. It is advisable to slowly move away..."

She stepped back, and Nadia pounced on her... or at least tried. She pushed Sophie hard in the chest, but her momentum was halted by the blonde girl, who grabbed her shoulders and dragged her away from Sophie, throwing her on the ground. Nadia let out a scream, which sounded more like a roar, and lunged at her friend, who held her by the shoulders.

"Nadia, you're losing control... remember to breathe... breathe!" she insisted, while the other girl was trying to free herself, kicking and flailing.

But the blonde girl did not let go: "You can fight it," she kept saying. "Remember, *control*! You can do it, I know!"

Nadia gave another roar which could have been fury or pain. Sophie continued to stare at the scene, paralyzed, unable to get up and run away. After a few seconds that seemed very long, it looked like the fury had slipped away from Nadia, who began to breathe more slowly. Her body, which had been rigid with tension, sagged like a wet rag into the arms of the other infected.

"I'm sorry... I'm sorry..." she whispered, in tears. "It is so hard..."

The other consoled her, hugging and stroking her hair: "It is difficult for everyone. It just takes some time..."

"Don't tell Cain!" Nadia pleaded.

The other girl shook her head, but Nadia got up and went to Sophie, who instinctively tried to back away.

"I'm sorry, I'm really sorry!" she said in a feverish tone. "You won't tell Cain, will you? Will you?"

"No, I... won't, no." Sophie stammered, terrified.

"You promise?"

Sophie nodded vigorously: "Yes, yes... I promise."

There was a moment of awkward silence, then Nadia turned to leave.

"You have a nasty cut on your back," the other girl pointed out.

Indeed, when Nadia had fallen, she must have struck a sharp rock, because her back was crossed by a deep vertical cut.

"I heard that you're a doctor, aren't you?" the blonde girl asked, turning to Sophie.

"Ah... er... yeah," she confirmed.

"Could you give it a look?"

Sophie felt the ground around her to find the gloves and the mask that she had dropped, then put them on with trembling hands and walked over to Nadia.

"You'd need some stitches," she remarked, carefully pulling aside the bloody tatters of her shirt.

"Can you do it?" Nadia's friend asked again. Nadia herself seemed to have lost all strength, as if even talking was beyond her energy.

"Er, yes, but I don't even have a first aid kit here..."

"We can walk to the hospital."

Sophie could not see how she might refuse without appearing extremely unkind.

"Ok."

The walk to the hospital was slow and awkward, but Sophie took the opportunity to ask some questions. She discovered that the blonde girl's name was Karla, and she had lived here for about eight years, while Nadia had survived the infection six years before.

"You have to excuse her," Karla explained. "At times it's hard to keep tabs on the dragon."

Sophie frowned: "What do you mean?"

She had read too many brochures of the medical police, which said that the infected had no ability to reason and became uncontrollably aggressive.

"Obviously it isn't exactly so," Karla explained when Sophie mentioned this. "But there is some truth in it. At first, your perceptions change... I can't tell if it's hormones, or it's just a psychological thing, but every single emotion becomes stronger and more difficult to control, especially anger. It's a bit like living through a second adolescence. But you get used to it, you know. It takes a little habit, some exercise of meditation... it's all about exercise, really."

Sophie remembered the way James, when he was irritated, stopped talking for a moment to take a breath.

Karla added: "Some people, though... "

The girl paused, and Sophie noticed that Nadia gave her a glaring look.

"Oh, come on!" said Karla. "It's not a secret, and if she stays here for a while she'd better know." Nadia merely shrugged, unconvinced.

"As I was saying," Karla continued, undeterred, "Um, it's hard to explain for someone like me, who's not affected this way, but some people develop a bond with the dragons... something like a telepathic connection."

Sophie thought of the talk she had heard in the city: *the dragons call them... they whisper things in their heads....*

"So the dragons... talk to them?" she asked.

Karla smiled: "It doesn't work like that. Let's say that sometimes they share the strongest emotions, which are... you know, amplified. Some say that it would be possible to develop the bond to make it deeper, but Cain is absolutely contrary.

He says it does no good to have a dragon in one's head, because they are essentially evil."

Nadia gave a snort, as if to disagree.

"That's what he says," Karla remarked, shrugging. It sounded like this Cain said a lot of things.

"Why did you ask me not to… tell Cain?" Sophie asked.

Nadia and Karla exchanged a meaningful look.

"He is very intransigent on this point," Karla finally said. "If he knew... there would be consequences." Her voice had a scared tinge.

In the meantime, they had arrived at the hospital, where Sophie found the equipment needed to stitch Nadia up. She was wearing gloves and a mask, and after a few minutes she felt calmer and calmer in being in contact with an infected.

Nadia's skin was harder than usual, she noticed, and she had to use a larger than normal needle, but upon the whole it seemed the same as the skin of regular people.

When they parted, Nadia thanked her and apologized again for what happened.

"No problem," Sophie said.

Nadia held out her hand, and Sophie, after a moment's hesitation, shook it.

Later she thought this was the first time she voluntarily came into contact with an infected.

Chapter 17

Erik's new job turned out to be as depressing as he had imagined.

Having to work in shifts destabilized him: sometimes he woke up at the same time as Thea and Peter and went to work as he always had done. Those were the best days, when he could pretend that nothing had happened and that his life was going on as always. Only having to wear that silly uniform clashed with the illusion.

Leaving the house at midday and coming back at night felt strange, but it did not bother him that much. Other weeks, however, he went to the hospital in the late evening and slid the exit badge in the early hours of the morning, then woke up in the afternoon, when the house was still empty but already dark.

There were moments, as he was just waking up, when he looked around the empty apartment, wondering vaguely what happened to everyone. Then he would remember that the change was not in the others, who were going on with their days as they always had, but in him.

Another aspect of his old job that he really missed was the fact that it gave him something to think about, which kept him mentally busy. Being a jailer at the hospital was definitely not very interesting from this point of view.

Now all he had to do was wait, patrol the hospital, check that there were no problems with the prisoners (until now there had been very few, and he never had to intervene personally), escort the attendants that brought meals to the prisoners, and then return to his desk to watch the safety monitor. His colleagues were mostly officers close to retirement or people who clearly had no ambitions or hopes of a career.

Martin Nagy had kept his promise to bring him coffee during the night shifts: it was dark, bitter and had a strong taste that Erik was not used to these days but remembered well from his youth. Once upon a time it was not so hard to find; in fact, it was even included in the food distribution rations.

Erik had also discovered that his colleague was particularly good at procuring any kind of item on the black market, especially his beloved cigarettes.

He suspected that Nagy had settled quite well in his position at the hospital, and, like a mouse in a cheese, had no desire to get out. He couldn't understand how this could be, since the detainees were not allowed to have any personal items, but he had noticed that even within the hospital there was a form of illegal market of which Nagy was the fulcrum. Often Erik would see him talking furtively to an infected or exchanging something with them through the system of drawers used for the meal trays. A part of him wanted to put a stop to it… but then, he thought, what for? Was it really such a terrible thing to sell cigarettes to the infected? Now that they were locked up, they could not possibly do any damage.

In a few days, as he had expected, Erik had learned to find his way in the building without difficulty, and the sight of the infected didn't make him as upset as at first.

Although Murray had assured that they didn't add sedatives or other medicines to the food, Erik was convinced that the prisoners were somehow kept under control by chemical means. Otherwise, how could they all be so calm and unaggressive? It was a known fact that the infected had violent tendencies and uncontrollable aggression instincts.

In none of his shifts, however, he had been brought to pod six. This pod was the most mysterious area of the hospital. As far as Erik understood, that was where the most dangerous prisoners were kept, though he did not understand why each of them was considered as such. When he observed the creatures on the monitor screen, he could make out nothing but shadowy figures lying down, sitting, or moving within their small living space. The only thing he had noticed was that it was undoubtedly the department that received more visits from doctors, nurses and other medical police officers. Sometimes the infected were even brought out for interrogations, but until now he was never called to assist them. Maybe the director didn't feel he had enough experience for these tasks, he thought bitterly.

Apart from the little satisfaction he received in the workplace, Erik was also concerned about Maja. His daughter had come to visit on some occasions, sometimes alone, at other times with that Marc fellow.

Despite Thea's jokes, who argued that Erik was merely acting out the part of the apprehensive father, he could not shake off the feeling that the young man was hiding something. In addition, Maja began to make speeches that made him wary: well, not exactly speeches, more like hints, jokes, small references that were nonetheless alarming. Sometimes she covertly criticized President Hartmann's appearances on television, for example; or she made a disapproving joke about the inhabitants of the first ring. Erik knew that young people, especially students, often had rebellious tendencies, although he didn't recall any instances of serious trouble.

He thought it was in the nature of young people to question the status quo, even though most of the time it was nothing more than a part of their self-search. Not that he, personally, had ever been attracted by that kind of activism: but then, at Maja's age he was finishing his studies at the police academy, thinking about getting married... everything was different back then.

In any case, although Erik was convinced that for Maja this was not more than a phase of fleeting post-adolescent rebellion, he was afraid that if she continued to hang out with Marc she would risk putting herself in a nasty situation. He certainly didn't want her to compromise her future career by associating with scum who were good for nothing but raising their voices and complaining without offering any alternative.

Maja should be thinking about studying and building a good future for herself.

Erik, however, had not dared to talk to her yet: he was afraid that dealing directly with the issue would do nothing but make his daughter even more stubborn in her position.

Would she perhaps accuse him of not understanding, of being too steeped in the existing system to ask questions, or even of being an old man scared of changes?

She probably would, he reflected.

When she was younger it was easier to talk to her. He remembered the time when his word was enough to convince her of anything - that there were no monsters under the bed or that she had to eat the vegetables on her plate. Everything used to be easier then.

Another night shift awaited him that evening. Erik took his place in front of the security monitor with resignation. He had four hours of absolute boredom ahead, then there would be lunch (or dinner? He was not really sure at that hour) in the officers' canteen. The food was bland

and depressing as the rest of the work, but at least it was one thing less to worry about. Then he would go to secure one of the armoured doors between one pod and the other.

Erik was accompanied by Bruno Martinelli, one of the older jailers. The man was extremely polite but had a tendency to doze off in front of the monitor. Erik never knew whether to wake him or not: in doubt, when he realized that his nap has lasted for a while, he intentionally moved the chair, making some noise, or got up and opened the door, causing his colleague to jolt awake. It seemed less embarrassing than pointing out that he was asleep again.

"All right, Persson?" Martinelli asked.

"Yes, thanks, and you?"

"Oh, at my age," he sighed, "I get by as I can." That was his usual answer.

The officer had a thermos of hot barley drink that he had brought from home, and offered a cup to Erik, who declined.

After the customary pleasantries, Martinelli dozed off in front of the monitor, while Erik stared at the screens almost without seeing them, lost in his thoughts. He wondered if he was wrong not to talk to Maja about his concerns. After all, wasn't it what a parent was for? Of course, she probably wouldn't listen to him, but perhaps it was his duty to try to make her understand his point of view.

At that moment his attention was attracted by a glimmer in one of the monitors. Frowning, Erik leaned in to see better. Apparently, there was nothing unusual: the rows of cells, the long corridor with two guards at the ends. In one of the cells, a man was standing in front of the toilet, which he was apparently using. It appeared he was the only one awake.

Erik blinked: he probably had imagined it... it was late, after all.

He looked at the watch: almost two o'clock. Soon there would be a change of shifts.

Although he had rested all day, even Erik, like his elder colleague, was struggling against sleep. Who knows, next week he might be on the same shift as Nagy: he wouldn't have minded a cup of coffee at that moment.

An alarm clock informed him that it was time for a change of shifts.

Martinelli awoke with a start: "Ah, it's time for a little break," he commented. "I was beginning to feel a bit tired."

Erik did his best to suppress a smirk. At that moment, however, another sound drowned out the alarm clock: a loud, penetrating noise.

"What...?" Martinelli said, a little dazed by the sleep.

Erik, however, recognized it at once: "It's the fire alarm."

He watched the monitors again: in pod six a heavy blanket of smoke was spreading, but not he could understand where it was coming from. Again, he saw movement in the cells: some prisoners were banging on the doors, perhaps inciting the officers to let them out. In the meantime, some officers were preparing a corridor that was usually deserted to accommodate the detainees.

Erik realized that they would have to move some prisoners, to get them away from the area invaded by the smoke. According to the monitors, there was no fire in any other area of the hospital. Between the shift change and the comings and goings of the other officers, the scene was a little confused. The transfer of prisoners in case of fire was a routine operation... and yet... something didn't quite sit right with him.

"I have to go and see," he announced.

"What?" Martinelli protested. "No, no, there is a protocol to follow... we have to be at the collection point, and..."

But Erik did not stay to hear him: his intuition told him to go and check. He raced to pod six, and as soon as he opened the separation door he was assailed by a wave of smoke.

Erik noticed that he simply had to swipe his badge to open the doors, without having to undergo retina scans. He imagined that the fire alarm put a simplified procedure in place.

He stepped into the room and felt water splashing on his head from the fire-fighting system. The cells were being opened by two officers, who escorted the prisoners into the cells of an adjacent pod.

"What are you doing here?" Dukas, another officer, addressed him; he was currently busy taking away a detainee. "You're not following the procedure."

Erik ignored the rebuke: "Everything all right here?"

Dukas shrugged: "It sucks. All this smoke!" he coughed. "See? My poor lungs! Who told you to come here?"

Erik made a vague gesture: "They probably thought you needed a hand... I'm going to take a look at the other cells."

"OK," Dukas merely answered.

Erik made a quick inspection of the cells: some detainees seemed a bit worried and pressed against the glass, trying to see better. It was probably because of the smoke, but the scales were invisible, giving the prisoners an almost normal appearance.

He began to wonder if he had done the right thing by disobeying the protocol: the situation seemed under control. He certainly wouldn't want to have problems with Murray or his other new superiors or make himself a reputation of a troublemaker. He decided to get out of there before his presence became too conspicuous.

While he was passing by a cell, a dark-skinned woman, whom Erik could not help but find surprisingly attractive despite the circumstances, stared at him, following his movements. She looked strangely familiar.

Before he had time to wonder about it, his attention was drawn to another officer, who was heading in a hurry towards the exit. He was the only other jailer, apart from him, who wasn't occupied with the evacuation. Erik decided to leave with him: this way he could sneak away without being too obvious.

"Hey!" he addressed the officer, approaching him. "I wanted to ask you something about fire extinguishing system..."

The colleague turned briefly to look at him, then sped up. Erik hurried behind, catching up with the man.

"Hey, listen…" his eyes ran over the colleague's uniform to the place on the chest where the name was indicated and read, "Nagy...?"

He looked at him: that man was not Martin Nagy. He was lean, short- statured, with a face that reminded him of a rodent. The uniform was clearly too big for him.

"What...?" Before Erik could react, the man gave him a punch in the face and ran away, opening the door with the badge that he had at the belt. He went through the first door, which shut behind him.

Erik swiped the badge as quickly as possible, following him. The fake jailer was fast, but Erik was in a better shape: as soon as the other man slowed down for lack of breath, he was on him. He anchored him to the ground with his weight, then instinctively reached for the handcuffs he always had attached to his belt but realized that handcuffs were not part of his new uniform. Therefore, he kept the man pinned down while the other officers came to his help. The prisoner desperately tried to jerk away, emitting sounds similar to an animal caught in a trap.

"Let go!" he shouted, "Let me go!"

"Who are you? What did you do to Nagy?"

The man merely let out a frustrated groan. When the other officers arrived, Erik pulled away, while someone else handcuffed the fugitive. While they were taking him away, the man caught his eye: "Why must I die? Why?"

Erik was taken aback.

"You have no right to do it! No!" the man continued to scream.

Dukas approached Erik and put a hand on his shoulder.

"Good job. How did you realize that he was the one who set off the fire alarm?"

It took Erik a moment to catch the meaning of his words: "No… I…" he finally stammered. "I was not sure. Only a suspicion."

"Well, it seems he used a lighter that he obviously wasn't supposed to have. I think someone will be in trouble for this story."

Erik nodded. It was likely that Nagy would have to slow down his flourishing trade, at least for a while.

"Come on, let's go. You look like you need a drink. Maybe we'll find some coffee," Dukas proposed.

Only when he was sitting in the guards' common room, with a steaming mug in his hand, did Erik realize that the man who had tried to escape showed no signs of the plague.

Chapter 18

After about a month, Sophie found herself to be the more or less official doctor of the island. She wasn't sure how it happened.

Maybe Nadia had talked about how she had stitched up her back, or maybe James had been secretly encouraging the whole thing. In any case, a few days after the incident with Nadia and Karla, a number of people began to show up at James' house asking for medical help or advice. There were some who had had small accidents by working in the fields or with animals; others had some minor medical issue (those involving stomach and teeth were especially frequent; respiratory ailments seemed to be less common among the plague survivors).

At first Sophie could not say she was enthusiastic about this trend. She tried to send some of them away, saying that she couldn't help them, that she didn't know the way their bodies worked, that she didn't feel like it... it was useless. People just kept showing up.

Sophie actually had a feeling that James did nothing to discourage them; indeed, he offered tea and biscuits to all those who waited, until she decided she might as well listen to them. In the end, more for convenience than out of real interest, she decided to move the meetings to the hospital. At least there she had some rudimentary equipment at hand.

She ought to have had a greater choice of drugs, of course: many of those she had were well past their expiration date, and she often had to increase the dose, because the bodies of the infected reacted differently than those of uninfected people.

Anyhow, her work made her get to know a little better those who, at least temporarily, were her fellow citizens.

There were people who seemed to be affected by the plague to a lesser extent: some had very few scales, and those only on their back and legs, so that at first glance they could be mistaken for normal people; others had parts of their face covered with hardened scales in metallic colours, which gave them a particularly scary appearance.

Sophie also found that, though mostly the scales looked greenish under direct light, many showed different colours: on some people, the scars veered decidedly to blue or violet. Others had warmer hues, purple or orange.

Another feature of the infected that she discovered was their infertility: no woman had her menstrual cycle anymore, and pregnancies had never occurred. Evidently, the biological changes that took place were incompatible with human conception.

From a behavioural point of view, however, the plague survivors were not unlike other patients. There were those who came to her only in emergency cases, and others who required a consultation every two or three days. They reminded her of Mr. Verlinden, one of her most loyal patients in the third ring.

One day, Nadia showed up with extensive burns on her arm. Sophie gave her a painkiller, checked that she was not in shock, then bandaged her arm and covered it with sterile gauze.

"How did you get a burn like that?" she asked once she had provided first aid.

Despite her initial animosity, Sophie had discovered that Nadia was not as grumpy as she looked. Actually, she was alright. She didn't mince her words, and Sophie liked that.

Nadia grimaced sarcastically: "How do you think I got it? It was my dragon."

Sophie's eyes widened: "Your...?"

"Dragon, yeah," Nadia confirmed. "What is it? Don't you know why we are on this island? This is where we keep them."

"The dragons are here?" Sophie stammered. "Where?"

"Don't worry," Nadia laughed, "They are far from the town. We keep them on the other coast, in caves... you know, they like cold and humid environments."

Sophie took some time to process this information. Sure, she knew, like everyone else, that the rebels had dragons, and that in some cases the beasts were used in attacks... but to think that those creatures were here, not far from her... she suppressed a shudder.

"So... uh, you have a dragon of your own?" she asked.

Nadia shrugged: "Um, it's not as simple as that. It's not like having a dog or a cat. No one can own a dragon: they are too dangerous, unpredictable and independent. But yes, there is a dragon to which I am bonded. In my mind, you know?"

Sophie nodded, even though she was not entirely sure she understood.

"Actually, I'm not supposed to consider it *mine*. Cain says that it's better not to deal with the bond. He says that it's too dangerous, that it pollutes the mind..." here Nadia's voice dropped to a whisper. "But I don't believe it's true. I feel it, you know? His thoughts are fascinating and at times very intense... but he's not evil. It's just... how can I explain..." Nadia struggled, searching for the right words. "Much bigger than us," she said at last.

Her eyes had lit up while she talked about the dragon, and heightened colour appeared in her cheeks. There definitely was a link between these people and the dragons, and it scared Sophie a little. At the same time, however, it was fascinating: in some ways it was like the propaganda spewed by the medical police, but in others it was completely different...

As if sensing her thoughts, Nadia leaned toward her: "Do you want to see them?" "What?"

"The dragons, of course! Want to see one?"

Sophie's gaze instinctively moved to Nadia's burned arm.

"I meant from a safe distance. They are pretty big, you know? No need to go too close to see them."

Sophie shifted her weight from foot to foot, uncomfortable.

"I'm not sure... "

"I can't believe you have been here all this time and have never wanted to see one."

To tell the truth, Sophie had not even thought about it. But now that she knew... she was afraid, of course. A *dragon*! In a sense it was the dragons' fault that the world was falling apart: the disease, the infected, the rebellions... on the other hand, a dragon was not something you saw every day.

Even in videos that were broadcasted on the television they never showed them in detail: the dragons always appeared like slightly blurry spots, taken from afar.

Sophie could barely distinguish their wings, at times, and the fire that came out of their mouths, but otherwise it was only a confused image.

"OK, but... can you really just take me to see one? I mean, is it even allowed?"

Nadia rolled her eyes: "Of course not. I mean, we'd be breaking a million rules or so... Cain would have a fit."

Sophie got the impression that the idea of breaching Cain's rules was a strong motivation for Nadia, and she was starting to understand.

Besides Nadia and Karla, several other people had mentioned him, seemingly at random, while talking to her. Some asked if she had his permission to use the hospital, others seemed concerned about the idea of doing something without informing him first. His name was like a black cloud hovering over all the inhabitants of the island. In the end, it was this thought that made her decide, more than anything else.

"OK," she said, with a bravado that sounded strange even to her own ears. "Take me to see it."

Nadia stood up in excitement, the pain in her arm apparently forgotten.

"Come on, Doc, let's get you roasted!"

Sophie stared, appalled.

"Oh, please, it was only a joke!"

They took a car to get to the other side of the island. It was much more old-fashioned than those used in the city (Sophie happened to drive one a few times), but it seemed more suitable for the local dirt roads.

On the other side of the island there was a mountain: Sophie was used to seeing its silhouette against the horizon, but she had never gone that far. After about half an hour of journey they arrived at the mountainside.

"This way," Nadia said, indicating the steep rocky slope.

"Are we supposed to climb it?!"

"No, look." She walked around the rocks and moved a bush to reveal a series of steps, steep but usable. "Hardly anyone knows this path, so we shouldn't have problems."

Nimbly, Nadia began to climb the steps, clinging here and there to the protruding rocks. Sophie was slower: she was not used to that kind of exercise, and when she looked down and saw how high up they had climbed, it made her slightly dizzy. This was absurd, actually: her apartment's window was much higher, and she had never experienced such fears when looking down... even on the emergency stairs of Lukas's apartment building, when she was escaping with Emma, she did not have the same feeling. Maybe it was because the buildings and their stairs were solid and reliable, while the mountain trail seemed so precarious... anyway, Sophie forced herself to continue climbing without looking back.

Suddenly she looked up and realized that from there she could see the entire island.

Despite the terror, Sophie could not help but appreciate the beautiful landscape.

She noticed that on the horizon there was another mountain, almost as tall as theirs.

"What's there?" she asked Nadia.

She shrugged: "Dunno. Whatever there is on mountains."

At last, they came to a recess of the rock wall, which crept into the mountain to form a cave. Sophie dropped to the ground, exhausted.

"I didn't think of bringing water," Nadia reflected. "I always forget that you, the not infected, have so little resistance. After a while we begin to take our strength for granted."

"Anyway, here we are. At the bottom of this cave there is an opening down which we can look."

Sophie's curiosity was strong enough to make her get up and follow Nadia into the cave. Indeed, there was an opening in its floor.

Sophie leaned over and realized that the mountain was almost completely hollow. It seemed that originally it was a natural phenomenon, but that the sides had been further carved artificially. The air was humid and warm. It was dark inside, and she had to squint to distinguish any form, until, suddenly, the entire huge cave was illuminated by a flame.

And she finally saw them.

Sophie gasped: inside the mountain there were a dozen of the most majestic and terrifying creatures she had ever seen. Sure, she knew that the dragons were big and that they looked ferocious, but nothing had prepared her to actually seeing one.

Actually, *big* was a gross understatement. The largest were absolutely enormous. There were two of them, looking very similar to each other. They had reptilian bodies, with leathery wings folded on their backs.

One of them was curled up, seemingly asleep, while the other was awake. When a second blaze erupted, Sophie shivered, seeing the creature's fangs, which were pointed and longer than a man's height, yellowish, crusted with something that could have been blood.

At first, she thought that their scaly bodies were black or very dark, but after a while she noticed that under the light their scales reflected metallic hues of different colours, dark red, petroleum-blue, even bright yellow.

"So?" Nadia asked, her eyes sparkling again. "What do you think?"

"I..." Sophie began. "I..." her voice died in her throat.

Nadia laughed: "Same."

They were frightening... yet Sophie could not help but think that they were also beautiful. Even in the narrow space of the mountain, she could see how their bodies, despite the size, were graceful and sinuous. She imagined them flying, finally spreading their great wings.

She wondered how the rebels managed to keep these creatures imprisoned in the cave... then noticed the heavy metal chains at their legs, neck and wings. Around the two larger specimens there were some smaller ones: their bodies were slightly awkward, thin and long, as if they had grown too quickly.

"Wanna see Taneen?" Nadia asked enthusiastically.

"Who's that?"

"My dragon!"

Sophie stretched her neck out towards the interior of the cave. "Can I see it from here?"

"No, he's too small. Come on, come on, it'll be fun!"

Sophie had serious doubts about Nadia's definition of fun.

After they had climbed down, an experience that turned out to be even more terrifying but definitely less tiring than the ascent, Nadia led her to the other side of the mountain.

Two people were stationed at the entrance, patrolling the area. Sophie noticed they were wearing heavy protective suits and helmets, and had automatic rifles strapped on their backs. Nadia signed to Sophie not to make any noise.

The entrance was a huge area to patrol for two people, so when the guards had gone far off enough, Nadia and Sophie snuck inside the cave.

"Will they shoot us if they discover us here?!" Sophie whispered once they were a safe distance away from the two guards.

"No, of course not, calm down," Nadia downplayed. "They don't go around shooting people for no reason."

"Those guns..."

"They're not to keep people out," Nadia interrupted her. "It's to keep them in," she explained, motioning toward the centre of the cave.

Seeing the area from above, Sophie had not noticed this, but the cave was divided into several compartments by walls made of metal and plastic sheets.

"Over here!" Nadia led her to an area similar to a stall, with many small cubicles.

Most were empty, but in one Sophie noticed a large, iridescent egg. She would have liked to stop to observe it, but Nadia pulled her by the sleeve of her jacket.

"Here, come on!" she urged.

The small stall in front of which they had stopped contained a specimen about the size of a cow, in a dark colour that glowed with deep red and orange shades. Its muzzle was pointed, reminding Sophie vaguely of a large bird of prey.

When Sophie first saw it, it was lying in a corner of the barn, but as soon as the creature saw Nadia it got up on its two hind legs and trotted towards her, the chains at its legs stopping it before it could reach her.

To tell the truth, Sophie didn't think it was particularly pretty. It had nothing of the beauty of the great dragons in the large cave... in her opinion, it looked a little like a big plucked chicken.

Nadia opened the door, went into the barn and began to stroke the dragon's scaly head.

"Hi... hi, you cutie! How are you? Have you slept a little?" she whispered, her voice full of tenderness. "He's cute, isn't he?" she asked, turning to Sophie.

"Um... it's very... very..."

Actually, she was in a bit of a strait. The young dragon behaved like a puppy, rubbing its great head against the girl's body and uttering rasping sounds of appreciation, but she would not call it *cute*. It was pointy and awkward, and, frankly, rather ugly.

"I'd offer you to touch him, but I'm afraid you would get burned. You know, they are very hot, we feel it too. Eighty degrees or so."

"Ah, er, that's too bad. Did you choose the name Taneen?" Sophie asked to change the subject.

Nadia nodded: "Yes, although actually it's not his official name. The rule is that each of them has a serial number, an alphanumeric code… How sad, though! I could not continue to call him D3AA9006."

"Yeah, that's quite impersonal. Is it a boy or a girl?"

"Neither. Or both, depending on how you see it. For them there is no difference."

The dragon raised its head and stared into Sophie's eyes. Its own eyes were a deep reddish-purple, with vertical pupils, similar to those of a feline. They were bright and shining, like precious stones set in its skull. Sophie could not help but get lost in that stare, which seemed to be strangely timeless. They were not the innocent eyes of a puppy, but those of an ancient creature that gave the impression of possessing forgotten knowledge, memories of former eras, as if just looking at them you could…

The dragon coughed, throwing out an irregular blaze from which Nadia moved away just in time.

"Sophie?"

She stirred, realizing that she was lost in her own thoughts.

"Look at the time! We'd better go, I heard some noises."

Sophie blinked, feeling vaguely fuzzy-headed: "OK."

When she returned to the village, Sophie was dying to talk to someone about what she had seen. She preferred not to discuss it with James, because she did not know what he thought about breaking Cain's rules, so she decided to go find Emma.

In the last few days, busy as she was with her work at the hospital, she had not seen much of her. Emma had not entirely overcome her atavistic fear of the infected. Several weeks earlier, however, she had begun to leave the house and walk around the town, without even wincing every time someone passed her by.

She didn't quite get along with Britt, her host, but sometimes she met with two ladies of her age who shared her passion for knitting, and who had involved her in the making of a large quilt or something. Sophie vaguely understood that they had to knit a certain number of patterned squares each.

Every now and then James asked Emma for blood samples, in order to build a sort of sample bank to be studied. He had asked her permission and the old lady had accepted. She seemed to trust James, with his calm and reassuring demeanour, although Sophie knew that it required enormous self-control on his part.

It seemed, in any case, that Emma has found a kind of her own space within the community.

When Sophie came to see her, she found Emma in her room, wielding her knitting needles at her usual fast speed. While she was telling her about the dragon, Sophie saw that Emma was growing more and more agitated.

"But... Sophie, how close did you get to them?"

"Not much, don't worry... just to the puppy."

Emma opened her mouth in an expression of amazement: "There are puppies?"

Sophie nodded: "Yes, some, and even an egg not yet hatched."

"What about the adults? How many?"

Sophie told her about the two mastodons within the cave.

Emma stood up, visibly upset, and began to pace the room. "Dragons…" she muttered. "Right here, so close..."

Sophie realized that telling her had been a mistake. Her friend was not ready to live with the idea of having these creatures only a few kilometres from her. She recalled that Emma had lived throughout the epidemic, the rebel attacks; maybe she'd lost her loved ones because of the dragons. She cursed herself for her insensitivity.

"Look," she tried to remedy, "I assure you that they can't get out and attack us."

"They are dragons!" Emma snapped. "How can they keep them imprisoned?!"

"Um, well, they have chains at the legs, the neck and..."

Emma appeared, if anything, even more upset: "Chains?" she murmured. "If they think that some piece of iron is enough to control dragons…"

"What do we know of dragons?" Sophie objected. "Apparently chains are good enough. The whole thing seemed well organized, as far as I could tell."

'Well organized' was perhaps a slight exaggeration, but in fact she didn't get the impression that those beasts were struggling to break free. The situation had seemed more or less under control.

Emma took a deep breath and sat back down in the armchair.

"Maybe you are right," She said, in a very unconvincing tone. "Yes... they surely know better than we do... they know what to do."

"Of course, yeah," Sophie confirmed, in the most reassuring way she could manage, but she noticed that her friend's hands were still shaking.

Chapter 19

Shortly after the false fire alarm, Erik was summoned to see Murray, who paid him compliments for his work and announced that from now on his duties would change, becoming 'operational'.

In practice, Erik found, it meant that he no longer had to do surveillance shifts and spend hours staring at the monitor. Instead, he would handle more delicate tasks, such as guarding the most troublesome prisoners and backing up the police officers who came to the medical prison for interrogation.

"Just so I know, will I get a pay rise for this?" Erik asked cautiously.

Murray laughed as if it was a joke: "Very funny, Persson. As if I had funds for staff..."

Another piece of good news he received was that he would not have to do night shifts, because normally the interrogations were carried out during the day. It didn't make any difference to the prisoners (the light in the cells was artificial, and there was no way to distinguish between day and night), but obviously the medical police did not want to work in the middle of the night.

Well, Erik thought, *at least I won't have to spend the nights in the company of narcoleptic Martinelli.*

"So, they're sending you to pod six," the latter said. "Poor you. I don't envy you at all!"

Erik gave a smile. It was hard to believe that Martinelli preferred monotonous drudgery to a real job in the heart of the action.

"You'll see," Martinelli assured him, noting his sceptical expression. "No one ever lasts long in that pod. After a while they all ask to be transferred. We'll see how long that takes you!"

After moving the few possessions he had at work into a new locker, Erik joined Dukas, the guard whom he had met during the alarm.

Nagy was suspended: it turned out that he was the one to provide the lighter Garcia, the wannabe fugitive, had used, along with cigarettes and other strikingly illegal items (a bottle of vodka and some unidentified pills) that were found in his cell. Nagy's possible complicity in the jailbreak had been immediately ruled out, but now he was facing an internal investigation for smuggling and trafficking. Erik definitely wouldn't have wanted to be in his shoes.

Dukas handed him a list with the names of the inmates and their cell numbers.

Erik began to peruse it: "What does the P next to some names stand for?"

"P is for plague. Not all inmates are infected," Dukas said nonchalantly.

Erik was stunned: "Not all…? But then why are they here and not in a regular prison?" he asked.

This was a medical facility, specifically designed for the imprisonment of the infected. Regular criminals (those who were tried for theft, fraud, murder…) were detained in an ordinary prison, a large and complex spectral building in the eighth ring he once had to visit in the course of his work. Not a nice place, Erik recalled, but it took years of trial for a suspect to get there.

Erik remembered that the inmate who tried to escape had seemed completely symptom-free, but the plague did not always leave obvious signs. At that moment he realized that Garcia probably had never been infected at all.

He thought he could still hear the man shouting: *'Why must I die?'*

Dukas shrugged: "I don't know. They have something to do with the plague, though… collaborating with the rebels, things like that."

"Were they tried for conspiracy or complicity in revolutionary activity?"

"I don't know, Persson!" Dukas exclaimed, sounding annoyed. "Can I give you some advice that will make your life more comfortable here? Let every man mind his own business."

Erik bit his tongue and resolved to be more diplomatic: it was his first day at a new job; this was not the time to make enemies among the new colleagues. There had to be an explanation … for example an internal agreement between the two structures to manage the resources more efficiently, he speculated. Maybe he could ask Murray, when he had the chance.

Erik began to read the names on the list, trying to make a connection between the names and the cell numbers. It would be more practical and less embarrassing not to have to constantly ask where this or that inmate was. There were also some code numbers, but certainly he would not be able to remember all those alphanumeric sequences.

Suddenly, a name caught his eye: Amanda Solarin.

It was the infected woman he had arrested a few months earlier. How could he forget? Her arrest had triggered the chain of events that brought him to lose his job and end up there... but surely there had to be a mistake. There was no 'P' next to her name.

"Why isn't Amanda Solarin reported as infected?" he wondered aloud.

Dukas looked at him: "Because she isn't, I guess?"

"That's not possible," Erik declared. "I went to fetch her myself, I remember it well. I had received her blood test results on my desk just before the arrest. She was infected, I assure you."

Dukas shrugged:" You can go and check if you want. Last cell in the left corridor. Fit as a fiddle."

Erik got up and walked to the cell.

Through the window he saw a tall and statuesque woman with short grey hair, sitting on the bed, apparently lost in thought. He remembered he had noticed her during Garcia's escape attempt. Now he understood why her face had seemed familiar.

He looked at her carefully: as far as he could see, she bore no signs of infection, but from this distance it was difficult to know for sure.

The woman looked up: "Let me guess, another interrogation? Today you came to pick me up earlier than usual," she addressed him sarcastically.

"No... I... uh..." Erik stuttered, surprised. He felt like a schoolboy caught cheating.

Solarin stared at him with an inscrutable expression.

"Have we met?" she finally asked, cautiously.

"Yes... well, not really, but... we kind of saw each other... during your arrest."

'*Saw*' was an extreme euphemism, actually. "Well, I was the agent who brought you in," he confessed.

The woman stood up and walked over to the glass to take a better look at him. She was really tall, Erik noticed, almost as tall as him.

"Ah yes, you were with the asshole who broke my nose. Thanks a lot. You know that even now I have to sleep on one side, otherwise I cannot breathe?"

Now that Erik observed her up close, he was sure that she didn't have the plague: her skin didn't have any scales or even wrinkles, but she had dark freckles on her nose and her cheeks.

"I thought you must be dead by now," said Erik.

"Because of a punch in the face? It would take more than that to bring me down."

Erik blushed. The idea of hitting a creature who was no longer human and was on its way to slow death was one matter but breaking an innocent woman's nose was quite another.

"I mean because of the plague. They sent me to arrest you because they thought you were infected but... well, there must have been a mistake, I think..."

"A mistake," she laughed bitterly. "Sure. Have not you noticed how I was released once the month of quarantine passed? I have to sneak in here every night... I just can't live without your delicious food, you know," she said, tapping her foot against the tray with the morning meal – a bowl of porridge the ingredients of which were hard to identify.

A sudden thought struck Erik: "You are being interrogated about the disappearance of Sophie Weber and Emma Lemaire, right?" he asked. Perhaps the investigation had really been passed to another department, and that was why he was told to forget about it immediately.

Solarin became more alert: "They didn't catch them, huh?" she smiled.

"No, as you very well know," Erik paused, cursing his big mouth.

The inmate, of course, had no idea of what had happened to her colleague and the elderly woman. Why did he have to babble? *What a fool,* he thought.

The woman laughed.

Dukas arrived, along with another guard and two medical police officers, who wore plain clothes with badges hanging from their necks.

"Move on, Persson, I have to take her to interrogation."

"Shall I do guard duties or...?" Erik asked.

"No, I'll take care of this myself," Dukas replied.

Amanda Solarin did not resist when she was handcuffed and taken away, but rather continued to laugh.

"See you soon, Persson. It was nice talking to you!" she called while she was being dragged away.

Erik stood in the hallway, not knowing what to think.

Chapter 20

Sophie didn't go back to visit the dragons' cave, but she began to think about its inhabitants much more often. Not just because of the great beasts - certainly, she had been impressed by the sight of them, but the main reason was Nadia, who spoke about Taneen all the time.

The girl, who was usually of few words and, Sophie had thought, a little grumpy, became a different person when she talked about the little dragon. Her eyes sparkled and her cheeks became redder. The fact that she could see him only seldom and in secret made her suffer very much.

"It's not fair!" she would exclaim. "There's a bond between us and the dragons! We should keep them with us!"

Karla was more cautious: "I understand that you want to be with him… but it would not be fair to him either. You really don't know how to handle him; he could be a danger to himself or to others."

Nadia snorted: "I *would* know how to do it. I can *feel* what he needs."

Sophie did not know what to think. She understood – or, at least, tried to understand - Nadia's pain at the forced separation, but she also believed it would have been very unwise to keep those dangerous beasts wandering down the road with nothing but a leash to keep them in check.

Though Taneen undoubtedly loved Nadia, she often ended up with a lot of burns and cuts all the same, because the dragon did not seem able to control his own strength. And he was just a puppy… Sophie shuddered to think of what the adults could do.

But hearing about Taneen's achievements was interesting: apparently, one of the main problems was flying, because it took a long time for the younger dragons to learn how to do it. It was understandable, given how they were kept confined at all times, with chains that greatly burdened their wings. Nadia claimed that Cain did not want the dragons to learn to fly at all.

At the same time, though, the rebels had used the dragons in battle on occasion, and so it was important that they could fly. The result was that, periodically, the people in telepathic contact with the dragons were allowed to take them out and try to make them glide from the hills, so they could learn to fly. According to Nadia, those were the best days of her life. She had suggested that Sophie should come and take a look next time she brought Taneen out, but Sophie was a bit worried that the situation could get out of control. However, she promised Nadia that she would think about it.

One day James showed up at the hospital and said he had come to take Sophie to the village.

"Sorry, urgent orders," he explained to the queued patients who emitted sounds of protest.

"Where are we going?" Sophie asked.

"Cain is back, he wants to see you. There will be quite a lot of people, so maybe it's better if you put the mask on."

She nodded: it was unlikely someone would touch her face, but in crowded places it was better to play safe. She followed James through the streets of the town, trying to gather her thoughts. She had heard so many rumours about Cain that she did not know what to expect from him. James spoke of him as a friend who helped him find his own place in the world, while Nadia depicted him as a kind of ruthless dictator who inflicted unnecessary cruelty upon dragons and the people bonded with them.

They arrived in front of a building in the centre of the town, which had once been the town hall.

"Sophie! Thank goodness you are here too!"

Emma and Britt joined them: Emma appeared very nervous, almost like when she had talked about the dragons.

"Don't worry," Sophie tried to comfort her while James and Britt spoke to each other about the rebels' last mission in Europa. "This Cain guy will most likely be entirely reasonable. I mean, nothing has happened to us so far, right? Why would he take it out on us now?"

Emma shook her head: "I don't know! I heard terrible stories... he's not like the others! With some of them you can try to reason, but he..."

The old woman broke off, because they had arrived on the first floor, on the threshold of a room where she saw a lot of people crowded around a desk. Sophie suppressed a shudder: she was trying to appear confident and optimistic for her friend's sake, but in truth she was very scared.

When James led them into the room, silence fell. Sophie looked around and saw a number of people whom she had never met before: a man with oriental features and heavy dark scales on his cheekbones looked at her with suspicion; a woman with very short hair, under which patterns of concentric scales could be seen on the skull, with open interest.

Then Sophie looked towards the occupant of one of the chairs at the desk, and realized it must be Cain.

Cain was not in a very central position, nor was he sitting on a chair different from the others, yet the focus of the room gravitated in his direction: all eyes were almost imperceptibly fixed on him.

When he looked up at her, Sophie could not help herself: "I know who you are!" she exclaimed in horror, instinctively stepping back. "You are the General! The one from the police's identikit."

A flash of tension crossed Cain's eyes, but it was quickly replaced by an amused look. The rest of the room chuckled.

"Ah, yes," he said. "I rather like this nickname, I must say. It sounds very impressive."

His voice was calm and deep, and for a moment Sophie was surprised it came from him. She had expected a completely different tone of voice... higher, colder, she imagined. Sophie observed him more closely. It was the same face she had recognized from the identikit, no doubt about it... and at the same time it was not.

The pattern of the scales had been represented faithfully, that was unmistakable. While most of the infected tended to show signs of the disease at the bones closest to the skin, his scales were placed seemingly at random, as if his body did not know how his skeleton was formed. A strip of scales crossed his face diagonally, and others seemed to make their way onto his temples, up under his thick brown hair and his very high forehead.

Unlike most survivors, his scales had a pale and ill appearance, like old hardened scars. The effect was alienating, much more than with the other infected, to the sight of whom Sophie had become accustomed.

His eyes had also been faithfully represented in the flyers: they were narrow, widely spaced, slightly bent downwards at the corners. In the posters they looked feverish and manic. In person, however, they just gave him a thoughtful look.

His body was never represented in the police identikit, and Sophie knew immediately why: it was easy to imagine him big and brutal, looming menacingly over an innocent passer-by. She had always assumed that he must be built that way. Instead, she discovered, he was a small man, even shorter than she was.

Although he was sitting, there was something asymmetrical about his posture, something vaguely out of place. She noticed that there was a crutch hanging from the back of his chair.

While staring at him with a mixture of curiosity and horror, Sophie wondered if the disease had interfered with his development as a child. But this was not possible, she inwardly corrected herself: no child survived the plague, it was well known.

"If she stares at you a little longer you will have to charge her a ticket," said one of the infected men in a cold voice.

Cain only raised an eyebrow, but James sprung to action and hastened to make the introductions: "Alright, these are Sophie and Emma. Emma is the person we spoke about with Amanda, the one who appears to have survived the plague."

Bystanders said nothing, but everyone looked at Emma with extreme curiosity.

"Sophie worked with Amanda, and helped Emma get to us. They fled from the medical police during Amanda's arrest, then hid here and there in the city for three days and finally managed to meet us. Since then, Sophie has worked here on the island, at the hospital, for some time."

The infected around her stared at her with something that seemed like admiration and Sophie knew that James had said exactly the right things to make them accepted.

Then he began to rattle off a series of names that Sophie was unable to remember: she only recalled that the man with Asian features was Ken, and the woman with a crewcut was called Famke. The guy who had joked about her staring at Cain was called Gregor. He seemed a bit older than the others and had a very pale complexion. His face was almost completely devoid of scales, but his sunken eyes and hollow face gave him a sinister look.

And then there was Cain, of course.

When James had finished introducing everyone, he spoke:

"Well, I'd say that's all. The reason we're all here is that we received reports about Elias and Amanda. They came in this morning, from a very reliable source," Cain began, without wasting time.

He stood up and walked to the front of the desk. Sophie felt her heart pounding in her chest and saw James's back stiffen.

"The good news is that Amanda is alive, and for the moment it seems that they have no intention to... terminate her," Cain continued.

Alive! After all that time! Sophie had hardly dared to hope, and yet...

"That bad news is that they are questioning her, and they seem determined to find out where we are."

James held his breath, and Sophie's heart sank: she did not know exactly how the police interrogations worked, but Cain's expression didn't bode well.

Seeing the look on James's face, Cain put a hand on his arm: "Jamie, they assured me that no violent means have been used on her yet. For the time being they are focusing on the use of thiopental. Not that it's a walk in the park, I know, but... well, it doesn't cause physical pain, at least."

James just nodded. He was too shocked to speak.

"We all know Amanda. She's strong, and she's doing everything possible to protect our location and the identity of our informants ... but we know it's hard to resist their methods for a long time. I think we should begin implementing the first phase of the evacuation plan and be ready to go as soon as we learn that our location has been compromised."

Famke gasped: "But the dragons... Cain, many of them are not ready. Some cannot even fly yet!"

He nodded: "I realize that, but I see no other choice. We can use the helicopters for the puppies, and the others... they must learn to fly as soon as possible."

The meeting went on.

"What about Elias?" James asked.

Cain sighed, and Sophie looked at the faces of the people in the room. They all looked very serious.

"I'm taking care of it," Cain finally said. "I don't think there is any choice."

"I don't think Elias would talk," Ken objected. "Surely that's not in his interest. After obtaining the information they want, why would they let him live?"

"You're right, but the risk is far too great. He endangers all of us."

"But Elias..."

"Sure, let's do nothing, like when he decided to leave on his own," Gregor said grimly. "I mean, it went splendidly, right? Nothing alarming like, I don't know, an arrest, or risking that he spills out everything about us."

Cain nodded. "I think you're right. We will not make the same mistake again. As to the evacuation..."

"You said you would do anything to get her out of there," James interrupted him, his voice full of repressed anger. "You said you would intercept the van after the arrest..."

"I assure you that we tried..."

"This is what you keep saying!" James snapped. "Words, always nothing but words! Meanwhile, my sister..."

Gregor stepped forward: "Sit down, James, you don't want to end up hurting yourself," he said, while one of his pale and knobby hands moved almost imperceptibly towards his right side.

Despite the seemingly calm tone of his voice, there was something very threatening in his demeanour. Sophie had the impression that he was a highly dangerous man.

James looked away and took a deep breath. Sophie knew he was trying to suppress the instinct to attack, as Nadia sometimes did.

Cain stepped towards him: "Jamie, I want to talk to you in private. Come with me."

He led him out of the door and began to speak quietly in the hallway.

Cain had a vaguely waddling and limping walk, but he seemed much more in control of himself than poor James. Sophie could not make out what they were saying, but she heard his low, reassuring, almost soothing voice.

It's all in his voice, she thought. *That's his best weapon. That's how he affects them all.*

She realized that Emma, who was standing beside her, stared at all the others with undisguised terror and had the look of an animal caught in a cage. Sophie touched her shoulder to get her attention and try to comfort her, but this only made her wince.

"I can't wait to be out of here," her friend whispered.

"Hang in there, soon it will be over."

She didn't understand why Emma was so scared, Sophie reminded herself, she hardly knew Amanda, so Sophie imagined that the information received was not very important to her. The only thing Emma seemed to be aware of was that she was locked in a room full of infected.

James and Cain came back inside. James looked gloomy but said nothing more.

Cain spoke of the possible evacuation again and said that fortunately there was another place where the dragons could be hidden. An infected with very dark eyes, who was called Xander or Sander, said he would take care of letting all the inhabitants of the island know about the evacuation plan.

Once the practical aspects of the matter were settled, the meeting was dissolved and everyone turned to go on their way.

"Wait, I want to talk to you two," Cain said, turning to Sophie and Emma. "In private," he added, addressing James.

With some apprehension, Sophie watched everyone else walk out of the room. What did he want from them?

Cain faced Emma, smiling and, she supposed, trying to look as normal as possible. Sophie was not entirely sure it was working. The smile stretched the scales on his face, highlighting them even more. Emma kept her face stubbornly low.

"Madam... Lemaire. Emma. May I call you by your first name?" he asked.

Emma made a feeble nod of assent.

"We have been looking for someone like you for years, even decades. Since the beginning of the epidemic. Someone whose blood might possibly put an end to all the deaths and the struggles that have divided us since the onset of the plague. Finding you is a revelation for us... a miracle."

Emma shrugged.

"It looks like you are still worried about your safety, but I assure you, none of us have any intention of hurting you. Indeed, we are extremely happy to have found you. Now," he continued, sounding more practical, "I know that James began collecting some blood samples, so we can analyse them. We do not know yet if it will be enough. For the moment I would prefer that you continue staying on the island, at least until we have made some progress in generating the vaccine."

"It's... yes, fine," she said, in a weak voice that was unlike her own. "Can I go now?"

Cain appeared puzzled: "Of course."

Sophie remained in the room, shifting her weight from foot to foot, not knowing exactly what to do. There was nothing special about her blood, and she had found herself in all this turmoil by accident. She wanted to ask Cain when she would be allowed to return home, but she did not know exactly how to introduce the subject.

"Sophie... that's your name, right?" he asked.

"Yes."

"First I would like to thank you for bringing Emma Lemaire here. James told me that you have been through a lot to... sorry, could you take off your mask?" he stopped in mid-sentence. "It's a bit awkward to talk like that," he added, frowning in an expression of amused bafflement.

The room was no longer crowded, so it was not a problem. Sophie took off the mask and, with some relief, finally breathed freely.

"That's much better. As I said, I know you have overcome great risks to bring Emma here, and this is something I am very grateful for."

"Yes. Well… OK, you're welcome," Sophie said, anxious to get to the point. "But now I've been here for a while and I don't know... I mean, I think... I have to go back home."

Cain blinked: "Well, in truth I hoped you could help us a little longer."

"Look, I know you want me to help with the research. James told me. But I can't, really. Amanda was the one who did all these things. I'd only waste your time."

"Really?"

"Sure. She was the one who was doing the real research. I would just... er, take care of the equipment, help with the archive, things like that."

It was a gross exaggeration, and Sophie knew it. But if she let herself become involved in this impossible project, she would never be able to leave the island.

The place and its inhabitants had proved less terrible than she had thought at first, it was true, but even so she didn't want to spend months, possibly even years, isolated there.

Cain looked at her for a long time. Finally, he said: "It's funny you should say that, because Amanda had always stressed that, if something ever happened to her, we would have to rely on you. 'Sophie is my right hand; if I know anything, she knows it too.' That's what she used to say."

"She was always too kind," Sophie said.

Cain raised an eyebrow: "Amanda? Are we talking about the same person?"

Sophie had no satisfactory answer. She blushed, aware of being caught.

Cain stood up and walked over to her: "Listen to me, please. I understand that you're not excited about staying here long term. We are taking every precaution to make sure you don't become infected, but even so, I realize that there's a risk. Think carefully, though: if you went back to Europa now, where would you go? The police are still on the lookout for you. There are flyers with your face on them at all the train stations. And I hope you're not thinking of simply reporting to the police and saying that you are not infected. You think they still believe that Amanda has the plague? They know very well that she is as healthy as a horse... and yet she's still in prison."

Sophie looked away: in fact, she had thought about doing something like that. She didn't really have a plan, but she had always assumed that, once she clarified the misunderstanding, somehow she could...

"You wouldn't be able to work, nor would you have access to food distribution. You'd be like the outcasts of the underground tunnels. Is that how you want to live? Months, even years, without ever going out in the sunlight? You can survive, of course, but it isn't much of a life. Believe me, I tried it myself."

Sophie didn't know what to say: the prospect of returning to the city was not rosy, certainly, but on the other hand... no, she could not imagine a life here, in the midst of those strange, unpredictable and dangerous people. This was not her place.

"I guess I'll have to make do," she said.

Cain made a long pause, and Sophie had the impression that it was a very calculated gesture. "What if I made you a proposal?" he finally said.

"What kind of proposal?"

"If you go back to Europa alone you would be out of the system, with no way to re-enter it. But we can help you. We have ways to give you a new identity: a new name, a new assigned apartment, a new food card ... even references for a new job. You would have to get away from the places you used to know and keep to areas where no one would recognize you. It would not be exactly your old life, but it's the closest thing you can get."

"But you want something in return."

Cain smiled: "You make me sound so mercenary," his voice lowered. It was almost a caress now: "I prefer to see it differently... I'd say that if you help us work on the vaccine, at least until Amanda is back, it will be our responsibility to re-integrate you into the society. You would be no longer alone."

Sophie hesitated: she could see the attractiveness of his proposal.

After all, she could tolerate some extra time on the island, provided that it was a temporary solution, of which she could see the end of. Part of her was alarmed at the idea of being bound to an organization of rebels ... but there was also a part of her that wanted to believe Cain, that wanted to stop worrying about the future and let someone else take care of it for her. Someone else who would deal with finding her accommodation, food and employment, just like the government had done before.

"Moreover, I understand that you and Emma have become pretty close in this period. I'm sure you wouldn't want someone else, someone who does not even know her, to experiment on her."

Sophie looked up: was that a threat? Cain was still wearing a quiet and amiable expression, but the implications of his statement were all the more sinister.

"Fine," she said then, slowly. "But we have to put a time limit. I can't guarantee anything. Most likely, if I can't find a vaccine after a certain period of time, then it is something beyond my abilities. Let's make it... three months, and then you must get me back to Europa."

Cain's eyes flashed: "Three months sound like a very short time for something like this. I would say you'd need at least a year."

No, Sophie thought, it was too much; she would not last a year here. "Six months," she said.

He stayed silent for a moment. "OK," he held out his hand and she took it. Like her, he wore gloves. Nevertheless, for a second she could feel the warmth of his hand.

When she emerged from the building, she went to visit Emma, who was very upset.

"That creature, Sophie... it was horrible! I could not even look at him... Those scales, and the way he walked... oh, it was absolutely grotesque!" she said, shivering.

Sophie shrugged: yes, Cain looked weird, but she had not found him that terrible.

"Well, to tell you the truth, I thought he was worse," she said, recalling Nadia's words about him being despotic and little inclined to dialogue. "All in all, he seems like a reasonable man."

Emma looked at her in surprise, then took her hand. "Sophie, what are you talking about?" she asked, almost gently. "That creature is no man."

Chapter 21

Though Erik had vaguely welcomed the idea of participating in the interrogations, it only took a few days for his enthusiasm to vanish.

He would enter the cell of an inmate with a colleague, handcuff them, escort them to the interrogation room and then wait in a corner as a safeguard in case the prisoner became violent in the course of the questioning. At regular intervals he was supposed to remind the officers that it was time for a pause: interrogations had fairly regular procedures that included breaks for the officers and medical checks on the prisoner. Sometimes, however, the officers preferred to continue, and in that case Erik had to go on waiting.

Sure, it was more interesting than passively observing the flickering black and white images of the surveillance monitor, and there was, in theory, the chance that he'd have to rely on his reflexes and take action to prevent a prisoner from attacking the officers, but soon he realized that it was a very remote possibility. Until now he had not done anything but stand and listen to long silences and denials by the inmates, and the monotonous and repetitive questions from his former colleagues.

The worst part, in fact, was not the boredom, but the feeling that he would have been able to do a much better job than the officers he had to listen to in silence. At times, observing the interrogated inmates, he would notice their stubbornly impassive faces change their expression slightly, or see them move uncomfortably in their seat. *Here*, he longed to say to the officers, *that's where you have to insist!*

But often the newbies did not notice those small signals; soon the moment was lost and he could not do anything, because he was not authorized to. This was life.

At the moment, for example, an infected named Elias Visser was being interrogated by two officers with whom he had worked on occasion, Gabriel Dupont and Olivia Lehmann, who were trying to get the prisoner to reveal the location of the rebels' headquarters. The stammering, embarrassed greetings of Erik's former colleagues had felt terribly humiliating... he could never imagine they would meet again on such terms.

Elias Visser must have been a little rodent-faced man before he was infected. Despite being disfigured by the disease, it was evident that he was pale and his face was tense. He was jerking one foot, as if in the throes of a nervous tic, and looked very tired. Nonetheless, he kept staunchly replying that he knew nothing.

Erik could not prevent his thoughts from wandering. Finding out that Amanda Solarin had been imprisoned here on the very evening of the arrest was disconcerting.

It shouldn't have been difficult to ascertain that she was not ill. As for the charges against her, claiming that she had joined forces with the rebels... certainly it was a very serious accusation, but this was not the place to hold and interrogate her. She should have had a lawyer present during the interrogations. It was pretty evident that the police had used the supposed disease to rob her of all her civil rights.

When he asked Murray about this, she only replied that it was not their job to ask why the prisoners were moved here, because these orders came directly from the central headquarters. The documents that accompanied Amanda Solarin were clear: she had to be interrogated and detained.

Murray had interrupted Erik's objections in a tone that left no room for argument: "Persson, I consider myself a reasonable and understanding person. I have always done everything to avoid discontent and ensure that things run smoothly in this hospital. As you can see, the inmates are not mistreated and their living conditions are not inhumane. Your crusade must end immediately," she stated sharply. "Remember what I told you during our first meeting? Don't forget what our role is. Inmates are here for a reason. We are at war and must trust the decisions of those who have the big picture. Or am I supposed to think that you cannot handle the stress of your new position?" she suggested.

Erik was left with no other choice but to declare that that was not the case and backtrack. After all, following orders was what he had always done, and until that moment he had never regretted it. However, the idea of playing along with the arrest of a person under a false accusation made him feel guilty.

And, deep inside, he began to doubt that Amanda Solarin's case was an isolated one. How many times had he heard anything of the fate of the captured infected, admitted that they were such, after their arrest? Hardly ever, certainly not in recent years. Erik had always thought he was protecting innocent citizens and guarding their safety, but what kind of safety was it that allowed anyone to be arrested and imprisoned on a charge that allowed no defences?

He realized he was paraphrasing one of Maja's favourite sentences against the government. *"What security is there in not being able to make choices?"*

Lately he began to listen more carefully to the discussions between Maja and Peter, cautiously chiming in. After all, his kids were now almost adults, he could talk to them. They were deeper and more interesting than he had previously thought... but too often he had to put up with the slimy Marc Werner too. As much as he tried, he could not understand what his daughter saw in this fellow and had to hide a grimace of disappointment each time his pleasure of Maja's company was marred by Werner's presence.

"Visser, if you go on like this we will have to resort to more forceful methods," Dupont's threatening voice shook him out of his reverie. "You don't want to return to the basement cells, right?"

Visser looked away and said nothing. Erik was sure that he was afraid. He wondered about the basement cells and shivered. His thoughts ran to Amanda Solarin.

Certainly, they would not have tortured a human, uninfected woman... *No, of course, not - that would be unacceptable.*

Dupont paused and left the room. Olivia Lehmann stayed, and was silent for a moment. She poured a glass of water and handed it to Visser, who accepted it with a trembling hand.

"Come on, Elias," Lehmann finally said, her voice low and confidential. "Give me something to work with, and we can end it here for a while... You could negotiate. You have the information we need. You could sell it well. Why do you keep hurting yourself instead?"

The well-known game of the good cop and the bad cop, Erik thought. The two officers undoubtedly lent themselves well to their roles: Dupont looked fierce and aggressive, while Lehmann was short and pretty. But he remembered seeing her fire at three infected without blinking, years earlier, during an arrest that they had carried out together. Appearances were deceitful, but Visser could not know this.

"It's nice that you want to protect your former comrades, really. I admire you, in a certain way," she said, her voice more persuasive. "But ask yourself, Elias, is it really worth it? We found you alone, away from the city and from them all. Did they leave you there? Maybe they had driven you away from the rest?"

"I... I went away," Visser admitted.

"Really? Why?" she pressed him, appearing genuinely interested.

"Cain," he hissed, his voice full of hatred.

"He took my dragon away from me," Elias continued.

"I understand," Olivia nodded, even though Erik was pretty sure she had no idea what Visser was talking about. "We could help you get it back."

Visser lifted his gaze, and now he looked positively hopeful: "Could you?"

"Of course," she assured, leaning towards him. "But you have to give us some information. Something that can be used to bargain for you. Come on, Elias, give me a hand... why do you have to take all this to protect that Cain guy?" she said with contempt.

It was evident that Visser was tempted by the proposal. "I need to think about it," he finally said. "Can I have a few days?"

Erik was astonished: the two officers were not as clumsy as he thought. The tactic seemed to work.

Olivia leaned back in her chair: "Well, you know, Elias, the more time passes, the less relevant your information becomes. The sooner you speak, the more you will be able to gain. This is in your own interest."

"If I speak you have to let me go," Visser said with determination. "And I want a helicopter or something that can fly. Can you do that?"

Yeah, sure, Erik thought.

"I think it's possible," Lehmann nodded. "So, where is Cain?" she asked.

Visser looked away: "Before I speak, I want everything to be perfectly clear. I want freedom and a helicopter," he said stubbornly. "When I have it written down, black on white, we can negotiate."

"Alright, seems fair enough to me," Olivia agreed.

The tablet in Erik's pocket vibrated to tell him it was time for a medical examination, and he gestured towards Lehmann, who nodded back.

"Now, I'm taking you back to a cell in this pod, okay? No more basement cells," she said to the inmate.

"OK," Visser nodded.

"We will talk again later."

"Yeah."

Erik escorted the prisoner to the door, behind which Dukas was waiting. Together they took Visser to a quiet cell that had just been cleaned up, so that the janitor came out of it just as they were taking him inside.

It's all part of the art of persuasion, Erik thought: if you collaborate you get a nice comfortable cell, otherwise you end up rotting in the basement.

A doctor presently came in. He usually carried out the routine checks to make sure the inmate didn't die or was seriously injured in the course of the interrogation. In this case it seemed an unnecessary precaution, but Erik had seen others leave the interrogation room looking not so great. The day before, for example, he saw Amanda Solarin taken back to her cell, supported by two guards. She did not look hurt, but she seemed confused and slightly drunk. Later Erik discovered that a kind of truth serum, which didn't work on the infected, was used on the human subjects. For the rest of the day Amanda Solarin was left in her cell, unconscious most of the time.

Erik had peered into her file while Dukas was in the bathroom and discovered that she had a brother who was suspected of being infected and part of the resistance. The medical police also had strong suspicions that Solarin cooperated with the rebels, but it was unclear what her involvement was or if she had any information of real value. *This was probably the reason why they didn't go as heavy on her as on Visser,* Erik mused.

After having left Elias Visser in his cell, Erik went ahead to Amanda Solarin's. He just wanted to check on her condition. Try as he might, he could not avoid feeling guilty about her whole situation.

The woman was awake. "You again," she welcomed him when she saw him in front of the glass. "What do you want?"

"Look, I'm sorry about your nose." Erik began. "I shouldn't have allowed that. We usually don't hit people, it's just that... well..."

"... You got carried away?" she suggested coldly.

"No!" Erik defended himself, aware that this was the classic excuse of a pathologically violent subject. "I am not like that!" he took a breath. "But we thought you were contagious, and that if we don't neutralize you, you might harm others. My partner was scared and I… I was scared, too," as he said it, he realized it was true. He didn't normally talk about his reaction to the infected in those terms (he preferred to talk about dislike, or zero tolerance or even hatred), but the truth was that deep inside, part of him felt nothing but a blind terror.

"Well, I'm sorry for what happened. I wanted you to know," he concluded.

Amanda Solarin stared at him with an unreadable expression. "Thank you," she finally said. "I appreciate your honesty."

There was a moment of silence.

"Can I do something for you?" offered Erik. "As long as it's legal," he added with a half-smile.

"In that case, no," Amanda said. "Well, on a second thought, a bit of paracetamol would not hurt. The stuff that they shoot in my veins gives me a terrible headache. Let's pretend that you have given it to me for the broken nose."

Erik nodded. It was only paracetamol. Nagy had smuggled much worse until a few days ago. He was about to say something and leave, when he heard a scream coming from down the hallway.

"What's going on?" Solarin asked.

"I don't know."

Erik ran to another guard, a young boy named Simons, who was staring at Elias Visser's cell in horror. Looking through the glass, Erik saw the lizard man's body hanging from a pipe in the ceiling.

Chapter 22

From the moment she had made the deal with Cain about the vaccine research, Sophie began to study all the material left by Amanda.

She found that, although she was already familiar with many of her conclusions, which her employer had shared with her, Amanda had actually gone much further than her officially published studies suggested. This was very encouraging, but it also meant that Sophie had to spend more time studying and combing through archives than she had counted on. Besides that, she also made several tests using the blood taken from Emma.

Of course, the islanders were not going to give up so easily on the possibility to consult a doctor, and therefore, in addition to the research, Sophie found herself doing several hours of medical practice each day. The result was that for many weeks, she had no time for herself, nor any leisure to think about dragons, about Europa or about her future.

On the one hand she felt tired, but on the other she was also thrilled. After all the time in which she had done nothing but hang around, the sense of having a purpose, a goal, was definitely a good feeling.

"Now that you're settled here for a while, you might as well get a house," Karla had suggested. "You don't have to go on staying with James."

"I don't know, actually. We might have to leave the island very soon."

In fact, Sophie had no inclination to leave the comfortable accommodation she had found. She liked living with James; for the first time in many years she found comfort in sharing her space with someone.

With James she could speak about her research, which he seemed to be quite familiar with (no doubt thanks to his sister), life in Europa, and even the strange fascination she had for dragons. Since the infected were now constantly training the dragons in preparation for the flight, she could admit to having seen some of them without exposing Nadia's secret.

Though he was a good listener, James was also able to understand when Sophie did not want to talk too much. And he cooked very well, which was something she greatly appreciated. Although Sophie had always loved solitude, she was not crazy about the idea of living alone in one of those damp and forlorn cottages.

"Oh, the evacuation!" Karla commented with a dismissive gesture. "Do you know how many times they started 'Phase One'?" she said, sounding deliberately pompous. "At least five or six times since I came here, every time some of us get caught."

"Yeah, twice since last year," Nadia confirmed.

"It seems that Cain likes making us pack every few months. Don't worry, I'm pretty sure that nothing will come out of it this time either."

On the few occasions Sophie had some time, she was persuaded by Nadia to go and visit Taneen again. Following the decision to implement the famous Phase One of the evacuation plan, a woman named Famke began training the younger dragons in flight, without the participation of those who were bound to them, which made Nadia absolutely furious.

"If I could go with him, he would learn much more quickly… they don't seem to understand that!" she protested. "And they didn't even take off all his chains. It's a miracle if he can get up half a meter."

Yet, despite Nadia's gloomy predictions, Taneen and the other dragons were actually learning something. She and Sophie, sheltered behind a hill, had seen them flying awkwardly around a pole to which they were secured by a chain tied around their neck. Their progress was slow, to be sure ... but also undeniable.

Sophie found herself more and more fascinated by these creatures. They were so... intense, and much more intelligent than they appeared at first glance. Taneen had a very deep, albeit nonverbal, communication with Nadia, and she always knew how to interpret his moods. Sometimes, Sophie caught him staring at her with the strange impression that he understood her far more than she might expect. She had even begun to appreciate the creature's beauty, despite having thought him awkward and ugly in the beginning.

Part of it was no doubt due to the fact that Taneen was growing quickly, not so much in size as in shape: from the moment he was allowed to take off, his limbs had begun to grow in a more harmonious way, suggesting the elegance that he would have as an adult. In any case, Sophie was beginning to understand the Nadia's passion for her dragon.

Sophie had talked with Cain on two occasions after their first meeting: in both cases, he had showed up to ask her about her research. In truth there was not much to say, as she had just begun studying the material and did not have anything new to report; however, Cain seemed satisfied that Sophie had started to work. From his very precise and relevant questions, she had the feeling that he knew the subject better than it seemed. She didn't investigate, however.

Although he was always very cordial, even friendly, there was something about him that put her on the alert: something vaguely threatening, as if his eyes (which, of a colour between green and blue, would have been beautiful on another face) could probe more deeply than she meant them to.

For the rest of the time, she didn't see him very often. Although he was, as it seemed, the leader of the community and of the rebels' resistance, he often disappeared for long stretches of time, to somewhere on a remote corner of the island.

"Why does he go there? Sophie asked Nadia, intrigued.

Nadia shrugged: "No one knows. Minding his own business, I suppose. He's a weird guy."

"And no one has ever followed?"

She laughed. "I would not dare to do it ... would you?"

Sophie thought about it: "Actually, no," she admitted.

She promised herself not to think too much about the movements of the elusive Cain.

Sophie was trying hard to get on top of the whole vaccine issue.

The day she finally got to analyse Emma's blood personally, she repeated the antibody tests three times. She could not believe the result. When she was reasonably sure of what she had discovered, she rushed to see her friend.

"Sit down, dear, you look upset... what is it?" Emma greeted her.

"Emma..." Sophie said. "You never use protection for your hands and face, right?"

The old woman shrugged: "Well, no... I mean, I thought that I definitely can't contract the plague again, right?"

Sophie ran a hand through her hair, confused: "No... I mean, yes, that's what I thought. But I'm starting to have some doubts."

Emma paled. "Doubts?"

"I ran some tests today and... well, the result is very strange. I don't know how to explain it..."

"Please try, I ... I need to know."

Sophie nodded: it was true, Emma deserved an explanation.

"Well, you see," she began, "The immunoglobulin G, a type of antibody, gives information about past infections, while immunoglobulin M tells of ongoing infections. Unlike the other infected, you have a higher value of the Igg, than the Igm. This is because they still have an ongoing infection, despite not being in danger anymore, while you recovered completely."

"I understand."

Sophie nodded:" Yes... the problem is, it seems to me that your Igg values are... too low."

"What do you mean?" Emma asked, frowning.

"They don't suggest that it's a disease you contracted a few weeks ago... if I found this kind of value for another disease, let's say toxoplasmosis, for example... I would assume that it's something you've had years ago."

Emma stared at her, saying nothing for a few moments. "Oh," she finally said.

"Yeah..." Sophie shrugged. "The only possible explanation is that these plague antibodies, as exceptional as they are, fall apart very quickly. For now, you are still immune, but..." she sighed, "there is a definite possibility that you won't be immune forever... or, actually, for long. And that's why you have to promise me that you will begin to use gloves and a mask as I do, and that you will avoid as much as possible any kind of physical contact with the people here, OK?"

"Yes, yes, of course," Emma agreed. "I hardly ever have contact with anyone even now," she laughed nervously, almost hysterically. "I promise you that I will be more careful."

"Ok, good. This makes me feel better."

Sophie did not mention the other problem that she saw arising from this news: her agreement with Cain did not include the release of Emma and her reintroduction in Europa, but if the old lady ran the risk of being infected, it was clear that she could not stay among the rebels forever.

One night, Sophie was sleeping peacefully, when James stormed into her room.

"Sophie... Are you awake?"

She got up with a start: "Um... no... I mean..." she rubbed his eyes, feeling befuddled. "Now I am. What's going on?"

"There's an emergency," he said. "I need you to come and help me."

"An emergency? Does it have anything to do with..." *Amanda,* she was going to say. *Or maybe Emma?* She was not sure, but she suddenly felt wide awake.

"No, it's..." James seemed uncertain. "Well, get dressed and come with me to the hospital. Wear your protective gear," he added.

Sophie wasted no time on washing her face, but she put on protective clothing, gloves and a mask. A few minutes later they were walking at a good pace in the crisp night.

"Now are you going to tell me what happened?" she asked.

"A person was wounded," James explained.

"Oh." Was that all? Sophie did not understand the reason for so much mystery. "Is it serious?" she asked. "How were they injured? Where?"

"You'll see in a moment," he assured. "You'll have to be discreet, though. Sophie, please, promise me you will not speak about it."

She looked puzzled: "No, of course I won't..."

"Not even with Nadia and Karla."

"I said I won't. Professional confidentiality, remember?"

Amanda had told Sophie that once upon a time, all doctors had to take an oath, a very ancient one, that originated in Greece thousands of years ago. They didn't do it anymore these days. Sometimes Sophie wondered if she could even consider herself a real doctor.

Her words, however, seemed to convince James: "OK," he said.

An old green jeep, its paint almost completely peeled off, was parked in front of the hospital. They entered the building, and James took Sophie to one of the rooms still in use.

A figure writhing in pain was lying on a stretcher. When Sophie got close enough to see his face, she stepped back in amazement.

"Cain!" she exclaimed.

The man raised his head, his face contorted in a grimace of pain. Sophie saw that his clothes were soaked with blood. After a moment of surprise, she recovered her nerve.

"Help me take his shirt off," she ordered James.

She took a pair of scissors from a drawer and, while James held the patient down, she cut off Cain's shirt, or what was left of it: it was torn in shreds. Under it, she saw deep cuts, in part cauterized, mixed with burns. By now, Sophie had seen that kind of injury all too often not to understand what had caused it: dragons.

But Cain never got close to the dragons, Nadia always said so. Perhaps he had been attacked? She had no time to lose on guessing: she had her patient to think about. First she gave him a painkiller, then carefully wiped all wounds, bandaged the burns and set about mending the cuts. But when she began stitching him up, Cain still writhed in pain. It seemed that the painkiller was not as effective as she thought it would be: Sophie had already noticed that she had to use higher doses than normal on infected people, but in Cain's case the increased dose was not enough either.

"I can't stitch him if he moves like this," Sophie said. "But I'm afraid to give him more morphine, I might… overdose…" *And kill him,* she thought, though she did not say it aloud.

"Increase the dose," Cain gasped.

"I have already used much more than …"

"It doesn't matter…" he interrupted. "For me it's different…"

"I can't…"

Cain grabbed her arm: "Nothing will happen… I promise you…"

Sophie looked at James, who shrugged. She didn't know what to do: she did not want to take any chances, of course, but it also seemed inhumane to leave him suffering. In addition to the cuts that she had to mend, there were burns that had to be very painful - at least third-degree. She saw Cain's forehead beaded with sweat and noticed how pale he was.

"OK," she finally said. "You're sure you can handle this?"

Cain nodded, with great effort: "Yes … quite sure."

Sophie took a syringe and injected him with more morphine. After a while, Cain's body relaxed, and Sophie hurried to stitch the cuts.

"How can he be conscious after such a dose of morphine?" Sophie wondered, turning to James.

"The bodies of the infected follow different rules, but Cain's got its own rules."

"Why?"

James shrugged: "I don't know. Maybe because he's one of the first people who was infected."

That intrigued Sophie. "Really?" she asked. "How did it happen?"

"I don't know. You should ask him, perhaps, when he is feeling better."

Sophie chuckled, embarrassed: "I don't know if I would dare," she admitted.

"I assure you, he might be hideous, but he's not as evil as he looks," James said with a wink.

"I'm still… awake… just so you know," gasped Cain.

James grinned. "Sorry, boss. We didn't mean to gossip before your unconscious body."

Cain laughed, which turned into a coughing fit. Sophie glared at James: "Don't upset him!"

She was surprised to notice the familiarity that existed between the two, despite their differences. For the first time, Sophie realized that they were actually friends.

Once she had finished stitching and bandaging, there wasn't much left to do. Cain's temperature was very high, but she could not tell if it was a fever: the infected usually had higher body temperature than normal people. In any case, it was better for Cain to spend the night in the hospital.

"He is not in any condition to be moved," Sophie stated. "But you can go home now," she told James.

"I think it would be better if I stayed here, should there be any problem," he argued.

"James…" Cain said with effort. "You must go check on… you know what…"

James appeared uncertain: "I…"

"It's very important… there is no other who can…"

"All right, I'll go," James agreed. "I'll be back in a couple of hours."

Shortly after James left, Cain began to stir. "The dragon!" he exclaimed. "He's close, he's right here... he wants to set himself free!"

"There is no dragon," Sophie said. "Please, calm down!"

Cain seemed to look right past her: "You don't understand... he always knows where I am. He knows how to sneak in my thoughts... I have to stop him..." he shouted, grabbing her by the arms.

Sophie thanked her lucky stars for the protective gear she wore, or she would surely have been infected. Cain looked like a different person: his usual self-assured way was gone, replaced by a blind terror that he didn't seem able to control. His eyes were feverish, like those of a madman. He attempted to rise, and it took all of Sophie's strength to push him back down on the stretcher:

"Please, listen to me. What you're feeling is not real. It's the morphine, you understand? You're high." *I shouldn't have given him so much. Damn!*

"But the dragon..."

"There is no dragon. Calm down, I beg you."

Only when he agreed to lie down again, Sophie realized how scared she had been. Even though he didn't look particularly impressive, his arms were stronger than she had expected. She wondered whether he'd be able to throw her to the ground if he hadn't been so weakened by the pain and loss of blood. *He probably would.*

"They took James's sister," he suddenly said. He still looked very confused, but at least he didn't seem to be aggressive anymore.

"Yes, Amanda," said Sophie.

"I am so sorry... it shouldn't have gone this way..." Cain groaned.

Sophie pitied him. He seemed genuinely crushed by the thought of Amanda's imprisonment. She brushed his wet hair from his forehead: "It wasn't your fault," she said, trying to comfort him.

Unfortunately, it didn't quite work. Cain shook his head: "Nothing should have gone this way... my brother... I had a brother, you know? David. He... he was such a good person... well... he was the only..."

Despite the situation, Sophie could not help but feel intrigued: Cain had a brother? It seemed impossible to imagine him as a part of a family; but then again, he had to come from somewhere.

"He taught me everything..." Cain went on, "...reading, riding a bike, playing chess. Only he could get close to me, you know? It was just me and him... until... until... I don't know... I don't know what happened..."

Cain stopped, apparently losing his train of thought. A few minutes later, Sophie heard his breathing become more regular, and finally she realized that he had fallen asleep.

Sophie felt Cain's brow with a gloved hand, noticing that his temperature had lowered: he was sweaty, but his face was not flushed as before.

She began to clean up the room, washing away the blood and sterilising the instruments she had used. Then she made tea with a kettle that she kept in the next room and drank it slowly. Finally, she allowed herself to curiously observe her patient for a long time. Cain was lying on the stretcher: he was still wearing shoes and trousers, but his chest was uncovered except for the bandages that she had just applied.

The proportions of his body were vaguely wrong, although she could not say exactly how: perhaps his limbs were shorter than normal, his legs more crooked, his chest stockier. If she had to liken him to anything, she would have said he reminded her of Taneen, the first time she had seen him, in part because of the uneven scales that he had here and there along his body. Unlike the dragon, however, Cain would never turn into a more powerful and elegant creature. She noticed that his hands, too, were covered with patches of greyish-pink scales. *This must be why he always wears gloves.*

He's so ugly, Sophie thought. But no, it was not entirely true. He didn't look weak or sickly: the muscles of his chest were lean and defined, albeit crisscrossed by scales and scars, as well as those of his arms.

When Sophie saw him for the first time, she hadn't noticed anything but the usual characteristics of the infected, the pattern of the scales and his different way of walking... but now she paused to notice other, more ordinary details.

He had a hint of a beard around his mouth and chin, but not on the cheeks, which were smooth as if hair couldn't grow there. Where there were no scales, his skin looked fair and clear. Sophie knew that everything about him was the exact opposite of what a man should be... and yet, she found herself thinking, there was something about him, something that left her speechless. *Like a dragon.*

The thought embarrassed her, and she looked away, looking for something to do. Emma was right: she was losing touch with reality.

When Cain awoke a few hours later, he was back to his usual self. Sophie was almost asleep on the chair: she was very tired after all the excitement of the night, and his deep and rhythmic breathing had lulled her into a numb semi-consciousness.

"Good morning," he said, quietly and, she thought, suspiciously.

"Ah... hello. How are you feeling now?" Sophie asked, stretching on her chair.

Cain looked around, examining the bandages that covered his wounds. "Well enough, I think," he said finally. "Thank you for your assistance."

"It was my duty," Sophie replied.

Now that he was back to his own self, he seemed even more reserved than usual, as if he was wondering what he had done or said under the influence of the painkiller. Sophie checked his wounds and changed the bandages, noticing that the burns had already begun to heal. The wounds she had just stitched up, too, were almost completely sealed; she also noticed that, though Cain certainly didn't look in his best shape, his fever was gone.

"You are recovering faster than I would have thought possible," she said. "You must have special regenerative powers, or something like that."

Cain gave a tense smile: "Something like that."

There was a moment of nervous silence.

"Sophie, thank you so much for last night," she saw him groping for the right words. "I hope I haven't done or said anything inappropriate that I can't remember..."

She decided to save him from embarrassment: "Nothing serious," she said with a smile. "You rambled a bit about dragons coming, something like that. Don't worry; short term confusion is a very common side effect."

Most likely he wouldn't have wanted to remember speaking to her about his brother: it was too personal and knowing he had done so would only make him uncomfortable. Pretending it never happened seemed the best thing to do.

Cain looked relieved: "I understand. I didn't do anything embarrassing, I hope... I don't know, tell bad jokes or something?" he chuckled.

The thought made her laugh: "No, don't worry. But how did you get yourself in such a state?"

He did not lose the slight smile, but something in his eyes became alert: "An accident with the jeep. I was returning to the village and lost control of the vehicle."

Sophie only raised her eyebrows but said nothing.

They were supposed to wait outside for James to take Cain home, but he seemed unable to stand on his own feet, so Sophie helped him get to the exit. Without his crutches, he had a swaying, irregular walk.

"There is one last favour I need to ask of you," he said. "Don't tell anyone about the events of last night. I know that may seem like a ridiculous request, but I must count on your confidentiality."

Sophie nodded: "I already promised that to James. But..." she bit her lip, not knowing how to go on. "The least you can do is tell me the truth about your accident."

Cain stared at her without saying anything.

"I know that your injuries were caused by a dragon. I have been here for months now, do you think it's the first time I've seen something similar?" she said. "If you want my help, I think I deserve to know the truth."

Cain continued silent.

"If you don't want to tell me about your business, at least don't tell me lies," she went on, gaining courage as she spoke. "I don't think of myself as a particularly nosy person, but no one likes to be lied to."

"Alright," Cain said finally, slowly. "The truth is, I'd rather not go into the details of my accident. But yes, you're right, it was a dragon. Is this enough for you?"

Sophie nodded:" I think it is," she sighed. "Let me know if you need more painkillers. These burns might take a while to heal."

Cain shrugged: "I probably won't need any more. My injuries usually heal pretty quickly. My superpower, remember?"

Sophie smiled.

"You know…" Cain said, thoughtfully. "I was thinking... you're quite friendly with Nadia and Karla and have met many people on the island."

"Yes," Sophie confirmed, not understanding what he was trying to get at.

"Maybe you could help me deal with them. I know many feel a lot of discontent about... how some things are handled here."

Discontent was something of a euphemism, Sophie thought. Nadia hated him through and through.

"But the dragons, the plague, and all that is connected to them... I'm sure you understand how dangerous they are."

Sophie thought about it: "Well... I don't know. I mean, yes, I know they are dangerous, but the bond that some people have with them..." she shrugged. "Maybe it could be a useful thing."

Cain just looked at her for a moment. He really had a very intense gaze, and Sophie realized that she couldn't avert her eyes.

"I wish we could talk more about it, but..." he sighed. "Not now. I ask you to trust me, however, and think about what I told you. Do you agree?"

"Yeah, sure," she found herself answering. She didn't know why. She didn't really agree, but she could not say so.

After all, being involved in the politics of the island was something that could come in handy, even for Nadia and the dragons. *Better me than someone else, perhaps someone with bad intentions.*

"I'm glad you came to the island," Cain said.

"Yes, well... I... me too," Sophie stuttered. It was not exactly the truth, but somehow, that was what she felt at the moment.

Once Cain left the hospital, Sophie reflected on his words. What did he want from her? *Usually*, he had said, as if his accidents were quite common. Assuming that they were accidents in the first place, of course: in fact, his wounds seemed more the product of a struggle.

But why did the dragons wanted to hurt him?

Or, Sophie thought with a shudder, maybe he was the one who wanted to hurt them?

Chapter 23

Erik was sitting on the couch in the living room, next to Peter who, for a change, was tapping incessantly on his tablet. Under normal circumstances he would enjoy the day off, but these days he could not stop thinking about the death of Elias Visser.

Police officers and the medical administration of the prison had no doubts: according to them it was a clear case of suicide. Visser had used the sheets to fabricate a crude noose, and died instantly, the pressure breaking his neck. No clues of any possible reason for the suicide, or anything that would suggest a murder were found in the cell, which was unsurprising, as the deceased hadn't been there for more than a few minutes before he died.

When Erik had been notified of the result of the investigation, he couldn't help but express his doubts: "But that doesn't make sense!" he exclaimed. "Visser was negotiating for his freedom. He saw a real possibility of being released. Why would he kill himself?" he asked Lehmann and Dupont, taking advantage of the confidence given by his old job.

Olivia Lehmann shrugged: "Unfortunately this happens more often than you imagine. Maybe it's the guilt that leads them to kill themselves before betraying their comrades, or perhaps the experience of the interrogations..." the agent leaned towards him, lowering her voice. "I confess that even I don't completely approve of certain practices that we are forced to use. But what choice do we have? In any case, many of the lizard men are unstable. Visser was obviously one of them."

"Yeah," Dupont nodded. "In the end, anyway, nothing should surprise you when it comes to the infected. The disease messes up their minds on many levels... let's face it, they don't really act in a logical way," he concluded.

Erik, however, was not convinced. Since his transfer to the prison, it was becoming more and more evident to him that the infected were not crazy wild men with unpredictable reactions: granted, some could be aggressive, but this was a situation that occurred in all detention facilities. From what he had been able to see, most of the infected did not behave so differently from human prisoners. *If Visser had been human, there would have been further investigation.*

Out of habit, perhaps out of boredom, Erik could not stop thinking about possible ways in which a murderer could have entered Visser's cell. The hospital had very tight security, and inmates were never in direct contact with anyone who was not part of the staff.

The first way that came to his mind was the administration building, where the security checks were less strict. However, from there it would have been very difficult to reach the detention areas, so he discarded this hypothesis. The murderer could have infiltrated the hospital through the service of cleaning and maintenance, though. In regular prisons, these tasks were usually assigned to the prisoners themselves, but of course this could not happen here, so the service was outsourced to a cleaning company.

Erik had discovered that every maintenance worker had an identification badge similar to that of the security staff, but they didn't need to undergo retinal scans. When they needed access to a level which required it, they were accompanied by a guard. He also noticed that, though the badges were supposed to be for personal use only, the workers would often use each other's badge (Erik suspected that their employers, to avoid hiring extra staff, required them to perform a greater number of hours than was accepted by the union, and the exchange of badges masked this shady practice). In any case, it was a serious gap in terms of security.

Besides the janitors, part of the medical staff was civilian as well. For them the controls were very tight... but he could not rule out the possibility that some of them were linked to the rebels, like Amanda Solarin. Of course, if he began to suspect everyone, he would have to suppose that even guards like him, or the officers themselves could be spies... but Erik found it really hard to believe, as he had been reluctant to suspect Zoe Hernandez or Hoffman. He could not, however, get rid of the uneasy feeling that all his activities were closely controlled by the rebels, as if they had eyes and ears everywhere, first in the police headquarters and now in the hospital too. He felt he was constantly observed.

As for Solarin, that was another question that gripped him. He could not resign himself to the idea that she had been arrested and was being brutally interrogated without the possibility of an appeal. He had begun to carefully comb through her file and discovered that she was also a brilliant researcher who had worked for years in search of a vaccine for the dragon plague. So even if she had contacts with the rebels, she was not a subversive who wanted to spread the disease and destroy the social order. She wanted to cure the disease, and she might even have succeeded. She seemed like the kind of person to have on the right side, not one to be locked up in a basement and tortured.

"Hey, Dad, are you listening?" Peter startled him.

"Um... to tell you the truth, no," he admitted. "Sorry."

"Mom told me to ask you if I can go out tonight," he said, looking hopeful.

"And where would you go?"

Peter snorted: "But I've just explained it!" he protested, "Maja and Marc are going to this place where there's a band playing. Can I go too?"

"Maybe Maja isn't really in the mood to babysit her little brother when she goes out with her boyfriend," Thea suggested, entering the room.

"Her boyfriend? Is it official now?" Erik winced.

Peter laughed: "Dad, they've been dating for, like, centuries."

"Bah," Erik commented dryly. "We'll see how long it lasts."

"I hope it lasts a long time. I like Marc. He always listens to me carefully and doesn't treat me like a child," Peter said.

"I don't know... It's just..." Erik grappled for the right words to express his feelings. "He has too many teeth."

Thea looked sceptical: "How can he have too many teeth? He must have thirty-two of them, like everyone else."

"I'm positive he has more," Erik insisted. "When he smiles, he looks like a shark."

Thea laughed. She was so beautiful: when she laughed, she looked once more like the girl he had fallen in love with. It was such a shame that lately she was always so gloomy and distant. Not that he did not have his own faults: instead of enjoying his day with his family, he did nothing but thinking about moles and murders.

"Anyway, can I go?" Peter insisted.

"Come on," Thea attempted to reason with him. "Why would you want to go and ruin their romantic evening?"

"You know what, Peter? I think you should go," Erik chimed in, shuddering at the thought of his daughter clinging to that guy, maybe with cheesy music in the background. "And since you like Marc so much, spend some time with him, tell him all about your conspiracy theories. I'm sure he will be delighted."

"I'll send a message to Maja to tell her to come and pick me up!" Peter lit up, tapping again on his tablet.

"Go on, send it along!" Erik urged him.

"You're wicked!" Thea whispered to him.

Erik shrugged: "I know."

Anyway, when Maja and her *boyfriend* (Erik had a twinge of disgust at the thought) arrived, they were all smiles, and if Marc was disappointed, he was careful not to let it show. Erik was preparing his uniform for the next day: he'd have to get up early in the morning and was planning to go to sleep soon.

"Isn't it a bit late to go out?" he objected.

"But Dad, nobody starts playing before eleven!" Peter protested in alarm, perhaps afraid to lose the opportunity to spend the evening out.

"Hmm, if you say so..." Erik muttered, feeling the pockets of his uniform. "Thea, have you seen my badge and my tablet?"

"I think I saw them on the coffee table in the living room," She replied.

In the living room? He really should have tried to be tidier. When he looked on the table, however, he didn't see his badge or his tablet.

"Come on, Peter, are you ready?" asked Maja. "We're leaving!" She seemed impatient but looked happy. *Well, in the end that's what matters.*

"I'm coming, let me just put on my shoes," Peter shouted from his room.

Erik felt a tap on his shoulder and turned around. "Excuse me," Marc Werner said, with one of his oversized smiles. "I think you were looking for these," he added, handing him the tablet and the badge.

"Ah yes, I was just looking for them," Erik admitted, reluctant to accept any favours from this fellow, "Thanks."

"My pleasure," Marc said, still smiling.

Too many teeth, thought Erik, shaking his head, while the three left the house. *Far too many teeth.*

Chapter 23

On the next day Erik discovered that Simons, his young colleague, was suffering from suspected post-traumatic stress. Apparently, the discovery of Visser's body had greatly upset him, and the hospital psychologist gave him a few days of rest.

"So overdramatic!" Dukas said with a shrug. "Wait until they put him on duty in the basement! What will he do, run away screaming?" he laughed, watching Erik as if awaiting his approval. Erik offered a set smile, but in his heart he sympathized with the young guard. He had probably seen too many corpses to be traumatized, but he understood Simons's distress much better than Dukas's crass insensitivity.

"Anyway, since the boy wet his own pants," Dukas went on, "We've got to replace him. Today Solarin's interrogation is all yours. Come on, let's bring her to the interrogation room."

Erik hesitated: he did not know why, but the idea of assisting the interrogation of Amanda Solarin made him uneasy. Though he could not claim to have witnessed real torture against the questioned infected (which allegedly took place in the basement cells), the persuasive methods of the officers could be very rude, if not violent. He didn't like the idea of having to stand by while two officers mistreated the woman.

However, he had no choice, so he followed Dukas to Solarin's cell.

"Come on, stand up!" his colleague urged her. "You've got some talking to do."

"Such a pleasure, I can't wait," she said dryly. "What happened to Simons? Did he go back to playing with toy cars?"

"He was shocked by the premature demise of your friend Elias," Dukas replied. "Don't get any ideas, eh! It was not a pretty sight, and I really wouldn't want to pull another corpse down."

"I don't have the slightest inclination to become one," Solarin assured.

That was comforting, Erik thought.

Along with Dukas, he escorted Solarin to the interrogation room, and settled the timer on his tablet. Dupont and Lehmann arrived shortly thereafter, accompanied by a doctor.

"Your arm," the latter ordered Solarin, then injected her with something. After a few minutes, her gaze seemed to become clouded and her posture slumped.

"So, Amanda, tell me about your brother James. Where is he now?" Dupont asked.

Amanda smiled dreamily: "Jamie. I have always called him Jamie."

"Yes, Jamie. Where is he?"

"We were born together, barely a few minutes apart, but I have always considered myself the eldest. Even if technically he came out first... actually, this means that the foetus that I became implanted before his..."

She went on talking incoherently for a while. Whenever she spoke of her brother, Solarin recalled some anecdotes from their childhood, often contradicting herself. Sometimes she claimed that her brother had died as a young boy, at other times that he was there in prison with her. It was difficult to separate facts from fantasy.

"Amanda, James is not here in the hospital. He's with the infected, with a man named Cain. Where are they?" Dupont insisted.

"Behind the bed there is a tunnel, which passes through the sewer. That's how I'll run away from the hospital... I will walk the tunnel to the manhole," Solarin stated.

Lehmann rolled her eyes, as if to say 'here we go again'.

"Amanda, there is no tunnel in your cell. We checked many times. Where are James and Cain?" Dupont asked.

Erik's mind began to swirl: the tunnel to the manhole... sure, there really was one! It was not behind the bed in her cell, though, but next to the stretcher in her study. And the manhole was the one that he and Zoe had found months earlier. Amanda's delirium was not as random as the officers believed.

"Cain... Cain says that no one is indispensable. Not even himself."

"So you know Cain. You are in touch with him!" Olivia Lehmann encouraged her.

Amanda shook her head: "I fear for Sophie. Who knows where she is? Cain will never let her go. No one has ever come back..."

"Sophie... Would that be your assistant Sophie Weber?" Dupont checked the file. "Is she your contact among the infected?"

Everyone is expendable, thought Erik. This included Sophie Weber and... Elias Visser, perhaps? Was he sacrificed because he was going to confess? *So there has to be someone who is passing information from the inside.*

"Sophie and Lukas will be here soon. I have to give them some work to do. We are already late and the patients will be here before long!" Solarin exclaimed.

It soon became obvious to Erik that any further response Amanda Solarin might give would likely be too confusing to provide any actual information. The two officers seemed to have the same notion, because when the timer clicked, they sent Solarin to her cell without further insistence. Amanda was curiously inconsistent and could hardly stand up, and Erik gently eased her down upon the bed. When he left the cell and went back to lock up the interrogation room, he heard Dupont and Lehmann whispering to each other.

"She does nothing but rant, this stuff is useless," Dupont said. "I'd say that this settles the matter. Next week we'll switch to Phase Two."

"Oh gosh, I really don't feel like it," Lehmann commented. "You know, the infected are one thing, but torturing civilians makes me sick."

At these words, Erik turned pale.

Chapter 24

After Cain's accident, Sophie doubted for a long time whether it was appropriate or not to tell Nadia about it. After all, she was involved in an indirect way, as one of the dragons that could have attacked Cain was her own. There was definitely something fishy about that whole business, and Sophie would have been sorry if anything happened to her friend or the little dragon.

However, there was the issue of confidentiality: she didn't like the idea of talking to Nadia about something that she was explicitly asked to keep secret. And in any case, she was uncomfortable at the idea of violating the privacy of a patient. That had always been one of her red lines. So in the end she decided to say nothing.

She had tried to talk to James, but these days he was distracted, and she realized that he was not listening at all.

"Sorry, Sophie, but I have other matters to think about now," he said abruptly.

He had just found out about the death of Elias, another infected who apparently had been kept in the same prison as Amanda and was very concerned. Sophie was disappointed, but she understood that he had far greater concerns, so she decided to keep her doubts to herself. She regretted her decision shortly after.

She was doing some work in the lab when she heard noises from the outside. She left the hospital to find a crowd of people gathered in the square in front of the house where Cain lived. At the centre, she saw Nadia. Her friend seemed distraught: her face was red and tense, contracted in an expression of anger and fear.

"You can't do this to me!" Nadia shouted. "You have no right!"

"The decision has been taken," Sophie heard Cain's voice. She was surprised by how cold he sounded. It took her a moment to spot him at the edge of the group of observers. His expression was hard and controlled, the exact opposite of Nadia's, but the hand holding the crutch was stiff with tension. Sophie wondered what could possibly have happened.

"This is not… fair!" Nadia yelled. "You can't take my dragon away!"

Sophie gasped: take Taneen away? No, it was too cruel, even for Cain.

"It wouldn't have come to this if you had followed the rules on contacts and visits. But it is clear that I can't trust you, so I'm forced to send him away."

"It will kill him! It will kill us both!" Nadia replied. Now her voice was more like a whimper.

Cain rolled his eyes: "Don't be melodramatic. The dragon will be fine. He will be taken to a safe place, as required by the evacuation procedure and..."

"Melodramatic?" she shrieked. "You have no idea what you're talking about... I... we... there is a bond between us and the dragons! Why do you continue to pretend it doesn't exist? It's... unnatural, perverse, it's..." she was stammering for words.

"Nadia, we've talked about it, not once but many times. Dragons are dangerous. This bond must be kept under control..."

"You are just jealous!" Nadia spat out.

Sophie sensed a subtle change in the mood of the crowd: from discomfort to open curiosity, as if waiting to see what Cain would say. Apparently, Nadia had hit a nerve.

"Do you think I'm the only one who figured that out?" she continued, unstoppable. "Everyone says so. Everyone. You are a control freak, and you're just jealous because you'll never have your own dragon, and that's why you blame us and..."

Cain exchanged a look with a woman at his side (Famke, Sophie remembered), who grabbed Nadia by the shoulders.

"That's enough," she ordered.

"No!" Nadia struggled. Two other henchmen, Gregor and Ken, grabbed her.

"Take her somewhere to calm down," Cain ordered to the two, then turned to Famke. "You take care of the dragon. I want it off the island within a week at most."

Famke nodded and Nadia let out a cry of pain that seemed to go beyond despair. Within moments she was taken away.

The crowd that had gathered looked alternately at Cain and in the direction where Nadia had disappeared. Some muttered among themselves. The atmosphere seemed full of fear and discontent, and Sophie could well see why. She could not imagine anything crueller than separating someone from the dragon to whom they were bonded. Nadia was right: it went against nature.

"What are you looking at?" Cain snapped suddenly.

Someone standing in front of him jumped back, and everyone started to disperse to the square and side streets. Sophie, however, approached him, determined to talk.

"Was that really necessary?" she asked.

Cain stared, appearing surprised by her vehemence: "Of course it was necessary, otherwise I would not have done it."

"I think that separating Nadia from her dragon is detrimental to both..."

"And on what basis do you believe that? Huh?" he pressed. His voice was still low and controlled, but Sophie could see the anger in his eyes.

"Well, my medical expertise..."

"Your medical expertise!" Cain repeated with contempt.

Sophie was furious: "Yes, exactly, my expertise, which you weren't so contemptuous about when you needed it for the research or," here she lowered her voice to be heard by him alone "...to stitch you up the other night. If such a deep bond exists between two people, or beings, or whatever you want to call them, cutting it off so suddenly could have dangerous consequences for both. I think that's a bit like trying to separate a baby from its mother. It cannot be right!"

Cain rolled his eyes: "A dragon is not an infant. I appreciate your concern, but there are too many things you don't know and..."

"Of course there are!" Sophie said, taking a step forward. "You never tell me anything! Nobody tells me anything! You keep uttering mysterious hints about the dangers of dragons and the connection with them, but never say anything definite!"

At the end of her tirade, Sophie was breathless. She realized that there were only a few centimetres between her and Cain. One step more and they would have touched. For a moment she wondered when was the last time she had shouted at someone like that, allowing her anger and frustration to come out so openly.

For a moment they simply looked each other in the eye. The air around them seemed strangely charged. Sophie almost wanted to take another step forward, towards him... but this was nonsense. Touching him meant a risk of infection. The moment quickly passed. They both stepped back, almost at the same time.

"Sophie," Cain said, "I understand how you feel, but the business of the dragons is... tricky. A thorny problem. You haven't been here long enough to fully understand. I must ask you to trust my judgement."

At first, he seemed embarrassed, but as he spoke, his voice took his usual distant tone. For some reason, this annoyed her.

She took a breath: "How can I trust your judgment if you don't even take mine into account?"

Cain just looked at her, as if he didn't know what to say. She turned around and walked away from him as quickly as possible.

Sophie poured some tea into Nadia's cup, and noticed that her friend's hands were shaking. Since she had been kept from seeing Taneen, it seemed that her health was deteriorating: she was nervous and restless, ate little and slept even less. There were deep dark circles under her eyes, and the scales on her skin seemed oddly pale and translucent.

Karla was worried about her: she went to Sophie to ask for advice. There wasn't much she could do, though: she had advised Nadia to rest, eat potassium-rich foods, and take a walk every day, but she was painfully aware of how it all was, at best, just a palliative measure. Nadia needed her dragon, and nothing else.

"When did you say he will be transferred?" she asked.

"I'm not sure, they haven't actually told me anything. But Karla heard it's going to be tomorrow morning. I think they will use one of the boats, he can't fly long distances yet..." Nadia blinked, and a tear trickled down her cheek.

Sophie felt a pang: that forced separation was so unjust. She wondered if there was anything she could do, but nothing occurred to her. Her attempt to intercede for her friend with Cain did not bring any result.

"I have to go and see him one last time!" Nadia said.

Sophie shook her head. "Nadia, you have to keep away from him. That would be just putting both him and yourself in danger."

After all, the whole unfortunate situation would never have occurred at all if Nadia had followed the rules rather than sneak into the cave every other day. However, Sophie knew better than to say so.

"You don't understand," Nadia accused her grimly.

Sophie rolled her eyes: she was beginning to find this habit, shared by Nadia and Cain, of disparaging her understanding every time she expressed an opinion different from theirs, extremely annoying.

"Listen," Nadia continued, her voice suddenly urgent. "I was talking to other people... and we thought that maybe you could help us."

"What people?"

"Well, Marie, Paul... ah, and also Heinrich and Jane."

All the people telepathically connected to a dragon. Sophie sensed a prickle of danger.

"Nadia... Don't do anything crazy," she admonished her.

"On the contrary!" she assured. "We were thinking that you could study the telepathic bond that we have. Do some tests... you know, the ones where they attach sensors to the head, and see areas that light up... that sort of thing. Prove that this attachment is normal, that it's *scientific*."

"But what's the point? Everyone knows that this – this relationship between you and the dragons does exist, no one doubts..."

"Yes, they know that it exists, but they don't really understand. They don't know how strong, how intense it is...they think we can ignore it, cut it away just like that..." she began to mutter, probably thinking about Cain.

They wanted to be legitimized, Sophie realized. This kind of data could shake the trust of the small community in Cain's approach. Although he was in charge, if an opposing faction appeared, it would shake things up. The problem was that the telepaths were asking her to support them, to give them the means to challenge his authority... it was exactly the opposite of what she had promised Cain.

On the other hand, she saw what state Nadia was in, and wondered whether this suffering was really necessary. Helping her and the other telepaths seemed so right. Meanwhile, Nadia kept looking at her with feverish hope, waiting for an answer.

"I don't know," Sophie said eventually. "You know, I don't really have much time between the vaccine research and all the patients... I mean, such a study is not something you can do in a day…"

Nadia slumped on her chair, clearly disappointed.

"You won't help us."

"It's not that I don't want to... it's just that..."

Her six months were almost finished. She had not yet found a vaccine for the plague, although she had certainly made some progress. She had a formula that seemed promising, but she didn't know on whom she could try it. No animal had ever contracted the plague, and she certainly couldn't test it on humans.

If only Amanda were here... maybe she would know what to do. In any case, she couldn't start researching the bond with the dragons - there was absolutely no time.

When she emerged from the hospital she ran into James. He was wearing a protective suit and had a backpack.

"Going somewhere?" Sophie asked.

"Back to town," he said, strangely reticent.

"To do what?"

James looked uncomfortable: "Nothing special. I just feel that... well, I'm worried about Amanda, and I want to be around in case it's necessary to intervene."

"Cain said he was working on it."

James snorted: "Yes, well, he's been working on it for too long, and in the meantime Elias died. You know, when he went to this mission..." he shrugged. "We were afraid he would end up giving us all away."

"Do you think that Cain had him killed?"

He looked at her with condescension: "I know he did. He admitted it himself."

Sophie stared: "He would never do such a thing to Amanda!"

However, as soon as she said that she realized that she didn't have the faintest idea of what Cain would or would not do.

James looked away: "I don't know... but I don't want to take any chances. So I want to go to the city. You never know."

Sophie nodded: "I see."

Later that day she went to see Emma, looking for advice.

"It's you," Britt received her with her usual scowl.

"So it seems," Sophie replied in puzzlement.

"I thought it was Cain again."

Sophie raised her eyebrows in surprise:" Cain was here?"

"Yes," Britt confirmed, "After your skirmish."

"It was not a skirmish!" Sophie exclaimed.

Britt made a gesture suggesting that she couldn't care less for such subtleties. "Whatever. Anyway, he came here to see Emma. I don't know what he told her, but she was terrified."

"But that's terrible!" Sophie exclaimed.

When she saw Emma, first thing she asked her if she was all right, and what Cain had said.

"Nothing, nothing..." the old lady replied. "He took a blood sample from me. I don't know what he needed it for, but... Oh, Sophie, that creature scares me so much!"

Sophie told her about her doubts, about Nadia's request and her mad desire to see Taneen again. The old woman listened for a long time without speaking. In the end, however, when Sophie asked what she thought, she was surprised by the answer.

"The study seems tricky to do. But I think you should help your friend to see her dragon one last time, or at least be there when they carry him away."

Sophie blinked: she was sure Emma would warn her to mind her own business and not put herself in danger.

"Why do you think that?"

"Well, you know, when you love someone so much, those last moments before parting, though they might not seem important to others, are extremely precious to you," she said simply.

Sophie thought about it for a moment: "That's true," she admitted.

"Nadia will never forgive herself if she doesn't at least try to see him one last time, and if she is alone she could do something foolish. Even if she doesn't manage to actually meet him, the mere fact that you have seen her dragon and maybe have some information about where they are taking him will be a comfort to her... All in all, the dragons are a bit like children for these people. You know, when I think of when I lost..." her voice caught in her throat.

Sophie felt guilty for having made her relive the terrible moments of her past:" Oh, Emma, I'm so sorry ..."

Emma wiped her tears on the edge of her sleeve.

"You must think I'm an old sentimental fool."

"Not at all," Sophie assured.

She didn't imagine that Emma would have such an empathetic reaction to Nadia's plight, but, now that she thought about it, she could see that she was right.

She always tried not to dwell on this too much, but she remembered how many times, as a child, she wished she had had a few more minutes to spend with her family, and then with her grandmother… it was insensitive of her to underestimate Nadia's pain.

For the first time Sophie noticed that Emma was much more intuitive than she seemed, and that, despite not being very talkative, she listened to the people around her very carefully. She still seemed a little upset, so Sophie stayed with her until she had recovered, and then set off to find Nadia.

The air at dawn was cold and damp, especially near the sea. The small port of the island was entirely taken up with a cargo ship so dirty and battered that Sophie wondered if it would hold up to the journey.

She and Nadia were crouched behind a car, and watched Cain's men on the ship transporting supplies, computers, all kinds of electrical equipment and, Sophie noticed with a shudder, weapons. Even Cain himself was on the pier: it wasn't difficult to discern his small twisted figure. Sophie wondered, as she had often done that morning, why she agreed to help her friend with this crazy plan.

"Mind you," she said, "We see Taneen, say goodbye, give him a kiss, and go, OK?"

"Look," Nadia said with a fervent voice, pointing to a spot not far from them and ignoring Sophie's words. "He must be in there."

Sophie noticed a wooden crate on the pier, with holes to let some air in. It was secured by ropes, which presumably would be used to hoist it on the ship's deck. The figures on the crate said D3AA9006; Sophie remembered that was Taneen's official name. An acute groan, similar to the cry of a bird, came from the direction of the box.

"He's crying," Nadia murmured, looking on the verge of tears herself. "I have to go…"

She made to leave the shelter of the car, but Sophie held her back.

"Wait! Look at this."

Famke, the gruff henchwoman who was in charge of training the dragons, was approaching Taneen's box. She shook it briefly and ordered him to be quiet, then, when she was sure that her teammates were not looking, she pulled a piece of candy from her pocket and handed it to Taneen, stroking his big scaled head while he was munching. The groans stopped.

Sophie had to laugh: "You see? Famke looks tough, but her heart is in the right place. Taneen will be just fine."

Nadia ignored her again: "As soon as she goes away, I'll go and see him. You take a walk, get Cain distracted and find out everything you can about the ship and where it's going, OK?"

"Yes, yes. But you do pay..."

"... Attention, I know. Don't worry. I'll be extremely careful."

Sophie took one last worried look at Nadia, and then walked towards the main road, pretending to come from there, and approached the group of people that stood on the pier, among whom Cain stood.

"Hi!" She greeted them, trying with little success to sound casual and relaxed. "What a crisp morning, isn't it?"

They all went silent, and Gregor stared at her with a murderous glare: "Ah, the patron saint of lost causes. You're here for your friend's dragon?" he addressed her.

"What? No! It's just that I woke up early and couldn't go back to sleep..." Embarrassment made her extremely talkative. "... I thought, why don't I take a brisk morning walk, something which I always recommend to my patients, and I saw some activity here, and so I thought, 'hey, why not come and say hello?'"

Damn, just shut up! she told herself. She was not a very good liar. Even Cain stared at her with a puzzled expression.

"Oh, all right!" she decided to admit. "I wanted to see where you would send Nadia's dragon, and make sure that he's all right. I thought that knowing it would make her feel better."

It was not the whole truth, but it was definitely more credible.

Gregor took a menacing step towards her: "How thoughtful of you. Do you want me to take her away?" he asked Cain.

Cain shook his head wearily: "No, it doesn't matter. There isn't much to see, and in any case the ship is about to leave."

Sophie noticed that all the cargo, except Taneen's crate, had already been moved onto the ship. Gregor and the others walked away, leaving Cain and her on the pier. Sophie breathed a sigh of relief: Gregor made her shudder. She felt somewhat embarrassed around Cain after their discussion a few days before, but then Nadia had asked her to keep him busy, so she tried to make conversation.

"Where are you taking all this stuff?" Sophie asked. "Or is this also confidential information?" she added with a smile.

"To another island, much like this one. Our backup plan, let's call it," he said.

"Have you had any news of Amanda?" she asked, and this time she didn't have to feign her interest.

"She's still in the hands of the medical police, but we are making progress. We have sources very close to her captors that are giving us valuable information. We'll get her out soon," he assured.

Sophie was going to tell him about what James had said, but then she bit her tongue. Did Cain know about his departure? She was not sure, and she didn't want to risk him finding out because of her.

They walked on the edge of the pier. The sun was now high in the sky, and the fog had lifted. The day was clear, and the sea around them shone under its rays, which coloured it with warm metallic highlights. In other circumstances, Sophie thought, it would have been a nice walk. Who knew where Nadia was, though. Had she been able to say goodbye to Taneen? By now she had been away for a while, but she didn't know if she could dare to return.

"I thought for a long time about what you told me the other day," Cain said suddenly, "About trust."

"Really?" she asked, surprised.

Cain appeared uneasy: "Yes, I've thought about it and... basically, I think you are right, in part. I cannot ask you to trust me if you are not aware of everything that happened with the dragons. It's a difficult subject and it is related to how we were infected with the plague in the first place. So, I think it's fair to tell you everything."

"Well... thank you. I think that would help me a lot," Sophie said.

"Maybe we could talk about this later? I have a couple of things to attend to today, but tonight I will have time to explain it all."

"Of course, that sounds... great."

Cain smiled, and for a moment Sophie had the impression that he was genuinely pleased with her answer, as if he had feared a rebuff.

A sudden noise from the pier startled her. Ken ran toward them, gesturing for them to lower themselves on the ground.

"What's going on?" Cain shouted.

"The dragon! Nadia is trying to set it free!"

"What?!" Sophie could not help but exclaim.

Cain stared angrily at her: "Do you know anything about this?"

"Yes... no... well..." she stuttered. "That was not the plan!"

"We'll talk later," Cain turned to Ken. "Stop that girl at all costs, shoot her if necessary," he ordered.

"No!" Sophie cried, horrified "You can't do that! It's all a misunderstanding!"

"Sophie, stay out of this."

"Let me just talk to her, I'm sure that we can solve..."

The dry thud of something heavy hitting the ground interrupted them. With a shudder, Sophie saw that the Taneen's crate was broken: the dragon was standing on the broken wooden planks, and only a heavy metal collar attached to a chain was holding him back. Sophie realized that he had undoubtedly grown since she first saw him: his legs had developed, and his whole body seemed more robust and harmonious. He didn't look like a plucked chicken anymore: now he looked like a prehistoric lethal beast.

Sophie winced when she saw Nadia: she was next to the remains of the crate, trying to break the ring that kept Taneen bound with a hammer.

"Nadia, stop!" she shouted.

Nadia caught her eye, and Sophie caught a fleeting expression of regret; then she resumed hammering away at the metal ring. Suddenly she heard Gregor's voice, very close to her.

"Got her," he said.

"Shoot," Cain coldly ordered. Before Sophie was able to articulate her horror, Gregor fired. Nadia screamed and collapsed to the ground. Sophie didn't know how badly she was hurt; she only distinguished a silhouette that was moving feebly.

At that moment, the dragon seemed to go crazy. When the bullet struck Nadia, he emitted a loud bark, trembling in the grip of fury.

"Stop it before it sets itself free!" Cain shouted.

The chain attached to the collar of the creature tensed and stretched more and more... until with one last, violent tug Taneen broke free. The dragon rose on his hind legs and let out a mighty roar. The bullets that rained around him didn't seem to dent his armour of scales. Before Sophie could move, Taneen flung himself in the direction from which the bullet had come from: hers.

She only had time to see his jaws open wide, and a scorching spurt escape from his throat. Sophie closed her eyes, expecting to be hit by the flames: then, suddenly, someone grabbed her and threw her down. She felt the heat of Taneen's fire above her, very close, then the impact against the ground and the weight of someone's body.

When she opened her eyes, she saw Cain's face, dangerously close to hers.

"Are you OK?" he asked.

"Yes," Sophie said in a faint voice that didn't even seem to belong to her.

"Come on, get up!" Gregor urged them. He seemed to have dodged in time. Cain stood up with an effort; Sophie was feeling very confused. Taneen, meanwhile, was coming back, ready to attack again. Once more, he swooped down on them... Sophie heard a hiss, and someone's firm grip pulled her to the ground once more. Sophie turned around, half expecting to see Cain again; instead she found that it had been Gregor to pull her away from the danger.

The dragon gave a desperate roar, and Sophie saw that a large syringe was stuck in the creature's neck. Taneen fell to the ground, where he crashed with a thud. Behind him, Sophie saw Famke, with her gun levelled.

"Fentanyl," she explained. "How many times have I explained that you have to hit them in the neck? Everything else is useless!" she barked, turning to her companions.

Cain cleared his throat, then ordered to immobilize the dragon with multiple chains and transport it to the ship while he was unconscious.

Sophie ran to Nadia, who, she discovered, had been hit in the clavicle: the bullet's exit wound was on her back. For a normal human it would have been a devastating injury, but the greater physical strength of the infected meant that the bullet had caused much less damage than Sophie would have expected.

Nadia, however, was inconsolable because of Taneen: "What will they do to him? They can't take him away," she kept repeating hysterically.

"Why on earth did you try to free him? What were you thinking? It was madness!"

Nadia stared at her for a moment, glassy-eyed: "It was he who told me to do it. I had to," she simply said.

At that moment Cain arrived, trailed by Gregor and Famke.

"Take her away," he told them, pointing to Nadia. When the two pulled her up, she let out a groan of pain.

"You can take her to the hospital, her injury..." Sophie began.

"No," Cain interrupted, in a tone that allowed no objection. "This time we'll handle it. I let this unacceptable situation go too far. This time there will be consequences."

"You can do whatever you want to me, I don't care!" Nadia said defiantly. "Just know that whatever happens, I will find Taneen! You can't keep us apart!"

"I will make sure that you and that beast don't ever get together again, you have my word!" Cain hissed with hatred. "And if you try to oppose me, you will go the same way as Elias."

He did not even raise his voice, and yet there was something in his tone, a cold repressed anger, that made Sophie shiver. Looking again, she noticed that his eyes had become clearer and metal-hued, and the pupils had thinned.

Famke and Ken dragged Nadia away. That was quite inhumane in her condition. She was probably in shock, and, though the infected were stronger than humans, it was still a gunshot wound.

"Listen to me, please," Sophie said. "The situation got out of hand, but I don't think that Nadia deserves..."

Cain turned towards her and Sophie realized that speaking had been a mistake.

"Wasn't what you just witnessed enough? We could all have died!" he snapped. "And don't think for a second that I forgot you were involved in this sham of a rescue mission!"

"It wasn't supposed to be a rescue mission, I thought..."

"Don't you understand how these creatures make people lose control? I can't make up my mind if you're reckless or lying!"

"But Nadia just wanted…"

"Stop this!" Cain roared. "I thought I could trust you, but obviously I was wrong." he paused, catching his breath. "Come to me tonight, and we'll see if you change your mind about dragons."

Sophie was speechless. Only a few minutes ago they had talked like two friends, and despite the situation she had perceived his charm.

But what had seemed like a flattering invitation before, now sounded very much like a threat.

Chapter 25

When Erik Persson entered the staff room in pod six, he saw Simons was back: he seemed a little tense and jumped up in his chair when Erik opened the door.

"How are you?" Erik asked. "Are you feeling better?"

Simons nodded half-heartedly: "Yes, yes, just fine," he assured.

"Have you already done the eight o'clock round?"

The boy shifted uncomfortably in his seat: "Um... I was waiting for you. I thought maybe we could do it together, like starting from the two opposite ends, so that we finish earlier and..."

"Ok, OK," Erik interrupted him. "Maybe this morning I'll do it, alright? Why don't you stay here and..." he tried to think of a quiet, non-threatening activity, "Mark down the surveillance shifts hours?"

Simons looked at him with pure gratitude: "Sure, good idea, I'll do that!"

As he walked down the corridor checking that everything was in order, Erik thought that Simons absolutely had to be redeployed elsewhere. Maybe he could ask to be moved to administration: he was precise, meticulous and he didn't mind filling out forms. Yes, he thought, administration would certainly suit him much better.

When he arrived at Amanda Solarin's cell, he found it empty. He immediately checked the interrogation rooms, but they were empty too.

"What happened to Solarin?" he asked his colleague.

Simons looked at the timetable on the computer: "They are interrogating her downstairs," he explained.

"You mean torturing?" Erik exclaimed.

The boy paled: "Really? I don't know... here it just says interrogation... maybe they're not... you think they are?"

Erik, however, had no time for coddling his post-traumatic stress: "Sorry, I have to go to..." he hesitated "... to check on something."

He pushed the elevator button, but it took so long that he decided to take the stairs and rushed to the basement. When he stopped to slide the badge and look into the sensor for the retinal scan, he was sweaty and out of breath. He passed a series of seemingly empty rooms until he found Dukas standing outside a door. He was sitting at a desk in front of a computer.

"Is Solarin here?" Erik asked.

"Yeah, why? Is there a problem?" Dukas said.

"I... I'm not sure..." Erik said, trying to find an excuse. He was not quite sure why he felt the need to know what was being done to this woman.

Dukas shrugged indifferently. "You can take a look at the monitor."

Erik walked around the desk and found himself staring at black and white images that showed what was happening behind the locked door. A human silhouette which had to be Amanda Solarin was tied to a surface tilted back, and her face was covered with a cloth. From what he could see Gabriel Dupont was pouring water over the cloth. The woman's body shook as though in convulsions.

Erik's heart sank: he knew that Amanda must feel as though she is drowning. During his training he was once required to experience a sample of the same technique, even though much less water had been used on him and the whole thing lasted less than a minute. He still remembered the water in his lungs, the gag reflex that made him vomit, the acid fluid that had burnt his throat. And that was just a demonstration... they couldn't do this to a human, a civilian, whatever the charges against her were.

Erik whipped out his badge and opened the door.

"Hey, what the...?" Dukas protested.

When he entered the room, he immediately smelled vomit, and then heard an ominous gurgling noise coming from under the cloth that covered the prisoner's face.

"What's wrong?" Olivia Lehmann asked, apparently nonplussed. She had her sleeves rolled up, but apart from that detail she could have just stepped out of a quiet meeting at the police headquarters.

"You have to stop. The interrogation was rescheduled," Erik said confidently.

"Ah. How come?"

"Well... Boyer called from the headquarters. Apparently, he has some highly confidential information for you," he invented wildly. "He said that on no account are you to proceed with the interrogations before you implement the new security protocol. To know more about it, call Perez or Schmitt."

Boyer was a big shot from the first ring, Perez was in charge of computer security procedures and Schmitt was a gruff agent close to retirement who on principle never answered the phone or any message. All of them would be very difficult to track, and if Erik knew anything at all about how the medical police worked, Dupont and Lehmann would spend at least three days getting bounced from office to office before they realized no one knew anything about that call. But at that point it would be easy to pretend he didn't remember the event or convince them that he had misheard.

"Damn, that sounds serious. Thanks, Persson." Dupont said.

As the two officers were leaving, Erik removed the cloth from Amanda Solarin's face and tried to clean her up as best as he could. She didn't look good and continued to cough up water.

Dukas came into the room. "We need to call someone to clean this up," he said dispassionately.

"Can you take care of that? I'll take her back to her cell," Erik offered.

Dukas hesitated. In theory, the procedure required that prisoners should be escorted by two guards, but apparently he believed that Solarin wouldn't pose too much of a threat just then, because he finally nodded.

"OK, see you upstairs."

Amanda Solarin did not seem able to walk by herself, but Erik managed to lift her up to her feet and support her on the way to the elevator, and then up to her cell. She said nothing along the way, and Erik noticed that she seemed to have trouble keeping her eyes open.

He sat her down on her bed: "I hope you are OK... I mean, that it isn't..." he stammered. To be honest, he didn't know what one could say to a person who had just experienced the feeling of drowning.

"You'll be better in a while," he finally said, hoping to sound encouraging.

Amanda Solarin didn't answer, which was unusual for her.

"Can I do something for you? Um... do you want a glass of water?" he asked awkwardly.

Finally, she opened one eye and looked at him askance. "Are you fucking kidding me?" she whispered huskily.

OK, maybe she had enough water for the day, Erik thought. But at least she was sounding like herself again. "No, I thought ... never mind. Just call me if you need something, OK?" he said, moving towards the exit.

"You know, I was about to confess before you stopped them," she went on, as if she was talking to herself. "I would have told them everything I know, about Cain, the rebels, even about my own brother. It's funny, but, when I thought about this part of the interrogation, I've never been afraid. I'm strong, I thought, they can't bend me," she coughed. "Instead, I would have done anything to get them to stop. I didn't care if they killed me later, as long as they would stop." Her grimace might have been meant to be a bitter smile. "I guess I'm not as strong as I thought."

Erik didn't know what to say. Deep inside, he always hoped that everything was just a misunderstanding, that Solarin had nothing to do with the rebels. But now he knew that she had really helped them all along. Erik knew this was supposed to justify any means that were used to get information out of her. And yet...

"Look, all these things you are telling me... you've got to tell them to a lawyer, not to me, nor to those two," he finally said. "You have a right to a trial and a defence. Maybe you're guilty, and in that case you will spend the rest of your life in jail, but..." he shrugged. "Well, not here, and not like this."

"Good speech, Persson, that was very enlightening," she commented sarcastically. "You know, I haven't made many calls since I arrived. Where do you think I could find a lawyer?"

Erik thought about it: it was none of his business and he knew he should not meddle... but if Amanda Solarin was here, it was his responsibility too. How would he feel once Dupont and Lehmann got the information they wanted from her and had her executed?

"I... I'll see what I can do," he told her. "You just hold on a few more days. If all goes as planned, Lehmann and Dupont shouldn't bother you."

She looked surprised. "What are you going to do?"

Erik sighed. "Actually, I don't know," he admitted "But I know someone who might."

Erik didn't dare to make the call while he was in the hospital, nor on the train home. He waited until he got into his apartment and closed the bedroom door. Then he pulled his cell phone out of his pocket and dialled Lara Meyer's number.

"Erik!" she greeted him warmly. "I haven't heard from you in a while! How are you? Are you still assigned to the custody hospital?"

"Yes, I'm still there," he confirmed. He wanted to explain his dilemma quickly but didn't know how to introduce the subject.

"So... what's going on at the headquarters?" he asked.

"Oh, nothing much. The same old thing. They sent in two new agents to replace you and Hernandez."

"Are they good?"

"They're OK," Lara granted. "But they are two grumps. I liked you two better. By the way, I saw Zoe on the train the other day. They sent her to check the third ring's accesses in the end."

"Blimey, poor Zoe!" Erik said. It was a tedious and worthless job, compared to operational work. Once again, he realized that, as much as the hospital was depressing, he was treated much better than his colleague.

"But do tell me, to what do I owe the pleasure of your call?"

Erik decided to dive in: "Um ... let's say I had some time to reflect here and... I know that you, as a lawyer, have always been aware of every ethical issue, and I was wondering... not that I'm talking about a definite case, just hypothetically..."

Meyer, please, read between the lines! He prayed. "I was wondering, what happens in practice after a person is arrested?"

Lara laughed: "Well, you tell me. You're the one who works in custody. If you want to, I can quote the legislative decrees that provide for the immediate transfer of the infected, but..."

"No, no, I mean… should it happen that someone gets mistaken for an infected, but actually isn't one... would there be some law to regulate their release or their transfer?" he asked.

"Ah, come on, Erik, that's nonsense! Don't you remember how we work?" she answered. Erik seemed to perceive a falsely cheerful tone in her voice. "You know very well that these things cannot happen. Oh, I'm sorry, but I really have to go," she went on. "Come and see us at the headquarters sometime! We'll go out for a drink together! Bye!"

Within seconds, Erik found himself staring at the silent phone. Lara had hung up. Before he had any time to register his disappointment, it rang again. The call came from a hidden number.

"Hello, Persson here," he answered.

"It's me," Meyer said in a matter-of-fact tone. "This is a secure line. Shoot, what did you see?"

"I... OK, there are prisoners here who are not infected. There is also Amanda Solarin, the last arrest I made, remember?"

"Yes, I remember her case very well," Lara confirmed.

"She was arrested because she was reported as infected. I got the arrest order with all the tests that proved she was infected. But she's not. And according to her file, she was taken to the prison on the same evening of the arrest. There has never been a trial, and she has been there ever since. She's being interrogated using methods that are absolutely illegal to use on civilians!" he was getting worked up. "Can they do that? Have you ever heard of such a case?"

Meyer hesitated: "Actually, yes, Erik, the rumour has been around for a while. There are some... er, associations of people, mostly relatives of the detainees, who are trying to discover the truth about what happens to those people, but it's really hard to find reliable information. And there have been episodes... we suspect that some were intimidated and were told to forget it... well, it's better not to talk about it too much."

Erik was puzzled. "Why have I never heard anything like that?"

"No offense, but you're not the kind of person I would have expected to sympathize with this cause."

"Why?"

"Ah, come on!" Meyer laughed. "You're the classic upright type! You know, the cop who seems to never doubt he's acting for the best."

"But that's not true," Erik said. "I have lots of doubts."

"I was wrong, then. Do you have evidence that they are detaining Amanda Solarin without justification, though?"

"Well, first of all she is locked up in the hospital while she's not infected, though the documents that you have at the headquarters state the contrary. Second, I witnessed the interrogation and... Lara, it isn't a pretty sight," he concluded.

"I can imagine. Let me think..." Lara was silent for a few seconds, and Erik imagined seeing her tapping her pen on the desk as she always did when she was thinking.

"Right, I've heard of a judge, someone who might look into this case. I can't make promises... but it would be best to have unequivocal evidence, something that would thoroughly shake him. Do you have records of these interrogations?"

"Personally, I don't, but there's a surveillance camera. I could download the videos from the hospital archive and smuggle them out."

"It's a big risk," Meyer remarked. "Could they trace the videos back to you?"

Erik thought about it: "Probably yes. But I could use someone else's credentials to get them."

He thought of Martinelli, who always left the badge lying around and wrote the passwords on a piece of paper he kept on his desk. It was still risky, but somehow the idea of doing nothing seemed even worse.

"It would be best to have those videos as soon as possible. With a little luck we could have her case reviewed by tomorrow."

"So I must get them today."

"Do you think you can do that?"

He could go to the hospital at night, when there would be no medical police officers around... He knew the surveillance system of the building and knew that the administration department had only a few cameras, which could be easily circumvented. He could connect to one of their terminals and...

"I think so," he said. "But we have to hurry; I don't believe Solarin can take it much longer. How do I call this number?"

"Send me a silly message to my phone, and I'll call you back."

"OK, see you soon!" Erik said and hung up. When he turned around, he saw that Thea was behind him.

"Oh, hi," he said.

"Who were you talking to?" she asked in a dry voice.

"Lara Meyer. You know, from my old office."

"Of course I know who Lara Meyer is," Thea said, appearing upset. "You always talk about her."

"Always? Come on, surely not," Erik said, uncomprehending. Then it dawned on him: "Are you jealous?" he laughed. "Really?"

Thea blushed: "And what if I were?"

Erik put his arms around her: "Ah, I know, I am irresistible. It's wise of you to closely guard all this bounty…" he joked.

It was true that Lara was beautiful and charming, and perhaps he used to look at her slack-jawed, as Zoe said, but he had never even dreamed of taking this any further. He was married, and he was happy that way.

His wife still looked annoyed but gave him a smile. "Irresistible? Maybe twenty years ago. Now you're big-bellied like the cops from the thrillers on TV," she teased him.

"Excuse me?" he pretended to be offended.

He was about to respond with another joke, but when he remembered what he had to do that night he suddenly was in no mood for laughing.

Chapter 26

During the rest of the day, Sophie put together all the documentation that she had about the vaccine and locked it away in a place she deemed safe (a locker in one of the abandoned halls of the hospital, which she had incidentally found the combination for). She had no illusions about the strength of the lock, but she doubted anyone would think of looking there.

The formula she had found looked promising, but she had no way to experiment. She had tried to test it on small samples of her own blood and tissue, but of course trying it on a living, complex organism was a different story.

She figured that tonight, when she talked with Cain, she could use her work as a sort of bargaining chip. Not that she feared he would hurt her... would he? She tried to banish the thought. *There is no actual danger*, she told herself. After all, Cain had shielded her with his own body to prevent Taneen from burning her alive. He had saved her life, but in the frantic moments that followed, she hadn't even had the chance to say a few words of thanks. In the confusion of that moment, she had not even thought about the risk of touching his skin and contracting the plague.

When this danger occurred to her, many hours later, she immediately splashed a drop of her own blood on the sensor, trembling with fear, but was relieved to find out that she was still free from the infection. Fortunately, both she and Cain always wore gloves, and, due to the low morning temperature, they were completely covered from the neck down.

But as she relived those moments, she also remembered his voice, his warmth ... there was a part of her that shuddered at the thought of being alone with him, and another part that was secretly thrilled. That morning she had seen his two faces: the attractive and charming one, but also the one that was dangerous and ruthless.

She had no idea what sort of punishment Cain had in mind for Nadia. He didn't seem inclined to cruelty, but he didn't hesitate when he ordered to shoot her. The lack of any emotion in that moment upset Sophie even more than the raw fury she had seen in his reptilian eyes.

She felt nervous and anxious: just to do something, she tried to fix her hair, which, after the ruthless cut she had made before leaving Europa, had grown in untidy locks and was unnaturally darker towards the tips, where the remains of the black dye could still be seen. Her appearance would certainly have earned her some curious glances in the city, where she probably would have looked like an outcast from the underground tunnels, but on an island populated by dragons and lizard people her hair surely wasn't the strangest thing around. After a failed attempt to make her hair look neat, she gave up.

She wished James were home so she could tell him about her doubts: she was sure that he would have reassured her as to Cain's intentions and probably encouraged her to go and see him without fear. But James was on a mission in Europa, and Sophie felt very alone.

The sun was still high in the afternoon sky, so it was far too early to go and see Cain.

She decided to visit Emma: her friend's comforting words would definitely soothe her. As she walked towards Britt's house, Sophie thought about how, during their daring escape from the city and in the following months, she had come to appreciate the old lady's calm demeanour.

When she arrived at Britt's house, she immediately felt that something was wrong. The gate was open, one of the vases was overturned and the door was ajar. She entered the house, but it looked like there wasn't a living soul inside. Sophie's heart began to beat wildly.

"Emma!" she called. "Where are you? Britt!"

Suddenly she heard a moan coming from upstairs and rushed there.

"Britt!" she exclaimed, as she saw the woman lying on the ground in the hallway. Approaching her, she saw that her nose was swollen and that she had been hit on the head. A trickle of blood was running down her neck.

"What happened?" she asked her, helping her to her feet.

"I... I don't know exactly, it's all so confusing..." Britt stammered. "Emma..."

"Is she hurt? Is she in danger?" Sophie pressed.

"Cain... He came here... trying to get... Emma."

Sophie felt the blood draining from her face.

"At the time I didn't think there was anything strange... he has been here before. Maybe he looked a bit upset, but... I don't know, actually. After a while, I heard the sound of something falling and something like... a struggle..."

"Struggle?" Sophie repeated in a faint voice.

"I knocked and asked what was going on... the door opened suddenly and struck me in the face. I fell and I felt another blow on the neck. I think I passed out and... oh, Sophie, I think I saw a knife!"

"When did it happen? How long ago did he take her away?"

Britt looked around, still in shock: "Oh... not so long... maybe ten... fifteen minutes..."

Sophie ran her hand through her hair: it was all her fault. She was the one who had put Emma in danger. She remembered the last words Cain said to her that very morning: *'We will see if you change your mind about dragons.'*

Did he want to blackmail her using Emma as a bargaining chip? Or maybe his plan was even crueller? At that moment she remembered Emma had told her that Cain had run blood tests on her... if he analysed them, he would definitely find out that her antibodies were decaying rapidly. Perhaps they were already gone. And that meant that Emma's life had become expendable... Sophie didn't even want to think about it. She had to do something.

"Sorry, Britt, I have to go!"

Sophie rushed out of the house, and then remained still for a moment, not knowing where to go. She wanted to ask someone for help, but Nadia had been imprisoned by Cain who knew where, James was far and Emma... She realized that she had no choice: she had to face Cain alone.

She ran and, when she got to the former town hall ,she was breathing hard and feeling a sharp pain in her side, but she ignored it. For the first time she realized how sinister the building appeared, standing alone in the middle of the square. The houses around it were completely empty, and it felt like being in a ghost town.

The door wasn't locked: Sophie walked in and called Emma's name, but got no reply. She was about to climb up the stairs when she heard the sound of a car approaching from a nearby street. Before she could react, she saw a jeep with peeling paint getting away from the building and swerving to one of the roads leading out of town. The car was moving fast, but Sophie was sure she saw two people in the cabin.

She had seen that jeep before - outside the hospital, on the night that James had brought Cain there. She had no doubt about it: Cain was taking Emma somewhere... but why? With a shudder, she remembered why Cain had been in the hospital that night: the wounds caused by the dragons... Maybe his ruthless plan was to feed Emma to one of them? "*We will see if you change your mind about dragons*" Sophie kept hearing in her head.

This time she had to follow him. She had brought Emma to this terrifying island; she had let herself be charmed by Cain and his nice words... Emma had always seen through the reasonable mask that he put on in front of everyone else... she should have listened to her from the beginning!

Feverishly, she ran to Nadia and Karla's house, in front of which she found the car that Nadia used to move about the island. The keys were in the ignition: no one was afraid of theft on an island where everyone knew each other. Sophie decided not to waste time asking Karla for permission to use the car: it was Nadia's, and she was sure that her friend would have lent it to her without thinking twice. Sophie had never driven it, but she had seen Nadia do it many times.

She put the gear lever in the driving position, turned the key and pushed on the accelerator. After a few failed attempts, she managed to start the car and leave. After all, it wasn't so difficult, but the sudden speed made her a little afraid. She hoped she would be able to keep control of the car. By now the sun had gone down, and the streets were deserted. There was no form of entertainment on the island, and in general there was no reason to go out at night.

Sophie realized she was shaking, but she could not tell if it was from cold or fear: in doubt, she turned on the car heater (one of the few things that, as a passenger, she had immediately learnt to do), and prepared to leave the centre of the village. Outside the area where everyone lived, the streets were few and almost all blocked by rocks and ruins. It was not hard to discern the way that Cain had taken: on the asphalt there were signs of tire tracks covered in mud, and, when the asphalt ended and the road became only a dirt track, all she had to do was to follow the trail of his car.

After a while the road began to ascend, and Sophie could see the lights on the horizon. It was Cain's jeep. They were still far apart, but she could follow them. She accelerated further, trying to bridge the distance between the two vehicles. They were on their way to the mountain in which the dragons were kept, she realized: the destination seemed to confirm her darkest suspicions.

Yet when they arrived there, Sophie saw the lights carry on, passing the mountain and climbing down to the fields below. Where was he going?

When she passed the mountain, there was another silhouette clearly visible in the moonlight on the horizon, and she finally understood: when no one could or dared to follow him, Cain went to the other mountain. And in that mountain, there was a dragon.

Despite her reckless driving, the trip took seemingly endless time, and she failed to reach Cain's jeep. When she got to the side of the mountain, the road ended. Sophie found the jeep abandoned, with the doors open and the keys still in the ignition. *Where are they?*

This mountain, too, seemed to contain a cave, but the entrance was much narrower. There were no armed guards, only a heavy metal door, which was now open.

Sophie looked around in the cabin of the car, looking for something that she could use to defend herself. She finally found a heavy jack in the trunk and decided to take it. It was better than nothing.

When she passed through the metal door, she saw that the inside space was huge, even bigger than the other cave, and completely dark except for the moonlight pouring in through a hole at the top. It was probably an inactive volcano. She cursed herself for not having thought of looking for a torch: the light was very dim. and she could not see much. The silence was ghastly.

The cave seemed empty but, on closer inspection, one of the walls at the bottom would move rhythmically... *like breathing*, she thought. She had no time to dwell on that thought, however, because she heard raised voices somewhere above her. Straining her eyes, she could see stairs and metal walkways that ran on the wall next to her.

It took her a while to find the first steps, and then she began to climb them. She heard metallic pings, very close to her ... a sound that seemed particularly disturbing. She wondered if Emma was still alive. At that moment she realized that she had not thought about how she could stop Cain once she had found him.

He was slow and a bit clumsy in his movements, but his arms were strong. Sophie, however, believed herself to be more agile, faster and with a better sense of balance. She would not be as easy to neutralize as Britt, she hoped. On the other hand, Cain probably had much more combat experience; after all, he was the head of a terrorist organization.

Deep down, however, she hoped it would not come to that. She would appeal to his common sense, and if that wasn't enough, she would bargain with the vaccine research. As long as she had the time, and Emma was still unharmed...

Suddenly the ladder ended and turned into a walkway: she was standing next to an opening in the side of the mountain. Below her, she heard the roar of the waves crashing against the rocks. In the dim moonlight, she saw a small dark shape in the corner.

Cain was bending over something. She couldn't see Emma, though... *is it too late?* She wondered, with her heart in her throat. For a moment she thought she could hit him on the head with the jack while he was facing away.

Cain heard her footsteps and turned sharply. He seemed shocked to see her.

"Sophie?!" he exclaimed. "But... but... what are you doing here?"

His falsely innocent tone made her furious: "You thought you could blackmail me? Or did you just want to show me what happens to those who challenge your authority? Nadia had always been right about you!"

Cain blinked: "What?"

Sophie realized that the tension had made her incoherent.

"You brought Emma here. I followed you! Where is she? What did you do to her?"

"Sophie, you don't..."

"Don't tell me I don't understand!" she snapped, a hysterical note in her voice. "I'm sick and tired of hearing the same old story! I'm not as big an idiot as you think. Now tell me where Emma is, or else..." she waved the jack in front of him, hoping to appear threatening. Only then she came close enough to notice some details that left her puzzled.

There was a cut on Cain's temple that appeared fresh and not completely healed, and his hand, which looked wounded too, was jammed against the metal floor. Then she looked again, and saw that he didn't appear just surprised, but genuinely terrified.

And then, from behind him, she heard a voice that sounded familiar and at the same time horribly alien: "I'm sorry to rub it in, Sophie," Emma said, "But you didn't understand anything at all."

Chapter 27

Erik was standing across the street from the hospital entrance, smoking a cigarette and trying to settle his nerves. The cigarette was the last he had managed to obtain from the tobacco his neighbour had sold him. A few days earlier Erik had asked him for more, but he replied that he hadn't been able to find any yet.

Erik had spent the last weeks stretching out every single puff of smoke, but now he had reached the end of the packet. However, he honestly didn't believe that he would be able to face the deeds he was about to undertake without that little steaming comfort. He was aware that he was about to commit a crime: he, who had always been so loyal and irreproachable.

This wasn't just performing a task without due authorization, as he had done a few months earlier following the investigation with Hernandez, but a totally unjustifiable act from a legal point of view: downloading confidential material from the hospital servers and divulging it to a third party who would otherwise never have access to it.

He was afraid, he could not deny it. But he was also determined: what the medical police had done to Amanda Solarin was neither fair nor legal, and if he had to commit an offense to restore the proper course of justice, Erik was convinced that it was his duty to do so.

He sucked the last, delicious mouthful of smoke, then decided to throw the cigarette butt off. He looked around for a bin but couldn't find any. Reluctantly, he threw the butt on the ground. *What an idiot,* he thought. *I'm going to break the law, and I worry about throwing a piece of burnt paper on the sidewalk.*

He crossed the street and reached the entrance of the building. Casting a glance inside the gatehouse, he saw Martinelli dozing off, and another jailer whose name he couldn't remember reading a magazine. The man looked up at him and, seeing his uniform, gave him a quick nod and went back to reading.

So far so good, Erik thought, swiping his badge on the sensor. He expected to hear the familiar click of the shutter door, accompanied by a green light of confirmation. Instead a small red light appeared, along with an error message on the display.

There must be a problem with the scanner, Erik thought, and swiped the badge repeatedly on the sensor: each time, however, the same message appeared. This was unbelievable. Did the bloody thing have to start acting up tonight of all times?

"Hey, Persson, what's going on?" Martinelli greeted him. He had woken up and was leaving the guardhouse.

"It's the badge," Erik explained, trying to maintain a neutral and vaguely bored tone. "It's acting strange."

"Come, let's take a look at it," Martinelli said, escorting Erik inside the guardhouse and opening the access management program on his computer.

"How bizarre. Here it says that you're already accredited," he observed. Martinelli's colleague got up and went to look at the screen too.

This is all going wrong, Erik thought desperately. His plan was to enter without being too obvious: the guards at the entrance were supposed to assume this was a normal shift change, and if someone asked him something, he would have said that he had forgotten his tablet in his cabinet and had come back for it, or something like that. Now this would never pass, however. Talk about bad luck!

He wondered if he should put it all off to another night. Could Solarin wait another day? It depended on how soon Dupont and Lehmann would discover the hoax of the new security protocol.

"What does that mean?" Erik asked.

"It means you've already logged in but haven't logged out," the other guard chimed in. "Basically, according to the system you're already inside."

"But I'm here," Erik said, sounding stupid even to himself. "Maybe the sensor didn't record it when I swiped out?" he suggested.

"Let's see," the other guard commented, starting to type a series of quick keyboard commands. "So, here I see an exit at seventeen past six p.m., does that sound right?"

Erik nodded: that was the time when he had gone home that afternoon.

"But according to the program, you came back half an hour ago," his colleague went on, puzzled. "Hmm, there must be a mistake... it appears here that you are opening various doors in different buildings. It can't be a surveillance shift."

Erik felt the familiar pang of an imminent danger. Instinct told him that this anomaly was more than a bug in the system.

"Where?"

"Administration, maintenance, basement, first floor, pod six..."

Passing through administration and maintenance was the best way to avoid security cameras and diverting to the basement and the first floor would have kept an intruder from meeting anyone at this hour. Someone was doing just what *he* had thought of doing to find a terminal to connect! It could not be a coincidence. Perhaps Lara Meyer decided to ask someone else for help? But the cameras in pod six would surely have picked up an intruder...

"Oh look, here it says that you are opening the maintenance door again right now!" the guard said, shaking his head. "There must be a virus or something, dunno..." he suggested.

"I'll go and check," Erik declared. "Can you open the door?"

"Do you want me to come with you?" his colleague offered. "Martinelli can stay here and..."

"No, that's OK. It's probably just a bug in the program, that's all," Erik said. Martinelli would probably doze off in a few minutes, and he would rather have someone more alert at the entrance, in case he had to call for help. Also, he had the feeling that these events had to be somehow related to his plan of stealing the documents, and he didn't want to risk having anyone interfere.

"However, I see that the door openings are operating in degraded mode," the guard said.

"Meaning...?"

"No need of retinal scan to open, just the badge."

That's definitely a wakeup call! Erik thought. But if he called for reinforcements at once, he would jeopardize his plan of helping Amanda Solarin...

No, he had to go alone.

The shortest way to the maintenance office was to take the elevator or the stairs directly, but Erik decided to pass through the administration. If his instinct was right, the intruder was heading there as well. He ran across the empty administration office without turning the light on. In the faint light of the street lamps drifting in from outside, the place looked spooky.

He was about to leave when he heard footsteps approaching, and crouched behind a desk, his hand on his gun. He heard someone opening the door and entering, speaking in a low voice. With dismay he recognized the first voice, low but definitely feminine... it was Amanda Solarin! But what was she doing there?

The other voice was deeper and belonged to a man. This was not any of the guards or officers he knew. It was someone he had never met before.

"... I assure you, she's fine," the man said. "I think Cain has a crush on her."

"Sophie and Cain?" Amanda Solarin exclaimed. The low tone of her voice did not hide her surprise. "Are you kidding me?"

The man spoke as if he stifled a grin: "I know, who would have thought?"

Erik leaned slightly out of hiding to see the intruder. He was tall and wore a dark suit similar to the uniform used by the operative officers of the medical police, which included a gun that the stranger was holding up in front of him.

When he passed by a window, Erik noticed the scales on his face... he was infected. Despite the scales, however, he also saw the incredible resemblance to Amanda Solarin... this was probably the same brother of whom he had heard during interrogation. His name was James, he recalled. This was a true jailbreak.

For a moment Erik wondered if he could simply remain hidden and let them go. No one could blame him if he didn't stop them: he was alone, and it would be easy to say he hadn't seen them. He would be on the safe side and Solarin would be free...

It was not exactly what he had planned: after all, she was still a subversive, but at least she would no longer remain locked up in the basement with Dupont and Lehmann, or whoever might take their place. He was already lowering the gun when Amanda spoke again. She was close to the desk behind which he was hiding.

"Jamie, you shouldn't have come here. It's too risky."

"It was easy," he reassured her. "I just recovered the duplicate badge at the usual place of exchange, you know, the tube stop of Metz North, and then I entered without any problems."

"I'm surprised that Cain allowed you to come."

"Um," her brother sounded uncomfortable, "'Allowed' is a strong word …"

"He doesn't know?" Amanda was surprised. "And does he know that with this bravado of yours you jeopardized the duplicate of Persson's badge and tablet? Our mole can't take it again, it would be too suspicious…"

Erik was dazed. His badge and tablet had been duplicated? He could not believe it… There really was a spy, and it was someone very close to him! That was why the rebels had all the information… Was it himself who had unwittingly provided it? Without thinking, he stepped out of hiding and pointed the gun at Amanda Solarin's temple. "Lower the gun or I'll shoot her," he told the lizard man.

James was about to lower the gun, then hesitated.

"Persson," Solarin said, surprised but self-possessed, "The very one. What are you doing here?"

"I said lower the gun," Erik repeated. "So, who's spying on me?"

James and Amanda looked at each other.

"Who is it?" Erik asked again. "I want the name, or I'll shoot."

"You don't want to shoot me, Persson," Amanda said coolly "You wouldn't fire at an innocent civilian unless you had no choice, I know."

Erik felt a stab of anger: "You have some nerve to call yourself innocent! You don't have the plague, granted, but you are guilty of a list of charges that would make any lawyer dizzy."

James was still holding the gun pointed at him. It was a stalemate.

"If we give you the name, will you let us go?" James Solarin asked, staring at him with a hard expression.

"I can't let you go," said Erik. "But I will make sure that Amanda has a fair trial. It's funny, but I have come here tonight on purpose to find the material on which to base her release. How naïve of me," he commented bitterly.

"Wow, that's two rescue attempts in one night," Solarin mused ironically. "What can I say, I'm flattered."

"If you both surrender yourself, I will get you out of here," Erik insisted. "I already found a lawyer. You would be accused of subversive activities, but I will make sure that your rights are protected. After all you've been through, surely they'll recognize all the attenuating circumstances."

"And James?"

Erik shook his head:" For him I cannot make promises. But if you come with me without making a fuss, you have a chance."

The two looked at each other. "OK, I agree," James Solarin said, "We can negotiate." He lowered the gun and laid it on the ground. Erik bent down to pick it up... and at that very moment, taking advantage of his distraction, Amanda Solarin grabbed him by the wrist that held the gun, twisted it and kicked him in the stomach.

Erik doubled over in pain and heard a gunshot. He realized that he had fired, but the bullet had missed the prisoner and struck a computer. James had grabbed his gun again, while Amanda had Erik's.

"I appreciate your intentions, Persson," Solarin said, "but I'm not ready to spend the rest of my life in prison." She turned to her brother. "Now let's go before someone comes to check and raises the alarm."

James Solarin raised his gun toward Erik, ready to shoot. Erik was still on the floor, doubled over. He was in pain from the kick and completely out of breath. He had no hope of defending himself, and nothing to do but prepare himself for the impact of the bullet. Was this the way he would die? *What a fool,* he thought. If only he had minded his own business...

"James, what are you doing? Are you crazy?" Solarin exclaimed.

"Amanda, it's a risk!" James protested. "If he sounds the alarm before we are out..."

"Don't even think about it!" she snapped. "You know that..." she sighed. "Come, let's go."

James started to protest, then snorted in exasperation. Before Erik could react, James grabbed his head and punched him in the face.

Following the sickening crunch of his broken nose, while he was losing consciousness, Erik absurdly thought that now he and Amanda Solarin were even.

Chapter 28

Sophie turned around. Emma appeared unharmed and was brandishing a knife against Cain. Or was it against *her*?

"What... What are you doing?" Sophie stammered.

Emma smiled: "I'm sorry, Sophie. This isn't how I was planning to tell you."

"Tell me what? Emma, what..."

"For a start," she interrupted, her voice patient, "would you stop calling me Emma?"

Sophie was speechless. She looked at the woman in front of her and realized that, despite being the same person with whom she had spent so much time in the past months, she looked very different.

She had abandoned her usual bent and hunched posture and carried herself with pride and power. Her hair was no longer knotted in a bun at the nape of her neck but fluttered around her face like a mane. And her eyes certainly had never been so green, her pupils so wide and slightly vertical...

"What happened to you? What did he do to you?" Sophie murmured.

Emma, or whoever she was, laughed mirthlessly: "Who, him? Oh well, you could say he ruined my life. But that was many years ago. Now I am here to settle it."

Cain, behind her, said: "Mother, let her go, she didn't..."

"Mother?!" Sophie exclaimed.

"I told you many times not to call me that!" Emma snapped. "I hate it, it makes me furious!"

Sophie felt dizzy. Her eyes kept darting from one to the other. She wondered if her friend had gone mad or suffered from a split personality... or even if she had ever existed at all. Next to this stranger, even Cain appeared small and intimidated, a shadow of the domineering leader she had known.

"I'm sorry about this deception, dear Sophie, but I assure you it was necessary," the woman said. "I had to get here, and I would never have succeeded without your help. First, I must confess that my name is not Emma Lemaire. The real Emma Lemaire, whom you've never met, passed away a few years ago, and provided me with a convenient identity that passed all the checks of our infected friends."

"You... You wanted to infiltrate among the rebels? Are you working for the police, the government...?" Sophie asked, bewildered.

"Let's see... Yes and no. The government helped me, that's true: they cannot wait to catch the 'General'," she uttered this word with a mocking tone, "and the dissidents... but I admit I had my own reasons to do what I did."

"Your mind is warped, you are no longer yourself..." Cain said.

"On the contrary, I haven't felt so much like myself for many years. Since I've been on this island, I've felt his presence... it's like an awakening. I feel stronger, healthier, more alive than ever!" she said with enthusiasm. The moonlight illuminated her features: her cold reptilian eyes and the transfigured expression gave her face a kind of haunting and rapacious beauty.

Cain shook his head, apparently speechless.

"If you are not Emma, then who are you?" Sophie finally asked.

The woman looked at her as if she had suddenly remembered that she was there, then smiled: "My name is Kathleen Anderson. Once, many years ago, I was a researcher, much like yourself. I worked for the university. And I had a son... David," her voice became full of tenderness in pronouncing his name. "But David was not a child like any other. He was born with a rare condition of the immune system, a more aggressive form of the illness that had killed his father before his birth. It made him weak and defenceless against even the most harmless bacteria. He had to be segregated in the house, in a sterile and controlled environment, otherwise his fever would rise, his organs would block, he would have a crisis..." she shook her head, as if reliving her son's pain. "The doctors said he would not live above a few months. But he survived. I made him survive... and then I spent all my life looking for a cure."

"And you found it?" Sophie asked, interested in spite of herself.

"Yes, I found it. I found it... in the dragons. It was during that time that scientists found the first egg. Inside there was a small dragon, dead but still exceptionally well-preserved. They discovered that the species had been incredibly strong, resistant to heat, cold and diseases. And so I decided to use its DNA to help my child...

I synthetized a serum which I hoped would heal him. But, of course, I could not test it directly on him: David was very weak, and any mistake might mean undermining forever his health and survival. So, I simulated his illness on myself and injected the serum and... well, it didn't go as planned. For a few days I was in a fever and delirium. My body was filled with spots..."

"The plague," Sophie whispered, "The first case." So this was the reason for those antibody values: her first impression had been correct. Emma – no, Kathleen - had really had the plague years, not weeks before.

"Not exactly," Kathleen corrected her. "It was a milder and more harmless version of the disease that you know. After a few days the spots disappeared, and I healed... And that was when I heard him for the first time."

"Who?"

"Who? The dragon, of course!" Kathleen smiled again, and this time Sophie perceived something fanatical in her expression.

"He was there, inside my head. I felt his presence, his thoughts... and he was looking for me, because I had his blood. There were two of them originally, you know. The scientists found only the one that had perished all those centuries ago... but the other had awakened, perhaps during the nuclear war, and was wandering alone, without his companion. But now he had me."

Sophie shivered.

"With his presence inside my head I felt more intuitive, self-assured, even more intelligent, " the woman continued. "I created a new serum for David, and I injected him. And... can you believe it? It worked! David briefly fell ill, and then his immune system began to take action: he became a normal child, albeit skinny and a bit weaker than most. He never felt any presence of the dragon within himself.

It should have been the best moment of my life, but I could not enjoy it fully. I felt incomplete, as if I was missing something essential. By then I had a new goal: I had to reconnect with the dragon. He was my partner, my soulmate, you know? We shared so much, much more than the trivial and mundane details that humans can exchange between them. We were one, united in the essence!" she said with fervour.

"The telepathic communication is difficult to control: I wanted to leave to look for him myself, find out where he was... but I only received confused images of unknown places, caves, tunnels from which he could not get out. I tried to draw the landscapes I saw, to compare them with pictures from all over the world, but I could not find him. And then, after a couple of years, I realized with horror that the effects of the serum were disappearing," the woman sighed. "I could no longer hear him as before. At first there were only brief episodes of blackout, then the connection began to stop for days... I injected the serum inside me again, but I didn't get sick and the communication wasn't strengthened. By then I was vaccinated. In a couple of months, I lost him completely."

Kathleen was silent.

"So what happened?"

It was Cain who answered: "Then she created me."

"You decided to have another child?" Sophie asked, vaguely incredulous. Sometimes people tried to fill the void in their lives with a child, but Dr Anderson didn't look like the type to do so.

"Oh no!" she exclaimed. "Absolutely not. I never wanted to have any more children after David. However, I found other... volunteers, who didn't mind me experimenting with some compounds to put them in touch with the dragon. It wasn't difficult: after the last economic crisis the place was full of misfits who accepted any kind of work to make ends meet and maybe help their family. In short, I had a queue at the door. Don't get me wrong, I wasn't thrilled at the idea of sharing that bond... well, to be honest, I felt sick at the very thought. But, as unattractive as it was, that perspective was still better than resigning myself to life without him. But it didn't go as planned: the serum that I had injected in me the first time had no effect in terms of telepathy, so I had to try new, increasingly more powerful formulations. The immune system of the volunteers reacted badly. In short, it was the plague as you know it. So..."

"No, wait, let me get this straight," Sophie interrupted her, struck by a sinister thought. "What do you mean, 'reacted badly'? What happened to those people?"

"They didn't make it," Kathleen replied simply.

Sophie was stunned: "They... died?"

"Well, yes."

"And... you... continued to kill those people? Just like that, without a good reason?"

"Without a good reason?!" Dr Anderson was indignant. "You are joking, I hope! I had to find my dragon! It was the most important reason, the only one!"

Sophie gasped. Only then did she begin to understand the lucid madness that was harboured in the person whom she had believed her friend.

"In any case, a few years passed. I had almost lost hope ... and then a woman came to me. She was desperate, she had no money and didn't know what to do with herself. To put it simply, she begged me to let her enter the trial program. So I injected her with the latest version of my serum... and soon I discovered she was pregnant."

Sophie looked at Cain, who was listening to Anderson's words open-mouthed. Probably even he had never heard this part of the story.

"She was so thin that I could barely see her, and she had managed to hide her belly under layers of loose clothing. When I discovered it, I was very upset. Pregnancy weakens the immune system, and if I had known I would not have wasted time and resources on her. In fact, that reckless girl did not survive. The child, however, did."

That child had to be... *Cain*, Sophie thought with a shudder.

Kathleen nodded, as if reading her thoughts.

"Of course. That was him. The only creature to have contracted the dragon plague *in utero*. Born already as we see him now, scales and all. A monster, so twisted and ugly... but he wanted to live, that I grant him. He screamed with such force that he became all purple, and his screams could be heard a block away. And when I saw his eyes, I knew at once that there was something of my dragon in him. However, as you can imagine, it would have been difficult to keep him in the university lab without someone noticing and beginning to ask questions, so I had to make do."

"So you pretended he was your son. You brought him home, you called him Cain and..."

"Oh, please," the woman interrupted, annoyed. "I certainly did not call him so. The code that identified his case was C41N, and in my mind, that's what he had always been. When David saw it, he had just learned to read, and exchanged numbers for letters. It was he who started to call him that. At the time he was five, and he was enthusiastic about the idea of having a little brother," Kathleen sighed. "What nonsense, keeping that stupid name even now. So ridiculously sentimental. How typical."

Cain closed his eyes, appearing completely devastated. The revelation about his origins must have been even bitterer than he had imagined.

"In any case, let's move on. I took a fulltime babysitter to look after him and asked her not to take him out of the house. When the poor woman came down with a high fever and was covered in scales, I realized that the child was not only a carrier of this strange new illness, but that he was also tremendously contagious."

Sophie did not have to ask what became of the ill-fated babysitter.

"At that point it was clear that he must never get out of the house, or the disease would spread quickly. I abandoned my research, lost all funding that I had managed to keep until then, to take care of him," she said contemptuously. "But every sacrifice was rewarded when, at times, I could see the eyes of my dragon through his. That child would take me to him, I was sure. I only had to wait until he was old enough. I thought that, having the bond from birth, it would be second nature to him, so powerful and instinctive. What I could not foresee was his rejection of this bond.

As I tried to encourage him, to help him express his potential, that monster closed like a clam, and pushed the dragon to the edge of his consciousness. It was a constant struggle. Rather than accept him, he closed him out. This caused tantrums in which he lost control, destroyed anything that came close to him, had convulsions. I would have given anything to feel that wonderful presence next to me again, and I could do nothing but watch that ungrateful brat refusing the gift and throwing all my work away. If only he could have lived in harmony with the dragon, as I had done..."

"Harmony?" Cain repeated. "That creature is evil! It has always been! He filled my mind with images of pain, destruction... it scared me to death."

"You never understood, you never even tried!" Kathleen accused him, approaching him.

"He wanted to burn down the whole world, and still does."

"A dragon is pure will, it is power! You've always been too weak to appreciate it!"

"You were blind then and you are now. David, however, knew..."

"Oh, David?! Don't you even dare to mention David!" Anderson shouted; she was now beside Cain and towered over him. Cain went silent and looked away.

"He killed him, you know," she said, turning to Sophie. Her voice was horribly cold. "David. He killed his own brother, when he was only thirteen. David had tried to help him in one of his crises. Look at him, now he's acting all goody-goody, 'oh, the dragon is evil, unlike me, I'm as good as a little lamb...'" she mocked him. "Don't believe that for a second."

"It was an accident," Cain's voice sounded like a howl of pain. "It was the dragon that made me lose control, I tried..."

"Oh, sure, the dragon, right. The truth is that you have never been able to take responsibility for your actions. Every bad thing that ever happened was the dragon's fault. Always! And it was David who paid the price."

Cain said nothing. He blamed himself too, Sophie realized, recalling his morphine-induced delirium.

"In any case, after what happened I couldn't risk him harming anyone else. I couldn't get rid of him, no, he was my only hope of finding my true partner. I had to keep him sedated since then, and I succeeded for five long years."

Sophie thought of the infected who was held captive in the city, in Edmund Harris's lab, with pale limbs, thin as a skeleton...

"I had lost everything because of him: my son, my job, my dragon..." Kathleen continued, her voice cracking. "I managed to keep him under control until his body began to get used to the drug. So in the end he tried to kill me, and until tonight he was convinced he had succeeded. But I am stronger than I look... I still have the blood of the dragon within me."

"I never wanted to kill you!" Cain defended himself. "I just wanted to..."

"What did you want? To run away? Go and spread your illness?" Kathleen prompted. "Because that's exactly what you did. You ran away without even looking twice at my dead body, or what you thought it was, and then you succeeded in wiping out ninety-five percent of the population of Europa. An impressive result, no doubt about it!" she added sarcastically.

"I tried…"

"But of course, you tried, I'm sure. It's never your fault, in the end, is it?" she shook her head with disdain.

"However, imagine my surprise when I heard of other dragons, and started to see his identikit around. I always knew that I had to hunt him down, but it took quite some time to find the right plan."

Cain seemed destroyed, as if the most terrifying ghost of his past came back to haunt him. Something didn't quite make sense to Sophie, however: "But how could you not recognize her?" she asked Cain.

"My face has changed much since he last saw me," Kathleen replied. "During the years I've underwent some extensive surgery to completely change my features, waiting for this moment. Age, then, did the rest," she shrugged. "Maybe he could have recognized my voice, but I have always been careful to speak quietly and softly in front of him. Who would ever suspect a sweet old lady like me?" she laughed.

"Sophie," she continued, suddenly serious again. "I am sorry that you have been involved as well. My plan was different; it should have been Amanda Solarin, who was already known to the police as a dissident, to bring me here. You shouldn't even have been present at the time of the arrest, but the police officers who came to get her were a bit overzealous, and so… here we are. At first, I was afraid you would give up. We started to run around in circles, and sometimes I had to… well, let's say, give you a nudge in the right direction."

Sophie felt herself blushing at the thought of how easy it must have been to manipulate her. A thought struck her suddenly: "The cathedral," she said, "It was you who caused the flood. There never was anyone hunting us."

"Oh, my dear, what else could I do?" Dr Anderson justified herself. "You seemed a little too keen to stay there… I could not allow you to blow up my whole plan, could I? I had to take risks, like tonight, when this idiot came to me, accusing me of lying about the plague and demanding an explanation. He did his own blood tests and, noticing the antibody values, didn't believe my explanation."

Kathleen shook her head. "Sophie, I hope you will forgive me for lying to you... I had to. But it was worth it, you know. He is here," she explained, with a loving smile.

"Here?"

"In this very mountain. You see, in the end my useless stepson managed to do what I had tried for many years. He found the dragon, but instead of releasing him he created an even more terrible prison for him. He could not kill him, so he put him through unimaginable tortures."

"I didn't torture it!" Cain protested. "I tried to break the bond with it..."

"It doesn't matter anymore," she interrupted him. "Since I'm here, so close to him, since I touched him... I feel him again. We're back together, as one. This evening, he and I will leave together."

She smiled fondly: "Sophie, I must say that I was really touched by your loyalty to me. Since the first time I saw you, you've changed, grown so much. Come with me now! Let's forget this foolish and weak creature and go back to Europa. The dragon and I will be invincible, and you with us!"

Sophie gasped. "You're going home?"

"Sure! I don't mean to brag, but I've been quite influential since I gave the government the vaccine. And now, with the dragon, they will be entirely in my hands."

"You mean that... you've had the vaccine all this time? But why did not you spread it?" Sophie asked.

Kathleen shrugged: "It was not my decision. It's all about politics, you know. After the illness, Hartmann's faction took the power, and keeping the vaccine under wraps was a way to maintain control. They promised me that they would provide me with the means to search for my dragon so, you know, I had to agree. The population was growing too much, in any case."

Sophie felt her legs going shaky: "All those people died... and you did nothing?"

"I understand how you feel. Of course, I'll give you the vaccine immediately. Damn, if that's so important to you, I promise you I will spread it. Now they won't be able to refuse me anything!"

Sophie's mind was running around in circles. *My family*, she thought. All those people... ninety-five percent of the population... and the vaccine had always been there - in fact, it existed even before the disease...

"What will happen to Cain?" she finally asked.

"You don't have to worry about him," said Kathleen. "I'll take care of it."

Cain looked up: "In all these years, haven't you forgiven me for David? I loved him too!" he said, desperate. "Did you do all this just for revenge?"

"It's not about David," Sophie said to herself, and only after a moment she realized that she had spoken aloud. Kathleen and Cain turned to look at her. "You didn't do it for David. You did it for the dragon, didn't you?"

Kathleen sighed, almost bored: "I confess, all this has nothing to do with David."

With one fluid move, she grabbed Cain by the hair and pulled him against her. "This," she hissed, "is for David."

Before Sophie even had time to scream, she plunged her knife, which she had been holding in her hand the whole time, in the neck of her stepson, and slit his throat with one swift motion. Then, seemingly without effort, she threw him out of the cleft of the mountain, and his body was engulfed by the waves.

"What have you done?" Sophie shouted, rushing to look below. "Why?"

Was he still alive? She wondered. A normal person would have died for sure, but Cain... maybe there was hope?

"What do you want to do, jump and save him?" Kathleen laughed. "Sophie, you won't do anything so crazy, you're not the type. Let's go, now."

Sophie could not look away from the waves beneath her. *Cain was right,* she thought. He was right about dragons, about everything... and now...

"Sophie, I'm losing my patience. You have to choose: do you want to come with me and live, or stay here and die?"

Sophie looked at Emma – no, Kathleen - and then at the point in which Cain's body had been thrown into the sea. She thought of her grandmother, about the seedlings in her apartment, about her home. She remembered Amanda right before she was taken away by the medical police, the pale infected approaching her in the underground subway, and Nadia with her dragon… she felt once more the smell of Cain's skin when he was next to her.

"I'm sorry," she said.

She jumped.

Chapter 29

"Persson ... Hey, Persson, wake up! Are you OK?"

Erik opened his eyes with an effort. It felt like his eyelids were as heavy as boulders. The first thing he saw was the face of Martinelli, who seemed very concerned.

"Ah, thank goodness!" he exclaimed, relieved. "When I saw you down there, I thought... but tell me, what happened?"

Erik sat up, trying to organize his thoughts. Amanda Solarin had escaped. An infected punched him in the face (with gloved hands, thankfully). There was someone who was watching everything he did, had a duplicate of his badge and hacked his tablet... was his home phone under control too?

Home. His home was no longer a safe place, he realised. He had to go straight home, to check that Thea and the kids were fine. They had to leave immediately. Move to another apartment, of course, and in the meantime... they would find a solution. He tried to get up but fell back to the ground. His head was spinning.

"Hey, calm down! Don't you want to tell me what's happening?" Martinelli asked, a little angrily. "I don't get what's going on. I saw some strange movements on the monitor and I found this near the exit... and then I came looking for you..."

Erik looked at the piece of plastic Martinelli was holding. It had to be the duplicate badge that James Solarin had used. Clearly, he had decided he didn't need it anymore.

"Sound the alarm. There has been a jailbreak," he said. His voice sounded tremendously nasal, and he realized that his nose was still bleeding.

Martinelli paled. "A jailbreak?" he repeated. "But... how...?"

Erik looked up and saw his own reflection in the window: he looked terrible, with swollen eyes and the lower half of his face covered in blood. No wonder that Martinelli had thought the worst. He felt his pockets and found a paper tissue: he tore it and shoved the bits into his nostrils to stop the blood flow. He began to feel somewhat better, like he was a little more in control of himself.

"Amanda Solarin has escaped," he explained. "Call reinforcements now and start the maximum-security protocol throughout the hospital. I have to go."

It was like closing the barn after the horses had bolted, Erik thought, but that was the procedure.

"You can't go!" Martinelli protested. "The police will come, you'll have to answer their questions, I won't know what to say..."

"Sorry, it's an emergency!" Erik said, heading for the exit, leaving his colleague standing there disconsolately. Would Martinelli actually sound the alarm? He hoped so. In any case, he would worry about it later.

The ride home seemed endless, though the train arrived immediately and darted fast through the traffic-less tracks. He looked at the time: just after midnight. By now everyone would be in bed, he imagined. He would wake Thea first: it would not be easy to get her to leave home without explanation, but he feared that telling everything while the rebels could still hear them would be too dangerous.

He still felt dizzy, and his heart was pounding. *A cigarette*, he thought, if only he had a cigarette... But he wouldn't be allowed to smoke in the train car anyway.

Finally, he arrived home. He expected to find the house shrouded in silence and darkness, but when he opened the door he found the lights on and the sound of voices coming from the living room. Instinctively his hand flew to his holster, and with horror he realized that the gun wasn't there anymore. *Of course*, he remembered, Solarin took it.

Gingerly he walked down the hall... and found himself facing Thea, Peter and Maja who was, as always, accompanied by her ubiquitous boyfriend.

When Thea saw him, she screamed. "Erik! What happened to your face?"

Peter stepped closer: "You got into a fight?" he asked enthusiastically. "Cool!"

Erik looked around, confused: "I... a work accident. How come you're all awake?"

"Maja and Marc took Peter home - after the concert, remember?" Thea said.

Ah yes, Peter was trailing his sister and her boyfriend again. Now he remembered.

"Are you sure you're OK? You look like one possessed. Did someone take care of your nose?" his wife asked, touching his makeshift swabs.

"Shall I fetch the first aid kit?" Marc Werner offered. Erik looked at him, annoyed; how come he was always in the way? Maybe he just wanted to help, but the fellow was so irritating. He needed to have a quiet moment to talk with his family, and... He was trying to formulate a civil response when a thought stopped him.

It was Marc Werner who had found his badge and his tablet when he lost them. Erik remembered his concern, his courtesy, his cold smile. Marc who, overnight, had begun to show up at the house as if he were one of the family. Marc, who always followed Maja and played up to Thea and Peter with those mellifluous ways of his and his shark-like teeth... *he* was the mole.

It had to be Werner. That's why he had always instinctively found him false, unpleasant. Maybe he could fool others, but not him. His first instinct was to throw him out of the house there and then. Maja was not safe next to a guy like that... none of them was. Could he arrest him on the spot... or not? He was not sure that a prison guard could perform arrests.

He took a deep breath, trying to calm down. He could not arrest Werner without a proof, following mere suspicions. He had to investigate. Meanwhile Thea, Maja and Peter continued to stare at him as if he had gone mad.

I have to lure him into a trap, he thought. He could do it tonight.

"I'm sorry," he said. "I have to make an urgent phone call. I'll probably go out again later... work stuff," he explained, shrugging apologetically.

He picked up his cell phone and pretended to dial a number. Then he walked out of the room, carefully leaving the door open, and began to speak.

"Hello, boss... yes exactly, I just got here. I had to retrieve the tablet... I have some information which might be useful. I know that the two fugitives will attempt to communicate with a mole here, someone linked to the police ... they have spoken of a *usual place of exchange*," he paused, as if to allow his interlocutor to respond. "I don't know where, though.

But if they use any means of communication, we'll intercept them immediately. As soon as they turn their cell phone on, we've got them."

The spy was listening, he was sure. This would attract Werner to the tube station of Metz North, as he had heard from James Solarin, Erik thought triumphantly. He would not dare to call them for fear of being hacked; he would have no choice but to warn them of the imminent danger in person. And his showing up at the place of exchange would be the ultimate proof of guilt.

He pretended to end the call, then went into the other room. His family and Werner were still there, but the latter was saying goodbye, as it was high time to go home and he did not want to intrude. *Of course*, Erik thought, *go ahead* ...

Taking advantage of the general confusion, he took Peter's phone, locked himself in the bathroom and dialled a number from memory.

A voice thick with sleep answered: "Hello, Hoffman."

"Hi, Hoffman, this is Persson," he whispered. "I apologize for the late hour, but I thought you'd want to hear this. You know the mole you were looking for? I think I have a way to frame him, but we must hurry."

An hour later, Erik was in an alley next to the entrance of the old tube, about a dozen meters from the place of meeting, along with his old boss. Awakened in the middle of the night, Hoffman looked tired and wrinkled, but seemed somehow more professional and less pompous.

A keen eye knowing what to look for would have been able to discern ten snipers positioned on rooftops and around the corners of the houses. Everything was ready. Once the spy showed up, the snipers had orders to shoot at any suspicious movement. Neither Erik nor Hoffman wanted to take risks: for sure the mole would have interesting information, but he could also be very dangerous.

"Are you sure he'll come?" Hoffman asked.

"I can't be sure," Erik said sincerely. "But I think he will."

"Persson, I want to trust you, even if you're not part of my team anymore. But if you made me mobilize a whole a team of snipers for nothing..."

"Wait!" Erik interrupted him. A dark-clothed figure approached the entrance to the subway, looking around. *Got him*, Erik thought triumphantly. Clutching an ordinance gun (courtesy of Hoffman) in his hand, he came out of the alley and got closer.

"Werner," he called. The figure turned, and Erik almost dropped the gun in surprise.

It was not Marc Werner. It was Thea. His wife, seeing him, seemed desperate and resigned at the same time.

"What...? I don't understand," said Erik. "Why are you here? Where is Marc Werner?"

"Marc?" Thea repeated. "What has Marc got to do with anything?"

"Someone hacked my tablet and my badge and passed information and I think he..."

He stopped in midsentence, finally grasping the truth. Werner never passed information to the rebels. Thea was the spy. It had always been her. That's why his moves had been watched even before the boy appeared on the scene. He should have known... but how could he? This was Thea, to whom he had been married for almost twenty-five years, the mother of his children... how could she do this to him?

"How long?" he only asked. He marvelled at how hurt his voice sounded.

"Erik, I'm so sorry," she said, sounding strangely comforting, in the same tone of voice she used with Maja and Peter when they were children.

"I said, how long?" he repeated tonelessly, as if he was not talking to Thea, but to any random suspect who had nothing to do with him.

"Two years," she said, "more or less," she faintly shrugged. That movement, so familiar, almost brought tears to his eyes.

"You did it because of me? You wanted to get rid of me?" he could not help but ask.

"No!" Thea exclaimed. "I did everything to protect you! They knew they shouldn't hit you... I tried to keep you away from harm!"

"Why, thank you very much. I am overcome by such devotion," he said, in a tone that sounded more sarcastic than he had meant to.

"Oh, Erik, let me explain..." Thea began, taking a few steps toward him.

"Stop!" Erik cried, but it was too late. A bullet whistled past his ear and, a second later, a red stain spread on Thea's chest.

"What the... don't shoot!" he shouted. Thea collapsed on the ground, and he threw himself down to support her, trying in vain to stem the flow of blood pouring from her wound. "Call for help!" he screamed again.

Around him, he vaguely heard footsteps, sounds, Hoffman's voice giving quick orders. Thea was becoming increasingly pale, and now both of their clothes were covered in blood.

"Oh, Thea..." he said, realizing that he was crying, "Why did you do that?"

Thea looked at him tenderly: she looked like she was about to say something, but only a wheeze escaped her lips.

A moment later, she died.

Chapter 30

The ship was damp, dark and smelly. On board, in the infirmary, they had Cain, or what was left of him. When Sophie managed to bring him back to the shore, he was unconscious and had lost a lot of blood. But he was miraculously alive, his pulse weak but stubborn.

Sophie had confused memories of the hours that followed: how she had bandaged the cut in his throat as best as she could, making sure the trachea was free, how she had returned to the village, in a ride that seemed endless at that moment, but which now she barely remembered.

She had to warn the others. She didn't know how long they had until Emma, or Kathleen, or whatever her name was, would alert the authorities, and there was no time to lose. Every minute was precious, she knew, but who should she alert? Cain was her authority, everyone's authority. James would have known what to do, but he was away. Nadia was locked up somewhere. Who could she turn to?

Eventually Sophie went to Famke, mostly because she was the first who came to her mind. With startling clarity, Famke listened to her disjointed story and finally raised an alarm that had sounded throughout the island. In twenty minutes, a crowd had gathered in an unexpectedly orderly way at the port, and in an hour they were all on the ships, including the dragons. Evidently the constant drills demanded by Cain had yielded their effect.

They had brought her and Cain on this ship, because it was the largest and the only one with the necessary equipment for emergencies. Sophie barely remembered having stopped the bleeding, performing the surgery and stitching him up and...

At some point, Cain was bandaged and attached to a breathing device. At that moment Sophie felt so tired that she had fallen asleep on the chair where she had dropped. She awakened on a cot, where someone had kindly transported her.

Cain was unconscious and the silence was broken only by the rhythmic noise of the breathing device. Sophie had no idea of the damage that his brain might have, or if he would ever be able to speak again. He might wake up at any moment. He might never wake up. There was no way to know but wait.

Only then a disturbing but obvious thought darted into her head. She left the cabin and ran into Ken.

"Dr Weber, are you all right?" He asked solicitously.

"Do you have a sensor for the plague?" she asked in a toneless voice.

"Yes, I believe there is one somewhere."

She had always been careful, but when she plunged into the sea to save Cain she had to abandon all caution. When she landed in the water, she hit a reef that bruised her leg and ripped off one of her trousers from the calf down. And while she was swimming and dragging Cain's body, the layers of clothes were so heavy... she had to take off many of them, staying in short sleeves, or their weight would bring her down. At that point she didn't know how many times their bodies had come in direct contact.

Ken returned shortly after with a tool similar to the one used by the medical police, but older and more battered. Sophie let a drop of her blood fall down on the sensor. A red light appeared. She tried again, but it was just an automatic gesture, dictated more by habit than doubt. Again, the red light appeared.

"I'm so sorry," said Ken seriously. At that moment, Gregor walked into the hallway.

"Oh, there you are, sleeping beauty. You know you were asleep on a chair, like an old woman?" he sneered. "Why the long face?"

"Shut up!" Ken reproached him. "She just found out she has the plague."

Gregor's face fell, his sarcastic look instantly gone: "Oh," he simply said.

Sophie didn't know what to say. She should have been terrified, desperate, in tears, but instead she felt only emptiness. *In a month I will die*, she thought with detachment. The statistics spoke for themselves: the dragon plague had a mortality rate of ninety-five percent.

She realized, to her amazement, that death was perhaps less frightening than the agony of the disease awaiting her. Her mind could not grasp the prospect of anything after that. It was simply too huge of a concept.

Yet she didn't regret diving. She had done what was right. Perhaps this was enough to give meaning to her entire life? She was not sure.

She marvelled at how calm she was. Should she cry in despair? She didn't feel anything. Maybe she was in shock.

She went back into the cabin where Cain was. Her hand pulled back from his face, ravaged by the scales, a lock of hair caked with sand and salt.

"Please, wake up," she said. She probably would not be there to see it, and most likely he would never be the same person as before. But Sophie only hoped that one day Cain would open his eyes again.

Epilogue

Kathleen Anderson smiled, enjoying the sea breeze whipping her face. The air was cold, but she did not care. The hot body of the dragon beneath her was more than enough to keep her warm.

She was feeling well, wonderfully well: as if she had become forty years younger within minutes. Or maybe even better, because even at twenty she had never flown on the back of a dragon.

She looked down at him and had the impression that he was smiling at her. Indeed, it was more than an impression: she could sense his joy, intense as her own, and the pleasure he felt in finally spreading his wings after years of captivity.

Around the neck and legs, he still bore the marks of the chains from which she had freed him. She was still furious thinking about the conditions in which her poor love had lived for so long.

When, in the cave, she had reached out to touch his pale scales, silvery in the light of the full moon, she felt something like an electric shock, and then...

It had been many years, but when she sensed the familiar presence in her mind it was as if they had never been apart. And now it was even better, because they were close and she could finally touch him, hold him, fly with him.

They were one, destined to be together.

She felt a vague weariness coming from the dragon. They had been in the air for no more than a few hours, but he was still weak; his wings had lost the habit of flying.

We're almost there, she thought, and felt a sense of comfort coming from her companion. In fact, on the horizon she could discern the lights of the mainland coast.

Nearby, there was a military base where they were aware of her undercover operation and where men knew they must not fire at the sight of a dragon approaching.

In the past months, while on the island, she was too occupied to find maps, charts, to accurately understand their position, to develop an itinerary for when they would be free. She had been afraid of not knowing where to head, with no roads and only the infinite surface of the sea below her, but she had discovered that the dragon was much more skilled than her; sharing her information with him had been as quick as a blink, and within moments they were traveling in the right direction.

They arrived at the military base: below her she could see the soldiers running from side to side, small and insignificant as ants. Now that she and the dragon were together, all those who had opposed her and her plans would be nothing but insects, as stupid and easy to crush.

We will have our revenge, and more.

The thought occupied her mind in an encompassing way. Kathleen had the impression that the notion wasn't completely hers... but what difference did it make now? They were one, the thoughts and intentions of the dragon were hers too.

While around her the military base appeared to be in total chaos, they glided gently down to a track that was probably used for helicopters. She was surrounded by men with rifles and looked at them almost tenderly. What did they think they could do?

However, it wasn't a problem now: she was coming in peace, as a friend. Those were her men. She knew that the poor kids were witnessing an impressive sight, one they would not forget, as they would not forget the little woman that easily jumped from the back of the creature.

But she was not the same woman that she had been until a few hours ago: now she felt powerful as a force of nature, and she knew she looked like one in the eyes of all the bystanders, who stared at her open-mouthed, not knowing what to do.

"Call President Hartmann and tell him that Kathleen Anderson must talk to him," she said to the man closest to her. "And take us to a place where we can rest."

The soldier looked around desperately, then ran away, probably to bring the message to a higher-ranked officer.

Kathleen smiled, satisfied: "Come, Fuzzi," she said. "Let's go and take back what's ours."

THE END

Did you like this book?

If so, I'd be grateful if you took the time to leave a review. Reviews are incredibly important for indie authors like me!

Let's keep in touch at:
www.facebook.com/themantovanisblog
www.themantovanis.blog

Acknowledgment

I would like to thank all the people that helped me in this project, especially my sister Maria Carla, who is a great alpha reader and a never-ending source of inspiration, and my dear friend and editor Hannah Ross.

A big thanks goes to Rachel Bailey and Amanda Brogan for their invaluable feedback on the ARC.

I'd also like to give a shout-out to my beloved family: Dario, Giacomo, Samuele, my mum Piera and my parents-in-law Graziella and Piero. Thank you!

Printed in Great Britain
by Amazon